MW01175045

Cardinal Divide

Essential Prose Series 172

Canada Council   Conseil des Arts
for the Arts   du Canada

ONTARIO ARTS COUNCIL
CONSEIL DES ARTS DE L'ONTARIO

an Ontario government agency
un organisme du gouvernement de l'Ontario

Canadä

Guernica Editions Inc. acknowledges the support of the Canada Council
for the Arts and the Ontario Arts Council. The Ontario Arts Council
is an agency of the Government of Ontario.

We acknowledge the financial support of the Government of Canada.

Cardinal Divide

Nina Newington

**GUERNICA
EDITIONS**
TORONTO · CHICAGO · BUFFALO · LANCASTER (U.K.)
2020

Copyright © 2020, Nina Newington and Guernica Editions Inc.
All rights reserved. The use of any part of this publication,
reproduced, transmitted in any form or by any means, electronic,
mechanical, photocopying, recording or otherwise stored
in a retrieval system, without the prior consent
of the publisher is an infringement of the copyright law.

Michael Mirolla, general editor
Lindsay Brown, editor
David Moratto, cover and interior design
Guernica Editions Inc.
287 Templemead Drive, Hamilton, (ON), Canada L8W 2W4
2250 Military Road, Tonawanda, N.Y. 14150-6000 U.S.A.
www.guernicaeditions.com

Distributors:
Independent Publishers Group (IPG)
600 North Pulaski Road, Chicago IL 60624
University of Toronto Press Distribution,
5201 Dufferin Street, Toronto (ON), Canada M3H 5T8
Gazelle Book Services, White Cross Mills
High Town, Lancaster LA1 4XS U.K.

First edition.
Printed in Canada.

Legal Deposit—Third Quarter
Library of Congress Catalog Card Number: 2019949202
Library and Archives Canada Cataloguing in Publication
Title: Cardinal divide / Nina Newington.
Names: Newington, Nina, 1958- author.
Series: Essential prose series ; 172.
Description: Series statement: Essential prose series ; 172
Identifiers: Canadiana (print) 20190173793 | Canadiana (ebook) 20190173963 |
ISBN 9781771834421 (softcover) | ISBN 9781771834438 (EPUB) |
ISBN 9781771834445 (Kindle)
Classification: LCC PS8627.E8655 C37 2020 | DDC C813/.6—dc23

for **Debbie Lafferty**

13th April, 1958 – 7th August, 2017

WEEK ONE

Chapter One

INSIDE IT'S HOT, dark. The smell of spruce needles in rain washes through my chest, something browner underneath. Pelts line log walls, in one corner a bed made of stout branches. Something hisses and sputters. The stove squats in the middle of the cabin like a plump cook in a tiny kitchen. The kettle is dented and blackened. Beyond it, an orange glow. Someone drawing on a pipe. Stringy silver hair.

"Moira McFie, meet my daughter, Meg Coopworth."

"Come here."

I look at Dad. He nods.

Her nose is long and sharp, her cheeks wrinkled and round. Eyes the grey-green of lichen flit over me. My breasts poke out from my chest like mountains.

"Pleased to meet ye," she says at last.

I duck my head, mumble, "Pleased to meet you too," the way Mum taught me.

"Have a seat on the bed, why don't ye?" Her voice is cracked but it swoops and banks like a swallow. I step back from her, from the stove that pulses with heat, sit down on the bed and sink my fingers into fur. The fur is warm as if the animal is still alive.

"Well, Ben." She was a famous trapper once, Dad said. Went on trapping long after most people gave up. I lie back. My eyes close. I'm slipping down into a nest lined with rabbit fur.

Something nudges my shoulder. Bounding away between dark trees, I blink, open my eyes. It's still dark.

"Did ye dream?"

The voice slips in among the deer. I nod.

"And what were ye?"

"A deer, running."

"Ah, that's fine."

I struggle upright. She hands me a mug of tea and an oatcake. "To tide ye over for the journey home."

Outside the hides are gone. "While you were sleeping," Dad says.

Rancid sheep fat still smears the air.

A few yards down the trail I look back. The cabin has disappeared.

The phone rings. I jolt upright, snatch the receiver from the cradle.

"Dreamcatcher Lodge, Meg speaking."

"Can I speak to Tanya please?" A woman's voice, urgent.

"She's not on tonight. She'll be here tomorrow. Can I help?"

"I'll call tomorrow." She hangs up.

I reach for the log book.

> *19th October*
> *16:00–24:00 Jay, Meg*
> *16:00 45 clients, 3 probation*
> *16:15 Jay starting room check, Meg on desk*

I fill in a few more room checks. End with:

> *21:55 Jay in ceremony, Meg on desk*

I swivel the chair to face the dome, eyes climbing courses of rough stone. Twelve feet up, the stone ends, just shy of a pyramidal skylight. I catch the cadence of the Lord's prayer, close my eyes, breathe in.

Hai, hai. Amen. The blanket at the door is pulled aside and the scent of sage and sweetgrass grows stronger. Clients file out, blinking, reclaim shoes, eyeglasses, jewellery.

"Good sleep."

"Good sleep."

They hug each other. Jay unwinds the purple and yellow sarong from around her black jeans, folds it up and puts it back in the basket before clicking open the gate.

Deborah's first in line for her meds. She knows the ropes, Deborah not Debbie, old white woman with her PhD and her cirrhosis, back for a fifth try.

There's a longer line for the phone. I set the egg timer for the first call.

"Smooth," I say, an hour later, bending over the log.

"Good thing," Jay says. "Two of us on, forty-five clients. Anything went sideways? Frig." She shakes her head. "Coffee?"

"Please."

Before Tanya came back to work here, it seemed like we'd be friends, Jay and I. We'd worked a few slow shifts together, talked about our lives while the clients played softball in the late summer evenings.

She rounds the dome, a thick china mug in each hand. Five foot six with short dark hair, greying at the sides, she always wears black and her hair always looks as if it was cut yesterday.

I follow her back into the office. She sits down by the computer, turning the chair to face me. Her skin is sallow, features rubbery but her eyes are sharp as her hair.

"How's it going?" she asks.

"Not bad."

"You look tired. New guy?"

"I wish. Well, no, I don't."

Jay waits.

There's a lump in my throat. My eyes prickle.

"I don't know what I'll do when my mother goes, whacked as she is," Jay says.

Fuck. I swallow. "It's been nine months. But sometimes, something." I shrug, take a drink of coffee. Jay's watching, interested. She knows my story. The outline anyway. And I need to say it to someone. "I'm going to find them."

"Have you ever tried?"

I shake my head. "Mum would have been so hurt. Besides, what was I going to find out that I wanted to know?"

Jay waits.

"But maybe it's why I can't seem to make a relationship that lasts, because I don't ..." My throat swells again. "Anyway, how's school?"

She studies me for a moment then says, "Great. I love it."

"What are you taking this semester?"

"History. More psychology. I'm doing my senior thesis on you-guessed-it ..."

"Jung?"

"I don't know what I'm going to do when I graduate."

"Get a Master's?"

She grins. "I promised Annie I'd pay off some of my loans first. Have to get a real job. Maybe I'll have this place out of my system by then. Shall we start on the overview?" She turns to face the computer.

I was the one who changed the subject. "What we were talking about earlier. My father has to know more."

"He's pretty old, right?"

"Really old. So I'd better ..." I shrug.

"You never asked him before?"

"He said he'd told me everything he knew."

"Why would he tell you more now?"

"With Mum gone. She ... for her there was only one story. I was a gift from God. It was God's plan I came when I did. End of story. You know."

Jay nods.

"Mum told all the stories. How Dad came to Canada. How they met. How they bought the ranch. How I showed up. The same stories, over and over. With her gone it's like a river dried up. You see the shape of the riverbed, the banks." Jay sips her coffee. "I don't know where I'm going with that. Anyway, I guess it's somewhere to start. Asking Dad. Because it doesn't really add up, that they were allowed to adopt me without a birth certificate. Without anything."

"Depends. You were what, ten, eleven? Late sixties? They were snatching kids right off the reserves, putting them up for adoption."

"People I used to work with all assumed I was Ukrainian."

"Everyone here thinks you're Cree."

Chapter Two

I PUT THE kettle on, scatter flour on the counter, turn out the dough I mixed when I got in from work. My hands push and fold, finding the rhythm, the rhythm of kittens kneading the teat. The dough becomes flesh, elastic and smooth. Cover it with the palm of your hand, you can feel it press against you. I brought a loaf in for Jay, not long after I started baking. Put it on the desk. She didn't pick it up, just said, 'It's a lot of work, eh?' Heather came in, sniffed the air. 'My mother always baked,' she said. 'Far as I'm concerned that's why God created supermarkets.'

First and last loaf I took to work. I bring a couple when I visit Dad but that's not enough to keep up with the supply.

I clean and dry the bowl, oil it, slip the dough back in and cover it. Make coffee, eat my toast and boiled egg then go for my walk. When I get back the dough is nudging up the cloth like the bellies of young girls at work, pregnant bellies rounding skimpy T-shirts. I rest my palm on the dough and it shrinks back into itself, but when I slide it out onto the counter, flatten it, fold in the sides, roll it back and forth, it swells again. *That's who my mother was.* Some girl in too much trouble too soon. I wait for a moment, the way I do when a thought like that surprises me. In case a memory hovers, shy by the half-open door. It never does, or if it does I can't see it. Or won't. I've had more than enough therapy to admit that possibility.

When the loaf has been in for twenty minutes I open the oven door, quickly swivel the pan, shut the door again. The smell escapes anyway and I breathe it in, the smell which is the thing itself, particles floating in the air. Actual physical remains. After Mum died I'd catch the smell of her. Back at the ranch it made sense that fragments of her body had come to rest in drawers, corners. Sixty-three years she lived there so of course she was in the air, stirred by our feet wherever we walked, a sweet sour smell. However tightly permed and scrubbed her outside was, there was a brothy ferment to her body, a gravy richness in the smell of her. It was the part of her that danced, I used to think, a wildness in her feet while her head stayed completely still which was the style and would have won her high marks if she had ever competed which she did not because she was a God-fearing and temperate woman, a God-fearing woman with wild feet who danced in the living room while Dad played the fiddle. Standing in my kitchen in the smell of baking bread I hear the clack of her heels on the hardwood floor. The woman who was my mother and who wasn't had a rigid mind and wild feet. After she died I smelled her here in this house which she never visited because I lived here with one man or another. Out of wedlock.

'Wed-lock. The word says it all,' I said to her once. Dad looked away but I caught a flash of laughter in his eyes. Sunlight glancing off water. Mum could stare you down. Reptile eyes. Brown with a slow blink. So there's no way her smell should have been in the air here but it was. In any corner you might inhale a particle of her until, one night, coming in from work, I knew something was different. In the morning I realized she was gone. Perhaps she hadn't been in this house but in the crannies of my own body and I used her up.

I turn off the engine, slouch low in the seat. October sun slants across fields bleached the colour of oats. The poplars by the slough cast indigo shadows. Ravens call from the alders. The low building doesn't interrupt the sky. Some evenings deer graze, a coyote lopes alone across the field. I reach over, sift through the mail. There's a white envelope, squarer than a bill. Spiky, slanting hand; fountain pen, blue ink. Dad's writing, but he knows I'll be out to visit next week.

Dear Meg,

At the risk of sounding melodramatic there is something we need to talk about before I die. Something that perhaps you should have been told long ago. Having reached this decision I find myself impatient to see you. Would you come as soon as you can?

Love,

Dad

P.S. No health problems. I'm as improbably hale as ever.

His face wavers in front of me, creased and angular, eyes the chalky turquoise of rock milk. Rock flour. I always think it's rock milk but it's rock flour, the fine particles that turn the mountain streams and lakes turquoise. Tears sting my eyes, seeing his face. His face thirty years ago, hair still blonde and thick. Even now he has a good head of hair. The Hetzl brothers tease him about it. Fifty years his junior and bald as eggs. *He's going to tell me.*

"Hey Meg," James's face appears around the office door.

"Hey to you, James, let me take my coat off, okay?"

"Sure," he says but his head floats in the doorway, a round brown moon, shadow moon to the crescent of his smile.

"Yes?" I step back out to the front desk. He's wearing a necklace of teeth strung so they all point the same way, little ivory tusks against his black T-shirt. "Can I skip the meeting tonight so I can work on my life line?" He smiles his loopiest smile. "I really, really need to get it done."

"Yeah, right, James, you're the hard-working man."

He turns. "Hey, Jay. My favourite staff."

Jay hoists an eyebrow.

He raises both hands. "I know, I know. Manipulation."

"Easy as breathing, eh James? Hey Meg." Jay's leather jacket is slung over one shoulder though it's not exactly warm outside. I've never seen her wear a toque. "Who else is on?"

"Haven't looked yet. Tell you what, James, work on your life line now, before the meeting. See how far you get."

"Aw ..." He catches Jay's eye and grins. "Okay." He saunters off.

"I need that look."

"This one?" Jay gives it to me: level hazel gaze, tiny quirk of amusement in one eyebrow.

"James would argue with me until I got mad. You just look at him."

"Me and Tanya, we have the eye. You're getting it. You've only worked here ... how long have you worked here?"

"Since the beginning of July."

"See, I'm coming up on three years."

"Excuse me."

Tanya's voice startles me. I step sideways, almost bumping into Jay. "Sorry."

"Like the hair," Jay says.

It's blue today.

"Did anyone go to the counsellor's office yet?"

"Not yet," Jay says.

"I'll go then."

"I'll count cash," I say.

"So is anyone else on?" Jay asks.

I squint at the chart. The lay-out's been changed again. "Heather."

"It's not like her to be late."

"She's coming in at five."

In the back corner of the office a low door opens into an over-sized closet. Inside are a coat rack, a small table and chair, trays of bulging Ziploc bags, and a safe, door ajar. I shove aside heaps of contraband to pull out the cash box.

"Done?" Jay's framed in the doorway. "You okay?"

"I got a letter from my father. He wants to see me. He has something to tell me."

Jay's eyebrows arc. "About where you came from?"

"What else could it be?"

"A little synchronicity, eh?"

"Dreamcatcher Lodge, Meg speaking. How can I help you?"

"My son, he's in trouble ..."

My sister, niece, uncle, mother, grandchild. "Let me put you through to Admissions. If you don't get Janet, leave her a message."

I hang up and reach for the log book. The phone rings again.

"Is Tanya there?" asks a clear young voice.

"She is but she's not at the desk. Shall I ask her to call you?"

"Yes, please."

"Is it urgent?"

"It's kind of an emergency."

"Shall I page her?"

"No. Thank you."

The door alarm beeps. Heather clicks across the floor.

"Hello Meg." She unwinds a black and silver scarf, shrugs off her mauve down-filled coat. In her late fifties, retired after thirty years in government service, an administrative secretary of no doubt ferocious efficiency, she looks like a tight-arsed white spinster, silver hair, sharp face, trim body, only if you look twice there's a sexiness to her, the red lipstick on her small mouth, big breasts she doesn't hide.

Tanya rounds the north side of the dome. Seeing us, she holds up the cap she's carrying, a bill cap with the familiar jagged leaf on the front. "Warren, Theresa's brother."

"Buddy with the tattoo on his face?" Heather asks.

"The one and only. Says he was wearing this when he checked in this afternoon," Tanya shakes her head. "Hate to think what else they let them bring in."

"I like the hair," Heather says.

Cobalt blue looks good with Tanya's copper skin. Her face is round, cheeks full and long so there's a groove to either side of her hooked nose. Her mouth is wide and when it turns down it makes a perfect arch. The day she came back to work here she plonked her mug down on top of the office fridge. **THE REAL BOSS**, it said. She scowled for most of the shift. I kept overhearing muttered conversations between her and Jay, how the place had gone to hell, clients never used to … But she's smiling now. "The girls like it too."

"That reminds me. Your daughter wants you to call her. She says 'It's kind of an emergency.'"

"They're arguing over what channel to watch."

"Somebody else called for you yesterday, a woman. She didn't leave her name."

"Probably Viola. Remember her?" She looks at Heather. "Went back out. Finally got her kids back and now she's high again."

She goes into the office, picks up the phone.

"Hey Meg, where's Jay? Sorry, didn't mean to startle you." James leans over the gate to peer into the office. I can't see his face, just the back of his head and, beyond, Tanya, eyebrows raised. "Oops." He pulls his head back smartly.

Alphas, Dad would call them, Jay and Tanya. At best I'm in the middle of the pack, as ready to grovel as growl.

James tugs a stick-thin, blank-faced girl forward. "Hey Meg, hey Heather, meet my cousin Shannon. My *kokum* is sisters with her aunt's mother."

"Just like where I come from." Heather's accent is flat as a rock skipping over water compared to James's lilt. "All anyone wants to know: Who's your father?"

"*Whoo's yeh faathuh?*" James repeats. "Where you from, Heather?"

"Nova Scotia." Her voice tips up at the end: *Sco-sha?*

"Ah. Well, like I was saying, this is my cousin."

"You again, James?" Jay lets herself in.

"Meet my cousin Shannon. My *kokum* and her aunt ..."

"James, you're related to every single person in western Canada."

"Not to you."

"How do you know?"

"Look at you."

"Because I look white? Seeing isn't believing, James. Seeing isn't believing."

"You Native then, Jay?" He's grinning at her.

"So do your life line, James." She nods at the alcove off the common area. "Nice to meet you, Shannon."

Shannon smiles a flat, plastic little smile. Her hair pulled up in a tight pony tail, she looks exactly like three or four of the other girls.

"Tanya back from the counsellors?"

"In the office."

We shuttle bedding for new clients, talk them through the pattern of the days. Some Wednesdays are a zoo but only six came in this week. Four women, two guys. Warren, short and muscled with a scorpion tattooed up his neck, the tail arching onto his cheek, and a tall, stick thin man in his forties who has yet to say a word.

"Suppertime, it's suppertime." Jay's voice booms from the speakers.

We meet back in the office, clearing space on the desk for our trays. "So," Tanya says, "they're not going to replace Georgie."

"Why not?"

"Budget won't cover an after-care worker."

"What are the clients supposed to do? Camp? There's no frigging housing."

"They had enough to hire Cathy to supervise us."

"This place makes me tired," Heather says.

"Heard it before. Heard it all before but here we still are." Jay forks up mashed potato shiny with gravy.

I push around the parade of carrots and peas, complaint, mockery, resignation lapping like waves.

"Meg?"

I look up.

"Nice job." Jay's grinning at me.

I look down. I've piled the peas and carrots on top of the slices of brown beef, buttressed the wall with mashed potatoes. If I'd taken gravy I could have made a moat. "If they'd just give me a sandbox," I say. My voice is supposed to be light. Now Heather is looking at me too.

"Heather," I say, "would you be willing to trade shifts with me? Take mine tomorrow?"

"Certainly, if I can." She gets up to look at the schedule. "How about Friday? No, we're both on then. Can you take my Monday? That would work out well for me actually."

"Fine. Thanks."

"I'll write it in, shall I?"

"Against the rules these days," Tanya says.

"That's right," Heather says, changing the names anyway.

"Excuse me?" A woman's head pokes around the door. "Can I make a phone call?"

"Not until six, hon," Jay says. "But if I were you I'd stick around, make sure you're first in line."

"Okay."

When her head disappears Jay mouths, "Who's that?"

Heather and I shake our heads.

"Wendy," Tanya says. "Which reminds me, two of the new girls, Janice and Mona, they had some kind of beef in prison. We're supposed to watch them."

Jay puts down her fork. "They let them come at the same time?"

Chapter Three

TRAFFIC ON THE Yellowhead grinds to a halt. I reach across, fold back the cloth, rest my hand on the warm loaf.

Brake lights flick off. The line moves forward ten feet. Stops. The loaf's the shape of a mushroom, the mushroom I found among the poplars by the river, fishing with Dad the first spring. Sun risen on the flat lands, pinking the mountains, shadows reaching. I pointed to it, the dome of the cap pushing up through the leaf litter. It was the exact reddish tan of Dad's pants.

The line of traffic edges out past an old pick-up truck that's shed half its load in the roadway. I looked at the mushroom and at his pants and he smiled. He told me they were made of tin cloth, his pants. But that didn't mean they were made of metal, it was the name the company gave the cloth. So the prospectors would know how strong it was.

At the end of the day the mushroom stood alone and perfect among the tree trunks. We stood there too, side by side. He never tried to make me talk. I can see him, fishing poles leaned against his shoulder, golden hair thick as a brush on top, a growl of brown at the back and sides, faded blue shirt, baggy pants.

They're still the only pants he wears, except for funerals. A new pair every five years. The same size, too. He doesn't even have a gut to hang over his belt the way the other ranchers do. Did. They're gone now, Ralph and Russ and Jimmy. A few wives linger, Betty living with her daughter, Agnes spry still and almost as old as Dad. She was always strong, a scrawny strength. Took over the ranch when her husband left which was no loss to anyone. I remember Dad saying that.

For him to speak against someone was memorable but everyone knew the husband beat on Agnes and drank and ran around. Word was one day she found him with their daughter who was fourteen. Told him she'd shoot his balls off if he ever came around again. She and her daughters, there were three of them, ran the ranch for years. They were stuck up, the daughters, wouldn't talk to me, but I don't know who they got it from because Agnes wasn't like that. I might stop and see Agnes.

Or not. I turn on the radio. A man is talking about dead zones. Dead zones and jellyfish. The dead zones come from fertilizer. Too much run off from the land. Jellyfish are the only creatures that can live in the dead zones. Jellyfish and bacteria. In the dead zones the jellyfish grow and grow.

Where the city ends I turn off the radio, leave the jellyfish among the traffic lights, but the round bales in the fields are like beached whales. Whales dying in the sun. I should expect this, Lip-tooth told me, when a parent dies. 'Your world is dying. For a child the parents are the world and we are all children,' she said, and she was pleased with her formulation. I nodded as if I was pleased too because I couldn't be bothered to say, 'What if the world *is* dying?' She would smile at me sympathetically, her lower lip sticking to her tooth the way it did, and I would want to tear her apart with my hands which would also be normal.

Driving past the shorn fields, the chocolate bloom of ploughed prairie earth, it's as if I am driving toward a shadow city, a city that has always existed just beyond my vision. I've heard its voices, alarms and celebrations, whispers in a wind I thought blew across empty land only it was there all the time, of course it was, the place I come from, the people I left. My father at last, my father who is not my father, my father will tell me where it is I come from.

Tell me what I can't tell myself. Hypnosis, EMDR, past life regression, nothing has worked. The life I remember begins the day a man driving an old orange tractor saw me at the edge of his field.

You forget for a reason. What they've all said. If you were ready, you would remember. So you're not ready. Perhaps you'll never be ready. Accept.

This Way to Heaven
Go Right—Stay Straight

How many years has that stupid sign been up? I scowl at the drab little church. Don't even remember turning onto 22. Missed the moment the mountains come into sight.

I signal and turn down the dirt road. Pump jacks. Clear cuts. All used to be ranch land, Dad said, but it was abandoned during one slump or another. The land begins to tilt and roll and there's the rusty ostrich, cut out of the hood of the old blue Chevy. The drive slices through a band of tamarack and spruce then the land smoothes and opens out, pasture now except for the ten-acre field the brothers ploughed in the spring, the best soil on the place, Dad says. He showed them where it began and ended, told them how he dug the toe of his boot in that ground sixty some years ago, the brothers nodding like two bald dolls.

Cresting the rise, the red roofs of the house come into view. A four-square white house like a thousand others except for the second, smaller but otherwise identical hip roof that pops up from the middle of the main one like a prairie dog poking its head out of its hole. I drive slowly past the brothers' trailer, the barns and the machine shed. Someone's smoothed out the driveway since I was last here.

The front door used to match the roof but the paint has faded. It's the pinkish red of rose hips now while the metal roofing's still a rustier red. Yellow leaves off the aspens have drifted up against the clapboards. The light's different here, softer. Moisture from the river, Dad says. And it's quiet. Home. This is home. My cheeks burn. All my thrashing around, whining about where I come from.

There's a movement in the living room window. I spread the cloth back over the loaf. As I'm getting out of the car, basket in one hand, the front door opens. Dad stands there, the shock of white hair, navy cardigan with leather buttons, sheepskin slippers. He's thin, so thin, and bending forward as if the years are hung from his frame the way he trained the apple trees, hanging stones from the branches. Wild white hairs spring from thick eyebrows, his nose a ridge of bare rock.

"Hello Dad."

"Come in, come in." His voice has never lost its crisp British intonations. He shuffles backward, keeping his hand on the door knob until he can reach the walking stick leaning against the wall.

I hold up the basket. "I brought you some bread for a change. Shall I make some tea?"

"Of course." He sounds odd, short of breath.

"Are you alright?"

"Tea would be nice."

Chapter Four

I FILL THE electric kettle I bought after I found Dad sound asleep, the kettle whistling itself dry on the range. The sink is still the same white enamel, the fridge has the comfortable lines of the retro cars they're selling now, but something is different.

My eyes settle on the window over the sink. Beyond the vegetable garden the brothers planted, beyond the invisible river, the mountains march across the horizon. Mum and Dad sited the house so you can see them from the kitchen, the living room. Upstairs in the tiny bedroom they shared, both windows face west. At dawn you can watch the first rays touch the face of the mountains.

That's it. The kitchen curtains are gone. Red and white gingham. They met in the middle at the top and were hooked back to the sides midway down. I helped Mum wash them and iron them every spring and fall until I turned fifteen and became a raging asshole. What's left is the bare aluminum rectangle framing the view. My father and his beloved mountains. My father the mountain. That's what I used to think, resenting his implacable reasonableness, his refusal to hit back. You could hurl yourself at him, beat yourself bloody against the rock of him and never make a dent. The only way to get to him was to attack Mum which, God help me, I did with all the venom at my disposal. 'If you can't be civil to your mother, you can leave this house.' The opening I'd been probing for, a way to make it their fault.

Christ what a fucking mess I made. And mended. The best I

could. I scald the pot, spoon in tea twice as strong as I like it, slip the cosy on.

"Can I cut you a slice of bread, Dad?"

"That would be nice."

"Butter and marmalade?"

"Please."

He looks weird, eyes skittering around the room, jaw so tight a muscle flutters in his cheek.

I don't even notice when I cut into the loaf. It's only when the bread smell hits my nose that I stop. Pay attention to the bite of the blade into the crust. But my mind's not on it. I smear the slices with butter then marmalade, carry the plates through, sit down in the other armchair.

"Shall I be mother?" I reach for the pot. He stiffens. Shit. That was always his line, arch and English, Mum smiling. Their little joke. I pour a cup for me, swish the tea around in the pot. Pour half a cup and hold it out. "Strong enough?"

"Yes. Thanks."

Milk and sugar. He stirs, watching the orange brown liquid swirl around the cup then looks up and past me. Sunlight glints on a long white hair curling from his chin. "Growing a beard, Dad?"

He puts down his cup, stares at me.

"Sorry. A joke. That hair." My stomach hurts. "More bread?" He's only taken one bite.

"No thanks." He picks up the slice, lifts it to his lips, puts it back down. We reach for our tea cups at the same moment.

"Sorry."

"Sorry."

Christ, my mouth is dry. The tea doesn't help. He's got his cup tilted in front of his face as if he's drinking from it but it goes on too long. When he puts it down he's going to start.

He sets the cup down on the coffee table and puts both hands on the arms of his chair. He levers himself up and reaches for his cane. "Won't be a moment."

It takes a long time, these days, his journey across the room, but it's never taken this long. I close my eyes. Breathe.

Open them again. Look. Lumpy oatmeal and crimson plaid fabric, shabbier than ever in the morning light. Vintage 1970s with its low back and rectangular arms, the chesterfield's sat in that exact spot under the picture window its whole life. Dad's chair is much older, made of oak and leather. The end of each arm flares out and curls down, the wood dark where his hands rest. The feet look like claws. Not bird claws, some mammal's. 'A carnivore,' I told Dad when I learned the word, something sinewy, ferocious. But the rest of the chair has stout curved legs and tapered spindles, a plump brown leather seat.

I'm tight as a fiddle string by the time he's lowered himself back into the chair.

He looks straight at me. "Meg. I don't know how to make this any easier. It's going to be a shock." There's something almost pleading in his eyes. "You'll think I should have told you. And perhaps I should. But your mother ..."

"Dad, I want to know."

"It happened long before you ..." He stops.

"Please, Dad. I want the truth, whatever it is. I need the truth."

His forehead furrows. He looks confused but then he nods. He's making himself look at me, his shoulders rigid. "Meg, I'm not who you think I am."

It's my turn to stare at him. He's going to tell me he's my real father. My blood father.

"Go on."

"I'm ... I'm not a man."

"What?"

"Meg, I'm a woman."

"What?"

"I'm not a man."

"You want to be a woman?"

"No, I am a woman."

"You're ... you're transgendered?" The word is as incongruous as a nose stud. Nipple ring. Dildo.

"No. Not." He stops, lays both hands palm down on the arms of his chair. "Meg, I was born a woman. By an accident, a chance, I, it's ... I can explain how later. I had reason to pass myself off as a man and I did."

"You're not a man. Everyone thinks you're a man but you're not."

"That's right."

"That's crazy." He's crazy. He's making it up. Why? The tips of his fingers are white, pressing against the oak. He doesn't lie. His eyes are on my face. Worried. For me. Why is he doing this?

My father. Who outlived all the other ranchers. The men. My unusually old father who hasn't lost any of his hair. Who was blonde and not very hairy but Cree men aren't particularly hairy either. My oh-so-modest father who never swam. "No tight jeans for you, eh?" It's crude, insulting, my voice. "You and Mum. Ben and Polly. Mum going to that church and all the time ..." I begin to laugh but it's crazy laughter.

"It's a shock, I know," he says. She says. Same light voice, gruff but not deep. Same wiry body. Flat-chested. Not even old man boobs. Course if I was that thin ...

Dad takes his hands off the arms of the chair. They hold each other, big, sinewy, sun-spotted hands.

"Mum knew?"

He takes a ragged breath. "Of course, she knew."

"She wouldn't set foot in my house because I was living in sin and all the while ..." I look at him. Her. "Why now?"

Violet shadows in the back of his eyes.

"Your mother didn't want anyone to know. Ever."

"And you did?" As the retort snaps out of my mouth that last word of his sinks in.

He shrugs, opens his mouth, but I cut in.

"How were you going to manage that? Keep it a secret in the funeral home? 'That old fella, he's not ...' " I tail off because Dad's nodding, because it's crazy and every direction I look it's unfolding into bizarre complications.

"We had a plan. But we assumed I would go first."

"Because men die before their wives?"

He gazes at me for a moment and it's the old steady blue-eyed you know what's right, you know what's wrong, you know I love you look and I'm twelve and I want to lie about something and he's there waiting for me to do the right thing and when I do, however careless or unkind or stupid the thing I'm confessing, his eyes will be glad and

I'll want him to be glad even though I hate the drag of the tether he's put on me and later I'll kick and buck and race away as far and as fast as I can from those eyes. It all twists up in me, sitting there, his eyes steady on my face. He was lying. She. She was lying.

"I was eleven years older than Polly. Of course we thought ..." He swallows.

Deep breath. "What was it, this plan of yours?"

"I'd go the way I always wanted to go. In the mountains."

I stare at him. "So, what? One day you were going to stroll into the wilderness, die of exposure. Conveniently, nobody would find your body. What was Mum going to do? Claim she didn't notice you were gone, that's why she didn't report you? No wait, I know. The Cardinal Divide. Today's the day, you say. Mum drives you there, drops you off. Goodbye, you say, and march off into the wilderness. Then what?"

He's studying me the way he used to, waiting for me to figure something out, and I do and feel sick because of course he'd take his gun, put himself down the way he put Moss down when the cancer drained the light from his eyes. The way he put down the colt with a broken leg. He'd do the job. Unlike my sloppy efforts at self-immolation. Tan pants, red braces, battered khaki hat, shot gun slung over his shoulder, he's walking up a narrow valley, wolf willow, sedge, the mountains clambering skyward. He's getting smaller and smaller. Even at ninety he could walk five miles. His ninetieth birthday, and his ninety-fifth, we drove up to the Divide, rambled over the thin turf, him pointing out the gouges where grizzlies had been digging for glacier lily bulbs. A thermos of tea and bacon sandwiches, triple-wrapped, in his old grey canvas knapsack. "Don't want to smell too good to the bears," he said, winking at me. On cue Mum looked around nervously. Christ. I look at him. Her. "I suppose you'd have filled your pockets with bacon sandwiches."

"Garlic sausage, I thought. More tea?"

He's holding up the pot but he has to use both hands to do it.

"Dad." I stop. Close my eyes. Hear him set the pot down.

"Meg, can you imagine what it would have been like for your mother, to lose not just me but her whole world? For it to crack apart. She wasn't strong. Not in herself. She needed her world to be her skeleton. Rigid, perhaps, but"—he lifts his shoulders—"it let her live a good life."

"Pretending to be something she wasn't." My voice isn't hard now. I've never, ever heard him talk like this.

"She was a woman married to a rancher living a quiet, God-fearing, hardworking life. All that was true."

"And her church's little campaign against homosexuals?"

He shrugs.

Another vista of strangeness opens up. "What about medical care?"

"I'm not the only one around here who doesn't hold with doctors."

"Yes but lately, didn't you …?"

"Meg?" His voice. Her voice. "Is this really what you want to talk about?"

I shake my head.

"Do you have to drive back tonight?"

I stare out of the window. The sun hasn't even set behind the mountains.

"I'm sorry, Meg." His voice is so soft it takes me a moment to parse the words. "You've every right to be angry and confused. When you were having such a difficult time, I used to wonder if this was a part of it. If somehow you knew and it confused you, added to the distrust."

"You wondered? Your life was a lie. That was your choice. But I didn't have a choice, did I? You preached honesty and all the while …" A black wave slams around inside my skull. "You lied. It was all a lie." It's getting clearer now, everything's lining up. "Why are you telling me this? Because you need me to drive you to the mountains when it's time. So you can die with your little secret intact and everyone can be sad Ben and Polly are gone and they'll put your name on the grave in the cemetery next to Mum's and you'll have won. You'll have put one over on everyone and you can die laughing in whatever cave you crawl into with your shotgun and your fucking garlic sausage. It's all about fucking power. The rest of us, we thrash around with what we're given but you, you can make things be what you want. Well, you better get someone else to drive you. Hey, take a cab, because no, the answer is no, I won't play along."

"Are you done?" Dad's voice is cold.

"I'm done." I stand up. My temples throb. My hands are in fists. I stumble on the table leg, brush past his hand. He reaches out. Suddenly I want to cry. I grab my coat from the hook. Don't look back. Turning into the driveway I almost clip Manfred Hetzl chugging along on the old Allis Chalmers. He raises a hand as I roar past. I drive too fast down the dirt road. Like a brushfire smouldering in the roots, it flares again. Acrid in my mouth. Smooth burn, going down. Sliding down, warm in my gut. That's Scotch. A dragon roar, out of nowhere. Scotch. My fingers tighten on the wheel. Christ. Hold on.

Chapter Five

FIVE HOURS. FIVE hours ago, I thought my father was about to tell me where I came from. Who my people were. So I'd have some ground under my feet. However shitty it was, the place I came from, I'd know.

A few heads turn when I slip in late, look around for a seat. I don't want to be here. Doesn't matter. *Take your disease to a meeting.* I sit with the restless in the back. Couple of old clients recognize me, nod. One looks away. Val's reading *Yesterday, Today and Tomorrow.* Tall elegant woman, slash of pink lipstick, *café au lait* skin. Large hands. I close my eyes, try to let familiar words wash me down. It is like a hangover, the chemical trace of rage. Sober, at least I know what I did. Slashed at Dad, who is a tired, old ... woman. Fuck.

A burst of clapping jolts me. Joe. His 29th anniversary. His sponsor's up there, telling stories on him. People laughing. Joe shaking his shaggy head. Big walrus moustache.

"Hello friends." Thick Newfoundland accent though he's been here longer than he's been sober.

My 20th anniversary in two months. Me standing there. 'Hello everybody. Well, it's been a busy year. My boyfriend and I finally called it quits so I'm single and not doing anything about it. Instead I make bread which might or might not be a healthy alternative.

'My mother died almost a year ago and I still burst into tears at odd moments.

'I quit my career to work a low-paid but socially useful human services job for an organization that's at least as impaired as its clients.

'I developed a need to find out more about my birth family even though it seems unlikely I'll find out anything I'll be glad to know. Actually, at this point, it seems unlikely I'll find out anything at all.

'But the big news is my father's a woman. Not my biological father, the man who raised me. Isn't.

'So, like I said, it's been a busy year. Wishing you all another twenty-four hours of sobriety, I'll take one for myself.'

Clapping. Or not. No, they'd clap. 'Thanks for sharing,' someone would say as I walk back to my chair.

"You okay?" Val asks after the meeting.

I shrug. Don't remember a word anyone said. Passed when it came to me. If I talk I'll cry. I'm like the river at spring break-up, all jammed up, more and more stuff stacking up behind.

Home. My home. This is my home. I'm forty-two years old. I own my own house. Unlock the door, punch in the alarm code. Flick on the lights. Coffee pot with an inch of coffee. Fill a glass at the sink. Gulp it down. Go through into the living room. Turn on all the lights, take off my coat. Chesterfield, armchair, coffee table, TV. The little round pine table by the picture window, two wooden chairs. Something should be different. Walk in the bedroom, the bathroom. Turn on those lights. I did this the day Bill moved out. My doll's house. What the realtor called it. Perfect for one. Tight for two. I like living alone. Except in my head I keep telling someone. Who would I tell? The therapist I fired? The sponsor I don't have. Friends I had, my old job, ten years we worked together. We met for dim sum in Chinatown one Saturday a couple of months after I quit. Without the office there wasn't much to talk about. Besides they live such straight lives. 'Hey, my father, turns out he's a woman.' Yeah, right.

I'm in the living room, every light in the house blazing, eleven o'clock at night and I don't know what to do with myself. I don't even want to make bread. I don't want to drink. Or smoke. Or get high.

Sit down. The armchair sags. Farm cast-off. Mum finally screwed herself up to buying a new one. Mum and Dad. Keeping the secret.

House not much bigger than this. My modest father. Bolt on their bedroom door. Why they built that bedroom. Not so I could have a room of my own. So they could keep their fucking secret.

Fuck, I'm mad.

The dubious luxury of ordinary men.

Fuck AA.

Whoops.

Resentment gets us drunk.

More Gospel.

Okay, okay.

Why am I so mad?

Three of us living there. Two in the know. Me, left out. Kept out. What else?

Dad lying.

Suddenly I'm so tired I can hardly keep my eyes open. I turn out the lights, tug off my clothes. Climb into bed, lie in the dark. Somewhere a thousand questions wait, like black flies clinging to a window screen.

Then he was a she. Lazy, taunting voice. Lou Reed. Club in Gastown, barman loved that song. *Take a walk on the wild side. Doop de doop de doo.* Decadent. *Annie and me, we used to shoot up, have sex. Six, seven hours at a time. It was fantastic. Morphine. Back in the day.* Jay told me that. Summer evening, clients playing softball. Me trying not to look shocked. Nothing shocks Jay.

I must have slept. Wake up, get up, try to do my routine. *My father told me ...* Stop. Look. Early sobriety, my head a highway with no rules, somebody told me, *Don't think, just look.*

Yesterday the river was a glassy expanse of green water. Today it's dotted with lily pads of ice, each rimmed with white crystals like fur trimming the sleeves of a fancy coat. *Look. Keep looking.* They glide along, the pads of ice, current carrying them wide around the bends in the river. From a distance they look separate, serene. But walking out onto the footbridge I hear them, a shushing, granular sound, distinct above the distant throb of traffic. Each ice pad has a skirt of submerged crystals. The drowned skirts brush against each other as the pads turn and turn. *My father told me ...*

For as far as I can see they're drifting toward me, serene and ruthless. I want to look away, to look up to where the glass cliffs of the city will be gleaming orange in the morning sun but my eyes are locked on the ice pads sailing toward me. They'll sail like this forever. Not true. Ice will sheet out from the banks, the pads jostling against each other in a narrowing channel until, one clear night, cold will weld them into a single plate. In the morning tracks will lead from bank to bank: coyote, fox, deer.

Dad loved the first snow. He'd take me with him to the cottonwood stand. We'd read the writing from the night before, paw prints, the brush of belly hairs. They were all around us, the invisible ones. Like the golden light that poured down through the leaves a few weeks earlier, so thick and rich you could feel it on your skin, I could feel it, the life around me which was the life in me, through me. We never talked about it but I knew he felt it too.

She.

Upstream a siren blares, loud, louder, then a second starts up, crossing the Capillano Bridge. And a third, same cadence but tentative, like a fiddler tuning up. It's coming from the trees across the river, growing louder.

When the sirens have faded into the distance, the coyotes fall silent too. Before the pulsing hum of traffic spreads back across the river valley, there's a moment of silence. The water between the ice pads shines turquoise and copper.

Perhaps it doesn't matter. I turn to face downstream, close my eyes, feel the sun on my skin. It's not that big a deal. He's the same person. She. I open my eyes. Sunlight glitters on the refinery stacks. They're strung with sodium lights. At night, they twinkle, cellophane orange, a city's worth of lights. At night, flames climb the sky, lick away the stars. Of course it matters. I look down at the ice pads sliding out from under the bridge. He lied. He lied to me every single day.

Chapter Six

"WHAT'S HAPPENING ABOUT aftercare?" Tanya is on one side of the desk in the office, Cathy on the other.

"We're working on designing a better program."

"In the meantime what are we supposed to tell clients?" Tanya's lips curve down to match the long curves of her cheeks, the hook of her nose. I've never seen a face that's all scowl.

Cathy draws herself up to her full five foot two. "I've told you all that I'm at liberty to say."

"Ah," Tanya says as if she has received a precious gift of enlightenment. "I'm sure they'll find that helpful."

Cathy stalks out, all of us watching her go.

Heather says, "He left them all his contacts, told them to use his ideas, even though they fired him."

"With Georgie, it was never about him."

"More than you can say for the lovely Miss Brenda."

"Or Scratch-My-Balls Bob."

"Or Hapless Howard." Heather glances at me. "Brenda's glorious predecessors."

"It was better when I was here, as a client, I mean," Tanya says.

"Or you thought it was," Jay says. "How much do the clients know?"

"More than we imagine," Heather says. "They're not stupid."

"They'd be dead if they were, most of them," Tanya says.

"What do you think?" Jay asks, turning to look at me.

I shake my head. Everyone waits.

After a long beat Jay asks, "Who wants to do the welcome?"

Tanya's voice echoes through the building as I head for the back door. "Welcome meeting in ten minutes in the Riel room. Please return boom boxes and table tennis bats now."

It's cold and dark and the wind is roaring in the poplar trees but the clients—hatless, in skimpy jeans, the young ones anyway—smoke and kid around. I nod and keep going around the corner of the building. I'm the only one who ever walks the perimeter. I read it in the list of duties when I was hired. 'You don't have to do that,' Tanya said, the first time I wrote it in the log. 'But I like doing it.' She raised her eyebrows. The Bloods are like the Cree, you're not supposed to tell people what to do. Expressing silent disapproval seems to be okay.

At the next corner, the wind slams into me. I close my eyes, open my mouth. *Blow through me wind, I can't do this.* I could keep walking, out into the night. My fingers brush the brick, tracing the curve of the building. Everyone's in the meeting when I get back inside except for Heather who's waiting for me by the desk.

"Everything okay?"

"All good," I say.

"I'll go into the meeting then." She hesitates.

I lean over the log book.

> 18:55 *Meg on room check*
> 19:00 *Heather, Jay, Tanya in Welcome meeting. Meg on desk.*

When I put the pen down, Heather's gone.

It was all a lie. Everything.

"Who's going into ceremony?" Jay asks.

"I'm on my moon," Tanya says.

"Me too," I say. Dad. Getting his period.

"Me too," Heather says, then cackles. I must have looked particularly dumb because she pats my arm. "There now, Meg. It's been a while since I hit menopause and you should be glad you weren't around for that."

Tanya looks up from the log book. "Want to know how to end a war?"

"Enlighten us," Jay says.

"Send in the menopausal women. Be over by dinner."

"Because they have to cook it," Heather says.

He would have been well past it by the time I showed up.

Theresa, a handsome woman in her early thirties with long black hair and perfect sculpted lips, hands me her rings and earrings. She must be this week's chief. She and the council go into the chamber. The others begin to gather, slipping off their shoes. The volume of voices builds. "Sssh," Tanya holds her finger to her lips, catching the eyes of three noisy girls.

The blanket that covers the door to the chamber is pulled aside. Deborah's first. Smudge person holds the abalone shell with one hand, sweeps smoke toward her with a bird's wing. A few of the new ones crane their necks to watch as she rinses her hands in the smoke, cups them to scoop it over the crown of her head, her eyes, ears, nose, mouth, chest.

The line shuffles forward, Heather in the midst of the women, all of them wearing sarongs over jeans.

In the office Tanya and Jay are talking quietly. Behind the last man, the blanket closes. On the bench outside the office, the menstruating women sit, staring straight ahead, keeping their special bloody magic to themselves. Too much power, that's the official line. It's not mine to argue but it still rubs at me. Or perhaps it is. Mine to argue. My culture. Even if I know squat about it. Wouldn't make me so different from half the people in here. City Indians. Urban aboriginals. Bannock the acme of my cultural experience.

Most of the rooms are dark. Sleepy voices murmur goodnight. I could navigate these corridors with my eyes closed, the women's end of the bedroom wing powdery, chemical sweet; the men's musky, like the ram pens in the barn at home, though here it's laced with pungent aftershave.

Rams and ewes. I know it's not that simple.

I'm missing two, a man and a woman.

They're in the cafeteria at separate tables, hunched over scrolls of newsprint. Cheryl, who wants to be an electrician, looks up and smiles. "Sorry. I got lost. Look at this, I'm not even ten yet." Her even writing covers six feet of the coarse paper. "I didn't think I would have anything to say, eh?"

James nods. "There's a lot to it," he says. "My life." His paper is multicoloured, a wild mingle of drawings and lettering in different sizes. "I'm almost done."

They're in their early twenties, both of them. Same age I was. How old was Dad when he came to Canada? Or she. They're both looking at me. "Will another fifteen minutes do you?"

Their heads are down, hands moving over the paper before I leave the room.

In the office Jay's finishing off the overviews. "Got anything to add, Meg?"

"Uh, James and Cheryl working hard on their life lines."

"Excuse me." We all look up. Pointed chin, tired eyes. New girl. Wendy. "Could you come? Someone."

Tanya and Jay are on their feet. I'm behind them, moving down the corridor. Wendy steps out of the way. Raised voices come through the door of room 19. Jay listens a moment, glances at Tanya then opens the door. Two women, one with black hair half way down her back, one with short red hair, stare at each other. Their hands are at their sides, curled. Neck tendons taut.

"Mona," Jay says to the redhead. She's squinty-eyed, skin dried out from too many cigarettes. "And you are?" Jay turns to black-hair, her voice one of polite inquiry.

"Janice." Broad slab of a face, pockmarked.

Jay turns to look at the label on the room door. "Janice, you should be in your room. Or do you want to come to the office, talk to us about what's happening here?"

"That cunt," Janice says.

"Let's go," Tanya says. "Both of you."

We step back and they troop down the hall to the office, Jay and Tanya following.

"You okay?" I ask the woman who came and got us. Wendy.

She nods.

"You sure?"

"Is it like this?" Her voice isn't much more than a whisper. She tips her chin in the direction of the retreating backs. "Fucking cunt," echoes down the corridor.

"Limited vocabulary, eh?"

A small smile reaches her mouth but not her eyes.

"No, it's not usually like this. I think those two have some history."

Her hair is a deep copper and wavy, her eyes blue-grey, skin the blue-white of skimmed milk.

"Is it ... well ... is it okay being ... not being ...? Some friends, when I said I was coming here. They said you had to be Native. Aboriginal. But the lady in admissions ..."

"Everyone's welcome. There's always a mix of aboriginal and non-aboriginal clients here. Staff too." She's pegged me for white.

"I wanted to come here. The spirituality. It's different. I thought ... If I don't get it this time ..." Her chin is quivering. She's biting her lip.

"Do you want to talk a bit?"

She nods. I sit at the foot of the bed. On the little table next to the pillow is a framed photo of a blonde girl, five or six years old, and a ginger-haired toddler.

She touches the photo as she sits down. "This is my third time. I'm thirty years old. I have a degree. I had a house. Children." She looks away. "Everything. This is all I've got left." She waves a hand at her own slight body. "If I go out again ..." Her eyes are blue tunnels.

Creator. God. Whatever, please. Help this woman. I look into her eyes, can't see the end. "You're in the right place. You don't ever have to pick up a drink or a drug again. So long as you remember this moment. How you feel right now. It's the gift of desperation. Hold onto it." The tiredness seeps back into her eyes, dims the shimmering blue. "I bet you're exhausted." She nods. "Go to sleep. We'll sort this out." I lift my chin at the other bed.

Fuck. Fury rakes my veins. Heather is sitting at the front desk, back turned to the closed door.

One of the women is saying, "I don't want to go back to prison."

"Drug court," Heather mouths, slipping the client list toward me.

Janice Yellowknee. Status. *Mona Bernsick.* Métis.

"So can you two work on not getting into it?" Tanya asks.

"Yes."

"Yes."

The office door opens and they file out. Jay and Tanya are looking at each other. Jay shakes her head, "Fuuuck."

"They didn't waste any time," Tanya says.

I say, "What the fuck were admissions thinking?"

"Thinking?" Jay says.

Tanya says, "It goes back before prison. This has been going on for years. Years and years."

"I'll do the incident report," Jay says. "Go ahead, you guys. I'll see you tomorrow, Meg."

I look at the clock. Five past midnight. "Where's Henry?"

"Getting himself a cup of coffee. He put his head in the door, pulled it right back out.

"Well, I'm off," Heather says. "Once again this place puts the *dys* in *dysfunctional* and once again I'm surprised which says I'm not all well up here." She taps her forehead.

"We wouldn't be working here if we were," Tanya says.

Chapter Seven

HEATHER'S TAILLIGHTS JOLT over the last speed bump. She turns right. I go left. Riding the range roads after midnight. Another thing I like about this job. The long way home. Out of the north a single white light grows bigger and bigger. Right on time. I could gun it. Or turn back, go through the city. Instead I sit and watch the cars clatter past. Rust red with a flat-looking ear of wheat stencilled in yellow. *Saskatchewan Wheat Board* printed along the bottom. Five in a row then a series of straight sided carriages with open tops. Coal? Scrap? Nothing? They reach back out of sight around the bend in the track. *I'm not even ten yet.* Cheryl, waving her six sheets. Good thing I never went to treatment. Handing in my homework. Nothing there. Ten empty cars. Clackety clack. The big empty. Wendy's eyes. Tunnels without end. The beast's got you and you know it and there's not a fucking thing you can do. Burn of scotch in my throat, tearing out of the farm. Yesterday. Yesterday I found out I knew less than I thought. Whatever I thought I knew, I don't. Because it was all fucking lies. It flares again. Fire in the roots. *Dad is not my father.* Clack, clack, clack. *I have no father.* Clackety clack. *No mother. No father.* The last carriage passes. Red tail lights disappear around the bend. I sit staring into the dark. The good old bottomless fucking pit. What I saw in Wendy's eyes. No human power can fill the pit. That's what they say.

Pray for her. Pray for me.

Pray to what? I need to talk to someone.

Chapter Eight

"CATHY'S IN," JAY mouths as I let myself into the office. "She's been here all day."

"I thought she took weekends off."

"Place can't run without her."

"It's just the two of us on tonight?"

"No karaoke, eh? They're going to watch a movie. You doing cash?"

"Yes." I open up the box, tally the coins. Five cents for every sheet of Bounce, pretty soon you have a dollar. Even the reek of fabric softener and cologne is comforting.

Footsteps in the office. Cathy, wide and bustling. *She could disorganize a nunnery.*

I sign off on the sheet, close up the cash box. Cathy's in the doorway and suddenly I can't breathe. Big body blocking the way. Can't see her face. "Excuse me."

"Oh, sorry." She backs up. "How are you, Meg?"

"Good."

Spaniel eyes, black hair pulled back in a ponytail. I keep walking toward her and she keeps backing up until we're out of the narrow space between the table and the back wall.

"How about you?" I ask.

"Relieved. I hired a new person today. He'll be good."

"That right?" Jay says.

"Doug Fletcher. You know him."

"Ah."

"He's coming in at six for orientation."

"Today?" I ask, trying for neutral.

Cathy glances at me. She may not be as dim as she seems. "I thought you two could show him the ropes."

"Time for a room check," I say.

"Coffee?" Jay asks when I get back.

"Where is everybody?"

"They've got some shrink in talking about triggers."

"So, who's the new guy?"

"Tanya's ex."

"Uh oh?"

"Nah. They get along. He takes the kids a couple days a week."

"His kids?"

"No. But they got together when the kids were little. He worked here long back. It's how they met."

She hands me a mug, pours one for herself. I glance at the clock. 4:45. I open my mouth but nothing comes. Jay's eyes settle on me.

"You were going to see your father. How did it go? If you don't mind me asking."

I shake my head. My eyes fill with tears. Crap.

She shunts the box of tissues my way, takes the chair with a view of the front desk.

I take a deep breath, toss the tissue in the waste basket. "Want to hear a strange story?"

"Of course."

"You know how Dad asked to see me."

Jay waits.

After a bit I get going again. "You know what I thought. But it wasn't that at all." I can't lift my eyes off the grey top of the office table. Jay is sitting very still. I've seen her do this with clients, letting the silence grow. I've forgotten how to move the muscles of my tongue. It's like pushing against a wall of paper. Trying to reach the words. "My father told me he's a woman."

Jay's eyebrows lift. Her mouth shapes 'wow.' She does it again, with sound this time. "Wow. How do you wrap your mind around that one?"

"Can't even start. I stall out on pronouns."

"When did he decide? Jesus. How old is he?"

"That's not it. He was born a woman."

Jay leans back in her chair. "Biologically?"

"So he says."

"What exactly did he say? If you don't mind me asking."

"It's a relief. To talk about it. I mean this is my father. My not-father. Christ." I close my eyes. He said, 'Meg, I'm not who you think I am.' I thought he meant he was my real father. My blood father. But then he said, 'I'm not a man.' I think I said, 'What?' and he said, 'I'm a woman.'"

"Who passes as a man? But not believing she's a man?"

"He said. She said—I close my eyes again—'I had reason to pass as ...' No, 'to pass myself off as a man.'"

"That's pretty clear." Jay pauses, staring at the back wall then she looks at me. "You believe him?"

I hesitate. "There are moments I think it can't be true. But ... little things. Suddenly they make sense."

"As if you'd known, unconsciously?"

I shake my head. "God, no."

"How long has he been, she been passing?"

"I don't know exactly. A long time. There's a lot I didn't ask. I got distracted by thinking about Mum."

"Your mother ..." Jay shakes her head. "Wow. Oh, wow."

"My hard-core evangelical homophobic mother."

"Makes you wonder, eh?"

"What?"

"How many other couples are passing. I love it."

I stare at her.

"Meg, think about it. All those Christian couples."

"Who aren't what they appear? Is that so great, to fool people? They trust you to be what you say you are and then you're not."

"Life's a stage, Meg. Everyone's in costume. Don't get sincere on me."

It's like running full-tilt into a brick wall. "Got to pee," I say. It's the only thing I can think of. I want to cry but when I shut the washroom door I don't. I just sit there. Outside I hear feet scuffling, laughter. Someone tries the door.

"Suppertime, it's suppertime," Jay's voice booms over the intercom. The door handle turns again.

Usually I get in line but staff are allowed to go to the front. I reach for a plate. White meat, white gravy, peas and a white bun. As soon as I get back to the desk Jay goes for hers. I force down a mouthful. The door beeps. Quarter to six. A tallish man with shoulder-length brown hair ambles in. He's wearing an old canvas army jacket, jeans, leather work boots so worn and soft they look like paws. He stops, looking across at the dome. Hawk nose, dimple in his chin, eyebrows a straight dark slash across his face. He turns to look at me, smiles, his eyes mild and brown.

"I'm Doug Fletcher." He extends a hand, warm, dry, calloused along the base of the fingers.

"Meg Coopworth."

He glances down at the plate. "I see the food's as colourful as ever."

"Hey Doug," Jay sets her tray down and gives him a hug. She's not the huggy type. "You can run but you can't hide, eh? Welcome back."

He dips his head. "Supervisor's office still in the same place?"

"Same old."

He nods to me, turns to go.

"That you Doug?" It's Mona, the redhead.

"Hey, Mona, right? How's it going?"

"Better for seeing you." She's gazing up into his eyes.

Jay, standing next to me, murmurs, "Good luck with that, Mona."

"Catch you later," Doug says, headed for the corridor.

"How long ago did he work here at Dreamcatcher?"

"Five, six years ago. He quit before my time. Went up north to make some money."

"He in program?"

"Long time."

"I haven't seen him around."

"He lives on an acreage over by Lac Ste. Anne now. They lived in the city, him and Tanya."

"Why'd they break up?"

Jay glances at me. "Interested?"

"Just curious."

"Good because, according to Tanya, he's gay."

Knock, wait, open doors on empty rooms. *I love it.* Well, Jay, I don't. I think I said that out loud. I'm standing in an empty hallway, talking to myself. The corridor stretches out ahead of me. It's getting longer and longer. Floor, walls, everything's flimsy. *Get a grip.* Get outside.

Janice turns her broad, indifferent face my way. I should tell her to go inside, help clean up. The tip of her cigarette glows as I turn the corner of the counselling wing. Wind slices through my jeans, my sweater.

I love it. Well, I hate it. Only I suppose I'm not allowed to hate it. 'We're a clan,' Jay told me one time. 'People hate us. Want to exterminate us. If we don't stick together, what do we have?'

Doug and Jay, chatting away in the office, while I'm out here freezing my ass off.

By choice, says some old sponsor voice, but it's all rolling together now, how all my life I've been on the outside, me and my crazy fucking story and now this. Dad got it off his chest and now I'm the one with the crazy fucking secret. Well fuck you. I'm stomping faster, head down. Something comes around the corner. Jesus. I stop dead, heart pounding.

Doug raises one hand. "Sorry. Didn't mean to give you a shock. I didn't know anyone was out here."

"Doing the perimeter walk."

He nods. "I always liked doing that." If he heard me ranting he's not showing it. He turns to walk with me. "Been working here long?"

Clients mill about, waiting for ceremony. James is standing by the entrance to the chamber, same black t-shirt, the necklace of teeth. He's watching the tall thin man walk toward the cafeteria. The new man's wearing brand-new black hi-top sneakers. Black long-sleeved shirt, cuffs buttoned at the wrist. His perfectly faded jeans look as if they've been ironed. James catches my eye, lifts one hand and lets it droop from his wrist. I stare at him, confused.

"What's his name?" Doug murmurs. "The one with the teeth."

"James."

James looks from me to Doug, quivers his hand then straightens the wrist. Oh.

"Well he *is*." James sounds defensive.

"He is or he isn't. He's got as much right to be here as you."

Jay must have been watching. She nods at Doug. "It's good to have you here."

"Mind if I go in?" He points his lips at the chamber.

"Go for it," Jay says.

He looks at me.

"Sure."

Black sneakers joins the line at the last minute, behind Doug. He has to duck his head going into the dome.

"Mr. Chatty," Jay says.

I want to ignore her. "You know him?" I ask.

"He goes to the Starlight. Gay bar Annie and I go to sometimes. Sits in the corner, reads his book, gets quietly hammered. First time I've seen him here. Something must have shaken him loose. Easy target if little James wants to curry favour with the hard boys ..."

"Like Warren?"

"Frig that's weird, that tattoo on his face. Frigging scorpion." She shakes her head, glances at me. "Listen, when you told me earlier ... Annie says I carry the observer bit too far. Of course you're not going to be running around going, 'My father's a lesbian, isn't that cool.'"

It catches me off guard. My eyes fill with tears again. "Sorry. I'm kind of a mess."

"You have someone you can talk to about this?"

"Oh yeah. People in meetings. You know."

"So where did you leave things with your ..."

"I can't start calling him Mum."

"Does he want you to? Is that why he told you? Because he's going back?"

"To being a woman?" I stare at her. "I hadn't even thought ... I don't think so. Christ. Dad in a dress."

Chapter Nine

THE ASPENS WHISPER. I knock again, louder, turn the handle, nudge open the door. "Dad, it's Meg."

Silence.

Two steps into the living room.

He's in his armchair, head tipped forward onto his chest. Weird angle.

"Dad."

Nothing.

"Dad." Louder.

His head jerks. "Wha?" Spittle in the corner of his mouth. Then he's awake, looking up at me.

"Sorry. Sorry. I shouldn't have startled you. I ..."

He knows what I thought.

He looks different. Frayed shirt collar. The cuffs of his grey wool sweater are ragged. He's usually so crisp. When he knows I'm coming. He gets dressed up for my visits. She. She gets dressed up. "Shall I put the kettle on?"

"That would be nice."

While I'm filling it I hear him stand, shuffle-tap across the floor. He's been using the ebony cane ever since Mum died. It hung in the back of the pantry, that cane, all the years I lived here. I pulled it out once. Mum found me playing with it. 'Put that back.' I remember the hiss of her voice, the weight of the cane in my hand, hard and black,

more like rock than wood. Tarnished silver bands, one on the end of
the handle, one on the tip. I am not thinking about Dad in the toilet.

I put the kettle on, go back to the sink, lean both hands on the
rim, gaze out at peaks gleaming in the last low rays. None of it mat-
tered when I thought ... But alive. In the flesh. Behind me I hear the
toilet flush. No wonder he never left the seat up. A bubble of laughter
rises in my chest.

He's back in his armchair, eyebrows damp. He washed his face,
combed his hair. Her. Her hair.

I get milk from the fridge, carry the tea in, sit down, make myself meet his eyes. "Look ... I don't know how to begin. What to call
you, even. But I'm sorry. I'm sorry about the way I spoke to you. The
other day. I ... it was wrong. I was wrong."

He waits until he's sure I'm done. "Thank you for coming back,
Meg."

I can hardly bear to look in his eyes. "God, Dad. I wouldn't do
that to you again. I promised. Remember?"

"Was I wrong to tell you?" His voice is light, uncertain. "Selfish?"

"I don't know. I wish I didn't know. Or that I didn't believe you.
But I do. And I don't want to attack you for telling me the truth.
Now." I can't help adding that last word.

"Meg, you have every right to be angry. It is an abuse of trust,
to pretend to be what you are not."

"Is it that simple?"

The melt-water eyes study me then he gives a tiny shake of his
head.

"Do you ... can you imagine ...?"

"Going back?"

I nod.

"I haven't. Imagined it. It's so long ago."

I didn't realize I was holding my breath. "Was it when you came
to Canada?"

"No."

"How old were you when ...?"

"Thirty."

I try not to stare.

"What?"

"A third of your life, almost. That whole story. How you came here as a young man, with nothing but a fiddle and the complete Shakespeare."

"Your mother loved that story."

"And you sat there while she told it. Dad." I stop. It's like standing on ice, watching it crack, one crack running to another. "I thought I was finally going to get some ground to stand on. Instead." I'm crying. "Shit."

"Meg." He lifts his hand, drops it back on his thigh.

"When you said you had something to tell me ..." Tears pour out of me. He's holding something out. A large white handkerchief. I blink, swipe at my eyes with it. "I thought you were going to ... it was stupid. I was just so sure."

His face crinkles up as if he's going to cry too which I never saw, even when Mum died.

"Oh Meg, I didn't think. That's what you meant. I thought somehow you knew. When you said you wanted the truth. Of course you thought ... but." He's looking straight at me, waiting for my eyes to meet his. "I don't know anything more about where you came from. Any more than I told you years back. I give you my word. For what that's worth."

I've never, ever heard him sound like that. "It's worth a lot, Dad." The first part comes out right but my voice crunches up on 'Dad'. I try repeating it. No go. He's watching me.

The last slant of sun reaches in, gilds his face. His skin which was always leathery and creased is translucent as onion skin. But what looks back at me from his eyes is a vein of ore that runs back into the mountain, further than I'll ever reach.

I take a deep breath. "When I look at you I see you. My father. The man who raised me. But then I do a double take. You were who I trusted. What I trusted. I don't know how to believe you now. I don't even know what to call you. I don't think I can call you Dad anymore."

He looks away, his eyes finding the mountains. A jagged line rimmed with flaming orange. After a minute he looks back at me. "How about Ben?"

"But that's not your name, is it?"

"I think I can call myself Ben after using the name for seventy years." His voice is chilly.

"But what were you called?"

"I haven't ..."

"Mum knew."

"Yes."

I wait.

Finally he says, "Charlotte Hunt."

"Charlotte." A girl on a lawn, a woman's voice calling, 'Charlotte,' the girl running toward the voice. It has nothing to do with him. "Where did Ben come from? Ben Coopworth? Did you just make it up? But you have ... you must have papers." Which is rich, coming from me.

There's a knock on the back door. A voice calls out, "Can I come in?"

I look at Dad. Ben. He nods. I go and open the door.

Victor Hetzl slips past me carrying a tray. He takes it through to the living room, nudges the teapot aside and sets it down. A covered casserole and a small bowl. Sour cream? "I made enough for you too, Meg."

He flicks on the overhead light. The clock on top of the bookshelf in the living room chimes five.

Victor asks, "Do you want to eat here or at the table?"

"The table, I think," Dad says. Ben says.

Victor sets two places at the square turquoise Formica table with the chrome edge and the legs that go straight down from the outermost points of the corners. It would fetch a fortune in some vintage store in Kitsilano. Dad's napkin is rolled up in the ring he carved out of a knot I found in the woods. The first thing I ever brought him.

Victor lifts the cover off the casserole and the air fills with smoky sweetness: paprika, beef, onions. "Enjoy," he says. A moment later the door clicks shut.

I look across the table at Dad, how bony his shoulders are. Perfectly flat chest. I always thought it was his metabolism. "Did you stay so thin because ...?" I didn't mean to say it out loud, don't know how to end.

His lips twitch. "Added years to my life"—he pauses—"watching my figure."

Wow, as Jay would say. *I love it.* I don't. I ladle goulash. Then we both stop because Mum would have said grace and I don't know about Dad but I can hear her voice so I look down at my bowl for as long as it would take. We pick up our spoons at the same moment. When I look at him, it's as if one eye sees Dad while the other keeps finding the woman. Finding and losing her. Panic swells in my chest. My palms sweat. Stop. Breathe. Eat. Pay attention.

The beef melts in the rich red sauce, sour cream a lush accent. What bread would go with this? Rye, with caraway.

"All from the ranch," Dad says, Ben says, resting his spoon, "all but the beef. Funny that. They're farmers, not ranchers, Victor and Manfred."

"Is this a regular thing, a dinner like this?"

"They like to eat. They say it's no trouble to make extra." He shrugs.

Early on they volunteered to do his shopping for him. It was a relief not to drive out every week. But I didn't know they'd taken over the cooking.

"It's good to have some life around the place. Someone to work the land. Even if it's just a bit. Reminds me of the early days. We grew it all, your mother and me. Kept our money for taxes. Polly was a fierce one for saving. But you know that."

I put down my spoon, questions piling up in my brain.

"Go on," he says. "Ask."

"What?"

"Whatever you want. Within reason."

"I don't know where to begin."

"It's why I decided to tell you. I didn't want to leave you with more unanswerable questions. After I'm gone. Whenever that is. Might be years."

"So you're not still planning ...?"

"I wasn't actually asking you to drop me off at the Cardinal Divide with a gun and a pocket full of garlic sausage, as I think you put it." There's a spark of laughter in his eyes. "That was for your mother. I don't care who finds out when I die, if you don't. If you do ..."

"Then what? Back to the gun and the sausage? Dad. Ben. It's not just after. What if you have to go to the hospital?"

"They'll get a surprise. It's quite freeing, not to mind."

"It was all for Mum then, the great lie?" It snaps out of me.

He leans back, eyes me. After a moment he says, "No, of course not. Living here. Neighbours. Friends. Maybe not close but people you could count on to help. Baler breaks down, they lend you theirs. Pull you out if you get stuck in a snow-bank. Kind, decent people, but narrow. Couldn't see them accepting us, if they found out. We'd have had to move, start over. I wouldn't have liked that."

Dad, so coiled into this place I can't imagine him anywhere else.

Mum and Dad, being driven out. Like something from the Bible. People throwing stones. Words and looks, more like. Except for Mum's lot.

"Why did she belong to that church? She didn't have to spend her time with people who would have hated what you were. What she was."

"Your mother was a complicated person." He stops. "I think I should start at the beginning."

I'm on my feet then. "I'll clear away first, shall I? Tea?"

"Meg, you don't have to."

"Clear away? Because Victor will do it?"

Dad pauses. "No, I meant you don't have to hear the story. Until you're ready. Or ever. You could decide you don't want to know."

"No, I couldn't."

Silence.

"Sorry. I want to be open. Accepting. There are moments. But then suddenly I feel. I don't know. Ambushed. I can't. The thing is I can't look at you and see the person I saw a week ago." I start to cry.

"Another death," Dad says. His voice is soft, sad. "For me too. I didn't understand. I thought, well, I'm still myself. I didn't see that telling you could change the past. Because I was never who you thought I was."

Something in me reaches out, gathers in those last words, folds them into my chest. I'm tired. Impossibly tired.

He's watching me. I'm too tired to look away. Too tired to think what is in his eyes. After a while he asks, "Do you have to go back tonight?"

I shake my head.

"Perhaps we should both go to bed."

I twist to look at the clock. Five to six. But it's true, all I want is to lay my face down on cool cotton, close my eyes. I nod.

"Go on then. I'll put these away." He heaves himself to his feet, leaning heavily on the cane.

"Let me at least ..."

He shakes his head. "Go to bed, Meg."

Chapter Ten

IN THE REACHES of the night I wake. The silence is vast, rippling. I lie there, heart clattering. Breathe. Breathe into it. Metal taste in my mouth. Sharp, hard little breaths. Keep breathing. *Come on, honey.* Kind Dora. I'm here. I'm here. But I'm fraying. Dark between the stars. Limitless space. The wind. The interstellar wind. Breathe. Let it be. Let it. Taking me. *Let it, honey.* Dora, big knuckled hand stroking my hair. *Don't fight. Let it come.* She'd know the moment the dark wave broke and I broke and the night took me into itself. *Good girl.* I floated, my breath the breath of the universe, universe breathing me. Nothing to break. Nothing to lose. Bliss to float on the waves of breath. Church of the Holy Peyote. Dora, strange angel, holding your head while you puked.

Downtown East Side Dora, last of the ghost dancers. My Higher Power. Taught me to break so I didn't break.

First year sober, kicking at the God thing, sponsor saying, 'Make it a door knob. Make it whatever the hell you want, long as you know you're not it.' I made it Dora. Six foot three Sioux spirit warrior. Angel of surrender. Purveyor of fine hallucinogens.

Panic's gone. Haven't had it come like this since the night after Mum died. It's not the silence, or the dark. Feeling powerless, more like. A little problem I have. Oh, and loss. Lip-tooth was big on that. How well I don't cope.

And if Dad hadn't told me? If I found out after. Christ.
But he did. Easier not to. But he did.

I wake to the hiss of water filling the kettle. Clink of china. The sky
is brightening. The bolt on the door snags my eye. This room. The
room they built to keep their secret. Their fortress. Only it's more
like a ship's cabin, the mattress tucked between the chimney and the
west wall. You have to clamber into bed from the foot end. I turn on
my side, study the slant-wise view out of the two little windows.

Downstairs, Dad will be sitting in his Morris chair, drinking tea,
gazing at the mountains too. They stand tall. Declare themselves to
the sky. Later they may brood in violet shadow but for now they are
frank, simple fellows. I gave them names soon after I came here:
Hook and Shell, Feather and Bone. Names you couldn't guess. Nail,
Hair, Tongue. Names I gave in my mind before I spoke again.

Dad's head swivels my way, a smile spreading across his face.

"Good morning, Meg."

"Good morning." It's not hard, in the slanting early morning
light, to see an old woman.

"Did you sleep well?"

"Mostly. What about you?"

He tilts his head to one side. "Tea?" He lifts the pot. There's a
mug ready for me. "Might be a bit stewed."

"I'll make some fresh." Dad's stewed tea could pave a driveway.

There's a pot of oatmeal bubbling slowly on the stove. I heft the
kettle, click it on, go to pee and wash my face. My face looks back at
me, same old mystery. I shake my head and the mirror gives me that.
I try a smile and the smile in the face of the woman in the mirror
reaches her eyes so the skin wrinkles at the corners, the wrinkles
fanning out. I did that a lot when I was newly sober, to see if I recognized her, the smiling person.

Chapter Eleven

REACHING IN THE fridge for milk, my hand finds the little brown bottle with its glass handle. I uncork it and inhale. It smells of menthol cigarettes to me but I can see Mum holding it to her nose, a smile softening the lines between her eyebrows. 'Wherever did you get this?' She passed the bottle to Dad.

'The Farmer's Market. You've had it before? I never heard of it.'

Mum looked at Dad. 'The camp where we met,' she said, 'there was a French fellow from New Brunswick who kept talking about how my oatmeal would be better with maple syrup. Everyone got pretty sick of hearing it but then one day he showed up with a couple of buckets of sap, borrowed my biggest pot. He'd tapped some birch trees. Nobody complained after that. When the camp broke up and we were leaving together, your father and me, he gave us a little bottle. "To keep your life together sweet."'

I walk into the living room, bottle in hand.

"Dad—Ben—did you really meet Mum in a logging camp?"

He looks surprised. "Yes."

"And Mum was the cook? And you used to be a prospector, before that? In the Rockies."

"The Selkirks. And the Monashees."

"But then you were a lumberjack?"

"Just for that season. Not all the men were big and burly. Besides, five foot ten was quite tall in those days, even for a man."

"And nobody suspected?"

"Apart from your mother."

"How did she know, if no-one else ...?" I stop, let the silence stretch.

Dad—Ben—says, "I really think I should start at the beginning."

"And I ..." Breathe. "I can look at you and I can say 'Yes, you could be. A woman.' But Mum. Married to a woman. It's crazy. Or she was."

"Meg, listen. I was in my late sixties when you came into our lives. Your mother was fifty-seven. She'd lived longer than you've been alive before you ever met her. She wasn't always so set in her views." He's watching me.

"What is it?"

"What you said yesterday. About feeling ambushed."

"There's more, isn't there? Wait, she was really a man."

"I really think it would be better if I began at the beginning."

"Sorry. I'm not making it any easier, am I? Do you want some oatmeal to go with that syrup?"

At last he puts down his spoon. "So." He spreads his hands on his thighs, pushing down as if he's about to stand up. "Some of this you know already. I was born into a reasonably well-off family in a small town in Suffolk in the east of England. My father was a solicitor."

"But his name wasn't Coopworth?"

"No. It was Hunt. I did have two sisters."

"Whose names were Lucy and Victoria?"

"Yes. And a much younger brother."

"Oh." I take that in. "Whose name was Benjamin?"

"No. Ralph."

"So were you the oldest?"

"Yes. My father's first name was Charles, hence Charlotte. My mother told me once they were so sure I would be a boy they never even thought of a girl's name. But no, it wasn't *The Well of Loneliness*. They didn't dress me up as a boy or even treat me like one. Far from it. My father wanted everything to look just so. Most of all, he wanted us to better ourselves. Marrying my mother, he'd married into a better class. They were in entire agreement about what I should do which was to put my foot firmly on the next rung of the ladder.

"My sisters showed every willingness to acquire the proper accomplishments and to use them in the proper way. I had no use for it, any of it, ever. I was a wolf cub in a litter of Pekinese. My mother was small, delicate. My father wasn't much bigger. I galloped into adolescence, feet and hands and height improperly growing. They tried to chop me down to size. That's how it felt. Only amputation could have made me the daughter they wanted."

He stops, eyeing me. It's the torrent of words that surprises me as much as anything. 'This isn't Dad,' I think, then don't know whether to laugh or cry. "What became of your brother and sisters?"

"I have no idea."

"You lost touch when you came to Canada?" That was the impression I got from Mum.

"Before that. I haven't seen any of them since I was seventeen."

"Oh. How old were you when you came to Canada?"

"Twenty."

"But you came as a girl?"

"Yes."

"On your own?"

"No."

Before I can ask about that, something's niggling me. "*The Well of Loneliness*?"

"Lesbian novel. 1920s. The hero's a woman called Stephen."

"I know *The Well of Loneliness*, but where did you come across it?"

He shrugs. "I'm not illiterate, you know." He leans back in his chair, eyelids drooping.

What did they have, a little lesbian book club? Mum and Dad. Ben. Charlotte. One or two other ranch couples I never thought twice about? I shake my head. There's one thing I'm pretty sure about. Mum did not think of herself as a lesbian.

Dad's snoring lightly now, chin tucked down on his chest. Usually his head tips back.

Looking at this house is like looking at him. One eye sees the square little Prairie house I grew up in. Through the other, it's their shell, thick and hard enough to shelter the secret. They let me into one but not the other.

WEEK TWO

Chapter Twelve

"WHERE ARE WE going?" the guy sitting across the aisle from me asks. Don. He operates some kind of heavy equipment in the oil-patch. "You're allowed to tell us now."

"The AA meeting in Beverly. "

"Beverly." Don shakes his head. "You guys pick these neighbourhoods on purpose?" Short back and sides, brown hair, little moustache. Everything annoys Don. Particularly all the no good welfare bum clients. He doesn't quite say drunken Indians but he's thinking it. Only he has to put up with it all because he's going to lose his job if he doesn't stay the full seven weeks.

Can't Get No Satisfaction blasts out of the speakers. I'm sitting next to Theresa. Head half-turned away from me, she's gazing out of the window. Dark fields slide past, then squat commercial buildings with big metal doors, then houses, rank on rank, too big for their lots, cars gleaming in the driveways. The bus rocks with laughter and catcalls. The ear-battering beat of the music is the wild throb of survival. I close my eyes, just want to swim in the crazy soup.

The bus swings left. "Ooh, trigger," someone yells. We're on 118th Avenue already, passing the East Glen Motel.

"Been there," one of the men shouts.

"Shut up." A woman's voice.

At the light by the library a sign reads, *This neighbourhood does not tolerate prostitution.*

Theresa's eyes are closed. She's a beautiful woman. Straight nose, perfect sculpted lips, hair black as a raven's wing. A beautiful Cree woman. No-one would ever take her for Ukrainian. She used to run an escort service. Jay told me. 'Hired a couple of her brothers as muscle. Bunch of girls working for her. Quite a businesswoman, our Theresa. Only then she started using crystal, right? Ended up on her back like the rest of 'em, brothers pimping.'

The bus jolts to a stop. Her head jerks. "Are we there?"

"Not yet."

She turns to look at me. "You've been sober a long time, eh?"

"A day at a time. You're leaving on Wednesday, aren't you?"

She nods.

"How does it feel?"

"Scary."

"Because of last time?"

"I was so sure. Too sure."

We all thought she'd be the one. One and a half out of fifty. Those are the stats. She went tree planting in BC. Good money, no meetings. The day the helicopter brought them out on break, she picked up.

Everyone piles out and lights up. Doug and I stand on the street edge of the cluster. He seems okay with just watching, a little smile on his lips. They're a soft, beige pink, his lips, the edges indistinct.

"I used to come to this meeting," I say at last.

"You live around here?"

"Few blocks away. Nicer neighbourhood."

His lips twitch.

"Not hard, eh?"

"You like living in the city?"

"No."

"Hey Doug. See that?" It's James, pointing his lips at a white SUV parked a few yards up the road.

"Uh huh."

"Know what that is?"

"Mm. No."

"You?" James looks at me.

I shake my head.

"Undercover cop."

"How do you know?" I ask.

"Antennas."

I look again. The car's bristling with them.

"Learn something every day," Doug says. "Thanks, James."

He nods, pleased, and saunters off.

"All who care to, join me in the Serenity Prayer." The guys doff their caps. Shining black hair, shaggy blonde, orange. Mona. The regulars are all seamed faces, grey hair or no hair. Beverly is old guard white working-class even though the main drag has a Caribbean restaurant now. My eyes travel round the circle again.

Amen. Hai, hai.

A barrel-chested man, bald pate ringed with sparse silver hairs, stands up. "My name is Vince and I'm an alcoholic. Welcome, everyone from Dreamcatcher Lodge and anyone else who's new to this meeting." He leans forward, scans the back rows. "I want to tell you, I envy you. You've got a shot at getting sober now. Don't have to wait to be an old fart like me."

People always say this at meetings. People said it when I got sober and it annoyed me then. James is leaning back, jiggling his knee. A couple of the girls are whispering.

The old men are old men. Stubbled faces, pot bellies. Dad didn't have to shave. I never thought about it. Dad squatting on his heels, gold hairs on his arms. Her arms. Something curled in the palm of his hand. 'A caterpillar. One day it will be a moth or a butterfly.'

"I was fighting four cops at once. When I was drunk I was ten foot tall and tough as a grizzly. Next thing you know, I'm on my face in the dirt and after that I'm in a cell, no belt, no bootlaces, puking in the jake."

Is it easier for a woman to pass as a man? The only woman here besides the Dreamcatcher crew is Amelia, heavy-breasted, pear-shaped. She does have a moustache.

"You know what I did, the minute I got out of jail? Went and bought me a bottle, get the taste out of my mouth."

The regulars have heard it a hundred times but they're laughing too.

I sit down next to Theresa again. She glances at me, half-smiles then goes back to the window. The driver cranks up the radio. We pass the library and the Lucky 97, lights green all the way. My street now. Couple blocks back from the mansions along Ada Boulevard. Four blocks south of crack and cops and tricking. Like layers of clothes sliding over one another, the worlds, all separate, all happening all at once. In my old job I fit right into the Highlands. Slipping off my pumps at the end of the day.

Voices erupt in the back. I half stand, twist around. Doug's got it. Laughter now. Theresa's cheek is pressed against the glass, her eyes closed. Last time she was in, she talked about the day child welfare took them from her grandmother, Theresa and her four brothers. Not before Theresa got a cracked skull and a bunch of broken bones. Foster care was worse. Her foster father raped her. Social worker too.

Theresa stirs then sits up. She rubs her eyes. "I know I have to go to meetings. But those guys ..." She tips her head back. "It's all the same disease but ..."

"Not all the meetings are like that. Are you going to stay in Edmonton?"

She nods.

"You've been to the *Mustard Seed*, right? That's my home group."

She looks away. "That neighbourhood."

Crap.

She looks at me. She knows I know. Her chin comes up. "I have a plan," she says. "I'm going into the concrete business. Couple of my cousins are into that. Driveways, pavements. Start small. Build it up."

Let her do it, let her succeed. Whatever You are.

"If you stay sober," I say, "you can do whatever you want."

"I could hire my brothers. We'd work together. A family business, you know?"

'The Pen boys,' Jay calls them. 'They'll always get her, those brothers. Welfare split them up. She's always trying to put them back together.'

"First things first," I say.

Theresa nods, turns to stare out of the window again.

She was old school, my kokum. Taken from her family, sent to residential school. *She never cried again.*

A few weeks after I started at Dreamcatcher, Dad asked me how it was, the work.

'At least I feel like I'm doing something useful. But it's frightening. Because I can't.' I shrugged, the wall of everything I couldn't make different rising up in front of me. I wanted to cry but I was sick of crying, sick of Mum being dead, sick of everything I couldn't change.

'You can't but you want to. That matters.'

Then I did start crying. It undid me, the gentleness, and I cried until I was dripping and red-eyed and my nose was chafed. He sat there while I cried and made little mm-ing noises, him in his chair, me on the chesterfield, then he made a pot of tea.

I thought we never touched because he was old and English.

Chapter Thirteen

"IT'S HARD TO describe what it was like, being a girl in those days. I was full of energy and curiosity but all I was supposed to do was wait. Wait for a man to shelter me from the world."

"So what did you do?"

"I waited. And read. I read Shakespeare, George Eliot, Dickens, Hardy, Mrs. Gaskell. Whatever I could find in the library of the holding tank for young ladies that passed as a school. At least it was better than the governesses we had for a while. I lived inside the worlds those writers made. I don't know if I can explain this. How little room there was to move or dream. To believe there could be anything different. I was thirteen when the War began. It was supposed to be over by Christmas. At first it was all speeches and cheering. The gardener's boy went off to fight. But so many died. The nearest gentry. They lost one son, then another, then the last. My mother had dreamed of the youngest son for me or for Lucy."

He stops, takes a drink of tea. "God help me, I thought it was an adventure. One that I was barred from, as I was barred from anything exciting." He shakes his head. "The other thing I did was act the leading man in any number of Shakespeare's plays. I was the tallest girl in the school and besides I had no trouble learning my lines. As long as I read them out loud."

"That's how you know such huge chunks of Shakespeare?"

"They didn't need a prompt, if I was on stage." The skin crinkles around his eyes, creases upon creases.

"Is that what you've been doing all these years, acting?"

He studies me for a moment. "No. The other day, when you asked if I wanted to go back to being a woman. It took me by surprise. I really haven't considered that as an option. When I was a girl, I was a girl. Frustrated by the limitations. But I didn't feel I was a boy. And yet"—he shrugs—"I don't feel as if I am a woman pretending to be a man. Does that make sense to you?"

"I think so."

"So perhaps I'm a woman or a man." He hooks an eyebrow at me. "Not 'and'?"

"I don't know if there's room for 'and.' Not yet. What's the matter?"

I shake my head. "I could be having this conversation with a friend in the city. With a client, even. But here"—I look around the living room—"it means Mum is really gone." Tears spill down my cheeks.

"Ah Meg."

I wipe my eyes. "Sorry."

"I miss her. Not every minute. That would almost be easier. The jolts of remembering. And then ..."

"And then?"

"The house is very empty."

After a while I say, "So Mum was the only person who knew?"

"There were two other women I'm fairly sure guessed the truth."

"But you didn't talk about it?"

"No."

"So you never told anyone else?"

"No. Why?"

"I was thinking what a bond that must have been. For Mum and you."

He studies me, surprised. Is it really so unusual for me to look at things from his point of view?

"For better and worse," he says.

"Did you ever consider telling me?"

"A few days after your mother died I found myself telling you, in my mind. The whole story."

"I meant when Mum was alive."

Slowly he shakes his head. "No."

I wait but he doesn't say anything more.

Chapter Fourteen

OUTSIDE THE WIND snatches at my hair. The sun is a pale suggestion of itself, as if snow is on the way. Instead of taking the path to the river I go back behind the barn where every bit of old machinery Dad ever owned is stored. Teeth and gears and tines, axles, tires. Bleached grasses tick against rusted metal. Here and there flakes of the old brave colours cling on. Green, orange, red. Poppy red.

'Put it on,' Dad said. We were standing in the driveway. A cold, sunny November day.

I held it straight out in front of me, opened my finger and thumb. It dropped to the ground. I didn't see it drop because I was watching his face. His eyes went flat and flint grey.

'You don't know anything.' His voice was as hard as his eyes. He marched off.

Mum, hanging clothes on the line, turned at the sound of his voice, a wet shirt in one hand, clothes pegs in the other. She looked down at the poppy lying in the grit.

'Meg.' Her voice was a whisper.

I bent over, picked it up, dusted it off, pinned it to my coat. I wanted to cry but wasn't going to give anyone that satisfaction. In another year I'd have ground it under my heel.

"Nice walk?"

"Just poking around. I was remembering the poppy."

"You didn't know. I didn't know how terrible that war was. The newspapers were mostly concerned with keeping up morale. Who was it said, 'Truth is the first casualty of war?'"

I shake my head.

"You're working today?"

"Yes, but I don't have to leave until one. Will you tell me more of your story?"

"Where was I? At home, waiting for my life to start. The head girl from my old school lived nearby. I talked to her after church one Sunday. I hadn't seen her for a while. Dorothy was her name, a tall, dark-haired girl with grey eyes and a sort of natural authority. She was a couple of years older than me. Her father was the local doctor. Her mother was dead. He was an unusual man, the doctor. He believed in education for women. She was supposed to be going up to Cambridge. She told me she was going to France instead, to drive an ambulance. She was home visiting for a few days before she shipped out.

"I went to see Dorothy that night. Just let myself out of the house after everyone had gone to bed. I'd never done such a thing before. It was raining. There was no-one around. The doctor was out on a call. But they were used to knocks on the door at all hours. The maid was surprised when I asked to speak to Dorothy. I was shown into the library. I told Dorothy I wanted to go with her. Did I know how to drive? They gave preference to anyone who could drive. She'd learn-ed so she could help her father with his rounds. I don't know where I got the nerve, really. I wasn't usually so bold, but I asked if she would teach me.

"'I'm only here for a week.'

"I didn't say anything, just looked at her.

"Suddenly she smiled. 'Why not? You always were a plucky thing.' As an afterthought she said, 'Your father will agree?'

"'Oh yes,' I said. It was a glaring lie, but she didn't notice. She had no idea what it was like to grow up in an ordinary family.

"The next day I told my mother I was going to Dorothy's to wind bandages. We practiced in her father's car while he held his surgery. Petrol was rationed by then but he was allowed extra. By the second day I had the hang of it, more or less. Dorothy wrote to the Baroness." Dad glances at me. "A handful of aristocratic ladies took it upon themselves, late in the war, to raise funds and recruit drivers for private ambulance corps. Mostly women. Freeing up the men to fight. The authorities were desperate enough by then for bodies in the trenches." A bitterness in his voice I've never heard before.

"The Baroness replied by return of post. They'd take me as long as I was eighteen. Dorothy's recommendation counted for quite a bit, I think. I was a few months shy but I saw no need to confess that to anyone."

He shakes his head. "I'd always been quite honest but I discovered I had a talent for duplicity. I could lie"—he snaps his fingers—"like that."

"So what happened?"

"We were due to catch the ten o'clock train on Monday morning. I packed a small bag on Sunday, hid it in the garden shed. I had a couple of pieces of jewellery from my grandmother. I took enough money from my father's dresser for the train fare. That night I sat at the supper table, looking at them all, not listening really, just fixing their faces in my mind, Lucy, fair like my father and me, Victoria with my mother's colouring, brown hair, hazel eyes. Ralph was in the nursery. He was only two. I went and watched him sleep.

"At breakfast I told them I wanted to go and train as a nurse. That I wanted to do my bit and had been accepted into a program. I planned to leave in a week's time. My father forbade me to go. I said I was sorry but I was going to go anyway. I had never imagined speaking to him that way. He told me I was not to leave the house. That if I set foot outside, as far as he was concerned, I might as well be dead. My mother wrung her hands but she didn't stand up to him."

"That wasn't what you were planning to do though, was it, the nursing?"

"No, but I didn't want to just creep away. I suppose I needed to give them a chance even though I knew my father would never agree."

"Why didn't they stop you?"

"They thought they had a week. And they were distracted by their outrage." He shrugs. "I really hadn't thought it out very well. I just knew it would work. And it did. A week later I was in France."

"You never saw them again?"

He shakes his head. "I'd broken through into another world.

Done something so unthinkable there was no turning back. I'd never imagined defying them in that way. But then there was Dorothy talking about driving an ambulance behind the lines and I wanted so fiercely and completely to go with her. It was my chance. I saw it and I took it. A week later I was in a world I could never have imagined."

He closes his eyes, opens them again to stare at the mountains. A couple of times I think he's going to say something. But then his eyes close and stay closed.

His head is tilted back. The morning sun touches the domes of his eyelids. Wrinkled skin falls away from the ridge of his nose to collect in soft creases along his jaw. Trying to picture a young Dad it's not so hard to see Charlotte. The soft mouth, thick, honey-blonde hair, that faint golden fuzz on peachy skin. The quiet stubbornness and quick reactions. The way he trained dogs, horses. He'd see what the animal was thinking. By the time it started to act he'd already be there, deflecting, redirecting. So quick it was as if it had changed its own mind.

He tried to teach me how to do it. I could read the tells but I never reacted fast enough.

Chapter Fifteen

"YOU WERE GOING off to drive an ambulance."

"So I was." His eyes stray to the mountains. "I'd rather not talk about the war right now." He still isn't looking at me.

"All right."

"It was over, six weeks later."

"It's okay, Dad."

He does look at me now. "Some things are never 'okay'." After a moment he says, "It wasn't easy, coming back. Everybody celebrating victory. Happy to welcome the heroes home. Unless they were wounded. Unless they couldn't forget."

He picks up his tea, puts it back down. "And for us, well, we'd lived. Full strength. Suddenly we were supposed to step back into our corsets." He says the word with such disgust I can't help smiling. He sees my smile, returns it, shaking his head. "There were not many options for genteel young women of no means. Through one of the other drivers I found a position as a glorified nanny. A servant with a pretty accent. Ignored by the other servants, condescended to by my employers. But what else was there for me to do? It seemed hardly better than the life I'd left. And I did miss Ralph."

"You never tried to get in touch?"

"I wrote. Once. To say I was alive and well. Gave them my address. I never heard back. I didn't see much of Dorothy. She didn't go up to Cambridge after all. Her father died in the Spanish influenza outbreak. She trained as a teacher, specializing in Sunday School. Then one day I got a letter from her, asking if I would be interested in taking part in a mission to bring Sunday School to settlers in Western Canada." He smiles, seeing my face.

"The Bishops of Saskatoon and Calgary had started a Sunday-School-by-post program but the Women's Auxiliary wanted to do more. The settlers were unchurched and their children were growing up as heathens. 'They could set a snare for a rabbit sooner than recite the Lord's Prayer,' according to the Auxiliary who, bless them, raised enough money to buy a motor caravan. They were going to take religion to those children, by God. Dorothy was to be the teacher but they needed a driver. The team would be sleeping in the van or camping out. Obviously it would be most improper for the driver to be a man.

"There were quite a few applicants. Almost all of us had driven ambulances in the war. Ideally they wanted someone who could perform running repairs. I'd once replaced a fan belt with a stocking. And I came from a respectable family. No doubt Dorothy put in a word for me. In any event, I was chosen. The Women's Auxiliary paid your return fare, second class, if you couldn't afford to cover it yourself, and you got your room and board, such as it was."

I shake my head, smiling. "You came to Canada as a missionary?"

"I had some belief, growing up. The war put paid to most of it. But I didn't mind going through the motions. Religion wasn't terribly important to me, either way."

"You didn't tell them that?"

"No. I let them assume I was a properly devout young woman." His eyes flit over to the clock. A moment later it chimes noon.

"Are you hungry, Dad?" Somehow it's getting easier to call him that again. "Shall I see what I can come up with for lunch?"

"There's soup in the fridge. Victor stopped by earlier."

"When?"

"While you were off on your walk."

I dump the soup into a pan. It's thick and orange, squash presumably. I set it on the range, fill a couple of glasses of water. Stare out of the curtainless window. Did Victor wait until I was out of the way? It sounds paranoid. But I wasn't gone that long. When I turn around the stove is spattered orange. In the pan slow volcanic bubbles burst. I snap off the heat, slide the pan off the burner. A last bubble spits scalding soup onto the back of my hand. Shit.

"Oh good," Dad says, seeing the bowls I'm carrying. "Curried butternut and apple." He sounds like a kid. "I never much cared for squash until I tasted this."

The soup is pretty good. Just enough curry to brighten the starchy sweetness of the squash. The apple lends some tang.

Farmers who can cook. *Too good to be true.* Bill, when the brothers moved to the farm. *Watch his bank account.*

I want to ask some questions but Dad never did like to talk while he was eating. Mum talked enough for two and always finished first anyway. He used to eat so slowly I'd be wriggling with impatience to get down from the table. 'Can I get up please? May I get up? May I get up please?' At last he'd put down his knife and fork. 'Off you go, then.'

When he puts down the spoon I ask, "Where do they come from, anyway?"

"Victor and Manfred? Manitoba."

"And their family?"

"From Germany, I think. Could be wrong. Central Europe. They've taken to this land the way they say the Ukrainians did to the prairies. Knew just what to do with it. *Chernozem.* Black earth. It's a Ukrainian name, you know."

"It's working out well for you, having them here?"

"Oh yes. They know how to work. You should see the root cellar. Cabbages and potatoes. Carrots in a barrel of sand. Great big crock of sauerkraut. Brussels sprouts hanging by their roots, the whole plant. Never seen it done that way."

"Do you give them money for groceries?"

"Of course." He looks me in the eye. "They refused to take as much I offered them." He glances at the clock. "What time did you say you had to leave?"

"I might as well go now." I sound as tart as I feel.

He doesn't say anything.

At the door I say, "Thanks, Dad."

He nods. "Drive carefully. And come back soon."

I open my mouth. Close it again. That's not like him. "All right. I will."

Chapter Sixteen

"HEY MEG. AM I glad you're here." Alison's reaching for her jacket. "I'll just go out for a quick puff, if that's okay with you?" Squarish face, permed black hair, she looks far too young to have four grandchildren.

The front door beeps again. Jay's actually wearing her leather jacket. Definitely means winter. Tanya's hair is still blue. "So I'm going to be a bridesmaid," she's saying. "Powder blue satin shoes, matching dresses. Me and my round brown face. Can you picture it?"

"Keep the hair," Jay says. "Hey Meg."

Tanya nods to me and goes on back to take off her jacket. It has fake white fur on the sleeves. She turns as she reaches the closet, holds out her arms, grinning. "Like it? The girls got it for me. Value Village."

I smile, don't know what to say.

"Height of style," Jay says. "You need a hat to go with it."

"Doctor Zhivago meets the voyageurs. How many are coming in today?"

"I'll look," I say, retreating to the front desk.

Alison bustles around the north flank of the dome. "I'm back," she announces wheezily. "Hey Meg, do you have a sister?"

"Not that I know of. Why?"

"New girl, she's the spitting image of you. I haven't gone through her stuff yet. She's got enough of it. Holy, you should have seen her hauling it all in."

"What's her name?"

"Danielle Laboucan."

"Ring a bell?" Jay asks.

"No." My voice is sharp. Jay's eyes rest on me then turn away.

Alison is pulling on her coat, looking for her bag. She looks up, points her lips at the corridor leading from the bedroom wing. "See what I mean?"

A short young woman with glossy black waist-length hair walks toward us. High cheekbones, pale, smooth skin, strong, sculpted lips. I glance at Alison, puzzled.

"Ignore the hair," she says.

Since mine is reddish brown and cut just above my shoulders that might help but I still don't see it. I have freckles and my lips are nothing you'd notice. Height and build are about the same, I suppose: five foot nil, bulky torso, flat butt and skinny legs.

"I see it," Jay says. "It's in the outline, not the details."

I shrug, irritated, then the girl turns to study the notice board. It's like catching a glimpse of yourself in a store window. Same smudge of a nose. Same big breasts that start at your throat. Even the way she stands, feet splayed, weight back on her heels.

"So how many are coming in today?" Tanya's in the doorway from the office.

"Seven," I say, looking down at the list. "Two are here already."

"Did anyone go to the counsellor's office?"

"Not yet." I look up. Danielle is nowhere to be seen.

"I'll go." Tanya heads for the counselling wing.

Jay's watching me. "How's it going?"

I reach for the logbook. "Not too bad." I write,

> 28th October
> 16:00-24:00 Jay, Tanya, Meg

"How many left today?"

"Five, I think. Should be in the book."

"I'll go and check Danielle's stuff, shall I?" I didn't mean to make it a question.

"Alison didn't do it?"

"I gather there's a lot of it."

I retrieve a pair of latex gloves, a couple of Ziploc bags. The passage smells of sweat and cologne.

"Come on in."

Gone with the Wind drawl. Nobody mentioned that.

Danielle's alone in the room. She's sitting on the left-hand bed, knees pressed together, clutching a book to her chest. Black book, gold cross.

"I'm Meg. How are you doing?"

She shrugs. "Okay, I guess." The accent is for real. Beside her on the bed is a giant suitcase with wheels, on the floor five lumpy black garbage bags.

"I need to go through your things," I say. "I'm sorry. I know it feels a little weird."

"Oh, hey. Do what you have to do."

"Where are you from?" I pull on the gloves.

"Georgia. I guess. Or I was."

The suitcase is carefully packed, nice clothes. Really nice. "So how did you end up in Alberta?" Designer jeans, cashmere sweaters.

"It's a long story."

Silk lingerie. "Tell me. If you want."

"You got time?" She looks at me, dark brown eyes, almost black. Mine are just brown. She does have freckles.

"They'll page me if they need me." One garbage bag is full of shoes. Hope her room-mate's travelling light.

"I don't know where to begin."

"Where were you born?"

"I grew up outside Atlanta." She pauses, watching me set aside bottles of perfume and mouthwash.

"Alcohol," I say. "The mouthwash you can collect when you leave. The perfume, razor, hairspray we keep in one of these bags in the office. You can ask for them anytime."

"Okay." She nods.

"Go on with what you were saying."

"My parents were from Austria. They immigrated in their twenties, tried for years to have kids, finally adopted me. They were in their fifties, kind of rigid. They did the best they could. But I started getting high. Turning tricks, dealing. My Dad died then my mom, not even a year later. I got in more trouble. Cops threw my sorry ass in jail. That was in St. Louis."

She pauses again, watching me flick through notebooks, shuffle a pile of CDs. If someone really wants to hide something I won't find it.

"So where were you actually born?"

There's a knock on the door. "Room check." Jay sticks her head in. "There's a slew of new clients coming in, Meg. We could use you up front. And you're Danielle? I'm Jay."

"Pleased to meet you," Danielle says.

"You need anything, talk to us, okay. Supper's in half an hour."

I pick up the bag of toiletries. "Let's take these to the desk. If you have any money, valuables, credit cards, we suggest you let us keep them in the safe. Then we'll get you some bedding."

"Suppertime. It's suppertime." Tanya's voice blares out of the speakers. "If you don't know where the cafeteria is, follow the crowd."

Jay looks at me. "Why don't you go ahead. We'll finish these two up." She turns her gaze to a sturdy man in his thirties with a dark braid and a thin, jaundiced woman who could be anywhere from thirty to fifty.

I slip in behind Geoffrey as he holds out his hand for a plate of lasagna. He reminds me of a heron, wading at the edge of the water.

"That's so gay." A girl's voice behind me.

"It is not."

"It is too."

I twist to look. Shannon and a gaggle of other girls.

"It's really, really gay."

There's a crash. Geoffrey's dropped his tray. His face is dark red. He's glaring at the girls. "You shut up. Just shut the fuck up. You don't know what the fuck you're talking about." Spit sprays from his mouth. His pristine hi-tops are spattered with tomato sauce. He stands, surrounded by broken china, lasagna, an apple. "You're nothing but ignorant little bigots."

Cutlery clatters underfoot as he stalks away. The girls are gaping, then one of them snickers.

The most obviously pregnant one says, "What's his problem?"

"All I said was something was gay."

"We weren't talking about him."

"He shouldn't have been eavesdropping."

Shannon turns to me. "He shouldn't talk to us like that. And he didn't even clean up."

"Everyone has a right to be here," I say.

"It's just a word. It doesn't mean anything." She opens her eyes wide.

"If it makes someone uncomfortable, maybe you should find a different word."

"Or maybe they should get over it."

The clients stalled out in line behind us are crowding closer.

"He's so *sensitive*." A man's voice.

"Okay. We'll deal with this later. I need a couple of volunteers to clean up."

"He should clean up his own mess," says most-pregnant.

Wendy comes forward and starts picking up broken china.

"Why are we in trouble? Why isn't he in trouble?" Shannon asks.

I gather the apple and cutlery. "James, would you get the mop please?" He glances over his shoulder at Warren who's scowling into middle distance, then does as I ask.

"He used the f-word. That's worse."

I guess it's good that they sound like regular teenagers, given the crap lives they've lived, but it doesn't make them less annoying.

Jay appears in the cafeteria doorway, scanning the room. She comes over, sidestepping the freshly mopped area. "Wondered what was taking so long."

Shannon opens her mouth.

I say, "I'll tell you in the office. Thank you, James. Let's get on with getting supper now."

"Good for Geoffrey," Jay says.

"Someone should talk with him," Tanya says. "Pity Doug's not on."

"Who's his room-mate?"

"Gordon, the Inuit guy."

"With a braid? Barely said a word?"

"Homesick," Tanya says. "They always are. Two thousand miles from home. Cathy thinks they'll be a good match."

"Doug'll talk to him tomorrow. She's given him a lot of shifts, eh?"

"You worked with him yet?"

Tanya shakes her head. "She doesn't schedule us together. Thinks she's being sensitive. I told her we were fine. Doug did too."

I'm not on again until Sunday. That means Jay, Heather and Doug are doing three nights in a row together. Am I being squeezed out? Is Tanya?

"You hang out?" Jay asks Tanya.

"He takes the girls every other weekend. They love it at his place. Long as they can get into the city too. He's good about driving them around. It's not so hard anymore, now they're old enough to be in the house by themselves when I'm working, but it's good to get a break."

"You still seeing that guy?"

"Joe? Nah. Mum's not doing well. She's lost a ton of weight. No energy."

"She been to the doctor?" Jay forks in the last mouthful.

Tanya shakes her head. "Stubborn," she says. "Jesus. I made an appointment for her anyway. Three weeks from now. They'll call if anything opens up sooner." She glances at the clock. "Who wants to do the welcome?"

I shrug. "I'll stay on desk, do up an incident report."

The list of new clients is under the log book. *Laboucan, Danielle N/S.* Non-status. Mother Native, father not. Probably. Laboucan? Hardly an Austrian name. She's not the first Laboucan who's been through here in my time.

Chapter Seventeen

"WE SAILED FROM Liverpool on the Empress of India on the 13th of April 1921. Arrived in Saint John five days later. We boarded the train almost immediately. I could hardly believe it. I was in Canada. I was looking out of the train windows for wolves before we'd reached the outskirts of town. Read too much Jack London. In point of fact the train was desperately overheated. To suit the Americans, we were told. I rode between the cars half the time, feeling the land pass under my feet, the sway of it, the big of it, my chest filling and filling. Forests so vast, rivers wild beyond my dreams. Then we left the hills behind. The first little station we stopped at in the prairies, I stood out on the platform, threw my head back and looked at such a sky as never spread itself over sooty old England, over blood-drenched France. I soared into that sky, higher and higher. Dorothy had to tug my sleeve. I'd have stayed there on that platform while the train pulled away. I shook my head, looked at her. She'd a long face, those clear grey eyes, dark hair pinned up in a bun. I could have kissed her for choosing me.

"'Did you know?' I asked her. 'Did you have any idea?'

"She shook her head, smiling. 'Come on.'

"We got back on the train just in time."

Dad pauses, gazing out of the window.

"What was she like, Dorothy?"

He considers a moment. "She'd a clear voice, not deep, not high, but she could quiet a roomful of rowdy children with scarcely more than a whisper. She was truly a devout woman. The war only deepened her faith. After her father died she went to live with her married sister over near Bristol. I suspect it was mostly the two of them who raised the money to have the motor caravan built. The Women's Auxiliary stocked it with pamphlets and hymnals and posters. We brought those with us on the ship, sent them on ahead once we got to Saint John. They were there when we got off the train in Saskatoon and so was the Bishop's secretary. The van however, was not.

"We stayed with the Bishop and his wife for three weeks. Dorothy taught some Sunday School classes. I went to the garage most days, watched what they were doing. Asked questions whenever they took a break. Poor men. At first they couldn't believe a woman was interested but they got used to me. We spent quite a bit of time considering our route, Dorothy and I. Not that we had maps of any worth. The plan was to cover southern Saskatchewan and Alberta that summer, reaching as far north as the season permitted, then to finish up the next summer. Dorothy was determined that we would drive down every half-way passable track in the district. And keep notes. In order, she said, that the women who came in following years should not need to take unnecessary risks.

"We went up some hellish roads, I'll tell you that. The further west we got, the worse the driving. And the worse the driving, the happier she was. There was nothing she liked so well as to break a spring on a mountain road with a storm threatening. One time, I was under the van, Dorothy passing me tools, when we found ourselves surrounded by sheep. A settler was walking them to market. We assured him we didn't need help. The next words out of his mouth were, 'Are you girls married? I have two bachelor sons.'"

Dad glances at the clock. "How about some lunch? There's more of that soup. And the bread you brought."

"It's good," he says, chewing thoughtfully.

My father, the gourmand.

"What's different?"

"I gave it a longer rise." I take another bite. "The texture's better and there's more flavour but does it taste a little rancid to you?"

"Mm. A bit."

"I think it's the whole wheat."

"That's why they take the germ out of it."

"I need to get fresher flour."

"You should talk to Victor." Dad's gazing out of the window. The sun is shining and it's not windy for once. "Manfred's made a new bench. Shall we try it out?"

It's set on the bluff above the river but in a slight dip. A slatted seat and back rest; the curving arms made of driftwood, river worn, bleached as bone. Wild roses grow around it, the hips mostly black now. Dad sits down with a sigh and pats the wood next to him. We sit, side by side, the usual careful foot between us, gazing at the mountains.

"I miss them," I say eventually. "I miss them in the city. I don't think I could ever live very far from them."

Dad nods. After a moment he says, "I cried the first time I saw them. I'd seen pictures in the papers the government put out. Promoting the West. But they looked so improbable. You didn't know what to believe. Not much, as I found out later. They were opening up the Peace Country then. Land of milk and honey. Never a mention of mosquitoes. Barely a word about the cold. I read whatever I could lay my hands on, the months before we sailed. The one thing they couldn't exaggerate was the mountains. But I didn't know that, driving day after day across the prairies. Then one day we came over a rise and there they were, on the horizon, shimmering, white against a dark blue sky. I pulled over, tears pouring down my face. Dorothy didn't say anything but her eyes were wide too."

After a while I say, "I'm trying to imagine it. The adventure. Coming to a new world. The country you're describing seems so brave, so ... so innocent."

"Innocent," Dad says, as if he's holding the word in his hand, turning it this way and that. "No, I don't think it was innocent."

"By comparison," I say. He's never seen the inside of a place like Dreamcatcher, never dragged himself through the gutters of somewhere like the Downtown Eastside. Or even 118th Avenue. "I mean, you and Dorothy discovering the West, seeing the Rockies for the first time."

"Innocent we were not." Dad says. "Not after the war." His mouth relaxes. "We were naive about some things. I was, anyway. I'll give you that. But how is your job? Tell me about it."

"I'm getting better at it. It's ... It gives me a different window, you know. My old job, everything was under the surface. Dreamcatcher is the opposite. The client's lives. A lot of them, anyway. Everything that's awful and crazy, it's right there. Drugs and violence and sex. But there's a life force running through the place. I don't mean to romanticize it. The chaos they grew up with. Makes me grateful for what you and Mum gave me but ..."

I stall out. "Maybe there isn't a 'but' there. I'm just grateful for the calm and order."

"But it's not the whole story," Dad says softly.

"No. Wherever I came from." I can't finish the sentence.

I stand, walk over to the edge of the bluff, peer down. Ice reaches across the shallows but where the water runs deep, undercutting the bank, it's dark and lithe as a mink. The second summer after I came here, Mum and Dad and I stood on the shoulder of the road at Saskatchewan River Crossing. Dad pointed up at the jagged peaks. 'See that snowy basin?' He waited for my eyes to find the right stretch of snow, the turquoise shadow of ice at its edge, 'That's the Saskatchewan glacier. That's where this river rises.' I pictured it bursting out of the ground like a sleek blue bird.

Where we were standing the water fanned wide and shallow over gravel. It rippled and frisked and it had the colour of his eyes in it. He was gazing up at the ice-fields. Mum was smiling, watching him. I thought, anybody driving by would think we were a family on a summer holiday, me and my parents. It could be true. I thought, it is true. But at the same moment something was caving in inside my chest. I kicked at the stones by the water. I kicked hard, over and over. Mum told me not to scuff my shoes. Dad said, 'Take them off and I'll wade in the water with you.' I shook my head. I wouldn't look at him. He crouched down next to me, picked through the pebbles until he found one flat enough to skip across the water. He handed it to me, looked for one for himself.

'Ben, Meg, turn around.'

I turned, heard a click, freaked.

The one and only photograph they ever took of me.

Did you ever regret it? That's what I want to ask. *Did you ever regret taking in such a weird, damaged kid?* But there's no point. I know what he'd say. No, they never regretted it. Not for a minute.

Dad's standing next to me now, leaning on his cane, looking down at the river below.

"The thing about Dreamcatcher," I say, knowing it's true as the words are out of my mouth, "is that I don't feel weird there. Because half of everybody there comes from some kind of nightmare. The stories are so over the top"—I shrug—"whatever I imagine, somebody's been through something worse."

"I wish I could help you find out. Not knowing"—he shrugs—"it's harder than knowing. Even if what you found out was horrible."

All I can do is nod.

"You're staying the night?"

"If you'll tell me more of the story."

"Then I might stretch out, take a proper snooze."

"Sounds like a good idea. I didn't get much sleep."

His eyebrows ask the question.

"Sometimes getting home at half-past midnight, it's hard to switch off."

I must have fallen asleep as soon as I lay down. I wake to a knocking on the front door. Think for a moment I'm in the city. Then I hear Dad's voice and one of the brothers. Victor, I expect. "Enjoy," he says, and the door closes behind him.

He's cooked dinner for me too. When we've put paid to two perfect pork chops, baked potatoes, Brussels sprouts and sauerkraut, Dad asks, "Where were we?"

"Under a van, somewhere in Western Canada. A passing shepherd was inquiring whether you were married."

"In spite of the fact that we were covered in mud from head to toe. He told us how happy his wife would be to see us and went on his way. He was right. They so rarely had a chance to talk to other women, the wives. They'd talk and talk. We'd sign the children up for the Sunday School by post, give them each a picture and a leaflet.

The choice was: Faith, Duty or Prayer." He glances at me, catching the smile.

"On Sundays, wherever we were, Dorothy would teach Sunday School. She'd bring out Nelson's Bible pictures—great big pictures meant to be hung on a wall—and use them to tell the stories. The favourite was always the story of the Good Samaritan. The children could scarcely believe anyone would be so evil as to walk by a person in trouble. That was one thing you never did, pass by a person in need of help. Not out on the ranches and farms.

"Those were hard times. 1921 was the sixth straight year of drought for southern Alberta. We drove up once to a place, log house, sod roof, door not quite shut. Sheep nothing but skin and bones around a dried up watering hole. No dog barked. There was always a dog. No-one came to the door. We climbed down, walked over to the door, calling 'hello'. I knocked on the door. It swung open. There was a buzzing I'll never forget and then the stink. Something lay on the floor under a shining heaving mass of flies. I felt Dorothy stiffen behind me. 'Dog,' I said. I'd seen the tail. Black, a white tip.

"'Sir,' she said. My head snapped up. In the far corner a man sat. I could hear his breathing now, past the buzzing. Hoarse, uneven breaths. His eyes turned to us. I'd seen that look in France. On the cot between the man and the wall I could make out the barrel of a shotgun.

"'Sir.' Dorothy started to walk toward him, slow and smooth. I never saw that woman scared.

"He didn't move at all. She sat down on the bed a foot away. Never even looked at the gun. 'Tell me what happened.'

"His mouth moved. Took him a while to work up to words. It had been a few days since he'd shaved. He must have been in his thirties. A dark haired, handsome man. Gaunt now, eyes red and swollen.

"'Strychnine. For the coyotes. I ...'

"He started to sob. Such misery dragged out of his guts. Like pieces of himself tearing loose.

"She let him cry. She had that knack. With the women too. She'd sit with all the time in the world. No need to mend or fix or hurry a feeling along. 'That's for God,' she said to me once. 'That's God's work.'

"He cried until he couldn't cry any more. She said, 'I'll make some tea, shall I?' When he nodded she said, 'You'll have to show me where things are' and he got up and followed her to the stove. Showed her a pail of water, box of kindling. While the kettle boiled he showed her flour and lard and sugar. I made biscuits while they sat together and drank tea, the flies buzzing all the while over the stinking corpse.

"'Have you been in the country long?' She started him talking. It was only when he had tea and food in him that she said, 'Where shall we bury your dog?'

"'Moss,' he said. 'Moss was his name.'"

I look at Dad.

He nods. "I never forgot that man. I don't know what happened to him. We camped there that night, prayed with him in the morning. Rains came not too long after. A blessing for the ranches but not for us. Roads turned to mud. Wet or dry, they were a terror, those roads. The way they made them, they'd scoop the dirt from either side of the track, throw it in the middle, flatten it out a bit. Clods would bake, hard as brick, in the sun. Until it rained. You'd have a single track with a three foot ditch on either side. That or a slough. Muskeg. A thousand ways you could get yourself stuck. When it rained enough we'd have to put on the chains. Dreadnought chains, they were called, heavy as hell. No way you could get them on without being completely covered in mud.

"That was the thing about Dorothy. We'd be up to our axles in mud, night coming on, she'd stand there, cheek smeared, hair un-pinned, and laugh. She'd a peal of a laugh. It would ring out over the country and you'd feel, 'Well, life's for the living and here I am.' You couldn't help but feel more alive." His eyes sparkle.

"Were you ...?"

"Was I what?"

I shift, the chair suddenly uncomfortable. "I don't know. In love with her?"

After a moment he says, "We were two good Christian women. Well, one and a half anyway. I can't imagine such a thought ever crossed her mind. They were, in that respect, more innocent times." He glances at me, seeing if I caught the concession.

It's my turn to wait.

"I admired her more than any woman I ever met. There wasn't a petty bone in her body." He looks off at the darkened window. "Perhaps I was a little in love with her. But not ... Neither of us. I can't imagine us ever having been ... We didn't touch. Though I used to brush her hair. So dark it was almost black. As the summer wore on, the sun brought out chestnut lights in it. I fanned it over my forearm, hair so thick I felt the weight of it on my arm. I brushed and brushed. A hundred strokes each night. At first she did it herself but one night it was a hopeless tangle. She asked me to help. After that ..." He shrugs. "But I'm certain nothing more could ever have crossed her mind."

I look at him and he looks back, studiously bland. "Dad ..."

Suddenly he smiles. It's a real smile, eyes and mouth joined by the furrows dug deep in his cheeks. "Sometimes, brushing her hair, I'd picture kissing her on the cheek. She had a creamy smooth skin. The back of my hand might brush her shoulder. But that was all. I felt such a deep admiration for her. I could never have imagined her doing anything"—he hesitates, looking for a word—"smutty."

"Oh Dad."

"I didn't imagine. Not really." He closes his eyes.

I wait. The skin stretched over the domes of his eyes flutters. Eventually I say quietly, "Enough for today?"

Chapter Eighteen

ENOUGH FOR DAD perhaps, but I'm wide awake. Might as well go to bed and read. I stall out on the little square of floor at the foot of the stairs. I'm seeing it the way it was, big crocks and tins in front of me, not stairs. A narrow counter. A cook stove with cream enamel and little black lines. A box of logs. This used to be all kitchen. And Mum cooked everything on the wood stove.

'Dirty old thing,' she said the day Dad and John and a couple of men from the neighbouring ranches carried it out of the house. It's probably still in the back of the machine shed, holding up buckets of rusty nails and bolts.

'Dirty old thing.' I hear Mum's voice as if she's standing next to me and I know suddenly she didn't want to get rid of it at all. It must have been the only way to make room for the stairs.

Why isn't it enough, what they gave me? Even if Dad was Charlotte. Even if most of Mum's stories were lies.

But it isn't. Mum's dead. I can't hurt her now. And Dad? It was Mum I wasn't supposed to hurt. Dad was strong. I was supposed to be strong with Dad so we could protect Mum. I shake my head. Where did that come from? Mum was no fragile flower. She was a farm wife, perfectly capable of chopping the head off a favourite old hen.

I turn to the pantry. Mum's domain the way the barn was Dad's. I take a deep breath but it only smells of dust and vinegar.

Chapter Nineteen

"SO WHAT WAS it like, this missionary van you drove?"

"Chassis like a tractor. About as well-sprung. Big curvy fenders. That was it for style. She was a boxy old thing, dark grey, 'Sunday School Mission of the Anglican Church' painted on the side in big white letters. We called her Hilary, St. Hilary really, but she was known by a few other names in the towns. The Booze Wagon. The Black Maria."

Morning sun's slanting in through the living room windows. I push aside the oatmeal bowls. He picks up his mug and sips, eyes resting on my face, lines branching from the corners. He's deciding something.

"Tell me," I say.

The smile reaches his lips. "All right. One day we drove down 3rd Street in Lethbridge. Neighbourhoods by the railway stations, they were often rough. Hotels and bars everywhere. Of course they didn't have signs out, the bars. Prohibition, you know." I nod. "It was almost dark and we were lost. Eventually we asked the way. I forget where we were trying to get to. People listening to the man who gave us directions were nudging each other, pointing at the van.

"The road we were sent on led out of town onto a narrow spit of land, coulees to either side, Belly River far below. Up ahead there were big frame houses, all lit up. They were painted pink and lime green and yellow. As we got closer you could hear music. It was coming through the open doors. All the windows had lace curtains. There were people in the street, milling about. Men whistled, called out to us when they saw the van. Women came out on the porches, some dressed in velvet and satin finery, some not dressed in much at all.

"Dorothy was driving. She stared straight ahead, going as fast as she could. Just past the houses the road ended. Land dropped away into the darkness. We had to turn around, come back through it all, men stepping out in front of us, laughing. She kept us moving, Dorothy, but only just. I was trying not to gawk. The men were just drunken men but the music that drifted from the houses—piano mostly—from the grandest house, I'd swear it was Schubert. It was like a dream. After all the dusty thrown-together little towns, the colours and lights and music. The fancy clothes.

"Once we were clear Dorothy pulled over, her face white. 'You'd better drive.'

"'Are you all right?'

"'It's degradation of the worst sort. Those women. Girls. Ruined. And where are the police? It's a disgrace. The law is nothing but a laughing stock. You saw. The authorities turn a blind eye. It's evil. And they laugh. They laughed at us.'

"I tried not to stare at her. She was usually so imperturbable. Suddenly I understood what she was saying, what we'd seen.

"'I thought it was different,' she said. 'I thought it was different here.'

"We changed places. I got directions from a sober-looking elderly man. Dorothy just stared ahead.

"At last I asked her, 'Aren't men the same the world over?'

"She gave an angry shrug, as close to tears as I ever saw her. Truth was, red light districts went up right alongside the banks and saw-mills and hotels when a town was settled. But you'd never have guessed from the papers that places like The Point—that's what it was called—existed in Western Canada. Once in a great while you might find a reference to 'the social evil' but that was about it."

"Weren't you shocked?"

"I suppose. A little."

He sounds so blasé. "You never were interested in judging, were you?"

"Never saw the point."

"Whereas Mum."

"Ah. Your mother was very interested in Judgment."

I wait but he doesn't say anything more. Eventually I say, "You're going to tell me about, about crossing over one of these days, aren't you?"

"'Crossing over'? I think you'd better make us more tea. A wraith like me, it might be too much."

"You're laughing at me."

"Perhaps. Just a little. But I should warn you, it's not very dramatic."

"I like hearing about your life before. It helps."

"And I like telling you.

"By late September we'd covered close on three thousand miles. If we hadn't driven up every single track to every last settler's house in the southern half of those two dioceses, we'd come awfully close. Dorothy had signed up any number of prospects for the Sunday School by post, and left each child with some nugget of Christian learning. She was aglow with the success of the mission. The Bishop of Calgary congratulated us. There was a special service to welcome us back.

"I don't suppose it came as much of a surprise to Dorothy when I told her I'd decided to stay on in Canada. The Women's Auxiliary would be happy enough not to have to pay my fare back. The Bishop of Calgary assured me the Bishop of Saskatoon would be only too happy to enrol me in *The Fellowship of the Maple Leaf*, a high-minded outfit he had started to entice British women to come to Western Canada. He was looking for women who were willing to do more than they were paid to do, quote, 'for the sake of Church and Empire.' They were to go out to the prairie schools to teach the children of the New Canadians, many of whom couldn't even speak English. But the women who came had a way of evaporating before they reached the schools. In England, after the war, there were many more women than men, but that wasn't the case here. I could have had my pick of husbands."

"But you didn't want a husband?"

"Shall we have some fresh tea?"

"Do you have anything without caffeine? I don't know how you get to sleep at night."

"There's a jar of dried mint leaves in the pantry."

Waiting for the kettle to boil, I'm thinking about all the different worlds sliding past each other. It's not that they're invisible. More like everyone's agreeing not to notice, until some joker gives the Sunday School bus directions to the wrong world.

"So you didn't want to get married."

"And I didn't become a schoolteacher. Dorothy and I spent a week at the Bishop's when we got back to Saskatoon. I spent most of it in the garage. In between spirited discussions of the van's assorted mechanical travails I mentioned I needed a job. The owner of the garage's brother was looking for a secretary/book-keeper down in Regina. He was having trouble finding a reliable man so he took a chance on me. It paid a lot better than *The Fellowship of the Maple Leaf*.

"My boss was building up a fleet of trucks, hauling grain to the elevators. Mostly he needed someone to keep the books straight, keep track of the trucks and the drivers. He was nice enough. His wife kept an eagle eye on him. She viewed me with the deepest suspicion. Convinced I'd scandalize her any moment. I was a great disappointment. Young men courted me all right but I wasn't interested." He shrugs. "After a while I was known to be stuck up. Thought too much of myself for the local boys.

"It was a penny-pinching, respectable little place, Regina. Started out as a village called Pile of Bones. From the piles of buffalo bones. But that name wasn't grand enough. By the time I was there it was about as far from the Wild West as you could get. It had become the Mounties' headquarters for the whole Northwest Territories. As a result the flesh-pits and saloons had all moved to Moose Jaw, an hour's train ride away. Moose Jaw was what was known in those days as a wide open town. Railway ran cheap day excursions there every Saturday. At work I overheard the drivers talking about it but they clammed up when they saw me. I remembered the music, the houses all lit up, down in Lethbridge. I wanted to go to Moose Jaw, see for myself. I had a couple of friends but I could never talk them into it and I couldn't quite bring myself to go alone.

"I'd walk for miles across the prairies, Sundays after church." He shakes his head. "I wasn't much more of a believer then than I am now but I didn't have the nerve to skip it. The war, the Sunday School van, Dorothy, head thrown back, laughing on whatever godforsaken track we were stranded on, all that seemed further and further away."

"Did you ever see her again?"

"The next summer. She came out with a different driver. Millicent Jones. I didn't much enjoy it"—he glances at me—"seeing those two drive off together. But I needed a job that paid. Time went by. Here I was in Canada. A land of opportunities. At work I'd listen to the farmers complain, the way farmers do, and I'd wish that I had the chance to do what they were doing. But the only way a woman could get homestead land was if she were a widow with dependent children. And I can tell you the bureaucrats in the Department of the Interior scrutinized every one of those applications. There'd been a move before the war to extend the Dominion Land Act to single women but it didn't go anywhere. I haunted the second-hand bookshop. Read whatever I could find about farming on the prairies. One Saturday afternoon the man who ran it took a book from under the counter. 'Thought this might interest you.'"

Dad nods at the bookshelf that makes a half wall between the front door and the living room. "Top left. Would you mind? *Wheat and Woman.*"

A plump, faded hardback, dust jacket long gone. Well-thumbed pages open to a folded sheet of paper.

"It was by a woman farming her own land right there in Saskatchewan. A single woman. Georgina Binnie-Clark. I bought the book, rushed home and read it. At first I was disappointed. She was a well-bred Englishwoman with a small private income. An income that allowed her to borrow money to buy the farm. Five thousand pounds, she paid for land a man could have got for nine hundred and seventy pounds under the homestead act. Nobody was ever going to lend me money to buy a farm. Not that she had an easy time of it, strapped by those mortgage payments in a way the men weren't. She'd bought the best cropland she could find but it was dirty. Wild oats and French weed.

"Sorry. This probably isn't terribly interesting. The thing is, the farm she bought was near Fort Qu'Appelle. She claimed she was writing the book to encourage other women who dreamed of farming. I wrote to her that Sunday. Wrote and rewrote my letter so many times I still remember it." He glances at me.

"Go on."

> Dear Miss Binnie-Clark,
>
> I came upon your book, Wheat and Woman, yesterday and devoured it at a sitting. I am a single woman currently working in Regina in the office of Burbidge's Grain Transport. I drove an ambulance in the closing weeks of the war. From Suffolk originally, I came into the country in 1921, intending to stay for a summer, and never left.
>
> I very much admire all that you have accomplished and would like to meet you and to see your farm. I have a week's vacation coming up in mid-July. If it would be convenient, might I pay a visit?
>
> Yours sincerely,
> Charlotte Hunt

"This was her reply."

He passes me the folded sheet.

> Dear Miss Hunt,
>
> If you can drive an ambulance I expect you can drive an automobile, a contraption I view with disdain, but a necessity nonetheless.
>
> Might I request that you drive my new old motor car from Regina when you come to visit? It is possible another woman interested in farming will be visiting at the same time. If so, I'm afraid you'll have to bunk up. Fortunately my sister Ethel is away so her room is available for guests.
>
> In other words, please do come. I look forward to meeting you.

I look across at Dad. He's smiling. I still can't quite grasp it, how long he was a woman.

"I'll tell you all about that visit, but let's have lunch then take a walk before the wind picks up."

Somebody's running a saw inside the old machine shed.

"That'll be Manfred," Dad says. "He said he'd make some more of those benches. I'll just let him know you'll be here for supper again."

"I can cook us something. It feels funny ..."

Dad's shaking his head. "Victor told me yesterday he's slow cooking a shoulder of lamb with rosemary and garlic. I can promise you, you don't want to miss it."

I open my mouth but Dad's already pushed open the door of the shed. The noise inside stops. What's my problem, anyway? That all those years he was just putting up with Mum's cooking? He could have done some of it himself. Only Mum wouldn't have liked that. She had very clear ideas about men's work and women's work. Jesus. It's still the weirdest part of this whole weird story. The bit I can't make sense of.

"It was a long dusty drive. The car was a beast. When I pulled in at last someone came around the side of the house to greet me, a tall woman in a big floppy hat and britches, a bevy of cats at her ankles. She took off her hat and I was startled to see her hair was shot with silver.

"'Hello, hello.' She'd a warm, firm voice, the voice of someone used to talking to horses. There were horses all around, some grazing, some by the water-trough, windmill turning steadily overhead. The breeze kept the heat off but it was still a pleasure to step into the shade of a couple of apple trees next to the house. The house itself felt small and hot.

"As soon as I put my bag on the bed she asked, would I rather rest or would I like to ride out on the land? I sensed a lot hung on my answer so I replied without hesitation that I should like to ride, not mentioning that it was ten years since I'd been on a horse.

"She must have seen my hesitation when I was faced with mounting the horse she led out. Or perhaps it was my skirts.

"'You can ride?'

"I grimaced. 'Side saddle, I'm afraid.'

"She threw her head back and laughed. 'Anyone who can stay on a horse side-saddle will have no trouble astride. As ever, custom confers the tougher task on the supposedly gentler sex.' She measured me with her eye. 'I've a pair of britches should fit you.'

"As easy as that I was wearing britches for the first time in my life.

"She held my stirrup, showed me how to grasp the horn of the saddle.

"It was true, it was much easier. We rode and I drank in the prairie with a woman I'd never met but instantly admired. She discoursed as if I were on the cusp of owning my own spread and must be spared unnecessary expense and labour.

"I listened but mainly I soaked it in, a woman riding her land, assessing, planning, doing. Doing, my God. The impatience of my whole life boiled up in me. *This, this is what I want*, I thought, and in that moment, in that company, believed with all my heart it could be mine. Would be mine.

"I learned over supper that she was in the habit of inviting women to come to the farm so that they might learn the skills necessary to farming without the condescension of men.

"I immediately pledged all future vacations. Though honesty compelled me to tell her it was unlikely I would ever acquire land of my own.

"That set her off on the Homesteads for Women movement, of which, it transpired, she had been a prime mover. Its supporters hadn't only been women. In 1913 they'd got up a petition to extend the free lands provision to women. It was signed by 11,000 voters, meaning men. The men had their own motives of course. If single women were allowed to homestead they thought more families with daughters would settle the West. It was a real issue, the shortage of women in Western Canada.

"Meanwhile in England 'The Superfluous Woman Question' was a matter of public debate. By the early twenties there were 800,000 more women than men in the old country. But would they extend homesteading rights to women? No. The government's response was that for a man to homestead successfully he needed a wife. If they extended the act to single women it would only serve to encourage women's independence.

"She was a tireless campaigner, Miss Binnie-Clark. After her second winter on the farm she went off to Ottawa to raise the matter. To no avail. By the time we met, her focus had shifted to passing on her skills and knowledge. Most of the good land had been claimed by then anyway."

He stares down at the book in his hand then sets it aside. "She gave me something far more valuable than information. She gave me confidence. I'd seen with my own eyes a woman doing what people said could not be done. Her whole motto was, 'If I can do it, you can do it too.' Which was and wasn't true. Like Dorothy she was possessed of a rare drive and determination and courage. Like Dorothy, she gave herself entirely to the work at hand. There was no saving herself, no scrimping of her energies. No hoarding, you know?" He looks at me, waiting until I meet his eyes. "It's not worth living at half-strength."

Slowly I nod.

The lamb is luscious, as good as any I've ever eaten. Neither of us says anything until our plates are completely clean. "No wonder you didn't want to miss that," I say.

Dad nods. "I'm a lucky ... person."

I look at him. He gazes blandly back at me.

"So what was she like, Miss Binnie-Clark?"

"Wonderful with animals. With people, relentless. Imperious. I think she had to be, to do what she did. She'd come out from England in 1905 to check on her younger brother. Reading between the lines, he was one of those remittance men who'd got into some sort of embarrassment in the old country. He and a friend were making a wretched go of homesteading. They were by way of being a local laughing stock. She decided that she should restore the family name by buying a farm and doing the job properly. She managed to seal the deal a day before a telegram arrived from her father ordering her to do no such thing.

"No one expected her to make it through that first Saskatchewan winter, by herself on the farm, gathering firewood and tending her animals. But she did, and she stuck to it."

He looks at me. "I was never made of such strong stuff. I went around my difficulties. Georgina, Dorothy, they confronted them. I'm not sure either of them ever told a lie. Not knowingly. Whereas I ..." He shrugs. "Well, I did what I thought I had to, to survive. But I admired the heroes. The heroines. Still do."

His eyes drift to the window. The dark glass gives back the room, the two of us sitting in our armchairs, the pot of tea. A simple, ancient scene, stuff of a thousand sentimental prints.

Chapter Twenty

THEN CAME THE *sound of wheels. A buggy drawn by a little Canadian pony, prairie-bred and fearless as fast, flew on its way between fences of flame until it reached the black waste of our own making which no flame could leap. It was Roddy McMahon, and his wife was with him, and her baby in her arms and two small children in the bottom of the buggy.*

'So you burned the old guard,' he commented. ''Twas a wise act. You've saved a burn-out all right.'

'The fires will meet in the dip by the gateway and extinguish each other,' I answered, 'but there's still a wide opening to the worst danger.'

I set the book down on the little shelf by the bed, reach back and turn off the light, the settlers' voices echoing in my ears. But when I shut my eyes, flames leap and embrace each other.

When I open them, cool silver light is pouring in through the windows. I slither down the bed, kneel in front of the glass, blankets draped around my shoulders. A three-quarter moon sails across the sky. Snow-capped peaks lap the horizon.

Georgina, Dorothy, Charlotte, living their full-strength lives. And me? Am I living at half-strength? Is that what Dad thinks? It was a lot easier to have life and death adventures on the prairies in early nineteen hundreds. But what's Dreamcatcher if not full strength? Maybe that's what I like about it. Except I'm always one step removed. Jay and Tanya, they're like Dad. Quick. Instinctive. Me, my flames extinguish each other.

There's a stillness in me then. I don't know what it means but it's true. And I don't know how to change.

I went around my difficulties.

Dad doesn't think he's a hero.

Heroes confront. Confront what?

Their difficulties, of course.

Fuck. This isn't getting me anywhere. I stare out at the moon, a freckled face framed by night-black hair.

I wake before dawn, tiptoe down the steep stairs, but when I get to the bottom there's a glow from the living room. The lamp behind the Morris chair is on. Dad, in his old dressing gown and striped pyjamas, is sitting in the circle of yellow light, reading the paper.

He looks up and smiles. "Good morning. You're up early."

"Morning, Dad."

"Tea?"

"I'll make some fresh."

Standing in the kitchen, waiting for the kettle to boil, watching him read in that quiet room, my heart feels too big for my chest. All the years he and Mum sat there, and now he gets up alone, pads about, making tea for himself.

When I go back in, his eyes are on the mountains. At the skyline a slight primrose glow traces the meeting of rock and air.

I stare, bemused. "That's not ..."

"It's the moon setting. The hunter's moon. It always seems to be particularly big and bright, this time of year."

The glow fades from the horizon.

After a while I ask, "Will you go on with your story?"

"Where was I?"

"At Miss Binnie-Clark's."

He doesn't hesitate. "Before the war she'd made the farm a sort of teaching station for young women from England, girls who wanted to learn to farm. Because it was a way they could make a living.

The professions were closed to them but if a woman could acquire some land, who was to stop her growing crops or raising livestock?

"After the war, though, the supply of Roedean girls dried up. Educated women had other ways to make a living. The few women who did come kept finding husbands. It was a grave disappointment to Georgina."

"Who had no interest in a husband of her own?"

"Not that I ever saw. She liked her freedom."

"You got along well?"

"Very. She was determined that I should have the skills she lacked when she started to farm. She'd been at the mercy of a succession of hired men and had come to the firm conclusion that any woman who wanted to farm should do all her own chores then hire a field labourer by the day when she needed him, even if she had to pay top dollar. By dint of taking my vacations at different times in the growing season, I learned how to break, plough, harrow and stook a field; harness a horse; milk a cow; feed and water the stock; clean and pickle seed grain; cut firewood and keep good accounts of the whole operation. I didn't have much patience for the book-keeping but I loved the rest. It was what I was made to do. In her company, I believed somehow I would find a way. Back in Regina, well, it was harder to imagine."

"What year did you go to the farm?"

"1926. I went again in '27 and '28."

"And then, in two more years, you were thirty."

"Are you going to stay the night again?"

"I wasn't. I'd like to catch the farmer's market this morning to see if I can get some fresher flour. But I don't have to. If you're going to pony up."

He considers me, a smile in his eyes. "I think perhaps I've told you enough for this visit."

"Scheherazade."

He grins.

"I left *Wheat and Woman* upstairs. Do you want it down here?"

"No, that's fine."

"It's almost as good as Jack London." I gather up my stuff and pull on my boots. "Thanks, Dad."

"I like having you here," he says.

Outside the wind is icy.

"Drive carefully." He's standing in the doorway, one veiny hand on the black cane. "Phone me when you get home."

He's never asked me to do that before. I watch through the window as he makes his way back to the armchair. He looks small suddenly, his head further forward, a hump above the back of his neck. Widow's hump.

By the car I hesitate. But what am I going to say if I go back in?

At the end of the driveway one of the brothers waves. No, he's flagging me down.

I wind down the window.

It's Manfred with a newspaper under his arm. "Morning, Meg. How you doing?"

"Good. You?"

"Very good. How was your visit?"

"Good." If it's any of his business.

"We were wondering whether, next time you come, you would stop in to see us. There is something we'd like to discuss."

"We could talk now."

He looks alarmed. "No, no. Next time would be soon enough."

"All right then. I'll be back mid-week, depending on my work schedule."

"Very good." He turns away.

Come on, Meg, you can do it. "Manfred."

He pauses.

"Thank Victor, if you would, for all the delicious meals."

He nods.

I watch him walk away. Skinny butt, dusty blue jeans. He takes off his ball cap, rubs the palm of his hand across the bald dome of his skull a couple of times, puts the cap back on.

Chapter Twenty One

VOICES WASH OVER me; throngs of shoppers crowd around; a homeless man sells me a newspaper. I jostle past the stall with the birch syrup, past puffy, tasteless loaves and rolls, past lurid scarves and toques, orange and black the theme of the day. Nobody is selling flour. I come to a stop in front of a new stall. Vats of pink pickled vegetables. Tubs of white, soft yogurty-looking balls in oil, sprinkled with herbs and some kind of red powder. "Labneh," the woman behind the counter says, "with sumac." She points to a basket of pita cut up into triangles. "Try, please."

I hold out a wedge and she smears some of the white paste onto it.

"It's delicious," a voice says over my shoulder.

I turn. Doug's smiling down at me, a basket in each hand.

I put the pita in my mouth. It's half way between cheese and yogurt, the labneh. The red powder isn't hot, it's lemony. "Yum," I say to the woman who's watching me, smiling. For a moment we're all three floating in a little bubble of friendliness, then somebody nudges me, reaching for the basket of pita samples.

"I'll get one of those please." I point to the labneh. To Doug I say, "What else do you recommend?"

"I only discovered this place last week. I'm going to try those." He points to the pink vegetables.

"What are they?"

"Pickled turnips, maybe."

"Are there other new stalls I should know about?"

"Have you tried the Vietnamese one?"

"The seafood pancakes?"

"It's early enough there are some seats free." Doug nods at the collection of picnic tables in the centre of the hall.

"And she does run out sometimes."

Neither of us says anything until we've cleaned our paper plates.

"God those are good," I say.

Doug's licking his fingers. "The only thing I ever regret," he says ...

"Is not having another one," I finish. "Moderation never having been a strong point."

"You're sober too, aren't you?" he asks.

"Nineteen years. You?"

"Twenty five. So how did you end up working at Dreamcatcher?"

"Somebody at a meeting suggested I apply."

He's looking at me, a smile in his brown eyes.

"Oh, you want the longer story."

"If you don't mind."

People come and go, drinking coffee, resting their feet, reading the free papers scattered across the tables. The roar of voices wraps around us. It feels oddly private. And as if I've known him for a while. Being in program can do that, even if we've never seen each other at a meeting.

"Three years ago I decided to conduct an experiment. I was sixteen years sober but still thrashing around. I mean I had a job, a real job, full-time, benefits. A live-in boyfriend. Owned my own house. But I couldn't settle. People I got sober with, they had good, orderly lives. And they were happy. Contented. Serene. So I decided to act as if everything in my life was exactly the way it was meant to be."

"*Acceptance is the answer to all my problems,*" Doug murmurs.

"My job, my parents, my relationship, my past, all perfect as they are."

"What happened?"

"My life got better. I felt happier. Steadier in myself. My boyfriend and I got on better. I thought maybe I was finally becoming a grown-up."

"And then?"

"Then my mother died. Out of the blue. I mean, she was eighty-eight but ..." I shrug.

Doug's watching me.

"A week after she died I woke up knowing three things. My job is meaningless. I don't love the man in my bed. The third one's a longer story."

He nods. "So what did you do?"

"I went back into therapy."

He snorts with laughter. "Sorry."

"No, it was meant to be funny, sort of. My mother left me some money which was totally unexpected. When it actually arrived in my bank account I paid off my mortgage, quit my job, terminated therapy. And my relationship. A couple of weeks after that I bumped into Heather at a meeting. I knew her to say hello to. She told me Dreamcatcher was hiring evening staff. 'Shit pay but meaningful' was how she put it. Something in me said 'yes', so I applied. What about you?"

"Mine's a longer story too, and I need to pick up the kids, who are part of that story." He twists around to look at the clock on the back wall. "Maybe we could do this again?"

"I'd like that."

Chapter Twenty Two

I STAND, HAND on the gate, breathing in the sage scented air. Out on the floor there's laughter, the click and trickle of a ping pong ball.

"Seen Doug?" Heather asks me.

I shake my head.

"He's signed in."

"Cathy," Doug says, rounding the north flank of the dome. "She lost my paperwork."

"Ah," says Heather, smiling at him. She's wearing jeans with rhinestones sown on the rear pocket and a dove grey turtleneck that looks soft as rabbit fur.

Doug smiles down at her. He's wearing the same ancient khaki jacket. Something orange pokes out of one of the pockets. Baling twine. Horses? It's easy to picture him in the saddle, relaxed and upright.

"And how are you, Meg?"

"Good, thanks. You?"

He's smiling at me now. "Very good." Reaching for a pen he fills in the log.

1st November
16:00–24:00 Doug, Heather, Meg
16:10 Doug on the floor

"It's as if he never left," Heather says, watching him chat to one client then another. "Sometimes I think nobody ever gets away from this place."

"Unless they quit after three days."

"Or never show up for a shift in the first place."

There have been a couple of those in the brief time I've worked here. Guys recommended by the Executive Director, both of them. I try to ignore what passes for management at Dreamcatcher. It seems to fit every stereotype about aboriginal organizations. But then my old whiter-than-white job wasn't exactly free of cronyism.

Heather turns on the computer. I look over her shoulder. An entry from Cathy for noon today. A session with five of the girls. They're opening up about their abuse.

"Cathy's in on a Sunday?"

"Place can't run without her," Heather says. "You know that. Woman's a candidate for Al-Anon if ever there was one."

"Who is?" Doug says from the doorway.

"Cathy. She's setting herself up for burn out. I've tried to tell her." Heather shrugs. "Well, that's her business. What bothers me is the bee she's got in her bonnet that the clients need to talk about their abuse issues."

"Well, don't they?" Doug asks.

"Yes. When they're ready, with their counsellor. But she's been getting together little groups, encouraging them to dig up the old shit." Heather tips her chin at the computer. "She's not trained. She was a private in the Canadian Forces. For twenty years. You know how thick you have to be, not to get promoted in twenty years?"

"She means well," Doug says.

Heather opens her mouth, closes it again. Waspish is how she looks. A word in a book Dad read to me. I pictured a yellow jacket arching its back. About to sting.

"Hey Doug, want to play?" One of the new clients, a young guy with buzz cut black hair and wide-set eyes, waves a table tennis bat across the front desk. "They let you out of the staff corral?"

"The staff corral," Doug says. "I like it. Did you make that up, Joey?"

He shakes his head. "James did."

He and Doug stroll off toward the table tennis tables, Joey in step with Doug, his walk acquiring the same easy amble.

"Poor little fuck," Heather says. They're scarcely out of earshot. "What chance does he have? Foetal Alcohol Syndrome. Oh, excuse me, it's Foetal Alcohol Spectrum Disorder these days. However you dress it up, he's got no attention span, no impulse control. Must be his sixth time through here." She shakes her head, mouth pursed.

"I'll do a room check," I say. No answer when I knock on Danielle's door but when I nudge it open a sleepy voice says "Hello."

"Sorry. I didn't mean to wake you up."

"That you, Meg?"

"It is."

"Do you have time to talk?"

"Sure."

Danielle struggles upright and turns on the bedside lamp. She waves a hand at the other bed. The Bible with its purple velvet page marker is by her pillow. Danielle rubs her eyes with her fists, hair mussed. She follows my gaze. "I took that Bible everywhere," she says. "On the street, everywhere. I don't know what I'd do if I lost it. They gave it to me when I was thirteen. That's how old I was when I accepted Jesus Christ as my personal saviour." She starts to cry. "He spared my life through all the crazy shit I did, for a reason. I know that. And I know I got to be sober to do what He wants me to do. Which will be revealed to me." She reaches for the box of tissues, blows her nose with a loud, wet snort.

The rap sounds better in Danielle's lush Georgia accent. Mum's accent slanted, harsh as the wind off the Bay of Fundy, mournful as the name of the place she came from. Port Lorne, Port Lorne, a seagull's cry of a name. In Mum's accent the love of God never sounded particularly comforting.

"I know I'm forgiven but ... I've been feeling so bad, Meg. I did so much bad shit. I sold drugs. I sold my own body." She starts to cry again. "I feel so dirty."

"You're living a different life now. But it's hard to forgive ourselves, eh?"

She wipes her eyes, blows her nose again. "I'll know I'm a Canadian when I say that."

"What? Oh, 'eh'?"

I'm just about to ask, 'Where were you born?' when her eyes well up. She reaches for a fresh tissue.

"I sure do cry a lot here."

"It's good. It's healing. You're doing really well, Danielle."

"Thank you, Meg. I feel so safe with you. I think maybe I might take a nap."

Heather looks up from the stack of folders on the desk. "All quiet on the western front?"

"Danielle wanted to talk. Shame about the shit she did."

"Peddling her bod, right? I never got to that, did you?"

"Nope. Screwed around a lot but I never made any money at it." I pause. "Do you know how she ended up here? She grew up in Georgia."

Heather shakes her head. "No doubt there's a story. There always is." She reaches for the phone. "Suppertime, it's suppertime."

"All Saints' Day," Doug says when he comes back with his tray. "Day of the very dead." He's gazing down mournfully at the frayed brownish grey slices of what might once have been beef.

"You grew up Catholic?" Heather asks, forkful of mashed potato on its way to her mouth.

"Just outside St. Albert. Saint City. What about you?"

"Catholic school all the way."

"You?" Doug asks me.

"My mother was in the 'Assembly of the Word of God'. Fundamentalist Protestant bigots. I went for a few years. My father"—I shrug—"he worships the mountains, I think, or maybe everything."

"I'm with him there." He smiles at me.

"So Doug," Heather says, "you grew up in St. Albert?"

"And a good little Catholic boy was I. Altar boy, all that. Even thought I might have a calling." He glances my way. "To the priesthood. My mother's dearest wish. But then I turned fourteen."

"And?"

"And I heard the devil's music. Janis Joplin singing *Me and Bobbie McGee*. Wind got under my feathers. 1970, I hit the road. I was seventeen years old. No one could teach me anything. Everything my parents were or cared about, I wanted different. They worked hard, saved their money, fit in. Never talked about where they came from."

Heather looks a question.

"Both sides of my family are Métis, going way back. But they raised me white. So what did I do? Grew my hair, stuck a feather in my headband. Hitch-hiked west.

"Got as far as Winlaw, BC. A happening place back then. Draft dodgers and deserters coming in from the U.S. They built some wild and wonderful buildings. I helped out. After a while I went the other way, down to New Mexico. The groups down there, they were well organized. The communes worked together, smuggling men across the border." He shrugs. "So many people, those days, were trying to live a different life." He looks down at his plate. "We had a saying, 'If it's white, it ain't right.' White flour, white sugar, white men." He looks up, shakes his head. "Sorry. I'm like some old geezer going on about the old days."

"Careful," Heather says. "I lived through those times too. Except I watched the goings-on on television. *Make love not war.* Precious little love but we were certainly making babies. Not like my mother though. I was one of nine."

"How many do you have?" Doug asks.

The front door beeps.

"Four," Heather says.

Chatting and cheerful, the first wave returns, slung with plastic carrier bags.

Doug carries the trays back to the kitchen while Heather and I check through sneakers and tissues, CDs and cigarettes and Halloween candy.

"Who's down for ceremony?" Heather asks, two hours later.

I glance at the board. "You are."

"Oh." She laughs. "That's why I write everything down."

"Think I'll walk the perimeter."

"Doug went to do that half an hour ago. He's probably hanging out with the smokers."

"Is everyone back?"

"Everyone except Mr. Chatty. Nobody high or drunk or beat up. If he makes it back sober too, it'll be a record."

"I don't usually work Sundays. Is it really that bad?"

"I'm exaggerating. But only a bit." She pulls out the basket of sarongs. "Hey, did you check out Warren and Shannon? They came back together."

Scorpion face and James' cousin. "Rehab romance?"

"Tanya noticed he was hanging around her."

"Should we put something in about it?" I nod at the computer screen.

"What's the policy these days? Used to be they'd kick people out."

"I think we're just supposed to tip off the counsellors so they can have a little chat with the clients."

"On the joys of the Detox Delight. Hell of a pool to pick your next partner from. Last time Warren was in—which was before your time, I think—he refused to take off his BC correctional outfit. Red pyjamas with little blue letters on the chest. Figured he was going right back there. Which he did."

"Didn't he arrive high this time?"

"Yeah. They bent the rules, let him detox here. That family, they could have a rehab all of their own."

"How's Theresa doing, do you know?"

"I saw her at a meeting Thursday."

"That's good."

There's a growing buzz of voices outside the office. The reek of cologne and perfume is stronger than usual. Off to one side of the throng, Danielle and her room-mate, Julie, are deep in conversation.

The new chief and smudge person go into the chamber and, after a murmur of prayer, smoke seeps from the blanketed doorway.

Doug comes around the dome, a clutch of table tennis paddles in hand.

"Joey got you playing again?" Heather asks.

He smiles. "Geoff back?"

"Not yet."

He glances at the clock. Five past nine.

"Did you have a chance to talk to him about the little tray incident?"

He shakes his head. "I will, if …"

The front door beeps. Geoff stalks in. He's wearing brand new black high tops. Blue star in a white circle on the ankles. Shiny white toes. He sets his bag on the counter.

"How are you doing?" Heather asks.

He shrugs.

"That good," Heather says.

He ignores her.

Doug says, "I'd like to talk for a few minutes after ceremony. Are you up for that?"

Geoff watches Heather check the bag then nods and walks off.

Heather blows out her cheeks. "Maybe I've been here too long. They're beginning to annoy me."

I don't know what to say. Neither does Doug, apparently. After a moment he says, "Emmett's the elder these days, isn't he?"

Heather nods.

"It might be good if he came and gave his two spirit talk. Have you heard it?"

He's looking at me as well as Heather. I shake my head. Meg no-spirit is more like it these days.

Out front glasses are piled on the ledge surrounding the desk. Clients stand in line, blinking, myopic and vulnerable. Heather wraps a fuchsia sarong around herself as the blanket is drawn aside.

"Going in?" I ask Doug.

"Nah." Lines fan out from the corners of his eyes.

"Do you keep horses?" I ask when everyone is in the dome except for two women on their moon.

"One, plus a neighbour's." He glances down. "Baling twine?"

I nod.

"Better than the other possible give-aways. Did you grow up on a ranch?"

"Sort of. What about you?"

"Farm," he says. "Good vegetable land. Some wheat. They leased out a bit of grazing."

"People don't talk much about that distinction but my father says there were major tensions, early on, between the farmers and the ranchers."

Doug nods. "Running a cattle ranch was an acceptable occupation for the younger sons of the English aristocracy. Versus growing vegetables. That put dirt under your fingernails. English didn't know how to work these soils anyway. It was the Ukrainians who knew what they were looking at."

"*Chernozem*," I say, enjoying the flick of surprise in his eyes. "Same as the plains in the Ukraine. Breadbasket of Europe. One of my father's favourite topics."

"My father too. That and the different strains of wheat."

"*Marquis* and *Red Fife*."

"*Club, White Drop*."

"*Golden Russian. Hard Red Calcutta*."

Doug's smile makes his whole face a relief map of gullies and rises, ridges, banks, sloughs. "You might be the only person I've met who can name more kinds of wheat than me."

"I'd love to bake with them, the old varieties. You can't even get Red Fife around here"

"The wheat that opened up the West."

"Because it ripened reliably here. Until then people starved if winter came early."

"White people," Doug says softly.

My face flames. "Sorry."

From inside the dome comes the cadence of voices reciting the Lord's Prayer.

"What do you think I am?" The question is out of my mouth before I've thought it through.

He studies me, shakes his head. "A lot like me, probably. Genetically, I'm your basic Alberta mutt. Cree, Scots, English, French, Ukrainian, maybe German, *Anishnaabe*. But you can't really tell by looks. My brother you'd have said was pure Cree. He got all kinds of shit in school that I didn't get. Mom's sister, same thing. She says their parents favoured Mom because of that, but then she's mad about everything."

Hai hai sounds from inside the dome. The blanket is pulled back. Clients start filing out.

"How was the labneh, by the way?"

"Delicious," I say as Geoffrey appears. Doug catches his eye.

Heather and I handle meds and phone calls. It's almost midnight when Doug reappears. He looks sombre.

"How did it go?" Heather asks. "Mr. Chatty tell you his life story?"

"Poor bastard," Doug says. "Good thing he had booze."

"Saved his arse until it started killing him?" Her voice is gentle, though.

"Why do people hate?" Doug asks. He sounds young, on the verge of tears, his face crumpled.

Neither of us says anything. After a moment he shrugs. "At least he's here. He came pretty close to not coming back today but"—Doug's face changes and his voice rises a little—"*I'm damned if I'm going to let a bunch of ignorant, badly-dressed little punks drive me to drink.*"

WEEK THREE

Chapter Twenty Three

"HEY, YOU'RE ON again." Danielle puts down her book. "C'mon in."

"How's it going?"

"Good. Little weird. Being here."

"Want to tell me about it?"

"Have a seat." She waves her hand at the other bed. "Julie won't mind. She's real nice."

"Being here's a little weird?"

Danielle shrugs. Her hands are pudgy little girl hands. "I guess I didn't know Canada would be so different. The way people kid each other, even. Let alone the hockey thing. And the whole pointing with your lips bit which is Native, right? Like it's rude to point with your finger."

"How did you end up here? You started to tell me."

"You were so nice, that first day. I was nervous, you know? But I could tell you were kind. A good person. Crazy it was only six days ago."

"Six days is a long time when you're first getting sober."

"Oh, I had ninety days before I got here. Got sober in jail. I told you I was in jail, right? In St. Louis, Missouri. One day I had to go see the governor of the jail. She told me I had no right to be in the U.S. Because my parents never did the citizenship thing. Naturalized. They weren't naturalized Americans. And I wasn't born there. So when I got out of jail they were going to deport me."

"You were born in Canada?"

"Yeah. She told me I could go to Austria or I could come to Canada.

115

I spent my whole life in America. I couldn't believe it, that they were saying I couldn't live there. Like it had to be some crazy mistake. I got a Legal Aid lawyer who knew jack shit about immigration." She shrugs. "There wasn't a whole lot I could do about it. I said the Serenity Prayer about a hundred and fifty times a day, read my Bible, went to the A.A. meeting. Tried to trust I'd be taken care of. God wouldn't have carried me this far to drop me in the shit. Excuse my language.

"The day I got out of jail two officers met me at the gate. They put me and my stuff in a van, drove me to the middle of the Peace Bridge, told me to get out. I didn't have any money. I didn't know a soul. I never even heard of Ontario."

Her voice is quiet. I look at her and the strange big love comes over me. It makes your heart swell and crack. There isn't anything to say but you hope they can feel it. "They told me, 'Don't come back.' There I was, me and my suitcase."

"What did you do?"

"I knew my birth name." She nods. "Laboucan. What I go by now. And I knew the name of the reservation where I was born. My folks told me that. It was near the Rocky Mountains. I panhandled some money, got the phone numbers of a couple of Laboucans on the Firestick Reserve. Called up the first number. Woman answered, Judy. Turned out she was my aunt. She told me to hang tight. Next day she wired me the bus fare."

I'm trying not to stare at her.

"Suppertime. It's suppertime." Heather's voice crackles out of the loudspeaker in the corridor.

Danielle stands up. "I'm hungry all the time these days. I must have gained five pounds. Are you coming?"

"Sure. Yes. But I'd better stop in the office."

I watch her walk down the hallway in front of me. We really don't look alike. Except from the side. But Firestick?

"Go ahead," I say to Heather and Tanya. "I'll watch the desk." As soon as they've gone I pull out the bottom drawer of the big filing cabinet. *Laboucan, Danielle.* There's hardly anything in the file but the aunt is down as the next of kin. *Judy Laboucan.* With a phone number. I put the file back just as Heather reappears, tray in hand.

Chapter Twenty Four

I DIDN'T EVEN check my messages last night. Slept in this morning. There's a hang-up call from Dad. 8:43 pm.

Mum did the talking on the phone. What there was of it. God forbid she'd run up a long distance charge.

No one answers. He could be out for his walk.

It's not like him to have called. Dad with his cane, humped back, stick thin legs inching across the floor.

I wrote the brothers' number on the cover of the phone book.

"Hello, this is Meg."

"Ah, Meg. Victor here. What can we do for you?"

"Um, I was just checking on Dad. I ... He called last night."

"You want to talk to him? He and Manfred just went out to the truck. They're going to the doctor's. A routine appointment. Nothing to worry about."

"Oh. Oh well, thanks. I don't need to talk to him. Just wanted to make sure he's all right."

"Of course. We'll see you next time you visit, yes?"

"Yes."

I stand, phone in hand, looking blankly out of the kitchen window. Six feet away is my neighbour's back door. It opens and she steps out. Quickly I turn away. Janet Somebody. McDonald. More than I know about Dad's doctor. He always flatly refused to see one.

The brothers must know who he goes to. I should have that information. I've been leaning on them too much. They're willing and I let them. But what if they decide to move on? I did consider moving to the farm after Mum died. But the church ladies enjoyed fussing over Dad. Betty, especially. And things weren't over with Bill. He certainly wasn't going to move to the sticks. So when Dad said two brothers wanted to put a trailer on the land in return for doing work around the place and they'd be happy to do his shopping for him, it sounded like an answer. A breathing space anyway. Then he said they wanted to build up the vegetable garden. They'd give him a share of whatever they harvested.

'Grow-op,' Bill said.

Clearwater County's not exactly B.C., climate-wise, but I did begin to wonder if it was too good to be true. Only, when I met them, they were so straightforward about their situation. And their plan made sense. Manfred had worked for CN for thirty years. They'd got a little money from selling their parents' ranch. 'On the interest from that and the pension we can live simply,' he looked at me with earnest brown eyes.

'If we buy a place, no more interest. Then we have to work,' Victor said.

'Not that we're afraid of work.'

'We like to work. At what we want.'

'To grow good food. Tend the land.'

'We'll give your father half.'

'Sharecroppers,' Manfred said. 'We'll be sharecroppers.' He grinned so cheerfully at this prospect that I couldn't help smiling too.

'Too good to be true,' Bill said when I got home.

'Half of nothing's nothing,' I said, 'They probably don't know how to grow a radish. But they seemed nice.'

'It's your inheritance.'

They really haven't given me any reason to worry. The opposite, in fact.

If I did move out there I'd have to quit Dreamcatcher. Too far to drive. Closer to Firestick.

I should have taken that phone number.

Oh, really?

Leaving aside the ethics of taking confidential information from a client's file, what exactly would I say?

'Hello. You don't know me but people say I look like someone who was born on your reserve. No, she didn't live there. She left when she was a baby. She was adopted. So was I. More or less. Only later. I was wondering, um, if you might recognize me. Or someone might. Or I might recognize them. Except I don't remember the first ten years of my life. No, I don't know that I came from your reserve. It's just ...'

The phone rings. Jesus.

"Meg? This is Cathy."

"Hey Meg," Doug smiles at me from by the coffee maker.

"How's it going?" Jay asks.

Cathy's clicking open the gate behind me. She brushes past, sheets of paper clutched in both hands. "Reworked schedules." She waves them around. Doug retreats into the back closet. "Meg's filling in. Tanya had an emergency."

Jay shakes her head at Doug who's looking alarmed.

"Silly me," Cathy says, staring at the pin-board. "I must have forgotten to print out one sheet. Back in a minute."

Once she's gone Jay says, "Doctor called to say they could fit Tanya's mom in this afternoon."

Doug nods. "She's lost more weight. We talked about taking her to Emergency but it's such a zoo. Anyway Ruth put her foot down." He glances at me. "Tanya's mother."

"Who is a force to be reckoned with." Jay shakes her head. "You think Tanya's got the look, you should see her mother. Funny though. The jokes she tells. Make a baboon blush."

"Here we go." Cathy rustles back in. It's not that she wears particularly noisy clothing but somehow you can always hear her.

Jay looks at Doug.

"Cathy," he says, "would it be possible to ask Emmett to come in and talk to the clients?"

"Is there a problem?" Cathy asks, broad forehead furrowing.

"Homophobia," Doug says. "It's making life hard for Geoffrey. And it could get worse."

"Warren's a powder keg and Joey and James want his approval," Jay says.

If I were Cathy I would not appreciate the tone of her voice.

After a moment Cathy says, "I don't see why not. Of course it's important the protocols are followed."

"Of course," Jay says solemnly.

Cathy bustles off.

Jay looks at me. "You ever heard the talk?"

I shake my head.

"I think you'll find it very interesting." Her eyes rest a little too long on my face.

"I'm sure I will," I say.

Jay raises her eyebrows, not missing my tone. I don't care.

Doug stands up. "I'm going for a walkabout."

Julie must smoke a couple of packs a day. Last thing at night is the only time I've found her in the room. Danielle's sitting on her bed as usual. She's wearing a pale pink cashmere turtleneck. Designer jeans. Somehow you can tell they're not fake.

"How's it going?" I ask.

She wrinkles her nose.

"What's up?"

"My counsellor. Angela. She's ... she's not very friendly. Not like you. It's easy to talk to you."

I shouldn't be pleased. "She's a good counsellor," I say. "She's been doing this a long time." I don't add that she scares the shit out of me, yellow-eyed glare, skin leathery as a coyote carcass hung on a fence all summer,

Danielle says, "I just need to talk. Get it off my mind, you know."

"Stuff from childhood?"

She shakes her head. "Shit that happened after I got here. Canada, I mean. Well, Firestick."

I lean back against the door jamb. "How was it, going there?"

"You got a minute?"

I nod.

"My aunt picked me up from the bus in Edson. I spent the first day with her. Judy's cool. Her house isn't much but she looks after it, you know. A couple of her kids used to live with her but she made them move out because they wouldn't stop using. She got clean and sober four years ago. She was so happy to have me there, being clean too. She said I was a sign from the Creator. She wants me to help her bring healing to the reserve. When I'm finished here. To make it a clean reserve like the one they made the movie about. Something Lake. It ... It all seemed real hopeful even though I was bummed about my birth Mom. Who's Judy's sister. She had me when she was fourteen. The nuns persuaded her to give me up for adoption. She didn't want to but they persuaded her. After that she just started drinking all the time. Then she hooked up with a trucker and they drove around a lot but she would come back to have her babies. My grandmother looked after them but she died last year." Danielle's staring down at the bedcover, dark hair hanging forward, covering her face.

"And your mother?"

"She lives on the reserve."

I wait. At last Danielle lifts her head and looks at me. "I put together sixty days in jail, didn't pick up through the whole deportation thing. Even when I went to my Mom's trailer and her boyfriend was drunk and she was smoking fucking crack—excuse my language— even then I didn't want to pick up but when I met my brothers ... I have three brothers and two sisters who didn't even know I existed until my aunt told them I was coming. When I met my brothers and they were shit-faced on a Thursday afternoon, I just ... I just felt like, who am I to think I can be any different? This is who I am, you know. I wanted to know where I came from and this is it." She starts to cry. "I never fit my adopted family and here is why. That's what I kept thinking. This is who I am. A drunk, junkie whore."

Tears trickle down her cheeks like rain on a windshield.

"You didn't pick up," I say, "You came here instead. You're changing your life. That's what counts."

"I prayed. I went in their bathroom which stank of beer piss, you know? Piss and puke. It smelled like a bar room bathroom nobody cleaned for a hundred years but I went in there and I kneeled down and prayed God to keep me sober and He did. I know if I do that every day I'll be okay, it's just ..."

She reaches for the box of tissues by her bed and blows her nose with a loud snort.

"It's just hard, eh?"

She nods. I hesitate. "Feel free not to answer," I say, "but how was it, meeting your mother? I mean I know she was high but ..."

"She ran around screaming 'my baby.'" Danielle's voice is flat. "Then she asked if I had any money, then she passed out."

Chapter Twenty Five

"THE BROTHERS WANT to talk to me about something."

"Mm." Dad's sitting in his chair, sun so low in the sky now it slants through the window an hour after noon.

"Do you know what it's about?"

"They haven't said anything to me."

His eyes wander off to the mountains. I can't make out his expression at all.

"Is it working well for you, having them here?"

"Very well."

"How was the visit to the doctor?"

Something flicks across his face. Surprise?

"Routine," he says.

The word Victor used.

"I was thinking I should have the name and number of your doctor, just in case."

"Of course," he says. "I'll get it for you." He doesn't move.

"I'll get it," I say, standing up, looking expectant.

"Bring me the address book then."

In the little wooden box by the phone is the neat pile of scrap paper Mum cut up for notes. A lifetime supply. Pens and sharpened pencils in the pinch pottery mug I made in Grade Six. The black leather-bound address book is on the shelf under the phone, gilt letters almost worn away.

Dad opens it with his gnarled hands, marks the spot with the little ribbon, passes it over.

Gazing down at the page of Mum's precise copper plate I smell gravy but only for a moment. The doctor's name stands out in Dad's slanting scratch. *Dr. Edith Nesbitt* 780 682 4340.

I look up. "Your doctor's in Edmonton?"

"Victor and Manfred don't mind. They say they always have errands to run."

"They've been driving you into Edmonton for doctor's appoint-ments? You could have told me you were in the city."

"I don't like to intrude."

"You wouldn't be intruding," I say but I know it's not quite true. I didn't really mind that Mum wouldn't set foot in my sinful house.

Dad spreads the blanket over his lap then reaches for his mug.

"This doctor knows?"

He nods.

I'm trying to picture the scene. The first appointment. "And she's all right with ..."

"Yes."

Eventually I ask, "How did you find this doctor? I didn't know they'd take patients from outside the city."

"It's time for my nap," Dad says.

Chapter Twenty Six

SMOKE RISES FROM the rusty chimney then bends to the ground. I knock on the flimsy storm door. Manfred opens it. His smile spreads to his brown eyes. I hold out the paper bag.

"Thank you, Meg. Come in." He stands aside, bulky as a hand-knit sweater where Victor is slight. With grey eyes and darker stubble. A twist in his sharp nose. They're both wearing jeans with black belts and big silver buckles. Manfred's gut strains his flannel shirt. Not the full rancher's paunch but it's grown since they moved here. They're in their fifties, I think. A faint air of tragedy clings to them. As if they once had everything—families, cars, houses of their own—but then whatever it was happened and here they are, making the best of things. Clean shirts, plaid, red or blue, are folded neatly on the bench along one side of the built-in table. A pile of socks, rolled. Two pairs of jeans, one larger than the other.

"Laundry day," Manfred says, scooping up the shirts and jeans.

I scoot along the bench while he makes coffee and look out the picture window. Like the house, the trailer's sited so the window frames the mountains. I reach for the sugar as Victor puts a mug in front of me. The brothers' coffee is tar strong and bitter. Manfred stirs three spoonfuls into his.

I look around. "I can't believe how much better this place looks." I stop.

"Than when we brought it here?" Manfred's grinning. "I remember your face. And you were right, it was a dump."

"Price was right." Victor slips onto the other bench.

"Yeah, the guy even let us use his flatbed to move it."

"Wanted to get it out of there."

"I just remember it being brown inside," I say.

They've painted it butterscotch yellow.

"Salvation Army," Victor says, nodding at the curtains which are acid green with white wiggly stripes. "Cheap and cheerful."

"It looks great."

We sip our coffee. After a minute I say, "I had no idea you were driving Dad all the way into Edmonton for his doctor's appointments."

"It's no trouble at all," Victor says at the same time as Manfred says, "We're glad to do it." They have that Manitoba lilt.

"He's a lovely man," Manfred says.

Victor deals three plates around the table, sets the bread board, loaf and knife in the middle. "More coffee?"

"No thanks."

He adds a dish of butter, a pot of honey. "Store bought. But next year perhaps we'll have our own."

I feel a little sag of relief. "Dad would like that."

"It's good for the system, raw honey," Victor says. "And if we want him to live to a hundred and ten ..."

"Where did you learn to cook?" I ask.

The knife slicing into the loaf stops. They glance at each other. Victor says, "From TV."

"Butter?"

"No thanks."

"Do you like the heel?"

"You take it, if you like it."

"Manfred does." Victor butters the heel meticulously and passes it to Manfred then picks up his own slice. "Your health," he says, waving the slice my way and biting into it. Manfred and I follow suit. All three of us chew thoughtfully then swallow.

"It's good," Manfred says.

"Very good," Victor says. "Just the right amount of rye." They're looking at each other. Manfred gives a tiny nod. "Why we wanted to talk to you," Victor says. "We like it here. This place. The land." He nods toward the window. "We like growing things just as much as we thought we would. It was a trial, this summer. Now we have an idea. But. Well, it's an investment, this idea."

Shit.

"We want to raise organic wheat. Alberta grown organic. Nobody's doing it. We think there's a market."

"Local food. Slow food." Victor tips his head at the TV. "It's coming. Even here. Your father has the equipment. It's old but Manfred can fix anything. The land along the river. That's good soil. Thanks to Ben fallowing the land between crops. Farming organically, you've got lower inputs but ..."

Here it comes: the pitch.

"But it's a commitment. Takes three years to get certified. We'd need ... Well, we'd need to know we could go on, even if your father. Even if your father passed away."

"Oh."

"A lease. Or something. Which depends ..."

"On your plans. If."

"When."

They look at me, heads tilted to one side, two eager dogs.

"Have you talked to Dad?"

"Not yet. We knew ..."

"Thought ..."

"He'd like the idea. But it would only work if you ..."

"We didn't want to put you in an awkward ..."

"Position."

The hell with Bill, I think, touched.

"We're not expecting you to answer right away."

I look down at my plate, blinking, thick white china, a band of red diamonds blurring around the rim.

"Are you alright?" Victor's brow is creased. "Did we upset you, talking about ...?"

"About after ..."

"You didn't do anything." I stand up. "Thanks for the coffee. I'll think about it, okay?"

Dad shakes his head. "Won't work. Not if they want a premium for organic. Have to sell to the Wheat Board. They set the price." His face brightens. "Unless they mill it themselves."

Dad and his schemes. Most of the land here wasn't good enough for grain. Hence the livestock experiments. Sheep when everyone else ran cattle. For a while he was going to make socks. He'd even found a special sock knitting machine. Mum figured out what it would take to wash and card and spin the wool. Nipped that plan in the bud. Around us the farms got bigger and bigger, farmers deeper and deeper into debt. Mum would never have that. Truth to tell she was just as determined to make the place pay, and just as willing to work dawn to dark. She always had a part-time job off the farm. On the cash register at the Co-op mostly.

Dad's looking at me, waiting for something.

"Sorry. What were you asking?"

"Did you find anyone selling fresher flour?"

"No but I haven't looked very hard."

"So what do you think?" He sounds oddly casual.

"About?"

"Leasing land to Victor and Manfred."

We both know that's not the real question. "Sun's setting," I say. Dad turns to watch. The peaks bite into the orange globe. When it's down to a slim rind and the sky is indigo, I say, "I can't imagine selling this place. But then I can only just believe that Mum is gone. There are moments I don't believe it." My voice goes shaky.

"I know."

"What would you like me to do?"

He shakes his head. "It's your decision." He reaches for his cane. "Excuse me."

When Dad has made his way back to the armchair I ask, "How did you meet the brothers?"

"They must have heard about my situation."

"They were looking in this area?"

"I suppose."

I know the set of his mouth. 'He makes rock look chatty,' Mum used to say. It wasn't a criticism. He just was, the way the mountains are. "Have they ever asked you for money?"

He glowers at me. At last he says, "No, they have not. Quite the contrary."

"They don't have access to your bank account, anything like that?"

"That boyfriend of yours, I thought you were done with him."

I stare at him. He never makes reference to my personal life, least of all in that pointy, sideways way. "What's Bill got to do with it?"

"He called me up, asked me those sorts of questions."

"Bill did?"

"I told him he was damned impertinent."

"Bill called you and asked you ..." I shake my head. "When? He never told me."

"I sent him off with a flea in his ear." Dad's accent gets more British when he's angry.

"The sneaky, condescending bastard," I say, "going behind my back."

Chapter Twenty Seven

"DID YOU GET out to visit your father?" Doug asks. He waves a mug my way. I nod and he pours fresh coffee. "How is he?"

Jay's eyes rest on me just long enough to catch the tiny shake of my head.

"Good," I say. "Amazingly good. He's a hundred and there's nothing wrong with him health-wise other than a bit of arthritis. He's just slow. Not his mind, how he moves. Everything takes forever. And he falls asleep a lot. But he still enjoys things. Goes for a walk most days."

I take a sip of the coffee Doug passes me. It's rich and dark and delicious. Doug's watching me, smiling. "Yum," I say. It comes out with childish gusto.

"It's called Alberta Crude. From Saint City Roasters. They're a new company over in St. Albert. Fair trade beans."

"In Edmonton," Jay says. "Who knew?"

"Life's too short for bad coffee."

It's easy, the three of us in the office, the murmur of prayer from the chamber, smells of sage and coffee mingling in the air. I can imagine telling Doug about Dad. Not right now.

I put my mug down. "There is one thing I'm a bit worried about. If you have any thoughts ..." They both look interested. "There are two brothers, Victor and Manfred Hetzl, who live in a trailer on the farm. They do a lot for Dad. Not just shopping. They cook for him, take him to doctor's appointments."

"Does he pay them?" Jay asks.

"No. It's in return for parking their trailer there."

"So what's bothering you?" Jay asks.

"They want to try growing organic wheat. They'd like me to agree to some sort of lease. So even if Dad ... well, when ..."

"Sounds reasonable," Doug says, "if they're going after organic certification."

"But you're planning on selling the place," Jay asks, "when the time comes?"

"Well no, I don't know."

"This is the land where you grew up?" Doug asks.

I nod. "It's not the best cropland but there are good bits. And it's beautiful. On the North Saskatchewan. South of Drayton Valley. You can see the mountains."

"How much land?"

"A section. They started with a quarter section in the Thirties."

Doug is nodding. "That's how my folks did it. Saved up their money in the boom years, bought during the busts."

"My mother was always smart with money."

"Not your father?" Jay asks.

"He doesn't care. Never did. This is how his negotiations go with the brothers. They say, 'We'll give you half the vegetables we grow.' Dad says, 'No, that's too much. Give me a quarter.' They fight him back up to a third."

"Sounds good," Doug says.

"Almost too good," Jay says. "Where are they from, these brothers?"

"Manitoba, up North. In the bush I guess. I remember Manfred said the nearest town was the kind where the bar-room doors swing out. On a Saturday night you walk down the middle of the street to dodge the flying drunks. He worked for CN long enough to get a pension. He can fix anything. Victor, I don't know what he did except he's a hell of a good cook."

"How old are they?" Doug is looking thoughtful.

"Mid-fifties, I should think. I have the feeling they've both seen hard times. Divorce, maybe bankruptcy. I don't know."

"Kids?" Doug asks.

"Not that I know of."

"They live together in the trailer?" Jay asks. She glances at Doug. His eyes meet hers for a moment.

"Sure."

"Look a lot alike do they? Strong family resemblance?"

I open my mouth to answer. Shut it again. I look at Jay then Doug. "They're a couple, aren't they?"

Jay lifts her eyebrows. "Could be." Her lips twitch. She's trying not to laugh at me.

Doug says, "Rural Alberta's not the friendliest ... If you're gay and you don't want to live in a city ..."

"Fuck." Dad. Victor. Manfred. All in the know. "Fuck this." Jay's eyes twitch toward the chamber. "I'm so fucking sick of people keeping me in the dark."

"Let's go outside, walk around," Doug says, his voice soft. "Come on."

I follow him out, not looking at Jay. Tears sting. Then the cold does. Neither of us is wearing a coat.

"Let's walk," he says, setting off around the corner of the building.

It's all turning faster and faster in my head.

"Go ahead. I used to yell in my truck all the time."

"Jesus fucking Christ," I shout. "Every time I start to trust him there's another fucking secret." The stars glitter. I won't cry. "Fuck. Fuck. Fuck. They've all been laughing at me the way you and Jay were. Don't fucking deny it." I catch myself. Breathe. "Sorry. I've got no right to attack you."

"Are you sure they are a couple?"

"It's obvious, once you think about it."

"And you're sure your father knows?"

"Yes." I stop. Doug gives me a moment. I'm certainly not going to explain that one.

"And he's okay with it?"

"Yes."

"How did they come to be there?"

"I thought Dad had seen their flier in the local co-op. But when I asked him the other day he was vague."

"They were lucky they found your father."

"Too lucky," I say.

I feel Doug glance over at me. Take a deep breath. Let it out. "Sorry."

"I hate feeling left out too."

Chapter Twenty Eight

THIS IS WHAT it comes to.

I slap the dough down, grind my knuckles into it.

He's got so many fucking lies going I'm surprised he can remember them all.

I scrape the dough off the counter, fold it, flip it, punch down into the warm elastic mass.

Why the fuck should I believe him about anything?

"Jesus Christ. Jesus fucking Christ."

Shouting doesn't help. But when I start to simmer down I think about the brothers. Who aren't. It's not just them being gay. They know about Dad. They must. I bet they discussed him telling me. Manfred on the tractor knew exactly why I went tearing out of there that first day. Probably beetled right over. Make sure Ben's horrible daughter hadn't beaten him up. The next time I came, Victor brought goulash for supper. Checking up. Then the squash soup when I was out behind the barn. Watching from the trailer, waiting for me to leave the house. 'How's it going, Ben?' Furrowed brow, worried voice. Fuck. I smack my fist down into the dough. Ow. Fuck. Slam the other one down harder. Fuck, fuck, fuck.

Stop. Right now.

It's all about you, eh?

Fired that sponsor.

Scrape the dough up, roll it into a ball. Cut it in two. Oil the loaf tins. Fold and roll and tuck each piece in. Like laying a child in a cot. Not that I've ever had a child myself, nor ever wanted one. Not for more than five minutes. Too fucked up. Planet's lousy with people anyway. But here I am, staring at two fucking loaf tins, tears in my eyes. Something's breaking. It might be my heart. How fucking corny is that?

Not cots. Coffins.

Dad isn't dead.

The father I knew is.

"Hello. Could I speak to Judy Laboucan?"

"Speaking."

"My name is Meg. I work at Dreamcatcher Lodge ..."

"Danielle, is she all right?"

"She's fine. I'm sorry. I didn't mean to worry you. This is a personal matter." *Breathe.* "I'm trying to find my birth parents. There's a possibility I came from the Firestick Reserve."

"Do you know their names?"

"No. It's complicated. I'd rather not go into it on the phone. I was wondering if you would be willing to meet with me. I'd be happy to drive out to the reserve."

"How did you get my number?"

"Danielle." I didn't even miss a beat.

There's a pause. "You work at Dreamcatcher?"

"Yes."

"Are you sober yourself?"

"Almost twenty years. A day at a time."

"What's your home group?"

This feels a little weird. Probably not as weird as I sound. "The Mustard Seed."

"You know René? Val?"

"Val C? She's a friend of mine."

"Okay," Judy says. "I have to go into Edson on Saturday morning. I could meet you at the Timmies at eleven."

Chapter Twenty Nine

"DID YOU SIGN Rodney's Big Book book yet? He's leaving a couple days early. Got a ride up to Yellowknife."

"Not yet. I'll do cash first."

In the back closet I open the box, start counting nickels and dimes. Rodney didn't ask me to sign his book. I thought one day I'd stop being the weird little kid who didn't talk. The last to be chosen for any team. Me and Danny Brown who was fat and picked his nose. It didn't help I just appeared in fifth grade. Most of the kids had been in kindergarten together. Maybe I went to school on the reserve. If they had a school there. I don't even know that. I must have gone somewhere before I came to the farm. I knew how to read, how to multiply and divide. I wasn't completely thrown by school the way I would have been if I'd been some feral child. The end of that first day, Mum waiting for me. Smiling as I walked toward her with my new satchel. Black hair under a pale blue nylon headscarf, heart-shaped face.

"Earth to Meg."

I jump. Heather's in the doorway. I can't see her face. My heart isn't slowing down. I stand up.

"You done then?"

"Not quite." I take another step and she backs up. "Excuse me, I need to get to the washroom."

I brush past her when we get to the corner of the desk.

In the washroom I hold my breath. It makes your heart slow down. Starves it of oxygen. Guy on the street taught me that. Diving for cover whenever a train passed by on the overhead tracks. Vietnam vet. Deserted. Not soon enough. Guy was his name, he said.

When I come out Heather's going to be looking at me funny. Maybe mention it to Tanya. 'That Meg, she doesn't like to be cornered, eh? You noticed that?'

Me, I wonder why I keep volunteering to do cash.

I wash my hands, splash water on my face.

Heather's in the office. Tanya's writing in the logbook. "I'll do a room-check," I say.

Nobody answers when I knock. I step inside, close the door behind me. On Danielle's side of the night-stand is a photograph stuck to a card. A gap-toothed woman with a round face and sparse brown hair stands in front of a trailer. Nothing written on the card. Nobody I recognize. Out in the corridor footsteps approach. I replace the card, step back to the door, open it when the feet have passed.

Danielle's outside with the smokers. Not smoking, just hanging out. *Integrating well.* I could ask to speak to her but I just nod, take a turn around the building. The air smells of snow. I should talk to someone about what I'm doing. Doug's face comes to mind. But he's not in tonight.

Except he is. I do another check after everyone is supposed to be in the Riel room. When I herd in the clients I flushed from their rooms, he's sitting next to Tanya. The air smells of sage and sweet-grass. Everyone is sitting in a circle. Emmett stands at the east end, marker in hand in front of a white board.

Cathy smiles as I sit down beside her. Doug's staring at the board where Emmett has drawn two circles, one inside the other. The inside circle he divided into eight segments labelled: *Infant; Toddler; Child; Youth; Young Adult; Parent; Grandparent; Elder.* His lettering is surprisingly small and spiky. Working between the two circles now, he's adding another label to each quarter, starting with *Infant* and *Toddler* in the north-east: *Earth; Water; Air; Fire.* Then he goes around again adding: *Physical; Emotional; Mental; Spiritual.*

He puts the cap on the marker and turns to face the room. "The circle is sacred. Our whole understanding of the cosmos begins and ends in the circle. Everything is connected. How many of you have seen the Medicine Wheel before?"

Almost half the room puts up their hands.

"Perhaps just with the four directions and a colour for each direction?"

More hands go up.

Fortyish with a round, unlined face and plump body, Emmett looks more like the guys in the garage where I get my car fixed than an elder. I've seen a picture of the previous elder, wrinkled as a turtle, beady black eyes glinting. Heard stories too about his obscure pronouncements and obscene jokes, his gradual descent into senility. According to Jay and Tanya there was serious disagreement over Emmett's selection.

He's looking around the room now, taking his time. "The Europeans, when they came to this continent, they weren't equipped to understand our conception of gender. They had only a crude duality in mind: man or woman. I'm going to talk to you about the Cree traditions I grew up with, but wherever you look among the peoples of Turtle Island, if you have the eyes to see, you'll find similarly sophisticated ideas."

Most of the clients are paying attention. Don, though, is staring out of the window, making no effort to disguise his boredom. As if to make up for him, Deborah leans forward in frowning concentration.

"Does anybody have any questions so far?"

After a moment Emmett turns back to the board. At the top of the outer circle he writes *Intersex* then, going around clockwise again: *Transgender; Lesbian; Bisexual; Heterosexual Woman / Heterosexual Man; Bisexual; Gay Man; Transgender.*

He turns back to the room. There's a different feel to the silence but nobody is exactly snickering.

"I am using the common English words, or some of them. There are no direct translations for these words in Cree because our whole understanding of gender and sexuality is different. Earlier you heard me use the phrase *two spirit person*. That is a name many Native gay and transgendered people have chosen to use but it exists only in

English. It is not a traditional phrase for any particular nation. In Cree there are different words we might use. One is *Kiskwe-kons-qwayo*." He prints the word carefully at the top of the board. "There is a story behind this name." He looks around. "In the beginning there was a being called *Kiskwe-konsqwayo* which is a name you might translate as *Changed in the head happy woman*. Now *Changed in the head happy woman* was different. She—or he—was not a man and not a woman. Because she was different the first people were scared of him. Because they were scared of him they derided her. So *Kiskwe-konsqwayo* made a promise to the ones who came after who were like her. They could always pray to him and *Kiskwe-konsqwayo* would help them.

"*Kiskwe-konsqwayo* now is used to refer to a gay person but what it means is 'someone who does a lot for others.' In English, 'gay,' 'homosexual,' those are about who has sex with who. For us it is about a person's place in the community. In our understanding, *Kiskwe-konsqwayo* has been a part of creation from the beginning. He/she is necessary to the whole. Spiritually and socially, there are specific responsibilities. For example, it is not so easy for heterosexual men and heterosexual women to stay together. You may have noticed this?"

A few of the clients laugh. Some, like Warren, stare stolidly at the floor between their feet.

"Among the jobs of the two spirit people is to help them to stay together and to live in harmony. You could say they are bridge-makers. Another part of their role is to expand the world, to usher in change. Just as with *Kiskwe-konsqwayo, Changed in the head happy woman,* those who bring transformation are not always greeted with delight."

No shit. My father, aka *Changed in the head happy woman*. And the two spirit twins. Who aren't. I look across the room. Doug's eyes move away. He was watching me. Has Jay told him about Dad?

"For us, if someone is transgender, it has nothing to do with someone being in the 'wrong' body. It is about that person being in the absolutely correct body; the body that is necessary to meet the spiritual requirements of the community. There is nothing and nobody, in our understanding, that is outside the circle. Every person has a part to play."

He pauses, lets silence build. Joey, who has been fidgeting most of the time, looks solemn. James, sitting next to Joey, is picking at something on the knee of his jeans. Doug is staring at the board now but he's far away, and sad. Geoffrey's leaning forward, hands on his knees. His chin is up but there's a rawness to his face, as if he might be about to cry.

Danielle, across the circle from me, is fiddling with the cross she wears on a gold chain around her neck. The shape of her face. It's not the classic oval of Theresa's face. Or Shannon's for that matter. It's more like mine. High-ish cheekbones. But her cheeks are round. Mine are heavier. Slabbier. More Ukrainian. Danielle glances across at me. I look away.

Emmett's still just standing there, relaxed, gaze resting on the empty middle of the room. At last he asks, "Are there any questions? Don't be afraid to speak up."

The cluster of girls next to James stirs. Shannon puts up her hand.

"If you were on a reserve and you said," she studies the board, "'Oh that's so *Kiska … Kiskwe-konsqwayo*,' would anyone be mad at you?"

There's a snicker from the cluster but Tanya's giving them the eye. Emmett considers then says, "It would depend on your intent."

"Exactly," Shannon says triumphantly. "Exactly."

I glance at Doug but it's a young woman with long lustrous black hair who says, "That's not the point, Shannon, and you know it. The important thing is the circle. Everyone belongs. Everyone. We respect each person's vision." She looks slowly around the circle. "That's what this place is about."

There's a smattering of 'Hai hai' and 'Here, heres.' The young woman's face is as perfectly sculpted as Theresa's, as unmistakably Native. Eleanor. She only came in last week.

One of the quiet ones half-raises her hand. Jenny. In her forties. A rope of scar tissue around her neck.

I miss the first couple of words but then her voice strengthens. "My *kokum* in Peace River. She was raising eight of us grandchildren. Our mothers were party girls. When it got too much for her, she would send word to one of two men who lived quite far away, in remote communities. One of the men would always come and help out. I used to watch them, how they moved and talked. I'd think, *my mum and my aunties do that. My uncles don't do that.* When I was older I learned there was a name for them, *eskwikan.* Somebody told me it meant 'men who have women's spirits who bring a lot of joy and happiness.' I remember that because it was true. That was what I knew growing up. I was so shocked when I came to Edmonton and I saw the abuse they got, men like that."

Emmett waits to be sure she has finished then he turns to the board and writes, *Eskwikan.* "Thank you," he says, turning back to her. "It is very important to hear this story. Would you be willing to tell it to a group of elders we are gathering together?"

She nods, pleased.

Danielle raises her hand. Her cheeks are pink.

Emmett nods. "Go ahead."

"I want to know about the traditions of my people," she says, Southern accent drawing out the words, "and I don't mean to be disrespectful but the Bible, the Bible says it is a sin for a man to lie with a man." She stops, chin sticking out. A few heads nod around the room. Don is looking at Emmett for the first time.

After a good long pause Emmett says, "Jesus said, 'As you do unto the least of these, you do unto me.' He welcomed the outcasts, the poor, the prostitutes." He looks around. "Until the missionaries came, our way was to accept. The Creator makes people as they need to be and we honour them as we honour the animals and the plants, the rocks and the stars." Next to me, Cathy is nodding, her straight black hair falling forward to hide her face. "Who are we to condemn the works of the Creator?" Now he looks directly at Danielle. "We can love Jesus without taking on the hatred and the intolerance of the church."

"*Hai hai,*" Doug says. He looks hard and remote as a hawk. It's the first time I've seen him angry.

"Can I ask you a question, Meg?"

"Of course."

"Is he really an elder?" Danielle's sitting on her bed, as usual. Next to her Bible is one of the hard-covered notebooks the counsellors issue as journals.

"Emmett? Yes."

"He doesn't seem ..."

"Old enough?"

Danielle smiles at me, the wide smile that makes her face look like a flower. Behind her in the dark, snowflakes drift down. They collect on the windowsill.

"It's not just that. I talked to my aunt a lot. About my people. Our culture. She never said anything about the two spirit thing. She said you could be a good Christian and follow tradition. That that was how our traditions survived." She looks at me earnestly.

"I think I'm out of my depth here. Perhaps you should talk some more with Emmett. He's willing to meet one on one with clients."

Danielle shrugs. "He's entitled to his opinions. But I know my aunt is not in favour of that sort of"—she hesitates—"*alternative* lifestyle."

"What's she like, your aunt?"

"Spiritual. She's very spiritual. She cares, you know? I mean, she wired me over three hundred bucks for the bus and she never even met me. Well, when I was born, for about a minute. She insisted on being with her sister in the hospital. Their mother was too trashed to bother. She's only two years older than my mother but she was like a mother to her. That's what Judy says."

"How many siblings does she have?"

"Eight. I think she's the only sober one out of the whole family. Except for me."

I take a deep breath. "I'd like to meet her. I was wondering ..."

"Hey, she said she'd come into the city next time I go out on pass. Maybe you could join us. I'll ask her."

Shit. "Actually, I was wondering if I could get her phone number from you."

"Maybe. I have to ask her. She's kind of fierce about her number. She had to change it. People were calling her when they were trashed, calling from all over the country, yelling about her wanting a dry reserve."

"Oh. Of course. Well, I'd better get back to the desk."

Chapter Thirty

THE GOLF COURSE has been taken over by dogs. People throwing balls and Frisbees. Children in bright colours running around in the snow. Not a lot of snow, just enough to change everything. Smoke stacks line the horizon, flares invisible in the flat white light.

Then it's on me, the feeling, nose pressed to cold glass, watching other families' lamp-lit lives. Won't someone notice I'm out here in the cold, the dark? Wanting what's not mine. Nothing I've a right to. No people of my own.

Come on. You were invited in. Welcomed.

But the claw gripping my gut is old and strong.

Feet, get me out of here. I half slide down the trail to the river's edge. Wind hisses a scrim of snow across the ice. Somewhere beneath my feet fish flick through moving water.

It grabs me the way a cramp grabs your leg. A moment's warning then you're gasping, fuck, fuck, fuck. It's always been like this. It always fucking will be. I'll only ever be on sufferance.

Walk. Just walk.

I knew it was a bad idea, letting the want get started. Dad coaxed me into it. Me, suspicious as a wild animal, him patient, luring me on. But it was there in me already, the wanting. Must have been. He just saw it, knew how to work it, the way he knew with the dogs how to bring out what was in them already. If I could cut it out of myself this moment I would. The wanting longing hungry fucking child. I can feel the blade, carbon steel, honed for the job. Flesh of my flesh. Fuck. Why I drank. Kill the fucking longing.

If you had succeeded you'd be a psychopath.

Only thing Lip-tooth ever said that got my attention.

Drink until I didn't want. Drink until I despised the wanting. I'd have killed it if I could.

You're still trying to manage your pain. What happens if you feel it?

'Universe ends. Of course.'

Poor old Lip-tooth. She tried.

Stare across the river. Wish the coyotes would sing. It's ebbing, the bad feeling. Helped, thinking about Lip-tooth. Does that mean I need yet more therapy? Can't afford it on Dreamcatcher wages. 'If you had succeeded ...'

Always felt like weakness, that I couldn't kill the hunger.

A good failure? Like getting beat by booze.

Across the trail ahead of me something's shuffled the snow. Look up into the bush that crowds the hillside. Fresh yellow wood. Poplar stump gnawed to a point. Thrash of twigs dragged over the bank. Patch of dark water rifts the river's icy surface. Beaver, silver bubbles trapped in his coat, glides through tea-coloured water, towing the branches down. Down to the secret lodge.

Chapter Thirty One

VAL WAVES ME over, squeezes my hand hello as the meeting begins. I close my eyes for the opening prayer, inhale subtle perfume. Musk under something lemony and fresh.

... and the wisdom to know the difference.

Val doesn't dress up for the meeting, she's just incapable of dressing down.

Looking round, people catch my eye, smile and nod. I guess it's been a while. Doesn't take long for me to forget I have a place I'm always welcome. Oh boo hoo. As if I'm living some terrible outsider life, me with my house and job, a father who's not some crazed alcoholic monster. Even if he isn't ...

I take a deep breath, let it out.

Val murmurs, "Good, isn't it? I come in sometimes, sit down and it's like I didn't notice until that moment how much baggage I was carrying."

I smile, nod, my eyes on her hands, big knuckles, long, square-tipped fingers, the thick bone of her wrist. Deep voice. For a woman.

Is she?

Does it matter?

Wish I could say no. That I'm not wondering what's between her legs.

The only requirement for membership is a desire to stop drinking.

It washes over me, the familiar cadence of the preamble. Whoever is reading is smooth. No stumbles. Newish guy. Jean. Métis. Handsome as Marlon Brando. He isn't reading. He's got it memorized.

I let my eyes slip sideways. Small breasts. Prominent cheekbones. The upswept sixties' hairstyle Val favours. *My Jackie O. look.* We got sober in the same meetings. She was a couple of years ahead of me. Exotic Val, father Ethiopian, mother Ojibwe. Grew up in Toronto but the tide of booze and drugs took her west, dropped her in Edmonton. Where she stayed. Selling French perfume in a Glenora boutique. For all I know, she owns the place by now. I've never considered that she might be trans. But she did remind me of Dora. Same dignity. Not that Dora wore suede soft as butter. Downtown Eastside they'd have had it off her back in a minute.

The topic's *letting go, turning it over.* A particular it. Or all of it. *Give it to God.*

Dear Dora,

I'm tangled in a stupid lie.

I don't even know if I want to find out what kind of hell-hole I came from.

And I'm still mad about the brothers.

I can see why they'd be scared. I know what Mum's fellow believers were like. It's not that. It's being the one who didn't know.

And thinking I was the one in the know with Dad. Feeling special. While all the time they were watching, knowing. The brothers. Who aren't. It's like a splinter I can't get out.

The woman who's sharing now, she's a dancer. Goes around the powwows. "The dance, it's not me. It's coming through me, you know? I have to let go. Let it come. It's in my blood, eh? I have two girls. They love to dance but they'll never be Fancy dancers. They don't have the blood."

She has a sharp face, Beth. Sallow with high cheekbones. Jet black hair gathered in a bun. I saw a poster once of a Flamenco dancer, how she stood, chin raised. Proud, I thought. That's what proud looks like. Fancy dancing the Cree Flamenco? Is that sacrilege?

What about the daughters whose mother is so proud and so certain they will never dance like her? Blood thinned by their father's whiteness. Some of the others look away when Beth is talking. But it's A.A. Nobody argues with her. When she's done, she passes. Newfie Joe talks about the bad old days, sleeping out in the river valley in the summer, shelters in the winter. On my morning walks I glimpse the camps sometimes: tarps draped over fallen trees, meagre belongings in plastic bags. How he thought he was in charge of his life when all that was left was making sure he had enough booze to get through the day. "More guts than a ten cent fish." He looks around the room. "Less brains." People laugh. "One day a guy volunteering at the soup kitchen du jour looks me in the eyes, he asks, 'Is this the day, Joe?' I say. 'Yes.'

"Everything changed." He shakes his grizzled head, snaps meaty fingers. "Just like that."

"Thousand times a person could ask me that question, I'd tell them to f--- off. That day I was ready."

It's always redemption. The fact that you're here, telling the story. To a roomful of people who listen, who laugh with you at the worst, the craziest stuff. Who know what you're talking about. Know the way I do, hairs standing up on my neck, my arms, when the moment comes.

I don't share. Can't think where to start.

"Got time for a cup of coffee?"

"Sure," Val says. "I've just got to talk to a couple people."

"See you at The Second Cup in ten? I need to feed the meter."

And I don't feel like milling about, chatting.

"What's happening, sistah?" Val sips chamomile tea.

"Not too much. Working at Dreamcatcher. Shit pay. Good work. Checking in on my father. How about you?"

"Good. But tell me how you really are." She smiles, even milk white teeth, pale pink lipstick. "I haven't seen you around much lately."

She means at meetings.

"Like I said, I've been spending more time with my father. Working extra too."

"Working in the addictions biz," Val says, "meetings can come to seem like work."

"I know. But it's not that. Honestly. I do have a question for you. You know a woman called Judy in the program, lives out on one of the reserves in the foothills, Edson way?"

"Judy L.," Val nods. "Been sober four or five years. All fired up to save the reserve. That the one?"

I nod. "What's she like?"

Val considers the far wall of the café a moment. "Nice woman. Hard life. Oldest daughter. Alcoholic family. Feels responsible for everything and everyone."

Val's done a lot of Adult Child of Alcoholics work. She's watching me now, waiting.

"I can't really tell you the details. Client confidentiality. But. You know my story, right? Well, people say I look just like her niece."

"Judy's niece?"

"Yes. So I thought I might call her up. Judy. See if I could visit. See if ..." I shrug. Val's looking worried. "That's the problem. I don't know what I'm hoping for."

"You need to find them, eh?" Val's voice is husky.

I nod.

After a moment she says, "You know I had a daughter when I was fifteen? There isn't a single day goes by I don't think about her. Sometimes I picture her deciding to find me."

How could I have forgotten? "I'm sorry, Val. I did know. I didn't mean to put my big foot somewhere so painful."

She's shaking her head. "It's okay. It is what it is. I'd just like her to know that I love her. That it was never about indifference."

It drives right into me, that word.

"My turn to hit a sore spot?" Val asks.

"Indifference. It's where I always end up. In relationships. I end up not caring. Like I don't know how to stay connected."

Val doesn't say anything, just watches me. Deep brown eyes. The longest, most elegant neck. Now I'm seeing the woman in her I can't imagine how I thought she might have been born a guy. Or how I forgot she gave birth to a daughter.

After a while I say, "I don't think I'm going to be able to make a relationship that works until I know where I came from." Concern shadows her face. "I know. I might never find out. It's not like I've got adoption papers. But I have to try. I was wondering, do you have Judy's number?"

"I do but I need to call her, ask if it's okay to give it to you."

"Oh, well, don't worry. I can get it from Danielle. The niece." I stand up. "Better get going. Good to see you."

"You too. Call me. Anytime."

Chapter Thirty Two

SHE LOOKS EXACTLY like the photograph in Danielle's room. Except she's dragging an oxygen tank behind her.

"Meg?" Her smile reveals the gap between her front teeth. She's short and plump, her eyes a clear hazel, steady on my face even as she sits down. After a moment she nods.

"How do you like your coffee?" I ask, standing.

"Double double," she says. "Please." She reaches for the purse she has set on the table.

"My treat. You drove down here."

"Had to get my prescription anyway."

She watches me go to the counter, order coffees and a dozen Timbits. I feel like one of Dad's ewes at the auction.

"Tell me the story," Judy says when I sit down again.

Christ, she doesn't go in for small talk.

She waves a hand at the tank parked by her chair like a small, obedient dog. "I run out of juice."

"It's a very long shot," I say.

"So this ranch where you showed up, no papers, no memory, nothing. How far is it from Firestick?"

"About forty kilometres."

"Did they go to the authorities, the people who took you in?"

"Not right away. My father wanted to but ..." I shrug.

"They didn't think you might just be lost?"

"I had scars on the backs of my legs. Older ones and some more recent. From being beaten with a switch, I guess. That's what my mother said."

It's not like being in some therapist's office, sitting in Timmies with Judy, wind blowing empty coffee cups around the parking lot. Grey, cold day, fluorescent lights not much better. Neither of us has eaten any of the Timbits. Now we each reach for one. I feel completely naked and weird. Not just me, Mum and Dad on display too.

I take a sip of coffee. The way Judy waits is different but I can't put a finger on why. After a moment I say, "My mother was sure God sent me. That I was meant to be there, with them. She didn't really care how I got there."

Judy nods as if she understands this.

"My father did ask around. The first person he talked to was a Cree man called John who worked on the ranch sometimes. He came from Firestick."

"What was his last name?"

"Smith."

Judy shakes her head. "What did he look like?"

"Craggy face, puckered scar on his eyebrow. He wore his hair in a braid."

"How old?"

"In his forties, I think. It's hard to tell when you're a kid."

"And that was nineteen sixty ..."

"Eight."

Judy is nodding. "John Yellowknee. He was my aunt's cousin."

"He spoke to me in Cree. At least that's what I think it was. I didn't recognize it."

"Or him?"

"I don't think so."

"Your foster father, what did he ask John?"

"If he recognized me. If there were any children missing from the reserve."

For the first time there's colour in Judy's face, a flush not just in her cheeks but across her forehead.

"And what did John say?" Her voice is harsh.

"Not that he knew of. He'd ask around."

"Nineteen sixty-eight. You've heard of the sixties scoop?" Before I can answer she goes on, "They shut down the residential schools. Just grabbed the kids off the reserves instead. Said we were unfit. Too poor. Too Indian."

Her eyes are glittering like the lumps of coal I've found in the riverbank.

"Just took them away. Gave them to other families. Didn't we want our children to have a better life?"

She stops, the colour draining back out of her face. What's left is ashen, empty. Her eyes are grey caves. She sucks on the oxygen. I drink thin coffee.

After a bit, her chin goes up. The glitter is back in her eyes. "We got smarter. Someone heard they were coming. The social workers. Child catchers. Families would take their kids, go into the bush. Live the old way. Course then they could get you because the kids weren't in school."

I nod. I don't know what to say, who she's talking to. White woman? Indian child?

As if she's reading my mind she says, "You must remember something."

I shake my head. "It's in me somewhere, what I need to know. It must be. There's no sign of a head injury or anything like that. But I can't get to it. I've tried."

"Perhaps you put it somewhere safe." Judy says slowly.

"Like hiding the children in the bush?" I've never thought of it this way.

"Our culture. Now we're trying to find it. Ever been to a sweat lodge?"

"Not yet. I want to though."

"They have them at the place where you work."

Is she deliberately not using the name? I've been told some people find it undignified. Gimmicky. But she used it on the phone.

"The prayers you offer in a sweat lodge, they're powerful."

She's reaching for her coat.

"I'll try that." I'm trying to keep the disappointment out of my voice.

"I'll ask around. I gave Danielle some photographs of her brothers and sisters. You could look at those."

"The thing is, I can't be her sister, not if her mother was fourteen when she had her."

"How old are you?"

"Forty-two, give or take."

"Four years older than me," Judy says. "I don't have an older sister but it doesn't mean we're not related. You and Danielle, you do look alike. She's a good kid, eh?"

"She's doing really well." I hesitate. "That was pretty amazing, you wiring her the bus fare, just like that."

Judy studies me a moment. "I was praying and praying on a sign in the sweat lodge. Asking the Creator, show me I should keep doing the work. For the reserve. In spite of all the crap I was getting. Next day she calls out of the blue like that. What was I supposed to do, hang up on her?"

She smiles, her round face opening just the way Danielle's does.

"Give me your number. I'll ask around," she says. "I'll call you if I find out anything. Meantime, you do some praying, eh? Tell Danielle I'm looking forward to seeing her next weekend."

Chapter Thirty Three

VICTOR OPENS THE door. Over his shoulder I see Manfred sitting in the kitchen. Dad must be in there too.

"Hello, Meg." Victor's voice sounds louder than usual. "Come on in. We were just finishing lunch. Are you hungry? There's cream of leek soup."

I stalk ahead of him into the kitchen, not bothering to shed my coat. Survey the scene. Dad knows me well enough to look uneasy.

Victor brings the chair we keep by the front door now. He's standing in the doorway when I say, "I wish you had not treated me like a fool."

Dad looks as if he's swallowed a goldfish.

Victor is watching Dad.

If anyone denies it, I'm going to scream.

Manfred looks up at me, sympathy in his brown eyes. "We should have told you when Ben told you his secret."

"At first we weren't sure how you were taking it," Victor says.

Manfred shoots him a look. "We should have told you," he says again, "but we were afraid."

I turn to look at Dad. "And you didn't tell me because ..."

He meets my eyes. "It wasn't mine to tell."

Fuck. He's always been able to do this.

Victor puts down the chair he's been holding. Dad leans back.

Manfred puts both his hands on the table. "Shall we go into the living room?" he asks, standing up.

There isn't room for all of us in the kitchen.

When everyone is assembled around the coffee table, I take a deep breath. "Okay, I'm really, really tired of being the one who doesn't know when everyone else is in on the secret. So is there anything else I should know?"

There's a pause. Victor and Manfred look at each other then Victor says, "Ben's doctor ..."

"Knows."

"We were worried, to be taking care of him ..."

"When you weren't here ..."

"And no doctor."

"So we talked to some friends ..."

"In the trans community."

"Transgendered," Manfred says.

"The doctor is?"

"Sympathetic."

"A lesbian."

"Okay." I glance at Dad. He might be enjoying this. "So how did you meet Manfred and Victor?"

"The *Edmonton Journal* ran an article about a new centre that had opened up. On 111th Avenue. For gays and lesbians and transgendered and somebody else."

"Bisexuals," I say. "On the corner of 101st Street." Bill and I used to go to the Vietnamese restaurant a couple of doors down. It's a dusty little store front on a corner. Metal shutters they can pull down at night. Tiny rainbow triangle next to the door.

"You remember Betty. Her daughter was taking her in to the Royal Alex. Out patient. Once a week. They'd offered me a ride if ever I wanted. I told them I needed a change of scene."

Dad standing at the intersection where 97th Street comes in, the little white figure flashing, counting down the seconds. Cars roaring past on either side. The thundering, brutal city. Dad on his way to the GLBT Centre.

He's watching me, waiting. It's weird. I'm not mad anymore. Not mad at all. "What was it like, deciding to go? Going?"

"Exciting."

"Weren't you worried someone would see you going in?"

"Senile old man," he says, "confused about where he is. Besides, I don't know a soul in the city anymore except you."

"So what happened?"

"I pushed open the door. Stepped in. Little bell rang. Old man appeared. Not as old as me but old enough. Told me I was free to look around, I could borrow books if I wanted to sign up for that. If I had any questions to go ahead and ask.

"I thanked him. Started looking at the bookshelves. I admit my heart was pounding but"—he shrugs—"I pulled down a few books. At random, you know. Then I noticed the shelves were labelled. African-Canadian, First Nations, Lesbian, Transgender. Titles caught my eye. *The Manly Hearted Woman. The Well of Loneliness.* He hooks an eyebrow at me. There was a bulletin board in the back. Lots of fliers. One down low with a fringe of numbers. None of the tabs had been torn off.

"*Gay male couple, discreet, hard-working, clean living, seeks a quiet country spot to put a trailer in return for working around the place.*

"I reread it. Thought, that's a long shot. Trying to picture any of the ranchers around us welcoming a gay couple to set up house. Then it hit me." He glances at me. "I wasn't used to Polly being gone, you know?"

He falls silent. His eyelids are drooping.

"So what happened?"

"I took the number, borrowed those two books. Wrote down a false name. And address. I had the feeling the guy at the desk knew what I was doing but he didn't ask for I.D., just put the books in an old grocery bag." Dad yawns. "It was time to get back to the hospital. Meet Betty and Jeanette."

His eyelids droop. After a minute his head tips forward. Victor and Manfred are watching him too, their faces tender. Other than the baldness, they really don't look alike at all.

"We didn't know," Victor says.

"We had no idea."

"When we met him ..."

"He told us his wife had died recently."

"We did think ..."

"Sometimes men who've been closeted their whole lives ... It's their chance."

"The only place we put up our ad."

"We met there. Went for coffee."

"Then he invited us out to look at the farm."

"We were worried."

"That sign on the church ..."

"If a couple of men moved onto his land."

"Worried for him as well as us."

"We were the ones suggested ..."

"He thought it was a good idea."

"We asked what we could do in return."

"He told us about you."

"What a good daughter you were."

"But two hours drive away."

"And he'd been having symptoms."

"What kind of symptoms?" I lean forward.

"Dizzy spells. Low blood pressure, it turned out."

"We said we'd be happy to drive him to doctor's appointments, or anywhere else he needed to go."

"That was when he went to make another pot of tea. He refused our help so we sat there. Looking out at the mountains. It was a bright sunny day. Almost spring. They were majestic, the mountains. And this house, it's so calm and settled, you know?"

"We could hardly believe it might come true. Our dream." Victor's eyes are a clear pewter.

"It didn't seem so bad, to pass as brothers, if that was what it took."

"Not everyone would believe it, perhaps, but nobody could say we were flaunting our sexuality." Victor glances at Manfred. "But you felt there was something else."

Manfred nods. "We were trying not to get our hopes up. Eventually Ben came back in with tea and slices of toast, all carefully buttered. A pot of marmalade."

"When we all had our tea he said, 'There's something I should tell you. It's a secret and it has to stay a secret or I won't be able to live here anymore. Do you understand?'

"He knew we did."

"'I don't want to answer a lot of questions but I'm going to tell you what you need to know. I was born a woman. I am a woman, I suppose. But I've lived as a man for seventy years'."

"We were gob-smacked," Victor says.

"It wasn't what we thought he'd say, that's for sure."

"I started to laugh."

"I joined in," Manfred says, "and then he started laughing too. He laughed until tears were coming down his face."

"When he stopped he asked if we knew *Twelfth Night?*"

"'Not well'."

"'Read it again. You'll enjoy it'."

"One of a kind," Manfred says.

"An inspiration."

On cue Dad lets out a frilly little snore. We all look at him.

"More than anyone I've ever met, he's lived life on his own terms."

"Has he told you the whole story?"

They shake their heads.

"We asked but he wanted to tell you first."

"He told us that right away, that he was going to tell you."

"But he told you first. He trusted you without even knowing you."

"It wasn't you," Victor says.

Manfred gives him a look. "He was worried," he says, "it was too soon after your mother's passing."

"What did you mean," I ask Victor, "it wasn't me?"

"He wasn't sure about your boyfriend."

"But I broke up with him months ago."

"Meg," Manfred says, voice gentle, "he was afraid you'd reject him. How we reacted, it didn't matter. Not by comparison."

"Did he say that?"

"No, but it was obvious."

I look at Dad and he's a blur. Tears are about to spill down my cheeks. But they don't and I go on looking at him. There's a tension around his mouth. He's too still. The others are looking at him too.

Victor grins. "I said to Manfred after we met him at the centre,

'It's not fair, a head of hair like that. What happened to male pattern baldness?'"

Dad's eyelids flutter then he's looking around, yawning, patting his mouth until he sees the smirk on Victor's face. He glances at me and has the good grace to look sheepish.

Chapter Thirty Four

"YOU MIGHT BE here for the night if you don't leave soon."

To the east the sky is perfectly clear but that doesn't mean any-thing. I've flown over this place. The land is flat for two thousand clicks then it starts to crumple. This is where prairie bangs into mountain. It's a complicated place, weather-wise.

"Would that be all right, staying the night?"

"Of course. You don't have to ask. Shall we take a walk while we can?"

I wait outside while he finishes putting his boots on.

It's warmed up, the way it does when snow is coming. The dead grasses by the machine shed are tawny brown, dun, bleached gold. Soon the land will be white and grey and dark green. My eyes keep travelling back to the grasses, as if I'm afraid I'll never see them again. As if everything might change forever.

I could tell Dad what I've done.

I could wait, see if it comes to anything.

We make our way around the field, skirting the frozen ridges of ploughed earth. There's no wind, the trees hushed, expectant. We both walk out to the lip, look down at the river frozen below, every pebble in the shallows collared with ice.

"There are beavers," I say, "in the river valley near my house. Down past the golf course. Felling young poplars, dragging them down to the water. River's frozen clear across but somehow they've kept a patch open."

"They'll do that," Dad says. "I don't know how."

I have the feeling I had the other day, about the lodge under the water where the beavers live. A whole other world, alive and out of sight.

"I suppose," Dad says, "the river will go on carving itself deeper and deeper."

Dad's stretched out on the chesterfield, sound asleep. I call my voice-mail then switch on the little alabaster lamp on the bookshelf. Scanning the spines I think about Dad and Victor and Manfred in this room, laughing until they cried. Years of secrets like wrapping paper scattered across the floor, the three of them shining in each other's sight. I pull out *The Complete Shakespeare*, take it into the kitchen.

The small, relentless flakes of a serious storm tap at the windows. Somewhere in Act Three I've lost track of who's who in what disguise. Instead I'm picturing Judy meeting Danielle next Sunday. The first thing out of her mouth is going to be, 'So you gave someone my phone number when I asked you not to.'

'What are you talking about? I didn't give your number to anyone.'

'Well, how did she get it then?'

'Who?'

'Meg's her name. She works at Dreamcatcher.'

'Meg? Meg called you?'

'She got my number from someone.'

'Wait. She did ask me for it. I said I had to ask you first.'

'Then where did she get it?'

'It's in my file. I put you down as my next of kin.'

'She took it without your permission?'

'Why did she call you?'

'You don't know? She didn't mention that she's looking for her birth family?'

Fuck. Just fuck. How the hell am I going to get out of this?

Everything stops for a moment then my mind gets going again. But I've learned. This much I've learned. Go back to the hiccup. The little pause. Breathe. Wait. What's happening here?

I know, the way I almost always do. *How am I going to get out of this?* That's addict talk. Sober self says, *Take an inventory. Have you done something wrong? If so, admit it. Promptly.*

Shit.

Call up Judy, tell her how I got her number.

No.

No?

No.

Everything's gone quiet inside.

Then pray for willingness.

And if I won't even do that?

Remember your last drink.

This is crazy. It's not that big a deal. I've made far harder amends than this.

Chapter Thirty Five

THE KNOCK ON the back door makes me jump. Victor stamps his boots on the stoop. Snow clings to his eyelashes. "Come on in."

He hands me a wide basket with a brown clay casserole in it.

"Thanks, but really, come in. I want to ask you a question."

He takes off his toque, shakes the snow away. Fresh flakes settle on his bald head. They melt as he steps inside and shakes off his boots. He looks into the living room. Dad's still asleep.

I put down the basket, lift out the casserole.

"Stuffed cabbage leaves," Victor says. "There's sour cream in the fridge. And homemade sauerkraut, only it's a little more like kimchee. What kind of bread did you bring?"

"I didn't, but I expect there's still some of the rye I brought last time."

"Perfect." He eyes me.

"What did you make of *Twelfth Night*?" I ask.

Whatever he was expecting, it wasn't that. He grins, shakes his head. "I think he thinks we shouldn't take it all so seriously."

"I got as far as Act III. I thought I was going to find some kind of key but really it's a goofy farce."

"Ben said once that when you get old, comedy creeps back in. Even Shakespeare outgrew tragedy."

"*The difference between tragedy and comedy is a sense of proportion.* I impressed the shit out of an English teacher once, repeating that. I thought it was Dad's idea but I guess it comes from someone famous."

"He was trying to get us to read *The Tempest*." He shakes his head. "Manfred tried. I think we're philistines."

"Not where food is concerned," I say, putting down the casserole and lifting the lid.

"Stuffed with ground pork and hazelnuts, plenty of onion. Parsley, garlic of course, a dash of soy sauce."

"So where did you learn to cook?"

"I worked in a butcher's in Gastown, making sausage. Good sausage. That's where I met Manfred. He liked my sausage."

I can't help it. The laugh snorts out. He grins.

There's a noise from the living room.

"Hello, Ben," Victor calls.

"Be with you in a minute," Dad calls.

We both listen to him shuffle and tap across the floor toward the washroom.

When he gets there Victor says, "His hearing is remarkable. It's better than Manfred's. Too much banging and clanging."

"He really did work on the railway?"

"Oh yes. Thirty years with CN."

"And you, after the sausage shop?"

"Worked in restaurants. Owned my own for a while. The recession in the early nineties." He shakes his head. "Catering after that. Until Manfred could retire. I didn't have a lot to show for all that work. Never owned a place in Vancouver. Rents kept going up. Neither of us wanted to end our days in the city anyway." He glances at me. "We did both grow up in Manitoba, just not in the same town. Never could get used to the rain in B.C., eh? Give me a dry cold."

We both hear the toilet flush.

"I know I need to answer your question," I say. "I'm just not quite there yet."

"It's not as if we'll be sowing seed any time soon. But the sooner we start the paperwork certification ..."

"I understand," I say, opening the fridge door to hide my irritation.

"I'll leave you to your supper," Victor says. He pulls on his coat and toque and steps into his boots. "Front door's drifted in," he says, opening the backdoor. Snow hurtles sideways in the lamplight. "Manfred will plough in the morning when the wind drops."

Why am I such a jerk? "Thank you," I say, "Victor. Really."

He nods and shuts the door behind him.

I'm so cranky these days.

Not enough meetings.

Meetings aren't the answer to everything.

After we eat I'll call my voicemail again.

And lying about the phone number, what are you going to do about that?

Dad comes out of the washroom. "Victor gone already?"

"Yes."

"I'd be the size of a house if I ate like this all the time," I say, wiping up the last of the nutty, savoury juice with a crust. The tang of the kimchee-kraut lingers in the air.

Dad's eyes are closing. Time for the postprandial nap. *I'm eighty now. I'm allowed a postprandial nap.* Dad when I was newly sober. I came home to make amends but I wasn't ready. Got in a huff about him saying he had a right to a nap. As if he was somehow criticizing me. *I couldn't walk down the street without picking up a resentment.* A man from New York City said that at a meeting one time, early on. Got a good laugh. Uneasy, in my case. Almost twenty years ago. Maybe I should resurrect the acceptance project. Work on being grateful for what I have. I like pottering about in the kitchen, washing up while the kettle boils. The curtain-less window reflects the lamplight, the chrome legs of the Formica table, the wooden cat-shaped clock on the wall, my own broad face. I look like a woman at home. Nothing complicated. The kettle boils and clicks off. I listen. There's the purr of the gas heater, the tick of the clock. Outside there's nothing but wind and snow. This is what I miss the most, I think, in the city. The absence of noise. But it isn't just an absence. I wonder if Dad could describe it. I tried to say it to Bill once, the feeling of a waiting emptiness, of something like welcome in the silence.

In the living room Dad snuffles and yawns. The armchair creaks.

"You awake?" I ask.

"Mm."

"Want some tea?"

"I'll join you in a pot of that peppermint. Shall I go on with my story?"

"Let me just call home. Check my messages."

I stand on the other side of the bookshelf, my back to him, as if he's going to hear whatever's on my voicemail. Punch in the numbers. My fingers miss the slinky coiled wire on the old phone. It hung on the wall by the front door. I used to drive Mum mad, stretching it out, letting it snap back. One new message. Breathe. It's Val, calling to see how I'm doing.

"Now, where were we?'

"Nineteen twenty eight. Two more years."

"You're going to be disappointed."

I wave him on with my hand.

"Very well. It was 1926 when I met Georgina. The slump that followed the war was over. So was the drought. Times were good for farmers on the prairies." He shakes his head. "Always the same old story, farming. At a dollar sixty a bushel, everyone piled in. Good weather on top of that and you had too much wheat. The 1928 harvest wasn't all sold by the time the next one was coming in. Price of wheat dropped. Whole thing was coming unwrapped even before the stock markets crashed. The boss had borrowed money to buy more trucks. But with wheat down to thirty-two cents a bushel, farmers dusted off their wagons, started hauling their own grain to the elevator. The bank took most of what he had and by the next summer I was out of a job, along with half of everybody else. I had some money saved and a friend who was in a similar situation. Mary Fraser. She'd been engaged to be married but the fellow changed his mind." He smiles, looks over at me. "Secretly I was glad. I didn't admit that, even to myself, but I remember the spring in my step after she told me.

"We bought tickets to Edmonton, third class. Train was all men but us. A couple of them appointed themselves our protectors, kept the rest at bay. They flirted but they were respectful. It was late when we pulled in. We thought we'd find a cheap hotel but it was like being a couple of pigeons surrounded by hawks. They were recruiting all right. Anything female would do. They even had women who'd come

in the ladies' waiting room where we were huddled up. Telling us they
had a nice clean place for us to stay. We didn't know who to believe.
Finally the ticket collector told us he was locking up for the night.
We asked him to lock us in but he wouldn't. Mary started to cry. He
told us the YWCA would be our best bet. If we waited a few minutes
he'd walk us there.

"Whoever said there was work to be had in Edmonton was
dreaming. Neither of us could stand dribbling away the precious bit
of money we had on the YWCA. Plenty of people were sleeping out
in the river valley. Mostly men. Some women but not by themselves.
I'd camped out all over the West with Dorothy, driving the bus. But
that was in the bush.

"We were walking along the bluffs not far from where you live,
Mary and I, looking down at the camps.

"'Nobody would bother you if you were with a fellow,' I said.
Mary looked at me strangely. 'Well they wouldn't.'

"'You couldn't. You wouldn't.'

"I stared at her. She was examining me, head on one side. Suddenly I knew what she was talking about and I knew that I'd do it.
'Just until we get on our feet.'

"'Your hair.'

"'It'll grow back. What's the worst that can happen? We'll keep
to ourselves.' She thought she ought to talk me out of it but I could
tell she was relieved.

"We went back to the YWCA. I put on Mary's spare clothes
which looked quite funny, her being six inches shorter and several
inches more on the front. We packed up and checked out. There were
any number of characters selling second-hand clothing. We ex-
changed all my clothes except my underwear for a pair of trousers,
two shirts, an undershirt, a jacket, socks, a pair of boots and a
couple of blankets. Then we went down to the river. We found a spot
in a thicket of willows near the bridge. Mary sat me down on a
stump, cut off my hair with a pair of nail scissors. I shook my head.
It felt as if it would float up off my neck. I ran my fingers through the
sharp hairs at the back of my neck, over bones in my skull I'd never
felt before. She went back out to the track, made double sure no-one

was around. I changed into my new outfit." He shakes his head, smiling. "Woman went into the willow brake, came back out a fellow."

"And you never ...?"

"One thing led to another." He shrugs. "It was never the right time."

"Seventy years and it was never once the right time?"

"Polly and I met, bought this land, built the house. It's just who we were by then." He gazes back at me.

His eyes are turquoise, the rings around the irises dark. For a moment it's easy to believe his hair is blonde again, thick and brushy. Freshly cut.

"So you see, it wasn't very dramatic."

"And you never told anyone except Mum?"

"Strictly speaking, I didn't tell her. She knew."

After a while I say, "Mum told all the stories, growing up. I thought that was just you. That you didn't talk much. But all the time you had these other stories in your mind."

Dad waits to make sure I'm finished. "They were there," he says slowly, "but it wasn't until ... It was so unexpected, Polly going first. A few weeks later I woke up in the night thinking, 'I have to tell Meg.' The two thoughts hit me together, that I could tell you now and that I must tell you."

"Mum wouldn't let you?"

Dad looks surprised. "I never asked her. It was unthinkable, that I would do that to her."

"Do what? Tell me?"

"Tell anyone." He reaches for his cane.

"So you didn't. But what about you? What did you want?"

"I made my choice."

"And that's what it was? A choice? A matter of convenience. For seventy years?"

He eyes me. At last he says, "I don't know how to answer that. But I do know it's time for bed."

Chapter Thirty Six

I LIE IN bed, the wind a giant blundering about in the dark. Images string themselves together. Charlotte driving the ambulance. On the little station platform, head thrown back, gazing at the prairie sky. With Dorothy, repairing the Sunday School van. Charlotte and Georgina riding out across the prairie. Charlotte and Mary on the bluffs in Edmonton. Then Charlotte goes into the willows. Out comes Ben in his men's clothes, his short hair. He strolls off into the future without a backward glance.

A woman went into the willows ... Gleaming like a pelt among brittle leaves, that coil of hair, abandoned but strangely alive.

'What did you do with the hair?'

It's like waking up from a dream. A voice so clear in my head. 'What did you do with the hair?'

Questions pile up like snow against the door.

When I wake again, the wind has dropped.

I'm up before Dad, before light, out in the iron cold, shovelling snow. The drifts against the door stand, sculpted, more stone than pillow, peaks and ridges inhospitable, remote. I carve a path through. Wind scoured the top of the car clean but in the lee the snow lies soft, smothering. I shovel the car free. Shovel fast. I'm sweating. The stars are fading. When lights come on I go inside. My skin burns in the warmth.

We eat breakfast in silence. Dad casts the odd puzzled look my way but I've got no words for any of it, and if there's one thing we know, the two of us, it's how not to talk.

When I've washed up and called my voicemail, I sit down again. He raises an eyebrow at me.

"You became a man just like that?"

"I was ready for a change."

"It can't have been that easy."

"People see what they expect to see."

"Except Mum. She knew. Somehow." I look at him.

"I don't know how. She just did."

"And everybody else took you at face value."

"It really was easy."

"Right from the start?"

"The first day was a bit nerve-wracking but nobody gave me a second look. Well, except for a couple of girls. That was a bit of a surprise." He grins. "We walked around for a while. I watched how men moved. Mary watched me. Corrected me when I was womanish. I changed how I walked."

"More strut, less sway?"

"Exactly. Stiffened up my shoulders. When I was ready I gruffed my voice and we bought canvas and some rope. A hatchet and a Billy-can.

"People were camped all the way down the river valley. Some had even carved caves into seams of coal. We found a site up a little side ravine. I'm not sure either of us got a lot of sleep that first night. Over the next few days it got easier and easier. It was fun, actually. The wall that cut the world in two, men on one side, women on the other, turned out to be no more than a stage curtain. That's how I felt, anyway. Mary though, I'd catch her stealing little looks at me. The more confident I became, the more uneasy she was. The whole idea was for people to assume we were a couple but I don't think she liked it much when they did."

"For some reason."

"I was just playing a part."

"A part that came naturally?"

"Mm."

After a moment I ask, "What did you call yourself?"

He looks surprised. "Ben."

"From the beginning?"

"Mary wanted to call me Charles. She thought she'd be less likely to slip up. I remember saying to her, 'It's not as if you get a chance to choose your own name very often.'

"She said, 'When I find a husband, I will.'

"That was a moment when I felt ..."—he hesitates—"relief. As a girl the only thing people seemed to care about was who I would marry. Marriage didn't interest me at all. It never had. So I always felt ... out of step. But as Ben"—he shrugs—"I could just be myself."

"So you weren't attracted to men?"

"No. Was I attracted to women? I'd say so now. At the time I had close friends."

"But you never ..." I stop. This feels too weird.

"Your mother was ..." He nods.

"And by then you were, you were Ben. Was that ..."

"The reason I stuck with it?" He studies me. "I did what I did and life unfolded. Could I have chosen a different path? I didn't. Would I have chosen a different path if it had been acceptable to be gay? Would I have chosen a different path if I were a different person? More inclined to confront than avoid. Possibly, but I wasn't."

"That's it? "

He shrugs.

"But Dad, what did you do about papers? A birth certificate, all that?"

"Those were simpler times."

"And the war? The Second World War. They had conscription?"

"I was too old by then. And a rancher. Which meant I was exempt."

"Why Ben Coopworth?"

"I like the name."

"But it wasn't your name."

"No, I suppose not."

"So where did it come from? You can't just make up a name and,

and buy land, get a driver's license, get married. Did you get married? Legally?"

"Yes." His eyes have the icy glitter. We both hear the rumble of the tractor. "He's got it running like a Porsche." Dad nods in the direction of the sound. "He's more of a mechanic than I ever dreamed of being, Manfred is. I preferred horses, really, but it wasn't practical."

"Dad."

"I think that's enough for now."

I take a deep breath. "I should get on the road then."

Dad shakes his head. "They'll have cleared 22 by now but I doubt they've ploughed out the side roads."

"So what are you willing to talk about?" I'm embarrassed as soon as the words come out. "Sorry."

Dad's face softens.

There's a knock on the front door. It's Manfred, stamping snow from his boots and swinging his arms.

"Thought I'd let you know the plough came by just as I was cleaning out the head of the driveway."

"Great. Thank you," I say.

"Saw you'd shovelled out your car already. Thought you might be in a hurry."

I've got hours until work tonight but I'm only going to get into trouble here. "I've got a bunch of shifts in a row," I say. "It'll be a while before I'm back out."

"Let me know you got home safely," Dad says.

"I will. I'm just going to get my sweater." Making the bed the view snags me. Mountains gleam under the morning's newly scrubbed sky. Mountains wrapped in blankets of fresh snow. Between here and there, Firestick.

Turning away from the window, *Wheat and Woman* catches my eye. I pick it up, take it downstairs.

"Mind if I borrow this?"

"Not at all. Drive carefully."

Chapter Thirty Seven

"WHAT'S THIS?" TANYA jabs her finger at the schedule.

"The new aftercare component." Cathy, trying to sound casually assertive.

"And I'm supposed to do what?"

"Teach the clients relaxation techniques. It's easy."

"No."

"Really. There's a tape ..." Cathy takes a deep breath, flicks the hair back from her face. "This is not optional. Brenda says ..."

"Instead of helping clients find housing we're going to teach them to relax about being homeless?"

"You'll have to take this matter up with the Executive Director." Cathy turns to stalk out of the room, catching several sheets of paper and a can of hairspray on the way.

When the gate clicks shut Tanya looks around the office, eyebrows raised.

"Brenda will get you for this," Jay says.

Tanya shrugs. "I'm not qualified to teach"—she drags the words out—"relaxation techniques." Her face breaks into a smile.

"Fuck 'em, eh?" Jay says.

"Dumb as my arse," Heather says. "That's what our Cathy is." She looks at Jay and me, shaking her head, red lipstick lips pursed.

I take a deep breath. "I can't help it," I say. "I feel sorry for her. Stuck between us and Brenda."

"She took the job," Jay says. "And don't forget, she's John Paul's plant."

"That's right. She was working for him over at Métis Child and Family Services."

"He took over the board here, saw we needed supervising and snapped his fingers. She does what she's told." Jay's looking at me.

"Like the good soldier she was," Heather says. "Johnny boy loves his soldiers."

"He and Bob were military buddies, weren't they? At least Brenda's better than Bob."

"Not a high bar. Brenda actually works."

"Mm. I don't think our Brenda's shown her true colours yet."

I feel like a kid listening to the grown-ups talk. "Think I'll do a room check." Walking down the corridor to the bedrooms I can't help wondering what they're saying about me. 'Even more out of it than usual, isn't she?'

"Excuse me?"

I jump.

Oil-patch Don is standing in his doorway looking at me, puzzled.

Because I was standing in the middle of the corridor outside his room, staring into space. "How's it going?"

"Okay." He goes back into his room and closes the door.

I turn and walk back up the corridor to Cathy's office.

"Come in."

Her desk is piled with art supplies. Bottles of white glue hold down stacks of papers. Tubs of beads pile beside her computer.

"What can I do for you?" Cathy smiles at me. If I was one of the others she'd be wary. "Have a seat. Just dump those folders on the floor."

"Thanks. Um, I had a couple of questions. About something that happened to someone long back. You worked for Métis Child and Family Services, didn't you?"

She nods.

"If a child showed up somewhere with no papers, no name, nothing … and he or she couldn't say where they came from, but the people took him or her in, is it possible the authorities would have let the child stay with those people?"

Her brow furrows. "How old was the child?"

"Ten or so."

"When was this?"

"The late sixties. 1968."

"And the child, was she Métis, aboriginal?"

"She might have been."

"And the people who took her in?"

"They were white."

"Were there any indications of past abuse?"

"Yes."

"I don't really know," Cathy says after a moment. "It's possible. I think it might have come down to the individual social worker. I mean they were closing the residential schools but ..." She shrugs. "You've heard of the sixties scoop?"

I nod.

"They were pretty busy taking kids away from their families. I'm not sure how much effort they'd have put in ... It would have been a lot of work"—she shrugs—"for a problem that had an easy solution." Her eyes are kind. "Did they do a home study?"

"Yes."

"And"—she hesitates—"was the foster family a good family?"

"Yes."

"That's good."

"Okay. Well, thanks Cathy."

"You're welcome. If you have any other questions ..."

I could have found a way to talk to Danielle before ceremony but instead I chatted with James who hung around the front desk most of the evening.

"Nervous," Jay says, when everyone's in the dome except the two of us and the girls on their moon. "He's got one more week."

"Does he have somewhere to go?"

"His girlfriend's. I think this might be his last shot as far as she's concerned."

"I hope he makes it."

"He's like an annoying younger brother. You can't help caring about him. Not that I have a brother."

Neither of us says anything for a moment, then we both speak at once.

"How's the search?"

"How's school?"

"You first," I say.

"'*Children re-enact under unconscious compulsion the unlived lives of their parents. C.G. Jung. Discuss.*'"

"Sounds interesting but I've no idea what it means."

"Children are destined to be their parents' worst nightmare? Whatever the parents find unacceptable and repress, right, that goes into their unconscious. So the parents are trying to keep all that stuff down, out of sight, but the kids have to express it. My mother, right, she joined her horrible church, shut down everything that made her vibrant and alive. What did she get? A lesbo daughter. Who they can all pray for." She shivers. "Gives me the willies, eh? Creepy fucking pastor. Always licking his lips. Consoling her. That weird furtive excitement they have."

"Sin's very interesting," I say. "I remember thinking that in church."

"It's where the juice is. *Whatever you repress, whatever you don't recognize in yourself, is nevertheless alive.*"

"More Jung?"

"Yes. So here's what I want to write about. What if you view Canada as a family? The settlers repressed aboriginal culture. Drove it underground. Declared it dead. Or at least doomed. But that was wishful thinking. Now it's demanding to be expressed. The country's unlived life."

"*Hai hai,*" sounds from inside the chamber. The girls on the bench stir.

"Annie says I'll get my ass kicked, trying to write about it."

"Because you're white?"

"She thinks I'm stretching the topic and I won't get my A."

The blanket's pulled back.

I watch the clients emerge, blinking. Something's tugging at me. It should be my conscience but it's not. Danielle's almost the last one out. We smile at each other. Apparently I'm not going to deal with the phone number issue, I'm just going to wait for the two of them to converge, Judy and Danielle. It's like watching a car accident in slo-mo. How everything slows to a crawl, the cars floating toward each other.

Chapter Thirty Eight

NO MESSAGES. NO hang-up calls. So she hasn't found out anything. Yet. I mix some dough, three-quarters white, quarter oat, lots of sunflower seeds. I'm still not sleepy. Perhaps a little nineteen twenties agricultural adventure will do the trick.

Make some chamomile tea. *Set the stage for sleep.* Who said that? Some helpful person, long ago.

Settled in bed, I open *Wheat and Woman* at random.

> *As you walk through the bright and sunny dormitories it seems the best possible arrangement that so many dear small bodies should be tucked safely and snugly into so many snow-white beds; but when you get back to the lake-shore trail again and watch the evening sky as it makes its rose and opal offering to the lake, when you sniff the pungent odour of prairie herbs, the heart-warming smell of the camp-fires which mark the freeman's tent, when you breathe in and breathe out the air of liberty, and the sway of the fascination of life in the open tugs at the heart-strings, you know that the children of Hiawatha pay the price for those opportunities of civilization.*

Jesus.

I go back a page, find the beginning of the paragraph where *quiet cheerful nuns preside,* where girls receive domestic training, boys a useful trade, *in order that they may be able to take possession of the opportunities which civilization brought to the wonderful treasure-land of their fathers.*

There's a photograph too: *The Industrial School for Indian boys and girls.* LaBret, Saskatchewan.

'And the dear small bodies buried out back?' Voice in my head, hardly more than a hiss.

Judy, that flush across her forehead, wind blowing wrappers round the parking lot, how they came and stole the children again.

Jesus.

Ah, yes. Jesus.

> *Father Hugenard and his brother-priests of the Roman Catholic Church have most truly bestowed on the children of the darker race the consolation of religion.*

Jesus fucking Christ.

Danielle and Jesus and Judy.

Are you my people? My lost people.

Lost children. Lost ceremonies. Lost land.

On the streets, drunk, I was always an Indian.

In my office, pumps, blouse, I heard it all: No good, sucking at the federal tit drunken Indians bleating about the noble past.

What did I do? Pretended I didn't hear.

Suddenly I get it, what's been tugging at me.

Dad's whole story, from when he landed in Canada until he became Ben, there's not a single Indian. Nine years. 1921 to 1930. No children of Hiawatha here.

But they were. They were there all along.

Not lost. Stolen.

Breathe. Slow down. Slow.
It's not working.
Hold your breath.
Drunk Indian.
Guy. Call me Guy.
Dora. Help me, Dora.
Hold your breath.
The dark between the stars, Dora. I'm shredding.
Disappearing.

Dora and the Ghost Dancers.
Desperate sacrament.
Let it, let it, let it.
Let it take you.
Dissolve or break. Let the great dark wave take.
Trust the dark, girl.
That velvet night.

Somewhere safe.
Let the wave.

I can't. Panic spikes.
Make it go away.
Jesus.

Relief. It's all we want, eh?
Consolation.
Annihilation.

WEEK FOUR

Chapter Thirty Nine

"SO ARE THE brothers brothers?"

"Nope. You were right." I poke at one meatball then another. They glisten in brown gravy.

After a moment Jay turns to Doug. "I haven't seen you in a while. What did you think of Emmett's talk?"

"I have heard stories about grandparents who were quietly accepting. Maybe it was the old way. But it hasn't been like that for a long time, on or off the reserves. Not for young people. More like relentless brutal teasing with plenty of straight out physical violence thrown in."

"Christianity doesn't help," Jay says.

"Starting with the fucking Catholic church."

"So was there really Eden before the Christian snakes slithered in?" Jay asks. "Is there something beautiful and whole to go back to? Healing in the traditional way? Or do you have to make something that works now? Stop hankering for the dead past. That's what Annie thinks. 'Hunter gatherers are so yesterday.'" She grins. "Me, I say, 'You can't walk away from the myths. They come and get you.' But she's the one with the blood."

Doug shakes his head. "Métis, we've got our own twist, but I can tell you, it's not gay friendly."

Jay looks at me. Talk. Okay. "I don't know whether I've got a right to an opinion." They're waiting again. "I like the way of thinking.

Everyone belongs as they are, and who they are could be fluid." I
stop. Jay's in the know and Doug isn't and it feels wrong.

"'We respect each person's vision'," Jay says. "She'll be Chief,
that Eleanor. If she stays clean."

"The one who spoke after Shannon did her little Miss Innocent
number? What's her story?"

"Great-uncle was one of the founders of this place. She was a
student at Concordia, first year. It was too much, I guess. Started with
speed. Helped her study. Dealer gave her crystal meth. Christ, it's
addictive, that shit. Glad it wasn't around when I was out there. Least
she knew where to go for help."

"At least there was help," Doug says.

"Excuse me?"

I push my plate aside, go out to the desk.

"Can I use the phone?" Pretty dark-haired girl, navy blue eyes
made up so they have the wide stare of a doll.

"Not until six." She must have come in this afternoon.

"Can you put me on the list?"

"What list?"

"For the phone." She says it slowly, eyes even wider.

"Hey Ash," Jay says from behind me. "How's it going?"

Ash shrugs. Ash, short for Ashlei. I saw her name in the book for
today. *M* for Métis.

"We don't do the list anymore," Jay says. "It's too soon for
phone privileges anyway. You know that."

The rest of the new clients arrive in a flurry. When it's time for ceremony I slip into line behind Danielle. Doug is between Edward the
Somali and Gordon the Inuit.

Sitting on the buffalo hide, breathing in the sage and sweet grass,
I need to feel something. *God, whatever You are ...* What? *Help me
find the truth? Help me face the truth?* But I'm back on the dear,
small bodies and the snow-white bedding. Stolen children, stolen
culture, stolen language. Trying to make it up again. Chief-for-a-
week, *Hai hai* and the Lord's Prayer. What's going to hold? What's
strong enough or warm enough or real enough to plug the fucking
hole where everything leaks out. Pour all the booze on the planet

down the hole, you still want more. Need more. I look around. How many of you poor fucks will still be clean and sober three months from now? Earnest Eleanor? Warren the Weird? Gay Geoff? Just Joey? Danielle? Danielle what? Fuck. Stop it.

Chapter Forty

"IS ANYONE SITTING there?"

Danielle grabs at the top of the seat as the bus lurches around a stalled car.

"All yours. How are you doing?"

"Good, I guess."

I give her a minute.

"Well, no, I'm scared. What happens when I get out of here?"

"You've got a month."

"Yes but where am I going to go? What am I going to do? I have to have faith. And I do. But ..." She shrugs. "My aunt wants me to come and live with her. On the reserve, you know. Turn the place around." She doesn't sound excited. The bus bumps along. Voices are raised then simmer down. Doug's in the back.

"It's just ... It's so poor." The word is thick and dark as molasses. "I know that's shallow. And unworthy. But ..."

Trailers with plywood over the windows, generations of derelict cars, a few horses on sour pastures. Now and then a tidier house. Never any vegetables growing. That's what I remember noticing. I doubt it's changed. Judy, four years younger than me, hardly able to cross the Timmie's without gasping for breath. Danielle's face is beseeching, freckled cheeks framed by thick dark hair, a soft pink turtleneck.

"It's okay to look after yourself," I say. "You won't be any use to anyone if you pick up again."

She's nodding. "I knew you'd say that. I trust you. Here." She pats her chest with her hand. "From the first moment I saw you. If you ... If it did turn out we were related and you wanted to be involved too ..."

The driver slows for the turn into the Rec Centre.

When they're all in the pool, laughing and splashing except Deborah who is swimming back and forth, head held well above the water, Doug asks, "How's your father?"

The lifeguard blows his whistle. He's pointing at the top of the slide. We both lean forward. The glass between the pool and the viewing balcony could do with cleaning. The jostling knot of guys at the top of the ladder teases apart.

"Dad? Pretty good, considering."

"Is he really a hundred?"

"Hundred and a half now."

"Did you have a party?"

"He didn't want one. My mother died a few weeks earlier. He's never cared about his birthday anyway."

My voice sounds weird but Doug nods. His eyes are a warm brown, friendly as a dog. He reminds me of a dog. Cheerful. Sensible. Each day a new adventure.

"Were they married a long time?"

"Sixty-three years."

"Wow. I'll never manage that." He sounds sad.

"If you started now ..." I stop. He can't even get married.

"I'd have to live to be a hundred and twelve."

The whistle blows again, then a second and third time. Doug's halfway down the stairs to the pool by the time I'm on my feet. Warren's squaring off against Edward. They're both more muscled than they look in their clothes. Edward's skin's a rich almost purple black, Warren's is blue and red, his whole chest and back patterned. The tattoos don't stop at his swim trunks.

Shannon's standing behind Warren, arms crossed over her chest. It's hard to read her expression but when Doug comes up she smiles at him. He says something to her. Warren and Edward each back up. The lifeguard looks relieved.

Shannon's still smiling at Doug. Women like Doug. I like Doug. I don't like him not knowing about Dad.

He comes back to the table shaking his head. "Way too much testosterone," he says.

"How's Geoffrey doing these days?" Twig thin and pale in baggy black trunks, he's standing in the shallow end watching Gordon who's in the water, supporting himself on his arms, legs making frog kicks.

"Sharing a room with Gordon's been a good thing. There they are, this totally urban gay man and a straight Inuit guy who feels lost, so far from the land and his community. I doubt they said more than ten words to each other the first week but I think somehow Geoff got it, that other people can be as lonely as he is, for completely different reasons. It's like he's shrugged off that suit of self-pity, now he's looking around at the world, saying, 'Okay, what's next?'" Doug looks at me. "That's what I love about this work. The transformations. That it's possible, you know?"

"Yes," I say. "Yes, I do know." I'm thinking I'd have given an arm for Bill to have been able to talk like this. Any guy I've dated. I guess gay men really are different.

Three long whistles sound. The lifeguard shouts, "Time's up." The queue for the water slide gets longer. Women as well as guys. We watch in comfortable silence as bodies hurtle down the slide. The crowd at the top dwindles at last.

"I meant it the other day," Doug says. "I want to hear the longer story. Maybe we could have coffee or a meal ..."

Without thinking I say, "I'd like that."

"How's Friday?"

"As in tomorrow?"

"I'm working Saturday and I said I'd be back-up for Sunday, in case Tanya's mother takes a turn for the worse."

"Tomorrow works."

"Got any ideas for where to eat?"

The bus smells of chlorine and cologne. *Get me to the church on time* blasts out of the speakers. Doug's up front this time, sitting next to Deborah.

Years ago I went out to Tofino, body surfed the breakers. A

thousand clicks of cold Pacific behind you, you feel the wave rise under you, swim like hell. There's a moment it catches you, lifts you, hurls you forward. Barrelling down the night-time street in the dimly lit bus I can feel it, the surge of life lifting me, lifting us, thrusting us on into the future.

Whatever the hell that holds. What if I really did come from Firestick? My mother could still be alive.

The bus jolts to a stop. Red light. Dandelion yellow sign. *Yvonne's Caribbean.*

Chapter Forty One

DOUG'S AT THE table by the window, studying the menu. Seeing me, he smiles and gets up. "Want this seat?"

I do because it's the one with its back to the wall and a view of the door but I shake my head, look around. "Good thing you got here early. Been waiting long?"

"I wasn't sure how long it would take to get into the city this time of day."

"How long does it usually take?"

"Just under an hour."

"That's not so bad, eh?"

"Worth it to me."

The waiter comes up. He looks worried. "You need more time?"

"I know what I want." I look at Doug.

"Me too."

He bustles off with the order. Doug's eyes follow him.

"He's Yvonne—the owner's—sister's son-in-law. And he always looks worried. She says he takes his responsibilities very seriously and that's a good thing. She's not too big on the Rasta men." I tip my chin at a table of handsome ebullient men with bulky red, yellow and green striped caps.

"You live around here?"

"112th and 66th."

"You didn't sound like a fan of the city, the other week."

"You mean when you asked if I liked living here and I said no? I surprised myself. But it's true, the noise bothers me more and more."

The waiter returns with glasses and a platter of dip we didn't order. I look across the crowded room. Yvonne, standing by the cash register nods once. I mouth, "Thank you."

"You come here often?"

"Used to." I reach for a sweet potato chip, scoop up some dip. Doug follows suit.

"Yum," I say. "This is new."

"I love plantain."

We both take more.

"And lime and cayenne."

"And cloves?"

"Mace too, maybe."

Yvonne's watching us. I raise my thumb. Doug nods vigorously.

"So what keeps you in the city, other than places like this which are thin on the ground out where I live?"

"I like working at Dreamcatcher."

"Me too, but you don't have to live here to do that."

"I guess if I was going to live in the country it would be on the ranch where I grew up."

"Over near Drayton Valley?"

"It's too far to drive in for work. I don't know how I'd make a living there."

"There are always ways. Especially if you don't have a mortgage. I make harnesses."

"For horses? Sorry, stupid question."

The waiter arrives with our plates.

"Thank you." Doug smiles and picks up his fork.

"How did you get into that? Making harnesses."

"I'd been going up north, on and off, working in the camps, but then something happened. I realized the girls needed me. We'd broken up, Tanya and me. I'm not their biological father but I've known them since they were one and three. It was more important to me to be in their lives than pretty much anything else. So"—he shrugs—"I used to make belts, sandals. Hippie stuff, you know. Back in the day. Not much of a market for that in Alberta but horses ... There was a lot of money coming into Stony Plain. Last boom, people bought acreages. What's an acreage without a couple of horses?

"I found an old guy over by Conjuring Lake. Gabriel Lambert. Worked with him whenever I could. He'd been making tack his whole life. He was happy to have someone to pass it on to. The knowledge he'd built up. It was a good time, the time I spent with Gabriel. We could go for hours without saying a word. It turned out he was Métis too but I didn't find that out for a couple of years."

He looks down at his plate which he hasn't touched yet. "You're going to have to do some talking. I was wondering how it went, with the brothers who ..."

"Aren't? I wasn't quite so mad by the time I talked to them. I'd worked out why it bothered me so much."

"*If we are disturbed ...*" Doug says softly.

"*The fault lies in us.*" I finish. "I've always hated that bit of the Big Book. I mean I don't believe it about all sorts of stuff. But ..." I shrug.

"It's saved my ass a few times," he says.

"Yeah. Me too."

"So why did it bother you so much, if you don't mind me asking?"

I watch him collect a forkful of rice and goat curry and fried plantain, his brown hair swinging forward, half hiding his face. Silver threads the dun brown. His moustache too is shot with silver. "It's all about trust, I suppose. The short version is: a) since my mother died I've discovered there are a lot of things that aren't the way they appeared to be, and b) I get mad at not being able to trust my father because there's a whole lot of stuff I need to know which I should know but I don't because I can't remember ..." Doug's brow wrinkles. "Never mind. It's too complicated."

He finishes chewing his mouthful, puts down his fork. "But I would like to know."

I look around. The people at the table next to Doug are in raucous conversation but the couple at my right elbow are barely talking at all.

"Somewhere less crowded. Perhaps we could get coffee afterwards."

"Fine idea. But you're still going to have to talk a bit." He picks up his fork. "How's the bread-making going? This curry is excellent, by the way."

"So is the jerk chicken. Actually everything I've eaten here has been good. As to the bread, I've hit a bit of a plateau. I'd like to experiment with techniques that bring out the flavour of whole grains but there's not much point without better quality flour."

"I heard there's a monk in Ontario who got hold of some viable seed of Red Fife. Just a handful. It'll take a while for him to grow it out, build up seed stock. Assuming it's the real thing." Doug looks down at his plate then smiles at me. "You'll get me talking again."

"Sorry." I'm smiling back.

He finishes off the curry and puts down his fork. "Where did you have in mind for coffee? Other than Timmies which won't be any less crowded. Beverly must have come up in the world if there's another coffee joint. But then look at this place. Even a couple of years ago Swiss Chalet was as cosmopolitan as you got in Edmonton."

"I'm drawing a blank," I say, "on the cappuccino bar. Want to get coffee at my place?"

I'd never do this on a first date but it's easy, hanging out with Doug. "Fine," he says. "Shall we go? Make some people happy?"

I twist around. "That's quite a queue."

Doug's standing up, heading for the register. No baling twine in his pocket. Same jacket though, and jeans faded to that point of perfect softness two minutes shy of splitting.

Yvonne wearing a blue and white tie-dye headkerchief and matching mumu. 'My Yoruba mama look,' she told me one time.

"Thanks for the dip," I say. "It was delicious."

She purses her lips and frowns. "Needs my grandmother's pepper sauce. Next time I go back I'll get the proper peppers, eh?" She finds our bill.

"We're splitting it," I say.

"Not if you're making coffee," Doug says, passing Yvonne a twenty, waiting for her to tell him the rest.

"Seventeen dollars and twenty cents," she says, her voice rich and brown as her skin, a guttural laugh in the bottom of it.

"You don't ask enough," he says.

She surveys him. "Is that so?" she says slowly.

He grins. "For such an excellent meal."

He turns away. Yvonne catches my eye, nods her head once, majestically.

I shake my head, smiling.

Yvonne tucks her chin in so several extra chins form, mock frowns at me. Bill and I used to come in here a lot.

I shake my head at her again and follow Doug out.

He left a five on the table. Good. I hate cheap tippers.

Chapter Forty Two

"THEY GAVE ME that." I wave the bag of *Alberta Crude* at my one and only fridge magnet: *I can sleep when I'm dead.*

Doug grins. "I confess I am an apostate in the Church of Timmies. Living in New Mexico, I got used to good weed, good tequila, good coffee. Good coffee's what I missed the most when I moved back to Alberta. The weed and the tequila ..." He opens his hands, spreads solid square tipped fingers.

Back in the living room, him in the armchair, me on the chesterfield, I ask, "So how and when did you get sober?"

He shakes his head. "First you're going to tell me this complicated story."

"How long ago did he tell you this? Or she?"

"He. I stopped calling him Dad for about three minutes but what's the point? He's not reverting to being a woman."

"So it's not really as simple as passing for convenience."

"No, but I'm not sure it's any of the other versions I know about either. He's clear that he didn't feel like he was born into the wrong body. The way he says it, it's more that he made a choice to pass and then it evolved. It wasn't even his idea, exactly. The woman he was with misunderstood something he said. She said something like, 'You wouldn't,' and he knew that he would."

"And that same day he bought men's clothes, cut off his hair and never looked back? There must have been some idea, some wish before that moment."

"I would have thought so. But he was quite impulsive. Or she was. She left home kind of on the spur of the moment, went off to drive an ambulance, even though she knew her parents would disown her. But that's another story."

"Which I'd also like to hear. But I'm trying to imagine. When he first told you, he said he was a woman, not a man. But later he said he was a woman or a man."

"He likes 'or' not 'and'. Possibly because he thinks the world isn't ready for 'and'."

"When did he tell you?"

"Three weeks ago."

"Wow. Then last week you found out the brothers weren't what they seemed either. No wonder you were steamed."

My eyes sting. You think you want someone to understand but then it hurts.

"Where did they meet? How did they meet, your father and the not-brothers?"

"An ad at the GLBT centre."

"Here in town? On 101st?"

I nod. "Don't ask. Every story sprouts another one. You'll be here all night." I stop, embarrassed.

"I want to go back to your story. If you don't mind. The day your father told you, you were expecting him to tell you something else. Something you should know but don't know because you can't re-member?"

"Jesus, you've got a good memory."

He shrugs. "I'm interested."

"All right. You know I'm adopted?"

"And that you don't know anything about your birth family."

"How about that I don't remember anything before the day I showed up at the farm which was when I was about ten years old?"

"Nothing at all?"

"Nothing."

"Wow. So where does your memory start?"

"At the edge of a field. A man driving an orange tractor. Who, it turns out, wasn't exactly a man. But I thought he was. A man with gold hair. Freshly ploughed soil. Poplar trees. Yellow leaves."

"And you don't remember anything at all before that?"

I shake my head. I'm not going to cry.

"What about your name? Did you know your name?"

I shake my head again.

"So 'Meg' ..."

"Is a name Mum and Dad gave me. I must know. I know I must. But I can't get to it."

"Do you mind me asking you questions?"

"No."

"When you were standing at the edge of the field, did you think, 'That's freshly ploughed soil'?"

I shake my head. "The soil was just lumpy and brown. But I see your point. I knew the tractor was a tractor. I knew the trees were poplar trees. But I don't think that adds up to me having come from a farm."

"So there you were at the edge of the field?"

He's not looking at me as if I'm a freak.

I can see Dad, dusty, wiping his sleeve across his mouth, long stride across the tumbled earth. Black and white dog slinking along at his heels.

"The man asked me if I was lost. I understood but I didn't say anything. Then he asked me my name. I didn't say anything then either. There wasn't anything in my mind to say. I just stood there. He asked some more questions then he turned and started walking away. I followed him to a house with a red roof. A woman was standing in the doorway.

"They gave me some water and a blanket. They asked me my name again and where I was from. I didn't answer. I couldn't. They gave me food then the man left. He came back with a different man who spoke to me in Cree. Not that I recognized it back then. The next day Dad went to the RCMP."

"He didn't call them that night?"

"No. Mum didn't want to call them at all. There were signs I'd been abused. Physically. Dad insisted.

"The RCMP didn't have any reports of missing children that fit my description. They put him in touch with a woman who worked in

Child Welfare. He talked to her then we all three went to see her. I don't really remember that visit. As soon as we got in the truck I kind of stepped outside myself, like I was riding alongside myself. Just watching. I didn't feel anything. I was in that state a lot, especially at the beginning."

I stop. I know the word for that state. Doug probably does too.

"Dad says the woman agreed I could stay with them while they went through the process of being approved for foster care."

"It sounds as if they knew right away they wanted ..."

"To keep me. Yes. Mum always said I was an answer to her prayers. As soon as they could they applied to adopt me. The first night I slept on the chesterfield. Then they set up a cot for me in the corner of the living room. It's a small house. There was just one bedroom. For obvious reasons they didn't want me wandering in of a morning so, as soon as they could, they built a room upstairs with a door they could lock."

"They locked you in at night?"

"No."

Doug's eyes rest on my face.

My cheeks burn. "That's where they slept. They went to a lot of trouble to make room for me. I do know that. There wasn't really even an attic. Dad cut a hole in the middle of the roof and put a sort of pop-up room there."

"Wow. He did it himself?"

"With the help of a couple of neighbours. It was the usual low budget operation. I think he spent that first winter gathering materials. I know he took down an old chicken coop. It was Mum's and my job to scrape the chicken shit off the old floor boards. We scrubbed them with bleach and let them dry for a few days in the sun and the wind. Even so, for years after that, on a hot August day, even with the windows open up there, you'd get a whiff of chicken shit.

"Those days Mum always said, 'I told you we should have put them bad side up. I'd have had them clean by now.'

"Dad always said, 'I told you we should have bought new boards.'"

Doug smiles.

"Sorry. You really are getting the long version."

"I like details. Don't stop."

"Well, so they moved into the new room and Dad built me a bed of my own in their old room."

"Had they been approved for foster care by then?"

"I don't know. Why?"

"I wonder if, back then, you had to have a room of your own for them to qualify?"

"Maybe. I remember the day of the home study. The social worker pulled up in the driveway in a big blue car that looked the way I thought a sailboat should look, as if it was leaning into the wind. Mum was fussing at Dad about the dust on his boots. My hair was pulled back so hard in a pony tail it made my eyes feel slanty. This social worker had yellow-brown eyes and pointy features. She asked me about my bed. It had a picture of sunflowers and mountains and a little white house with a red roof and another little red roof coming out of the top of it and a red door and a girl with dark hair looking out. 'Why that looks just like your house,' she said. I nodded. I could feel Mum's eyes on the back of my neck even though she was in the next room. 'Dad painted it for me,' I said, which was about as many words as I ever managed at that point. 'And is that little girl you?'

"I nodded again. She asked me to show her my clothes which were in a dresser. Her eyes crawled all over everything. The house was always pretty clean but Mum had gone overboard. She hardly let Dad and me indoors for three days before. You could see the social worker approved.

"We stood in the doorway together and waved as she drove away, red lights winking from the big silver fins.

"'Thank God that's over,' Dad said and Mum didn't even complain about him taking the Lord's name in vain."

"And that was it?"

"A couple of times I had to go and see a man in an office who played with his pens. Framed things on the wall that weren't pictures. Pale blue eyes watching me. A few times he wrote something down. I don't remember saying anything to him."

"A psychiatrist?"

"Probably. I think that might have been before the home study. I started going to school after Christmas."

"You'd been to school before?"

"I must have. It didn't freak me out." I shift on the chesterfield. "I think. I think that's enough about me."

"Of course. I didn't mean to pry."

"No. I'm ... It's me. I guess I'm surprised. I thought we'd be talking about Dad. You seemed to just take that in stride. Am I weird for being floored by it?"

"Of course not. I can't even begin to wrap my mind around my father telling me that. I'd be in shock for a year. But the two stories together ... It was a hell of a risk."

"What?"

"For them to take you in. To tell the authorities. Can you imagine inviting a social worker into your house when you were sitting on that kind of secret? They must have really wanted you. Did you feel it? Could you feel it, or were you too traumatized? Is this just my shit? I'd love to feel chosen. I always figured my parents loved me because they had to. Because I was their child, not because of who I was. Sorry. I'm putting my foot in it, aren't I? I should stop before I get the other one all the way in."

"No," I say. "I like it. I hadn't really thought of it that way. And you're right. They were scared, the day the social worker came to the house. I remember how stiff Dad was." I take a deep breath. "I know I just said I want to stop talking about this but there's something I'd like to run by you. If you've got time."

"There's nowhere I've got to be," he says.

"More coffee?

"Are you really all right with me talking your ear off like this?"

"Absolutely." When he smiles his whole face crinkles. Except there's a still place in the middle. The crag of his nose. His eyes are hooded, looking back at me. Domed eyelids, high cheekbones. I haven't really seen the Native in him before. "Go on," he says.

"It's about my last name. Coopworth. Which I thought was Dad's name. Only I don't see how it could be, legally."

"It's not the name he—she—was born with?"

"No. So where did Ben Coopworth come from?"

"Did you ask him?"

"Yes but he didn't really answer. It's obvious he doesn't want to talk about it. He's got a driver's license. And a S.I.N. number, all that stuff. He can't have just invented his name."

"He might have, if it was long enough ago. But there are other ways to get a name, meaning an official identity."

"Like what?"

"You really want to know?"

"Yes, I do."

"Well, the easy one first. Did he ever get married?"

"To my mother. Which would have required a birth certificate, wouldn't it?"

"I mean when he was a she."

"Oh. Not that I know of. He's clear he didn't ... she didn't want to get married. Which doesn't ... Shit."

"There are other ways. There used to be anyway, before computerized records. The simplest was to find a county where records of births and deaths were kept separately. You went to a cemetery or combed through the obituaries looking for a baby or a child who died. One who, if they had lived, would have been about the same age as you. Then you requested a copy of their birth certificate. Applied for a S.I.N. number. Built up the identity. The hardest part, the one that got people caught, was you had to let go of your old identity completely. That's pretty hard to do."

I stare at him. "Did you do that?"

"Not for myself. The time I spent in New Mexico, it was during the Vietnam war. There were people who needed new identities."

"Who stole them from dead babies. Dead children. Fuck."

"What?"

"Lost children. Stolen children."

"What's happening? Meg?"

Breathe. Come on. Heart's racing. Hold my breath. Okay. Okay. Fuck. Doug's looking at me, all crinkly eyed and worried.

"Sorry," I say. "I just. You'd better go."

"Are you all right?"

I look at him, about to say something sarcastic but words are gone and I'm just staring into the tunnels of his eyes. Two dark openings. I don't think anything. I'm just looking. Finally I pull my eyes away. "Sorry," I say. I want to say, 'Sorry I'm such a fucking weirdo.'

He shakes his head. "It's all right."

It's not but it helps, him sounding so ordinary.

At the door, when he's got his boots on, he says, "Thanks for coffee. Thanks for introducing me to Yvonne's." He hesitates for a moment then says, "Thanks for talking about real things."

I don't know what to say. I want him to be gone and I don't. "Thanks for listening, Doug."

He nods and turns to go.

"Wait."

I go into the kitchen, stuff the loaf of sunflower seed bread in a bag.

Chapter Forty Three

MEG NO SPIRIT

Meg No Name

A month ago I was all gung ho to find out where I came from. All that's happened is I know less and less.

I'm such a fucking basket case. How am I going to look Doug in the face? *You'd better go* after he listened to me witter on about my insane fucking life. I practically chased him out of the fucking door. Oh, except for the loaf of bread I have to all of a sudden stuff in his arms right when he thinks he's going to get away from crazy co-worker lady.

And he's on tonight.

Him and Jay and me.

Did you ask him? Doug's calm voice.

"Dad, I have a question for you."

There's a pause. I hear the chair creak, the one in the hallway by the phone. "Go ahead."

"Where did get your name? Coopworth, I mean."

"You've already asked me that."

"And you didn't answer."

There's another pause then he says, "There are things that aren't mine to tell."

"Keeping dead people's secrets is more important than what I need?"

I don't know where that came from but it hit the mark.

"I can't answer that question, Meg. I'm sorry."

"It's my name too. You gave me that name." I sound like a child.

"I know. I'm sorry."

"You stole it, didn't you? It wasn't yours to give. Did you steal me too?"

"I'm going to hang up now."

"Don't be such a fucking coward."

There's a silence but it isn't the dead phone sound.

"You were a gift we accepted with gratitude," he says at last. Then he hangs up.

I get out the flour, the bowl, but it's no good. My heart is thumping. I can't believe I spoke to Dad like that. Do I really believe they stole me? I keep thinking about the hair. I don't know why. But it's there in the willow brake, coiled up like an animal. It's alive, warm, golden-brown. I need to find it. It shouldn't be forgotten. I know this with the certainty of a dream but I'm not dreaming.

Winter is here, the river frozen. Beaver in their lodge. Silver bubbles. Silver fur. Moonlight under the water fur. The other. The other belongs to the sun. I thought his hair was like fur. Golden fur. The man on the tractor.

Did I really just show up at the edge of the field? Or did I make that up, that whole memory?

Or did they make it up? Mum and Dad. Telling me the same story over and over until I thought I remembered it.

Jesus. If they stole me ...

Stole me from where? Someone who didn't notice a child went missing. Or didn't care. Or couldn't afford to report it. Or ...

This is crazy. I have to be at work in two hours.

I pull open the drawer of the bedside table. They stare up at me from their black plastic frame. Mum dark, Dad blonde; Mum with shoulder length hair, Dad with his brush cut; Mum's heart-shaped face, Dad's oblong, furrowed. Behind them, wind-stunted spruce, spangle of flowers in the close turf. They gaze at the camera, the smallest hint of a smile at the corners of Dad's eyes, in the compression of Mum's lips. The wind had pushed Mum's hair back from her face. I must have taken this one July or another. The place where the waters divide. From one side the rivers flow north to the Arctic. From the other ... I can't remember. My eyes are locked on the photo.

What is there to trust if I can't trust you?
I want you to be what you seem to be.
I want it so fiercely my ribs ache.
A straight forward, hardworking couple.
What you tried to be.
What you wanted to be.
And weren't.

But what were you?
Two women hiding your love the way the brothers hid theirs. The not-brothers.
If that were all.
But it's not.
I don't know what it is but it's not just that.

I close them back into the drawer, step into the washroom.
And you?
I put my face close to the image. It returns my gaze.
And you?
You were a gift we accepted with gratitude.
Who gave me?
Gave me up?
Gave me away?
Gave up?
Gave way?
I ran away. Didn't I?
Whoever bore me didn't want me enough to come looking, did they?
No amber alerts for little No-Name.

Chapter Forty Four

A FANTASTIC WASP in wrap-around mirror shades, James swivels his head from side to side. "Step up, Dreamcatchers ..." He's almost kissing the mike.

Doug's standing over by the windows, listening to Mona. He hasn't noticed me, or he's pretending not to. You could hardly blame him.

The air is greasy with melted cheese, pizza boxes everywhere.

"Go Ashlei," someone calls. Knock-kneed on scuffed five inch high platform shoes, she makes her way to the front. The younger clients bang their palms on the tables.

Coal black ringlets frame a moon pale face. Emerald eye shadow spreads like butterfly wings, reaching to the edges of her cheeks. She takes the mike, licks her lips, then she's singing the lyrics *beneath this snowy mantle cold and clean, The unborn grass lies waiting*, her voice pure and tense. She doesn't make all the notes Anne Murray hits but my throat tightens when she gets to *Spread your tiny wings and fly away*. At the end there's a moment of silence then the clapping begins. She wobbles back to her seat, not meeting anyone's eyes.

In spite of James's urging nobody else comes forward so he cues up a hip-hop number and struts and curses his moments on the stage.

Danielle's sitting between slab-faced Janice and Warren with the scorpion tattoo. Her new best all-homophobes-together friends? But her face still reminds me of the pansies Mum used to grow, broad velvety petals, bright yellow centres.

What if they did make it up? The whole story about me showing up at the edge of the field. I close my eyes for a moment but it's better if I keep them open.

Sitting behind Danielle, Geoffrey's got his chair tipped back, legs stretched out, trying to look relaxed. He's about as relaxed as I am. Tomorrow Danielle goes out on pass. Meets up with Judy. When Judy finds out Danielle didn't give me the number, she'll be on the phone. To me? To Brenda, more like. Or Danielle's counsellor. The lovely Angela, she of the yellow-eyed coyote gaze.

Shit.

Everyone is clapping again. James raises the mike high in the air, acknowledging his fans. Geoffrey's chair thumps forward. He stalks up to the front, holding out a CD. There's a low buzz of voices. The two consult, backs to the room. James goes to the machine. Geoffrey turns slowly. Facing us, he stands completely still, chin up, eyes on the far wall. Everyone falls silent. Almost everyone.

Geoffrey opens his mouth and belts out *At first I was afraid I was petrified* in a strong, clear tenor as the opening bars of Gloria Gaynor's *I Will Survive* sound out. When he hits the chorus a few people sing along. It was the anthem in the gay bars, the years AIDS was cutting the men down in swathes. The second time we hit the chorus, Geoffrey lifts his arms, fingers summoning, and, the whole room joins in. Even Janice. Even Warren.

> *Long as I know how to love*
> *I know I'll stay alive*
> *I've got all my life to live*
> *And all my love to give and I'll survive*
> *I, I, I will survive*

It rises up in me the way it used to, that longing: *Let it be true. Let it be true for them all. Let them survive. Let us survive. Let us go on. Let us heal.* The only place I could pray back then, dancing sober in the bars.

When the music ends the room erupts. Geoffrey stands, tall and still, looking around. They keep cheering. Doug's watching Geoffrey, a little smile on his lips. Then he looks across at me and the smile widens.

"Shall we start on the overview?" Jay announces names as she types them in.

We have something to say for the performers. Don too. He collected money from some clients but he covered most of the pizza order himself. For the rest we're scratching our heads as usual.

"We should make a crib sheet," I say. "*Doing well. Progressing nicely. Engaged. Friendly. Participates ... *"

"Yeah," Jay says. "It's been going so smoothly I hardly know what to do with myself. I count on this place for my drama, my chaos."

"Won't last," Doug says. "Don't worry."

I suppose his home life's sane and serene too.

"Mona," Jay says.

"She's all excited about the karaoke. Thinks Ashlei should have an agent. Maybe she'll do the job herself."

"Mona? We're talking red-haired, hard as nails, in and out of jail Mona?"

"The one and only."

Jay's eyebrows go up.

"Why not? People change. We did."

"So what shall I say?"

"*Turned a corner? Committed to recovery?*"

"Good enough. Warren?"

"Spending quite a bit of time with Shannon."

"Now he scares me," Jay says. "That anger and no impulse control. Another one with FAS. So what'll it be?" Her fingers are poised above the keyboard.

"*Tense.*"

"And Miss Danielle?" Jay turns to look at me.

"Other than homophobic?" I return her gaze.

"*Progressing,*" she says at last, typing it in.

Chapter Forty Five

THE CLIENTS TRICKLE back in chattering groups. Danielle finally shows up, alone, just before supper.

"I'll check her bags," I say. "Come on, let's go to your room."

Sure enough, Julie isn't there.

Danielle puts the carrier bags on the bed.

"How was your Sunday?" I'm peering down into the first bag.

"Real good." I look up. "It was real good to see my aunt." Nothing but sweet in the drawl.

"Ah. Well, that's great." I lift two sweaters out of the first bag.

"She couldn't stay that long so I did a little shopping."

Not at Value Village either, I see, checking the other bag.

"I'm real fortunate to have an aunt like Judy."

"Uh huh."

"You like my new shirt?"

The loudspeaker in the hallway crackles. Tanya's voice booms out: "Suppertime. It's suppertime."

Danielle's off the bed and headed for the door in a blink.

I follow slowly behind, the corridor filling with jostling bodies.

"The karaoke last night," Heather says, "I heard it was quite something. Wish I'd heard Ash. They can always surprise you, eh?"

Tanya's in ceremony. Shannon and Julie are on the bench.

It's just the two of us in the office.

"How's your father?"

Why has everyone taken to asking about my father?

"*Who's yer father?*" I say in a lame imitation of her accent. "What was his name, that client who worked on the rigs?"

"From New Brunswick? Dale. No, Darrell. It's true. It is the first thing anyone there asks you."

"He was so happy when you opened your mouth."

"Homesick," Heather says. She shakes her head. "You couldn't pay me enough. Go back, live in a small town where everybody knows your business. Christ, knows your family's business five, six generations back. 'Fill yer boots,' I said to Darrell. 'Take my share too.' But it was all he wanted, to get back home. Your mother was from Nova Scotia, wasn't she?"

"From some little port on the Bay of Fundy. Over the North Mountain from the Valley. That's all I know about the place really. Geography. The Mountain, the Valley, the Bay. A few stories. Mostly about hard times."

"You never went to visit?"

"They weren't blood family. Anyway, Mum was all about Alberta. I don't think she ever went back.

"Amen. Hai hai."

The blanket is pulled back and everyone is filing out, hugging the girls on the bench.

"Good sleep."

"Good sleep."

When the rush of phone and meds is over I ask Tanya, "How's your mother?"

"Doctor says she has lung cancer. She says it's her time. When she decides something, ooh she's stubborn. We used to fight." She shakes her head. "Too much alike, eh?"

"She's at home?" Heather asks.

Tanya nods. "My sisters and me, we've been taking turns. Brother too, when he can get time off. I just sit with her. Sing to her. Traditional songs. The others, they want her to go to the hospital. She won't." Tanya looks at me. "You lost your mother not too long ago?"

"It'll be a year ago in January. She ... It was sudden. An aneurism."

Tanya nods. "That's hard."

"It was. It is."

"Quick or slow it's hard," Heather says.

"She's getting lighter." Tanya holds out her hand, palm up. "Like a leaf drying out." She spreads her fingers. "She'll blow away one day soon. We're both fighters, eh? But now we're the ones accepting. I can let her go. She knows that."

I nod. I'm nowhere near ready but I've glimpsed it too, moments he seems so papery, translucent.

"We never have as much time as we think," Heather says softly. "My father, he worked building railway cars his whole adult life except when he went to the war. He wasn't retired a month when he dropped dead. Of a heart attack. That's why I took early retirement. So I could do something that matters, not just type frigging memos. But speaking of typing ..." She glances at the clock.

When she's on, Heather does the overview, fingers flitting over the keys.

"Danielle?"

"*Enjoyed her pass,*" I say.

"Her aunt was coming into town to see her," Tanya says. "Judy. My *kokum* knew Judy's mother. A good woman. Do anything for you. Judy sounds the same way."

"I'd say so," Heather says, "sending a complete stranger bus fare half way across the country."

"She's got money to burn now, Danielle does." Tanya shakes her head. Glossy black hair swings from side to side. The blue streak's growing out. "She's always at the vending machines, that one."

Heather clicks 'Send' and shuts down the computer. "When are you on again?"

She's talking to me. "Tuesday."

"And you?"

Tanya says, "Depends on Mum. Cathy told me not to worry. Laura's finished with training. She's eager for shifts."

Heather looks at me. "Have you met her, the new hire?"

"I didn't even know there was one. What's she like?"

"Ambitious."

"As evening staff?"

"Foot in the door," Tanya says, arching her eyebrows.

Heather nods. "Be careful what you say around her. She's well connected. Know what I mean?"

"Another veteran?"

"No, but good friends."

Chapter Forty Six

THE LIGHT'S FLASHING on the phone when I get home.

"Meg, this is Judy. Give me a call, please. I have a question for you."

For example, where did you get my number? Why did you lie to me? Too late to call now.

"Judy? This is Meg."

A volley of coughing is followed by a couple of gasps. "Meg? Give me a minute."

I was sitting but somehow I'm on my feet, pacing in front of the picture window. My neighbours are getting into their cars, going to work. A few are walking small children to the school around the corner. Children the colours of jelly beans, padded and mittened.

"Okay." Judy still sounds as if she's barely got enough air to speak. "Been sick. Why I couldn't get into town at the weekend. I hope Danielle wasn't too disappointed."

"She didn't mention it." No shit she didn't. I sit down again.

After another bout of coughing Judy asks, "How old you were when you showed up at that ranch?"

"Ten. Or so."

"Ah."

"Could have been nine. Might have been eleven."

"Not six?"

"No. Definitely not six." I know I told her how old I was.

"In 1968?"

"September 1968." Breathe. "There was a six-year-old child who went missing?"

"Terri Bailey went off with her daughter. Everyone thought she must have gone to Vancouver. Get away from her boyfriend. But nobody saw her there. Not like she had money to rent an apartment."

"But her daughter was six?"

"Yes."

"So. So that's it?"

"Well, I can't say that." Judy's breath is short again. "She's not the only woman disappeared. No, she's not. But it's her name comes up when I ask about a child. I've got a few more to talk to. It's hard to get around, you know. This time of year."

"Can I give you some money for gas?"

"No need of that. Not yet."

"Should I, should I send you a photo of me? When I was a child, I mean?"

"Well. That might come in handy. I suppose." She sounds doubtful. I wait. "So many children taken. It hurts, you know? Showing someone a photograph from thirty years ago. 'This your baby?' People want ... if it was more sure you came from here."

I don't know what to say.

After a moment she asks, "Do you have any—what do they call them—distinguishing marks?"

"The scars on the backs of my legs from where I was beaten." It comes out exactly the way I'm feeling which is that I wasn't worth protecting.

Judy sighs and the sigh turns into a cough. "Gotta go," she says when she can talk again. "I'll call if I ..."

The phone goes dead. I didn't get her address. But maybe I'd just as soon nobody was peddling around the picture of me when I was a kid. 'You know her? You want her? Anyone going to claim her? No? Too bad, eh?'

Chapter Forty Seven

FLAT, GREY LIGHT, an icy wind, but people are still out and about. Snow's trampled and dirty. We didn't get as much as out at the ranch anyway. I'm going to have to apologize to Dad for that phone call. In person. We don't do well on the phone at the best of times. Calling him a fucking coward. But what if they did ...? Okay. I'm not ready. Breathe. Traffic rumbles over the Capillano. Pigeon shit streaks the girders. In the summer electric golf carts whirr under the highway here, past the stands of willow. Is this it, the place Charlotte turned into Ben?

Or was it the 53rd Street bridge which was a streetcar bridge for as long as they had streetcars? I hurry back down the trail as if what? Somebody's going to get to that coil of golden hair before me. Take it home. My stomach twists. I stop so suddenly someone coming up behind me almost runs into me. Woman with a Rottweiler on a leash casts me a not very friendly look. Dog too. I'm freezing my ass off looking for the place where Charlotte became Ben.

Seventy years ago.

I walk out onto the footbridge, out to the middle of the river. To the east smoke stacks poke at the sky. To the west, the city glitters. I look down. Through the gaps between the planks the ice-covered river is far below. It's not really that high, this bridge, but I'm dizzy. Scared. Breathe. Don't look down until my feet are on solid ground.

Except there isn't any. That's the whole fucking deal. What do I really know?

'What's your name?' He pointed at himself. 'Ben.' He pointed at me and waited.

'The child is cold and hungry and filthy, Ben. What does it matter what her name is?' I can hear Mum's voice.

The hair on his head was thick gold fur. He looked at me for longer, river in springtime eyes. Suddenly he was standing over me. I flinched. He stepped back. The woman was at the stove. She lifted the lid on a black pot, stirred with a long wooden spoon. A warm brown smell reached my nose and my mouth filled with spit but I was watching him. He kept his hands down, moved slowly away from me.

It wasn't in the story Mum told, that flinch. I've been over it a hundred times in therapy. My body was expecting something my mind doesn't remember. Won't remember.

After I ate the man went out. The woman took me to the washroom. She ran water in the enamel tub, pointed to my clothes. Her eyes were dark brown but sparkly, like a day so cold and sunny the air flashes with tiny rainbows of light.

Before the man went out, she said to him, 'God always answers.'

He said, 'Polly, Polly. She's probably lost. Someone is probably worried sick right now.'

I kept my eyes down when he talked.

In the washroom I do what she wants. I pull off the tattered sweater, slip off my shoes. She's waiting. Watching her I step out of the brown pants I'm wearing and my underpants, pull off my T-shirt. She nods toward the water. I turn to get into the tub, hear her suck in her breath. The water is hot. It stings the back of my legs. I sit stiffly in the water. She kneels beside the tub, dips a cloth in the water, rubs it on a bar of soap and holds the steaming cloth out to me. I take it, rub it over my cheeks, my forehead. She nods, her sparky eyes never leaving my face. She reaches out, touches my hair at my forehead. I lean back slowly and the water laps over my shoulders. It reaches my hair. I want to close my eyes, slide down until the water is warm all around me but I can't. I can't close my eyes.

Very slowly she stands up. 'I'll be back,' she says, 'with some clean clothes.' She starts to gather up my clothes from the floor. Something must have showed in my face because she stops, puts them down again. When the door clicks shut and her feet walk away I close my eyes, slide down the back of the tub until the water covers me.

I jerk back up. A door opened. Footsteps. Two people. Not hers. The man and someone else. Then I hear her feet hurrying back to this door. The handle turns and she slips in with something red and white in her arms. I see her looking down at the water. It's brown and scummy. There's a twig floating in it.

She hangs the dress on a hook and opens out the towel she's carrying. She holds it out like frayed white wings. I step out of the tub and she steps forward, wraps the towel around me. When she sees I have a hold of it she steps back. I dry myself carefully, including my hair, then I put on the dress. The sleeves hang down over my hands but she's brought safety pins. She fastens the cuffs around my wrists so all the material balloons out around my arms. The dress hangs down to my ankles. It has a shiny red belt which she fastens around my waist. Even on the last hole it is loose.

She holds out her hand to me and I put my hand into it, which is another moment I've dealt with in therapy, that I knew to do that, that somehow once there must have been someone I trusted because I did it simply, without thought.

Together we stepped out into the living room. The sound of voices came from somewhere out of sight. The woman held my hand tighter and we walked into the kitchen. The man with gold hair was standing by the door with another man, a man with wrinkled copper skin and black hair pulled back smooth over his skull. From under a jutting forehead dark brown eyes studied me. There was a scar like a W under one eyebrow. He said something I didn't understand. He waited. I watched him. His eyes were puzzled. In English he said to the first man, 'I don't know her. I'll ask around.'

'Thank you, John,' the first man said.

The second turned to leave. A black braid hung down the back of his denim shirt.

The woman's hand relaxed. I slipped my hand out of hers.

'Better?' the man asked me. After a moment he pointed to a bench by the woodstove. 'Have a seat,' he said. I sat in the corner made by the bench and the wall. The woman took a knitted shawl from the back of a chair on the other side of the stove. She offered it to me but I was warm now. I shook my head.

She and the man looked at each other. The man nodded at the door into the living room. I watched them walk across that room to another door. When he opened it I saw the corner of a bed with a blue and white and yellow quilt. They went inside and the door closed. Their voices were like wind in a spruce tree.

Back home I unlock the door, pull off my boots, walk straight through to the bedroom. I take off my jeans, stand with my back to the mirror, head twisted round. Like pale branches against a darker sky, the twig thin scars reach across my calves and the backs of my thighs. How many thousand times have I done this? As if, in the exact right light, at the perfect angle, I would be able to read them.

WEEK FIVE

Chapter Forty Eight

"LAURA, THIS IS Meg. You've met Jay."

Laura's honey blonde, possibly with help from the bottle. Shining, healthy hair, clear skin, deep brown eyes. "How are you doing?" Cree lilt. Five foot six, trim body of a runner. Maybe ten years younger than me.

"Good. You?"

She nods, a little smile on her sculpted lips. They're not quite so perfect as Tanya's or Eleanor's, the lips, but she's a beautiful woman. A beautiful Native woman.

"Have a good shift guys," Cathy says. "I'll be in my office if you need me."

"The safe doesn't lock?"

"Not in living memory."

Laura puffs out her cheeks then expels the air. "And they haven't fixed it because ..."

"Your guess is as good as mine. Want some coffee?"

"Where's Jay?"

"Supervising the clients while they set up for the AA meeting. There's an open meeting here once a week."

"Down in the gym?"

The tide of visitors retreats, leaving a scum of Timmie's cups. Some who signed in haven't signed back out. Which doesn't mean much. "I'm going to take a perimeter walk," I say. Jay nods. Laura doesn't offer to come with me.

I push open the back door, nod to the smokers and set off around the corner. The wind buffets me. I breathe deeply for the first time all evening then smell something familiar. Rounding the next corner I see two slight figures and a glowing tip.

A head turns my way. "Shit." A guy in a black hoodie races off around the building. The one holding the joint turns away. Perfect black ringlets.

"Ash."

She turns to face me, nothing in her hand now. "Oh, is it time for ceremony?"

I just look at her.

"Shit."

"Yeah. Who was that with you?"

"I don't know." She wraps her arms around her skinny body.

"Let's go to the office."

She doesn't move.

"Come on, Ash. I know you're standing on the joint. Let's just get this over with."

She starts crying, tears dribbling down her cheeks, mascara running.

Visitors and clients linger around the desk, chatting and laughing.

Jay watches Ash and me.

I nod once then point my lips at the corridor to the bedrooms. Jay glances around, sees Ash's room-mate in one of the clusters and, looking back at me, nods.

"Let's go to your room first," I say to Ash.

"What happened?"

"I caught her smoking weed with some boy. He took off."

"Visitor?"

"I think so."

"She denying it?"

"No. I'll fill you in later. I told her we'd come and get her when we were ready to do the paperwork but she shouldn't be in her room alone, should she?"

"No." Jay picks up the phone, hits the intercom button. "Chief and smudge person to the front please. Visitors, it's time to go. Thank you for coming. Don't forget to sign out." She hangs up the phone, looks at me. "Word'll be out any minute. We need to get them into ceremony as fast as possible. Three of us on meeting night." She shakes her head. "You, me and someone with all the finesse of a bulldozer. She's down for ceremony, right?"

I nod. "Where is she now?"

"Supervising clean-up in the gym. You good on the desk?" Before I have a chance to reply Jay's heading off down the corridor toward the bedrooms. And Mona's steaming toward her. She walks right up to Jay, blocking her. "What the fuck?" she says, face crunched up and flushed.

Jay doesn't give ground. She's a couple of inches taller and twenty pounds heavier but Mona's got that stringy redhead ferocity.

I can't hear what Jay says but Mona says, "I don't believe you."

Jay says something and Mona's face sags. "Silly bitch," she says and turns away.

A couple of guys turn to look at her then at Jay. "She talking to you?" one of them asks.

"Nope." Jay turns, catches my eye but I don't know what she's trying to tell me. She heads on down the corridor.

You can feel it like a swell, the disturbance. The clients are murmuring among themselves as they line up, glancing my way but nobody asks me outright.

Laura comes around the dome, herding a couple of sullen young men in front of her. She takes off her necklace, wraps a lime green and navy sarong around her jeans and steps into the line between the last woman and the first man.

Jay doesn't appear in the corridor with Ash until the blanket has closed. Shannon's on the bench with a couple of other women. They watch Ash and Jay approaching. When Shannon opens her mouth Jay puts a finger to her lips, tipping her head toward the dome.

I open the gate and Jay ushers Ash into the office. She's repaired her mascara. Her face is impassive under the mask of foundation but she's shaking.

"Hello?" Someone at the front desk.

Shannon. "Is Ash okay?" she whispers.

"Later," I say, nodding at the dome. Shannon hesitates then goes back to the bench. I stay out front, doing the paperwork to release Ash's meds. After a while the office door opens. Jay sticks her head out and nods to me. Ash is inside, standing, holding the phone, listening.

After a couple of minutes she slams the receiver down. "She can't come and get me. No gas in the car. No money. Just excuses."

"Call Harry, eh?"

Suddenly she's crying. Not just crying, sobbing. Jay closes the office door but I can hear anyway. "Fuck, oh fuck. I always fuck it up. Anything good ever happens I fuck it up. I'm so fucked up."

Jay says, "You can reapply in thirty days. Come back. If you're ready, come back. You don't have to go all the way down this road. You've got a real talent there."

The weeping subsides. "Here you go, hon." That'll be Jay handing her the box of tissues that lives on the desk. I can hear the cadence of the Lord's prayer inside the dome. Eventually Ash blows her nose.

An hour later she's still sitting up front, scant belongings in a nylon duffel bag next to her, other clients milling around, looking sombre. Meagan is crying.

Harry comes in at last. A slight silver-haired man, he greets Ash and Meagan, Shannon, James, a couple of others by name. "Ready then?" he asks Ash. There's no harshness in his voice.

As they're walking toward the door Jay opens the gate and steps out. "Hey, Ash." Jay holds out her hand. Ash takes it. "Take good care, okay? And come back when you're ready. Thirty days, all right?"

Ash nods but doesn't look at Jay.

"Take care," I say.

We watch them go. "I don't know how Harry does it," Jay says. "Heartbreak a minute."

"He seems okay," I say. "Not weird."

"Haven't heard anything. Probably would have. We get a lot of *Off the Street* kids."

"I hate terminating people."

"It doesn't get any easier, eh? Such a friggin' waste. Turns out Mona really does have contacts. She was lining up an audition. Fuck. Poor kid. Calling her Mum. Mum's trashed by nine in the morning. Ash left when she was fourteen. She was going to see her next weekend. First time in five years."

"Hope dies hard, doesn't it?"

"Kids quit hoping. Think they did, anyway. They come in here, start opening up." Jay shakes her head.

"Sometimes it's good."

"Sometimes. Meagan and her Dad."

"He got sober when she was little, right?"

"She still had to go out, give the old alkie genes a test drive. But at least she had something. Some love. Some order, you know?"

I nod.

"Me too. Mum liked to party but she couldn't afford it, waitress wage, kid to raise. On her own. I always knew she loved me. She had her men friends, back before religion got her, but I knew I came first. And Christ, if one of them had ever laid a finger on me, she'd have ripped his face off. Ash, her mother, useless slag. Too drunk to notice what the fucking boyfriend's doing. When she found out, who do you think got kicked out of the house?"

It floods through me, a giant wave carrying us all, the lost, the stolen, the unwanted, little match figures bobbing about, the whole sorry mess swept ...

"We all have choices," says a voice from the doorway.

"She's got a lot stacked up against her, don't you think?" Jay asks, standing up.

I turn my chair so I'm facing Laura.

"Excuses. I heard them all. Racism this, racism that. Big excuse to stay home and get drunk. White man lied so I get high, beat my kids. If it wasn't for everything holding them back, the things they'd do. Well, I never experienced any racism."

"Time for a room check," Jay says. "I'll do it."

"And what makes them weak? They're waiting for someone to save them. The government. Somebody."

A couple of women at my old job used to go on like this. It's weird hearing it from Laura.

"If I spent my time feeling sorry for myself, I'd still be there."

"Where?"

"The reserve I grew up on. You've got to take responsibility for yourself. That one tonight."

"Ash?"

"She chose to pick up. She knew the consequences. Nobody forced that joint between her lips."

"So what do you think keeps someone sober? Willpower?"

"What else?"

I shake my head but there's no point in arguing. "Where was the reserve?"

"In Saskatchewan, way up north."

"What was it like?"

"Useless. Anytime anybody got any money, whole reserve would get drunk. Grandparents, parents, little kids. Everybody. Party until it was gone. My own father molested me. I told my aunties. You know what they did? Slapped my face, told me not to talk dirty."

"That's horrible."

She shrugs. "I got out of there. No high school on the reserve. Had to go south. First day at the new school I walked into the counsellor's office, told her what happened. She was sympathetic." Laura snorts. "She didn't slap me, anyway. I worked hard, graduated from high school. All the girls I grew up with, they were having babies. I knew I wasn't ready. I wasn't healthy enough to have children of my own. Not yet. I went to college."

"What did you study?"

"Social work. Focus on Aboriginal child and family welfare. Thing was, I kept thinking, how would I counsel clients when I knew I let my own father get away with molesting me? So I called up my parents and my aunties, told them what I was going to do, then I walked into the local RCMP detachment, laid a complaint against my father. Asked them to arrest him."

"Wow. What happened?"

Laura does the filling her cheeks with air thing.

"Nothing. They couldn't get anyone to testify. One aunt, she'd walked in when he was doing it, eh, but she wouldn't say a word to the police."

"Jesus."

Laura shrugs. "I did my part, eh? I'd be able to look my clients in the eye."

"That's a pretty amazing story."

"I did what I had to do. I have a good life."

Her brown eyes look straight into mine.

"You're not ashamed." The words pop out as the thought hits me.

"What do I have to be ashamed about?"

"Nothing," I say. I want to say it's not as easy as that but, looking at Laura, I think perhaps it is. Perhaps the rest of us are just making excuses.

"Hello?" Querulous, older woman's voice. "Can I get my meds?"

Dishing out Deborah's pills I realize nobody interrupted us the whole time it took Laura to tell me her story, which has to be a record. Jay's still out on the floor somewhere. Was that my job, to keep Laura from stirring up the clients?

Chapter Forty Nine

THERE BUT FOR *the grace of God, there but for the grace of God, there but for the grace ...* The words click through, relentless as the boxcars passing in front of me, and there she is on East Hastings in the rain, drunk me, strung-out, liver-quitting yellow, skinned bones and bloat blearing at some passer-by who's not meeting her eyes. Sound of feet on wet sidewalk. Because suddenly she's sitting, back to the building, legs splayed out. One minute standing, next she's down and laughing but the laugh twists to a cough that's like a dog shaking a rag. Moss with a stick. *The kill.* That's what Dad called it, that shake. I'm crying on the wet sidewalk, bawling for stern sweet Dad and a black and white dog, my life shit in my mouth. Shit. I'm spitting, spitting it up. Feet making a big circle around me now. Clack clack clack. Gotta get the shit out, retching, yellow, bitter, nothing left, still retching.

'Hey Meggie, you okay?' Longest legs you ever saw, tight black miniskirt, plastic for the rain. Pink shaggy sweater. 'Meggie, you okay?' Six foot two Dora. Big hand reaching down. Carmine nails. 'You want up?'

'I'm done, Dora. I'm done.'

'C'mon then, hon.'

Crying. 'I'm done.'

Dora looking in my face, eyelashes curling like a giraffe's. Big brown eyes. 'What do you want to do?'

'I'm done.'

'Detox?'

I nod.

Honk behind me. Red lights on the caboose disappearing round the bend. I ease across the tracks, heading home. The car passes on the first straight stretch of road. 'The day you decided to change your life,' some counsellor said. I was supposed to be taking ownership of my power. To make Positive Choices. Only it wasn't like that. I tried to describe it to her. She got the patient look so I quit. In all my life it's the one thing I know for absolute sure is true. It was like an island rose up out of the ocean in front of me. I crawled up on the beach, sat and let the sun dry me out. One day I was a hopeless alcoholic druggie hell-bent on destroying myself. Next I was sober. Never had to pick up again. Which many would call the grace of God. Creator. Whatever. I don't trust the words. Fuck up a good thing, words.

Mum looking at Dad and me across the turquoise Formica table. 'Come on then, say something.'

Dad and I looked at each other, opened our mouths, 'What?' Same question, exact same tone. We started laughing, Mum too.

'What'll I do with you? As much talk in you as a couple of potatoes.' Dad winked at me.

Looks like a happy memory to me. Jay's voice in my head. Three of us around the table, square little house, wind ripping into the aspens. Mum and Dad and me, playing happy family. No. Yes. Fuck. The dark rangeland slips past me.

Drunk, I'd creep up to lighted windows, press my face to the glass. Let me in, let me in. But there I was, sitting around the table, laughing. That was me.

Except it wasn't my real family. My real family were probably drunk fucking assholes and I had the scars to prove there wasn't any happy family only maybe that was my foster family I was running away from and before them was my real mother who had to give me up for adoption because the dumb ass Catholic church made her. Maybe she really wanted me.

Or maybe she was another crack whore who popped me out and got on with her habit, whatever it was back then before crack.

So there were these two perfectly decent human beings who took me in when I showed up out of nowhere with nothing to say for myself. They welcomed me as if I was a gift from God and I ate their food and took what I could and six years later I spat in their faces and went dancing down my own little path to destruction.

That's the story, anyway. But, even if I did show up at the edge of the field, even if that's all true, none of it was the way it looked. Did I know? Did I know somewhere inside I was being lied to? Cold tendrils wrap around me.

Something catches my eye off to my left. An odd cloud. Lights. Wrong direction for Upgrader Alley. Wrong colour. Greenish. It pulses brighter. A curtain of colour sways across the sky. Pale yellow green, gold edge. For a moment the whole northern sky shimmers green then the light shrinks back to a little cloud pulsing just above the horizon.

A *sign*, Mum would have said. Everything was a sign to her. God managing her life. Every detail. Nothing happened by accident.

Fingers of light stretch out, pull back. How would it be to have God talking to you all the time? Like being a bean in a pod, soft pod-ness wrapped around you? No rattling about in empty space. No circumstance banging you around. Safe. Airless.

I've pulled over. Turn off the engine. Sit by the side of the gravel road, dark fields around me. I could make it a sign. The day my life changed. Again. I see Ash's pretty blank face. Feel the naked hopelessness. There's what you want with all your heart and there's you in the way, fucking it up. It's like a great claw rakes through your life, dragging you back, but it's you.

'Sinful you,' Mum would say. 'Satan. Don't let Satan in.'

Sasquatch Satan, big old feet, long hard claws.

Weird, sitting here, watching the lights, thinking about Satan. Everything balanced on this moment. All I can do is watch.

What am I talking about? What everything?

It won't go away, the odd hush, the extra stillness. I reach for the key, drop my hand. Guess I want to sit here in the cold.

Chapter Fifty

"WHERE ARE HEATHER and Doug?"

"Showing new clients to their rooms. Going through their stuff."

"I'd like to learn that."

"I'm sure you'll find them in the bedroom wing."

She's off with a swing of shining hair. I try the cheek-filling, air-blowing thing.

"Hello?" The tentative voice belongs to a reedy young man with sallow skin, large dark eyes, a cap of thick black hair. "I'm Roy Whitemud." He reaches over to point to his name on the new client list. *S. Status.* As he draws his hand back I see a series of pale scars across his wrist, like the rungs on a ladder.

"If you could sign in ..."—which he does with the same hand. They're not new, the scars.

"Do you have any valuables or medications to check in? Cell phones, cash, car keys?" He shakes his head. He reminds me of a new-born faun, wide-eyed, stiff-legged. "How about aftershave?" He shakes his head. His eyes go down to the plastic grocery bag at his feet. "Um. Do you need toiletries? Toothpaste, toothbrush, soap, shampoo."

He looks away, nods his head.

I rummage in the closet where we keep the bags of toiletries, a box for the men, one for the women, then pull out the tub of clothes.

"Will these do?" He looks down at the ziplock bag, then at the two pairs of socks and the white t-shirt. He opens his mouth. I say, "We've got too many. If you can use them ..."

Over his shoulder I see Doug strolling and Laura marching up the corridor.

"Hey Roy," Doug says.

Roy turns. Relief spreads across his face. "Doug, right?"

"You got it. And this is Laura."

The three of them head back down the corridor.

"Did you see the scars?" Heather asks, forking meatloaf into her mouth.

"Right handed. Right wrist," Doug says. "Just letting out the pain." He dips his fork in the mashed potato then sets it down again. "He bangs his head too."

"They say it helps them feel in control," Heather says. "Self-mutilation. I don't understand it myself. I'd rather thump the arsehole that did it." Her accent slants the word. *Arse*.

"Sexual abuse?" I ask.

"Nine times out of ten," Doug says.

Laura rolls her eyes. She's eaten the meat off her plate and the cauliflower. "Doug," she says, "you've worked here a long time?"

He shakes his head. "For three years a while ago. I've only been back"—he looks at me—"three weeks?"

"About that," I say. A smile tugs at his lips. Heather's sitting back in her chair, watching. Amethyst earrings under silver hair, the dove grey sweater. Her lipstick red but not hard red. Laura's wearing lipstick too. Just a shade pinker than natural. I haven't done the make-up thing since I quit my *job* job.

Doug's standing up. "Done?" he asks, reaching for my plate.

"Thanks."

Laura hops up too. "Show me where they go."

When the gate has clicked shut behind them Heather looks at me, eyebrows raised a couple of millimetres.

"Mm," I say. "'Good luck with that,' as Jay would say."

"Jay would say a whole lot more but not in a certain person's hearing. There's something going down. I've worked in offices my whole life. I know when management's up to something."

Out in the parking lot, two minutes after midnight, the sky is so thick with stars the Milky Way looks like a sash trailing across the sky. A burnt orange subcompact peels out of the parking lot. Laura's, followed by Heather's Honda Civic. I wait for Doug's jeep but instead hear a car door open and close then soft footsteps across the blacktop.

"Do you know the constellations?"

"A few. My father taught me."

"I know the Pueblo Indian names and some of the Cree."

"Does everybody pick out the same constellations or do different cultures pick out different patterns?"

"I don't know. Good question."

"I suppose it's the stories that count."

"It's what we do, eh? Us humans." He says it softly, the silent dome of the sky above us. "We need our stories. To help us with the unknowable. And the unbearable."

"Our myths?"

"Mm. The big collective ones but also our personal ones."

"I've been thinking about that moment of getting sober."

"You were on last night, weren't you?"

"When Ash picked up. Yes." We've wandered out to the edge of the parking lot, away from the lights. The stars are even brighter. "That moment when someone's really ready. No one can make it happen. Though rehabs try, I suppose."

"It's probably what keeps me going to meetings."

"The resurrections?"

"I suppose we are all born again."

"And again and again in some cases."

"I never went back out. Did you?"

"No. I knew in my gut I wouldn't get a second chance. Um. Doug, I'm sorry I got so weird the other night."

He's shaking his head. It's too dark to see his expression. "Don't apologize," he says, "I like real people."

Chapter Fifty One

A DINGHY SCUDDING across waves, I skim the surface of sleep. Used to watch the Sunfish in Burrard's Inlet. Looked like happiness, wind ballooning your sail, you leaning, counterweight to the wind. You, whoever you were, the sail, the board, the water, the invisible wind. Me, hung-over, shaking for the next. Drunk me. She's with me today, along for the ride. Maybe she's the one who needs to go to the farm right this instant. No bread to bring. I should bring something. Besides an apology.

Bring tobacco.

Right. Like Dad's some Native elder. I grab a couple of clean t-shirts, head on out. Take a different route out of town. At the lights on Jasper and 124th a trolley bus has come unhooked from the overhead wire. Driver's out, heaving the bar back up. I turn the radio on. Turn it back off. Look around. There's a cigar shop right across the road. Lights are on. Man opens up the door, flips the sign. Who in hell buys cigars at 7:30 in the morning?

The shop smells brown and rich, the owner a Turk perhaps, luxuriant walrus moustache, velvet black eyes.

"Good morning. What can I get for you?"

It smells of ships and harbours. Brine. Tar. The package on the seat next to me.

I drive with nothing in my mind but I'm full of feeling. When I crest the rise and the mountains spread out in front of me, tears spill down my cheeks.

When I pull into the yard, sun is glittering off a dusting of fresh snow. I sit looking out at the house, old machinery shed rusting away behind the shelter belt, t-shirts and boxers snapping on the line beside the trailer. Everything's got that extra edge. If I look the right way I'll see something I've never seen before. What I loved about acid. I climb out of the car. Overhead the sky is that limitless, inscrutable blue that makes you half want some old bearded God to point his finger, tell you what to do, because you could get lost, gazing into that blue. I drop my eyes to the line of mountains. They stroll across the sky, clouds bubbling up from behind them. Mountains are all here. There's nowhere but here. This. This. This. They insist, mountains.

"Are you coming in?"

He's in the doorway, head cocked to one side, squinting. The sun still low in the east.

"Dad. I'm sorry about the other night. On the phone. I should not have spoken to you like that."

He nods. "I was about to go for my walk. Want to come?"

His old brown boots are on but not laced. He's wearing the thick beige cardigan Mum knitted him.

"Yes."

I follow him inside. He lets himself down on the chair in the hallway and reaches for his laces. He's stiffer than I've ever seen him, his warped fingers fumbling the bows but I know he'd hate for me to offer.

"Ready?" he asks at last. He dons a jacket I haven't seen in years and an equally ancient sheepskin cap with earflaps that reappeared this fall. He picks up his cane.

He ought to have a dog. The thought is picked out in crisp lettering in my mind. "Would you like a dog again, Dad?"

His eyebrows lift. "I was just thinking, 'Where's Moss?' But I'm too old for a new dog. I'd worry, what would become of him?"

"I'd take him."

"City life's no life for a border collie."

"Or Victor and Manfred would."

It's his turn to look at me. "What'll you do, Meg, with this place? Do you know?"

I open my mouth to say 'no' which would be the truth only nothing comes out and I close my mouth again.

Now he's really looking at me. "What brought you here today?"

"Let's walk," I say. "I did need to apologize but you're right, that's not all."

It's so strong now it's like a guitar thrumming in my gut, the feeling something is going to happen.

We walk. Slowly. Slow as walking with a donkey, back when we had a couple to guard the sheep. Viola and Malvolio. Nothing walks so slow as a donkey. Except two donkeys. Dad and Moss would be moving the flock. It was my job to follow, leading the donkeys. They never did like Moss. 'Donkeys will kill a dog,' Dad said. He rode across the land, getting further and further ahead. I'd see Moss loop out on an outrun, drop to a crouch. If the wind was blowing the right way I'd hear Dad's whistles, the occasional 'Lie down. Lie down, sir.'

At last we're on the little bluff above the river. Dad sits down on the bench, pats the seat. I leave the usual space between us. In the opposite bank I make out a seam of coal. Coal in the banks in Edmonton too. "There are old coal mines under the golf course near my house." Dad's head swivels to me and I realize I spoke the words out loud. "Tunnelled in from the river bank. One day the third hole putting green sank. All that perfect grass looking up at the sky from eight feet down."

I look at Dad. "I've spent the last month trying to make the ground under my feet solid, getting mad every time I have to face the fact that it isn't. I've been so focused on what I can't trust I forgot what I can trust."

He's gazing out across the gorge. "Go on."

"The day I got sober, it wasn't anything I planned. It wasn't a better day or a worse day. Somehow, I was ready. I was done. I didn't decide, I recognized. It was like a door opened up in front of me and I could walk through it and I did. You could say that was a decision but it felt like an acknowledgement. Of something that was somehow already true. Does that make sense?"

Slowly Dad nods. "Yes. Yes, it does."

"There's a new person working at Dreamcatcher. She's ... I think she's like the heroes you talked about. She decides and she acts. She bends the world to her will. Doesn't have much patience for the rest of us. I've been stamping my foot, wanting the world to do what I want, feeling like a failure because I can't seem to make it happen. Somehow, listening to her talk, I remembered there's a different version that's more like the experience I had getting sober. You know what to do when it's the right time but you're not making things happen."

"There's a lot you can't make happen," Dad says, "however much you want to."

Neither of us seems to have any more to say. So there we are, side by side on the bench, looking out at the mountains. After a bit Dad pats the pockets of his jacket, a red and black chequered wool Mackinaw. It smells of hay and lanolin, wet dog and something else. The yellow brown stains on the front. I can see him, scrawny lamb slick from birth gripped against his belly. He snips the umbilical cord, sets the scissors on the window ledge, picks up the open jar of dark liquid. Dangling the cut end over the jar he presses jar to belly, tips back lamb and jar together. Iodine coats the cord and, if the lamb squirms, quite a bit else. Mum retired this jacket years ago, judging that one particular lambing had stained it past redemption.

He pulls something out of the pocket. "Do you mind?" He opens his hand to reveal an old brier pipe.

I stare at it, at him, and start to laugh.

"What's so funny? The other day I thought how I missed my pipe. So I dug it out. I never did throw it away."

"Of course not."

"Even found an old tin of baccy." He slips off his glove, reaches for the inside pocket. "I'm too old for it to kill me now. Too late to set you a bad example." He grins.

"And how is it?"

"Stale but"—he's tamping dark tobacco into the bowl with his thumb—"delicious."

"Well then, stop what you're doing."

"What?" His thumb pauses.

I pull the packet out of my coat pocket and pass it to him.

He turns it over in his hands. The cellophane crinkles. He's non-plussed for once. "But how did you ..."

"I didn't. It was a ridiculous urge that came over me. The last two days I've been in an odd zone."

"Balkan Sobranie, no less." He fumbles for the tab, pulls and un-wraps the cellophane. Holds the package to his nose, eyes closed. When he opens them he says, "One of the bravest men I ever met smoked this. Officer in the war. Jimmy Bowdoin-Smith. I'd never met anyone who laughed with such delight at the beauty and the absurd-ity of the world. Even there. Mud and rats and mustard gas. You'd think he was on a picnic, horsing around on the grass in the sun-shine. He found a buttercup behind a shell-shattered old barn, held it under my chin."

I can't picture the scene then remember: "When you were a girl."

"When I was a girl." He taps out the pipe on the arm of the bench, fingers the old tobacco for embers before sweeping it to the ground. He packs the bowl with the new tobacco, holds a match to it, draws the flame down into the bowl.

I watch it dip and straighten, dip and straighten. All the while the flame crawls down the wooden stem of the match. At the last minute he shakes it out, crushes the tip between finger and thumb, then he puts the spent match in his pocket. The tobacco glows in the bowl. He exhales a blue, fragrant cloud, aiming it away from me but it curls back and I breathe it in too. It's rich and dark as forest duff. I look sideways at Dad. He's gazing at the mountains, face calm.

The sun's warm on my back. This bench is better placed than the old one, out of the wind in a slight hollow. To my left wild asparagus fronds whisper in the breeze. Bleached and desiccated, they're still recognizable. In June we'd munch the slender shoots, raw and sweet-ly crisp. Somehow, in the busyness of the ranch he always made time to show me things like that. I glance at him again. One gnarled hand is wrapped around the pipe, the other resting on the head of the cane. The skin, always leathery brown, is paler now with the silvery sheen of driftwood, so little between air and bone. Thin as garlic skin, purple veins showing through. His hand at rest on the smooth black handle which is so dense it doesn't looks like wood. Strangely heavy. It felt like rock not wood, the cane.

'*What's this?*'

Mum looked up from the kitchen counter, flour on her hands. Mum in a pale blue apron, glasses slipping down her nose, knuckling them back up to look.

'*Put that back please, Meg.*'

'*But ...*'

'*Put it back. Now.*'

Looking at the long, dark shaft I'm giddy, as if the river bank, Dad, bench, asparagus, all are turning around it. The mountains, the ground at my feet. All turning, slow then faster, round the ebony shaft. I grip the bench, sun-warmed wood under my fingers, try to pull my eyes from the cane but it's the middle. The middle is dark. The middle is dark. The words spread through my mind, a stain spreading across water. Everything now is glittering about the black and silver and I'm shivering. It's evil, something evil. Evil. Evil. I'm so cold and it's in me. Get it out. Get it out. My hands are clawing at the wood. I hear them scrabbling and a voice, *Meg, Meg*. Evil, evil. I'm gasping, pulling away from the hand on my arm. The cane. The cane is on the ground. I slip from the bench. I'm kneeling by the black wood. I bring my head down hard. Something grips my shoulder, hauls me back.

"Meg. Stop this. Now." Voice like a whip crack.

I stop. Everything stops. I can hear my own breathing, ragged. Dad's too, rasping. His hand that stopped me. Christ, I was about to slam my head on the ground.

"Dad, what just happened?" My voice is shaking.

"I was going to ask you the same thing."

I close my eyes, steady my breathing. When I open them the cane is there, lying on the dusty ground, a stick of dark wood with tarnished silver tips.

"I'm losing it, Dad. I don't ..." I gulp.

"Tell me what happened."

Breathe. "It was the cane. I was looking at it and suddenly everything began to revolve around it. The dark axle. The middle of everything is evil, that's what I was thinking. The evil was in me. I was frantic to get it out. I was about to bang my head on the ground. It was the only thing I could think to do. To make it stop. The feeling. Of being evil. I can feel its cold breath on my skin, just thinking the thought."

"What were you thinking about before that?"

"Finding the cane in the pantry, asking Mum about it. She wouldn't answer, just made me put it back."

He's silent, staring at the mountains. After a minute he picks up the stick, rests his hands on the crook again. "Have you ever done that before, banged your head?"

"No. Not that I remember. It was the weirdest feeling. I had to do it. It was, well, it was like being possessed." I try to sound casual, reasonable, like my feet are firmly back in the world where that's a delusion. "I have been feeling weird. Almost like being on acid. They say you can get flashbacks. Or maybe I just ... I don't know ... got the idea in my mind. A client came in yesterday who bangs his head."

I glance at Dad. He's squinting at the ground, a funny look on his face.

"What is it?"

He shakes his head, one quick back and forth.

"Dad, please. I don't know what's happening. Since Tuesday night I've had such a feeling that something was going to happen. Today, the tobacco, for God's sake. I had no idea you'd taken up the pipe again. Either I'm losing my mind or ..." I stop.

"Polly believed that cane was evil."

"Why?"

When I bring the tea in he's staring out of the window. His eyes swivel to me when I sit down.

"I don't know what's happening any more than you do, Meg. But there are things I know. You'd better know them too. Your mother. She went through a bad patch. The year before you came. One night something woke me. She was in the kitchen in her nightgown in the dark, banging her head against the doorjamb. She'd split her forehead. Blood on her face, on the paint. I tried to pull her away. She fought me. Finally I said, 'Polly, stop it,' loud and slow and she did. Came and sat next to me like a little child. She sat on the sofa. I wet a towel, cleaned her up. I was scared.

"'Tell me. Tell me what's wrong.'

"'There's something bad inside me. I have to make it go away.'"

He stops. I must have been staring at him.

"That's how it felt. Exactly how it felt. Go on."

"There's not much to tell. She'd been withdrawn for a couple of days. When I, when I touched her"—he glances at me. I nod—"she lay there like a stick of wood. I stopped. Asked her what was wrong? She shook her head. It was as if she wasn't there."

"Did she do it again?"

"Several times that year."

"And after I came?"

He shakes his head. "She decided she had been possessed. When she joined that church. The pastor liked the idea. They all did. It's a strenuous sect. They enjoyed the exorcism very much."

"She kept the cane."

"To remind herself."

"Of what?"

"That Satan is always nearby, biding his time."

"Why did she think the cane was evil?"

"I'm not sure."

"But you have an idea?"

Dad's eyes drift over to the front window. Victor is walking across the yard carrying a tray. The wind nips at his scarf, whisks away the steam from a covered bowl.

Chapter Fifty Two

"TELL ME ABOUT Mum."

Dad's in his Morris chair, hands resting on the oak arms. I sit in the other armchair. He studies me. I refuse to feel as if I'm twelve years old. "What do you want, Meg?"

"What do you mean?"

He waits.

"I want the truth, Dad. I have no idea what happened earlier. With the cane. If that was something that came from me or if, somehow, it was Mum's. I need to know."

He goes on looking at me. I stare back at him. At last he tips his head sideways. "All right. Your mother."

"Why don't you call her Polly?"

He looks surprised, then relieved. "Polly then. Polly wasn't always the way you knew her. She only got religion a couple of months before you arrived. If you hadn't come I don't know if she would have stuck with it. You were proof that she was on the right track. She'd become angry, you see, that she couldn't have children, being married to me."

I stare at him. "But Dad, that can't have been news to her." I blush.

"The change of life, it set something off in her. Sorrow I suppose but it came out as anger. She blamed me. If she hadn't married me she could have had a normal life. I understood that."

"But she chose you. She knew what she was doing."

"Did she? Do any of us?"

"I don't know," I say at last, "but Dad, to blame you. That's crazy."

He takes a deep breath. "She was crazy by then. In a way. She was drinking all the time."

"Mum never touched a drop."

"After she got religion."

"She was an alcoholic?" I stare at him.

"At the end. She drank a little, when we met. Stopped when we got married. After the war she started again. Just a glass now and then. It was fun. She was fun. But then it changed. She didn't drink every day but when she did ..."

He shrugs. "Toward the end there, seemed it packed a hell of a wallop, whatever she drank. It wasn't that much, or so I thought. One day I came into the kitchen, there was a little white ring on the counter. I stared at it a while then I opened the flour bin, reached my hand down into the flour. It was cool, soft. My fingers touched something hard and smooth. I found bottles in the woodpile, behind the laundry soap, in the basket of mending. That night I told her what I'd found. She pretended she didn't know what I was talking about. Then she told me it was my fault. If she had a normal life she wouldn't have to drink. Then she cried, promised she would stop.

"It got worse and worse. That's when she started banging her head. I'd wake up in the night. Find her by the back door."

He stops, looks at me.

I take a deep breath. "It's alright. I asked you. Go on."

He lifts his shoulders, drops them. "I'd stop her. Sometimes she'd be meek, like a little child. Other times she'd start shrieking. Shrieking at me. How I'd ruined her life. Blood trickling down her face. Wouldn't let me clean her up. Wouldn't sleep in the same bed with me. I felt bad. That our life together wasn't making her happy. To put it mildly. But I got pretty sick of it."

"What did you do?"

"Me? Ran the ranch. Went for long rides."

"About Mum?"

"Nothing. It was bigger than both of us. That's what I came to. It wasn't my fault. Wasn't her fault. Not the drinking, not the other stuff. The remorse she felt was real. The contempt she felt for herself. She barely went out. Which was good because the one time a neigh-bour woman saw her forehead all split and bruised, she started giving me funny looks."

"Jesus, Dad. You must have been scared. Scared she'd give you away."

He studies me for a moment. "I was."

"And you must have felt very alone."

He nods.

"Did you ever talk about it to anybody?"

"Moira, once. She'd been married to a Native fellow, long back, went crazy with the drink."

"The trapper we went to see?"

He nods. His eyelids are drooping.

"You need your nap, don't you?"

I lean back, look out of the window, eyes travelling the line of moun-tains. Mum an alcoholic. It's not quite as shocking as it should be. But Mum banging her head. Then me. And the cane. There are too many pieces shifting about.

Mum. I picture the triangle of her face, wavy black hair shot with threads of silver. The pinch of her mouth. It was always there, that tension. White knuckle alcoholic, staying sober without the pro-gram? With religion though. Something to take the edge off. But it didn't quite.

I look around the living room, so familiar it's hard to see it, the worn furniture, the wallpaper with little blue forget-me-nots. I thought they were happy. Sadness washes over me. The two of them locked in their dance, alone inside the bubble of their secret. Like the little glass dome someone showed me once, when you shook it two skaters twirled around and around while snow flakes floated down.

Pushing open the storm door, an icy wind greets me. I reach back in, borrow Dad's tartan scarf. Why didn't Mum tell me? We could have gone to meetings together. Head down, eyes watering, I try to picture her standing up front, telling her war stories. Laughter as she lists the places she hid bottles

Shit, it's cold. Maybe just a turn around the yard. Banging from the machine shed, a trickle of smoke from the chimney. Where Mum raised the meat chickens every summer. My job to clean out after. Crap machines, Dad called them. He liked the laying hens. Gave them the run of the barn. Mum and Dad. Ben and Polly. The clack of Mum's heels on the living room floor. Feet flying, her head and arms stayed completely still. She'd be sweating, though, when Dad laid down his bow. They'd smile at each other. There was always some kind of juice between them.

She lay there like a stick of wood.

A head banger.

Banging her head until blood flowed. Banging her head on the white painted door jamb. Shrieking when Dad tried to stop her. Trying to kill the evil.

Cane on the ground like a black snake.

"Hey Meg."

I jump. Manfred's peering at me from the side door of the shed.

"Come on in, it's cold."

"Oh. No, no thanks. Just wanted some fresh air."

"Victor was wondering, will you be around for supper?"

"Yes, but I think I'll cook for Dad and me tonight. Could you pass that message along?"

Manfred's face closes. "Of course." He steps back inside and shuts the door.

Shit.

"Go ahead," Dad says when I've poured us both tea. "Ask whatever you need to ask. Really." He looks drained, sad.

"Why don't you start at the beginning, with you and Mum? Your version."

He looks surprised. Relieved too.

He takes a sip then puts the mug down. "As you know, she was the cook in the lumber camp where I worked one season. Up near Revelstoke. A younger, prettier cook than usual, according to the fellows." A smile tugs at the corners of his mouth. "They all flirted with her but I could see she liked me. Couple of them teased me for being so modest. She let them know she personally preferred men with some decorum."

"She knew the whole time?"

He nods.

"How did you find out that she knew? Did she say something?"

He picks up his mug but he doesn't drink from it, just looks at me over the rim. "There was a spot in the woods where I'd go to bathe. A little spring lined with rocks. Traces of an old cabin. Spruce and pine all around. It was a good mile from the camp. She must have followed me. She stepped into the clearing. At least I was still dressed. She walked up to me and where a person would stop, say something, she kept walking. She pressed herself against me and she kissed me. On the mouth. I stepped back sharpish. Kept on backing up.

"She looked at me. Those shrewd eyes, she looked at me and she said—I remember it to this day, the drone of flies in the clearing, moss that grew on the stones around the spring, light angling down between the trees—she looked at me and she said, 'I know what you are. And I know what you are not.'"

He puts down his mug, reaches for the pot, glances at me. I shake my head. He tops up his mug and adds milk before saying, "It was the moment I'd dreaded and there it was in the clearing with us, her knowing and me with nothing to say, just the memory of that kiss in my mouth. She said, 'Come here.' It was simple. It was so simple. All I had to do was to step through the angled shafts of light, step to her and hold her, but you have to understand I hadn't touched another human being. Not that way, not ever. I stood there in the clearing and then, I swear it, my feet began to move of their own accord. I watched as they carried me across the clearing and into her arms. She smelled of gravy and cabbage and wood smoke. Nothing in this world ever smelled better."

He looks my way but he's not looking at me. After a while he says, "That was Polly all over. When she made up her mind for something ..." He shakes his head.

"Did she ever tell you how she knew?"

"She just said she knew the first time she set eyes on me."

"And didn't say anything to anyone?"

"Polly,"—he hesitates—"Polly liked secrets."

I pour myself some tea but he doesn't say anything more. "What was she like back then?"

"Fun. She had a wild streak. I mean she was always thrifty. A hard worker. A planner. But she could kick up her heels. We'd go to all the dances. Every town with a community hall had one."

"You weren't ..." I stop.

"Weren't what?"

"Afraid people would find out. I guess I just assumed. The way you were when I was growing up. Sticking close to home."

He shakes his head, still smiling. "I used to worry. She'd say, 'Put a sock in it.'"

It takes me a minute. "TMI," I say but I can't help laughing.

"TMI?"

"Too Much Information."

"Sorry."

"It's okay. I asked you. Besides, it feels as if you must be talking about someone else. You can't be talking about the people who raised me."

Dad's levering himself out of the Morris chair. I assume he's headed for the washroom but when he gets across the room he reaches for his jacket.

"Going out for a pipe," he says.

"Dad, it's your house."

"Polly never liked the smell of it. I'm used to going outside for my smoke."

"Back then you were," I say. "A cold wind's come up."

"Funny thing,"—he's patting his pockets for matches—"all the years not smoking ..." He snaps his fingers. "Gone like that. Besides, doctor says the more I keep moving around the healthier I'll be."

"Bet she wasn't thinking of you taking up smoking. But seriously, I don't mind the smell."

He opens his mouth. He's about to ask about my plans again. For the farm.

"Is it alright if I stay the night?" I ask. "I don't have to be at work until the day after tomorrow. Then I'll be working a bunch of shifts in a row."

"Of course. You don't have to ask. But you should probably let Victor and Manfred know. Or I will."

"Actually, I thought maybe I could make supper tonight. It won't be as good, I know."

"That would be lovely. I'll tell them." He reaches for the phone.

"Um. I already spoke to Manfred. When you were asleep. Sorry. I should have asked you first."

"It's alright. I'm glad you're here. Now I am going to go out for my smoke. Then we'll see what we can scare up."

I call home while he's outside but there aren't any messages. Emptying the teapot, rinsing our mugs, I look at the flour bin. Dad built all these cabinets. Built the house and almost everything in it. The bin is hinged at the bottom. You pull on the handle and the top swings out. Inside is the old crock, a dusting of flour still in the bottom along with a couple of mouse turds.

The front door opens. I hear the stick on the floor. I don't need to look to see that it's the ebony cane. Just because it's the dark axle, you can't throw it out, a perfectly good stick. I walk over to the pantry. The back left corner is where she hung it, by the deeper shelves. The shelves were always lined with jars. There's only a couple left behind some tins of baked beans. I wipe one off, hold it up under the light. *Hedgerow Jam 1997* in Mum's careful script.

"That was a good year," Dad says from behind me.

"Shall we make more, this summer?" I ask. It's nothing I planned to say.

"If possible," Dad says.

Suddenly I'm crying.

"Oh Meg." He pats my back.

Shit. I turn and press my face into his shoulder. After a moment I hear him lean the stick against the wall. One arm wraps around my back. With the other he strokes my hair. I breathe the mushroom smell of him, the overlay of smoke.

"I don't want you to die too."

"Ah Meg." Dad's hand keeps stroking my hair.

"Sorry. I'm sorry, Dad."

"I miss her too." He steps back, feeling in the pocket of his cardigan. He passes me a handkerchief so old and soft the cotton is almost transparent. When I've blown my nose and wiped my eyes he asks, "What do you fancy for supper? I'd be happy with beans and scrambled eggs."

"Good thing," I say after reviewing the contents of the fridge. "You don't even have any bread."

Dad looks sheepish. "Check the freezer."

"Ah."

"I didn't want to throw any of it away."

"Maybe there'll be some lucky birds tomorrow."

Chapter Fifty Three

"WHAT MADE HER stop drinking? How did that happen?"

Dad puts down his fork. I gave up on the mealy beans in their acrid sauce a while back. "There was a revival in Drayton Valley. It was in the paper. She wanted to go. Which was surprising in itself but I didn't say anything. I dropped her off, went to see a man about a baler. Came back a couple hours later. Her face was shining. In the truck on the way home she told me she'd given herself to Jesus. Jesus had forgiven her. He loved her and she didn't have to drink anymore. A week later she still hadn't had a drink. I began to think maybe it would work. Then she told me Jesus was going to give her a child." He shakes his head.

"Jesus?"

"His Daddy did it." He hooks an eyebrow at me.

I stare at him then I start to laugh. It's not that funny. I stop as suddenly as I started.

"But then damned if you didn't show up. Out of nowhere. She knew what you were. A gift from God."

There's a lump in my throat.

"And so you were."

"Until I became a raging alcoholic nightmare myself."

"She prayed for you, every morning and every night. When you got sober, well that was more proof."

"And she stayed sober?"

"Never touched another drop."

"And she stayed married to you all the while they were preaching about the Homosexual Abomination?"

"When Polly believed a thing was God's will, there wasn't anything would change her mind, whether it was you being meant for us or whether it was us being married."

"Were you actually married? I mean legally."

"In front of a Justice of the Peace in Rocky Mountain House."

Which brings me back to that whole question. But I'm not going there. Not right now. "Have you ever felt you needed to be saved, Dad?"

Dad considers his half-empty plate then shakes his head. "Can't say I have. Not like that. I've felt guilty, ashamed, afraid, but not as if I was damned unless some power redeemed me. What about you?"

"I went to church with Mum but it didn't really take. It felt like he was using it, the preacher, hammering away at how you were lost without Jesus, a hopeless sinner."

Dad nods.

"It probably wouldn't have that much power unless you already believed you were bad."

"And you didn't?"

"Not like that. Defective, maybe, but not damned. I just don't expect to be wanted. If I'm part of a group I feel as if I'm there on approval. They might send me back. So I always have to prove I'm good enough to keep around. Apparently lots of adopted kids feel that way. Which doesn't change the feeling. I have to watch it, what I'll do so someone will keep me around. And what I'll do when I can't stand feeling like that anymore." I glance at him. "It took me a while to figure this out. I wanted your approval so badly, and I hated wanting it. Hated caring what you thought. It felt ... it felt like such an entrapment, to care."

I've been staring down at the table, trying to find the words but something makes me look up. He's sitting there, half eaten plate of beans pushed back. There's light pouring out of his eyes. I don't know how else to say it. Beams of golden light are streaming from his eyes. They reach me and wrap around me and I'm in a bright bubble of his seeing. Held in his gaze.

Wow. I never felt anything like this. With that thought the eyebeams fade and I'm sitting across from my father, the turquoise Formica table between us.

"What just happened?" I ask.

"I don't know."

"You didn't feel anything different?"

"What are you talking about?"

"Nothing I can put into words."

His eyelids are drooping.

"Take your nap, Dad. I'll wash up."

Standing in the kitchen, my hands in warm water, the weirdness of the
last couple of days hits me. Not the information about Mum because
somehow I knew. Not the specifics but I knew she felt in desperate
need of salvation. Felt the strain in her that shouldn't have been there
if she truly felt saved. I think perhaps she was always searching for
what I just felt from Dad. To sit in that golden light, knowing you're
acceptable as you are. Loved as you are. The eyebeams of God shining on you.

Don't mock it.

Okay, this is what's weird. It's like I've shed some kind of rind.
Become porous. Porous to portents. Everything swollen with signifi-
cance. Something I used to feel, taking hallucinogens. Because they
strip away the screens of habit. *A sacrament*, Dora called it. Peyote.
The Ghost Dancer's sacrament. *Respect it. Welcome it. Let it take
you. Let it break you.* Dora holding my head while I puked. The
wave curling higher and higher. *Let it. Let it.*

Let what?

I pull the plug. Greasy water twists down the drain. In the living
room Dad is snoring.

Poor Mum. Poor Dad. Only it never is poor Dad. Somehow he
gets things right. It takes people years in Al-Anon to figure out it was
nobody's fault.

I take a fresh pot of tea through to the living room. Dad's still
sound asleep.

Steam curls up from the hole in the teapot lid. When first I came
here I watched to see which way it flowed, as if it would tell me

something I needed to know. I wasn't much more than a pair of eyes, watching from the shadows. They went about their business, practical people, these strangers, and slowly I made out the sense in their motion and it comforted me, the precise way the woman moved around her kitchen, the quiet economy of the man as he hung his jacket, pulled off his boots. He smelled of horses, the slant of sweat over warm grain, and something greasier I didn't recognize. I watched from the bench against the wall, the woman glancing at me now and then, looking away as quickly.

Soon enough I'd follow her like a bottle lamb, out to the barn for eggs she piled, warm in my hands. Out to the garden. The first time she dug potatoes she must have seen my eyes widen, the red tubers rolling free of the dirt. She looked at me and I came and squatted beside her, running my fingers through the cool, crumbly soil until they met difference, roundness. We piled the potatoes between us. She threw a sack over them. A few rows on we wrapped our fingers in fading leaves, tugged onions from the loose soil, left the round bulbs in their brown paper skins to lie in the sun. "To cure," Mum said. "So they'll keep." Even at the beginning, when she didn't know if I understood, she talked to me, giving me the information I might need to feed myself in her world.

Mum. The first words I spoke. I asked Dad, 'Where's Mum?'
I followed his eyes. Turned.
'I'm here,' she said. Her eyes were shiny.

But somehow by the next winter my allegiance had shifted. I'd follow him out to the barn, break open the bales he tossed down from the loft, spread the flakes of hay among the mangers, eager sheep shoving each other aside, upper lips twisting forward. We'd stand, side by side, watching them eat, his big loose hands resting on the rail. The sound then of munching in the dusty air, sweet with dry grass, sharp with the reek of winter bedding. Motes dancing in the light that slanted in from the high gable window. As the winter went along the sheep grew wider until there was scarcely room for them in the barn. We'd stand in the frigid air and watch and they'd watch us, ears forward, jaws working, the sound of steady chewing.

The snoring has stopped. I look across at Dad.
"You're smiling," he says.

"I was thinking about the barn in March. It might be the most contented place I've ever been. A flock of gravid sheep chewing their cud. Light from the door shining through their ears so they all looked pink.

"At school, when they were badgering me to talk, that's where I'd go in my mind, to stand next to you in the barn, and I'd pretend the teachers were the sheep, their mouths moving and moving. Just the sound of chewing."

He grins. "When I was young and I had to go to church, I'd turn myself into the oak post at the end of the pew. It was carved, the top, into a wheat sheaf. It was very old and dark. I'd imagine being that wood. Feel it as my flesh. The grain of it. When the sermon was over my mother would have to elbow me to stand up for the hymn. I'd still be in my tree-ness."

"Did you miss them?"

"I missed,"—he pauses—"I missed my little brother. But my parents and my sister, I missed the idea of them, of a family, but no, I didn't miss them. The first time I heard about cuckoos, I thought, 'That's me.' It was a dirty trick the cuckoo parents played, sneaking their eggs into other birds' nests. The cuckoo chicks were too big, too hungry. Wrong. I suppose that's what I felt the most: wrong. I didn't even want to be like the others. I certainly didn't try. Mostly I day-dreamed about how, when I was old enough, I'd live on an island and catch my own fish, build my own house. I'd eat raspberries and trout and hazelnuts and read all night if I wanted to. Or I'd live in the Arctic with my sled dogs and hunt caribou and moose and make pemmican. Or I'd go to sea. Which might end up with me being stranded on a South Sea island. It wasn't until I was about thirteen that it dawned on me that women didn't do any of those things. Not on their own, anyway. My sister was always talking about getting married. What she'd wear, how handsome her husband would be. I never had the slightest interest." He shakes his head. "So no, I had no regrets."

He walked away. He just walked away. It's like being on the water, looking down to the bottom, seeing the shadow of a fish flit past. Not the fish itself but the shadow.

"That was what we couldn't give you."

"What? Sorry."

"Extended family. You know. Grandparents and aunts and uncles and cousins. Would you have liked that? "

"I don't know."

"I see now we'd turned inward even before you came. Polly's drinking, I suppose. And then, well, once you were here, if anyone had found us out, they'd have taken you away."

There it is again, that flicker. The shadow of the flick of a tail.

"I don't think either of us could have borne that."

"Mum walked away too, didn't she, from her family?"

"Not the way I did. She stayed in touch with her brother Frankie."

"That's him on the bookcase, isn't it?" I can summon the face of the beetle browed, heavy jawed young man. Other than the wedding picture and the photograph of Dad and me by the North Saskatchewan river, he's the only other human photograph.

"Did she ever go back?"

"Once, after her father died. To lay a wreath on her mother's grave."

I can feel Dad's eyes on me.

"And?"

"To make sure the old bastard was really dead."

"Mum said that?"

"She did."

"When was that?"

"A few years after the end of the war. Early fifties."

Chapter Fifty Four

NINE TIMES OUT *of ten.*

Lying upstairs, sliver of moon glittering through the windows. Waxing or waning? Dad can tell. Mum. Mum getting up out of this bed, going down to the kitchen.

She lay there like a stick.

Cane like a black snake.

The evil inside her.

Shit.

I can't lie here in this room thinking these thoughts.

In the kitchen I turn on the light over the table. Walk over to the door jamb. High gloss white, chipped along the edges.

A creak behind me. I spin around, heart hammering. Creak, tap, creak.

Dad's hair is standing up like a woodpecker's crest. He's wearing the old woollen dressing gown, coarse as a horse blanket, striped pyjama legs showing over battered slippers. He's halfway across the living room

"I'm alright, Dad. I just couldn't sleep." The relief in his face makes my throat ache. "I'll make myself a hot drink."

At home I'd make bread. I put the kettle on. When I hear the bedroom door click I go over to the bookcase with the photographs, pick up the one of Mum's brother. He's holding the yoke of an ox, the ox as pale as he is dark, a ponderous, ghostly presence. Together they regard the camera. In the background are a weathered barn and an elder-berry bush laden with dark clusters of fruit. I study it for a while but I have no idea what is in their eyes. I put it down and pick up Mum and Dad's wedding photograph in its silver frame.

Back in bed, pillow plumped behind me, inhaling the thin smell of peppermint which always makes me think of a mountain stream, I examine the photo. There's Mum, heart-shaped face pale in the frame of dark hair. She's wearing a white dress with lace around her shoulders. 'Lace from Montreal,' she told me, 'made by nuns. The dress I made myself.' The only colour comes from her lips, which have been painted a carmine red in the photograph, and Dad's hair, coloured a golden yellow. His eyes are crinkled as if he's looking into the sun. He's wearing an almost suit. Jacket and trousers the same dark grey or navy but you can tell the fabric is different. A narrow tie with a diamond pattern. He's standing ramrod straight, one hand on Mum's shoulder where she sits, dress furled around her feet. I hold the photograph further away. He's dense with himself. A furry golden animal, vibrating with happiness. She's more removed, looking out from further inside herself.

Behind them rises a jagged line of mountains, snow caps tinged pink by an imaginary dawn, the sky forget-me-not blue. One of three possible backdrops the photographer's studio offered. I never asked her what the others were. Perhaps she would have preferred a flowery meadow or a seaside scene. I wish I'd asked. I look at her face again. I didn't know her. Not really. I could have, if she'd let me. Why didn't she tell me?

It's not hard to answer that. The few women her age I've known in AA all talked about the silence and the shame. Sober, she became the woman she thought she was supposed to be. Only the dancing ... I keep staring at her as if I can make her look back at me. Slowly my mind slides closer to what happened this afternoon. I don't think it was mine, that feeling of being so bad inside. But was it really Mum? Some residue clinging to the cane? A visitation? It sounds ridiculous.

I put the photograph down on the shelf behind the bed and turn out the light. Lie back. *Let it. Let it come.* You can't see the moon through the windows any more but light lingers on the horizon. Inside the room there are pools of deeper shadow. I try to empty my mind. Focus on the breath. Witness my thoughts. Feelings. Images. Nothing.

I switch the light on again. Turn around in bed so I'm facing the bookshelf. Slide the backrest board to one side. The shelves are almost empty. Mum's Bible and assorted religious tracts are all that are left on the top shelf. Dad's books are downstairs now. Mum's books don't even fill the whole shelf. They're kept upright by the old tin pencil box. I pull out the box, letting the books topple. A tin box with a red salamander painted on the lid, it's the only thing my mother brought from Nova Scotia. Or so she said. An oblong tin, rusting at the corners, it once contained pencils, pencils stacked neat as logs on a truck, uniform, orange, hexagonal, unsharpened, not yet worn or chewed, a box of new pencils which to her held the promise of a world away from the men who slept in the woods under piles of branches, who came asking for soap in the spring. Soap to gnaw and unbind themselves after living all winter on cornmeal. I remember that, how she said the word *cornmeal*, as if in that one word was bound all the misery and poverty of those thin, grimy, constipated men.

Nothing but a dirt farm on the North Mountain. Not even a weir to catch herring. I grew up without a mother to speak of. Mum left behind after her sisters went to work in the factories in Saint John. How she wanted to go with them. *They laughed. Told me it was my turn now. They were going where there was work and if I missed them I could wave to them across the Bay when I wasn't too busy skivvying for Dad and the boys.*

Port Lorne. The name forlorn as the gulls' cries. The frigid Fundy. Massive tides piling into the Bay, sucking back out, stranding boats on the sea's bottom, trapping the unwary. I imagined it all: the unkind sisters, the stroke-dumbed mother, the reek of the man's moonshine, his hard hands. Wet woollens steaming by the cookstove, the boys off in the woods with their father when they were scarcely old enough to hold up an axe. The father missing two fingers from his left hand, how the stumps of the fingers went white when it was cold, how he stamped his feet and clapped his mutilated hand against his thigh. A tall man with a handlebar moustache, Donald was his name, and Frankie and John and Ronald and my mother Polly and Jean and Enid the oldest.

It was Frankie she felt bad about leaving. Frankie, the baby of the family, with his heavy, patient face. But I don't know anything about his life. There were really just a few stories, told and retold. It was true, what I said to Heather. Geography was more important than people. Summer storms blundering out of the south; the Nor'easter that dropped three feet of snow so the men had to dig the road out all the way down to the Valley before the ploughs could get up. Salt-laden gales hissing across the Bay, piercing the children's clothes as they walked the two miles to school. Snow on the window-sills inside the house. How the Valley with its railroad and tea dances scorned the Mountain.

I pictured a mountain like our mountains, grand and gleaming and remote, Mum and her people camped on the slopes like the no-madic herdsmen of Mongolia I had seen in a photograph at school. But when I asked if it was higher than our mountains, the mountain she lived on, she laughed and said the North Mountain was nothing but a hogback seventy miles long, a glorified doorstop between the Valley and the Bay.

Then she'd be on to the West which was the future of Canada. The East was what you left behind if you had the spirit and gumption to get out.

I pick up the photo again. On the brown paper backing is stamped: *Edgar McKenzie, Photographer, Rocky Mountain House, Alberta. 26th June, 1935.* Mum would have been twenty-four.

I turn the photo over, study the young woman. 'I was always good at arithmetic.' Mum keeping the books. At the kitchen table, sharpening her pencil. Keeping the farm on the straight and narrow. Only so much Dad was allowed to lose before she'd shut down the latest scheme.

It wasn't that Dad was a bad farmer. He'd have a good idea, make money for a bit but then other people would pile in, produce too much and the price would drop. Except for the ostriches. They never worked out. Cost too much to over-winter and besides, where was the market for ostrich meat?

'Vancouver,' Dad said.

'It's certainly not Edmonton.'

'People in Vancouver, they like something exotic. Don't they?' He looked at me.

I'd come back to make my amends, a couple of years sober. Mum caught my eye, shook her head. I never thought I'd be so happy to hear them bickering again. The mild, familiar skirmishes. The rock solid unit of them. Mum, always the voice of caution and sense. Except now there's Mum shrieking, beating her head bloody. Mum with bottles everywhere. Mum with ten thousand dollars to leave me in a codicil to her will I'm pretty sure Dad knew nothing about until the day in the lawyer's office.

Chapter Fifty Five

"WILL YOU TELL me what you know about Mum's childhood? I don't care if it's stuff I already know."

"Of course." He pushes back his half-eaten bowl of oatmeal. "She grew up on land that sloped down to the Bay of Fundy. They raised peas and beans for a cash crop. And apples that were shipped to England in barrels. Sold cream. Cut saw-logs in the winter. Her mother taught school before she married. She came from somewhere else, the mother."

"Do you know where?"

He shakes his head. "I don't think Polly ever told me. If she did, I don't remember."

"She had a stroke, right, that left her pretty much a vegetable?"

"Yes. When Polly was eight. Frankie was three. The older sisters took over the housekeeping. Mostly there was enough to eat but I don't think there was much love or kindness."

"When they were leaving home, going to work in a factory, Mum wanted to go with them." I stop, look at Dad.

After a moment he says, "They laughed at her, told her it was her turn now."

"She told me that too, in those exact words." I take a breath. "Did she ever say anything that suggested her father ... that he sexually abused her?"

Dad doesn't look shocked or even surprised. "She never said

anything explicitly, but after her mother died, which was a couple of years after her sisters left home, her aunt—her father's sister—gave her money for the fare to Saint John. Because it wasn't right for a young girl to be alone in a houseful of men."

"That's what the aunt said?"

"According to Polly. She had a powerful hatred for her father. 'He thought he was God.' I remember her saying that. 'Everything and everyone was his to do what he wanted with.'"

"The ... the head banging. At work there are clients ... It's pretty much always connected ..."

I can't believe I'm having this conversation here, with Dad, about Mum.

"He was a brutal man, I know that much."

"An alcoholic?"

"I'd say so."

He's thinking about something in particular. "What is it?"

"A story I wish I'd never heard."

"Tell me."

"There are things you hear that you can't forget."

"Please tell me."

He studies me for a moment. "Very well. She'd had a bit to drink when she told me this. When she was nine a neighbour's child came over, little blonde pug-faced thing clutching two whole dollars which was a lot of money in those days. She wanted to buy a heifer calf. They were standing by the pen with the calves. 'I'd like that one,' the girl said, pointing to a pretty little creature with black speckles in the white blaze. Polly's father picked up a mallet, walked up to the calf, hit it between the eyes. Killed it outright. Threw it on the manure pile. Little girl ran off crying."

"Why? Why did he do that?" I feel sick.

"I don't know. Polly said he didn't like the girl wanting to buy one of his calves."

"Jesus."

"She only ever told me that story once." He's watching me.

"Are there more?"

"No."

"That's it?"

"Not much else to say, is there? Are you all right?"

I can see a little blonde girl's face, eyes widening. The shock. An older dark-haired girl watching.

"More or less."

"I've never forgotten." His voice is quiet.

"No," I say, "I don't think I will either. But I did ask you to tell me." Neither of us says anything for a bit. At last I ask, "How old was she when she got out of there?"

"Sixteen. She didn't go to Saint John, she went to Montreal. She'd heard there was more work in the factories there. She only had her grade six. Her father made her leave school when the sisters left home. Claimed there was too much to do in the house. Besides, he didn't see the point of educating girls."

Dad's levering himself up from his chair.

"It doesn't quite add up," I say. "She'd have been what, eleven, twelve at the end of grade six. I suppose she could have been held back in school but I don't think so."

He shakes his head. "She won prizes in arithmetic."

"The pencil box?"

He nods.

"So if she left home when her mother died and that was two years after the sisters left, she'd have been thirteen or fourteen, not sixteen."

"I never spotted that."

"That's awfully young to be out on your own. How old was she when you first met her?"

"It was 1934."

"So she was twenty-three?"

"That's about right."

"And she was the cook at the lumber camp?"

"Yes." He picks up the cane.

"What did she do between leaving home and when you met?"

"It's time for my morning pipe."

Chapter Fifty Six

"THE TEN YEARS before you and Mum met, what do you know about them?"

"Very little. We mostly talked about our plans."

"You didn't talk about the past at all?"

He gazes blandly back at me. I already called him a coward. Am I going to call him a liar now?

"The cane," I say at last, "did she have that when you met?"

"Yes."

I wait. Okay. Time to change the subject. "The money Mum left me. Did you know she was going to do that?"

After a moment he shakes his head.

"Dad, please don't play games with me. I'm not that tightly wrapped right now."

After a moment he says, "I had no idea she had that kind of money. But then Polly was always secretive about money. When I found the bottles, realized how much she was drinking, I wanted to know where she got the money for that." He shakes his head. "She flew into such a rage."

It's as if his eyes have sunk back into his head. The bare rock ridge of his nose stands out, the grooves from nose to mouth scored deep.

"You got between her and her booze."

The skin around his eyes looks bruised. My chest unfolds, soft white wings spreading. The swollen, aching tenderness I get at work. In meetings. "Oh Dad."

He shrugs. "I gave up asking. We never went hungry. The bills were paid. The farm books were kept up, that's for sure. She knew to a nickel what I spent on fence wire."

The faint, familiar whiff of a well-aged resentment makes the love so strong it hurts.

His eyes roam around the living room. Eventually they turn to me. "The will the lawyer read wasn't the will he drew up the day Polly and I went in there together."

"Were you upset?"

"Mm."

He's got the deciding look.

"I do want to know."

"You've learned a thing or two, that place you work."

"Tell me. Please."

"Very well. I don't see how she could have saved up that much money over the years we were married. She did work part-time at the Cash and Carry then at the Co-op and she was always thrifty but ..." He shrugs.

"You mean she had some money before you met?"

He nods. "The way we got our first quarter section. It wasn't quite as simple as the story Polly always told. We were working for an old rancher. He had no money to pay us but he had land, that much was true. We had precious little money, or so I thought, but we could work. By God we worked for the old bastard. Each week he subtracted the wages we didn't get from the amount we'd agreed the land was worth. Only the land was worth less and less as the thirties wore on. At least we didn't go hungry. Part of the deal, we got a piglet each spring and we could plant up the vegetable garden, take half, he got the other half.

"What we didn't know was he'd borrowed money from the bank. Against the land we were supposedly buying. Foreclosure notice came. Old man was mad as hell. Only thing that gave him any comfort was the idea we'd be out our wages. Polly demanded to know how much he owed the bank. He told her it wasn't any of her business but she kept after him. Finally he told her. It was a quarter the amount we'd agreed the land was worth. She told him we'd pay that amount plus ten dollars. He laughed at her. Raw-boned old bastard, laugh like a jackdaw. He told her we didn't have a pot to piss in or else what were we doing working for him like dogs? She said he'd see the colour of our money in the bank where we could watch him pay off the mortgage. He kicked and hollered but in the end he sold us the land for forty dollars over the amount he owed the bank.

"I don't know where that money came from. We'd pooled everything we'd saved from the time in the lumber camp plus some I had from selling a claim I'd staked. I was sure it wasn't enough but she said I was mistaken. I was so happy we were getting the land I didn't think that much about it at the time. I spent every spare minute planning the house I was going to build us. A log cabin. I turned it around and around in my mind. Where the door should be. The window. We had the window already. Polly would split spruce shingles for the roof. I marked the trees I was going to fell. We went on working for the old man but now we were working for tools and equipment. Mostly it was the broken old stuff. Nobody ever threw anything away in those days. Christ, I collected bent nails, straightened them out.

"Finally it was the end of August, fresh snow on the peaks already. Harvest in. We'd dug a root cellar, filled that to the brim. We'd levelled off the spot for the cabin. Hauled good flat stones for the corners. I was set to fell the first tree. Polly came out with me. I picked up the axe. I was feeling excited as a child and solemn at the same time. She said, 'Don't cut that tree.'

"'Why not? We don't have much time.'

"'Because I've got a surprise for you.'

"'A surprise?'

"'It's coming on the train.'

"'What surprise?'

"'Guess.'

"I hefted the axe. I was annoyed, truth be told. She knew I was worried about getting a roof on before winter. She didn't seem to take it seriously enough.

"She came and stood between me and the tree. 'There's a house coming, Ben. A kit.'

"I let the axe back down, rested the head on the ground.

"'Everything we need. Floorboards. Even the nails.'

"'Have you gone mad?'

"She was laughing. I was scared as well as angry now. 'I've got trees to fell or do you want to freeze this winter?' I lifted the axe again.

"'Ben, Ben, I'm not joking. I'm not mad.' She took my arm. 'Come and sit down. I'll explain. It's a kit. It's already paid for.'

"'How?'

"'When you went to the feed merchant the other week I went to the bank.'

"'You borrowed money? Are you mad? But they wouldn't ...'

"She was shaking her head. 'No, it was my money, set aside.'

"'What money?'

"She leaned over, kissed me, which didn't make me feel any better. I didn't like it. I didn't like any of it. That she hadn't told me. That she had money hidden away. That we weren't going to build the house we'd talked about. That all the times we'd sat up in bed talking about what we'd build, how we could add on later, she'd had another plan going.

"'Why didn't you tell me?' I asked her.

"She leaned back. 'Because I wanted to make sure you were the good, solid, hard-working husband you seemed to be.'

"'Fine, but where did you get the money for a kit? That's $400 at least.' I stared at her.

"'I thought you'd be pleased.'

"I could never stand it when she cried. But I was still angry. Counted to ten, then twenty. When I could speak normally I asked, 'How much was it?'

"'$488. Freight included. And a dollar back for every knot you find in the wood.'

"'Where did that money come from?'

"'I saved it.'

"'How?'

"'None of your business.'

"She glared back at me. I knew the glitter in her eye. She always did have a temper."

There's a knock on the door. I jump.

"It's me." Victor's voice.

"Come on in," Dad calls.

I look across at the clock. It's only 11:30.

"Hello Ben, hello Meg." Victor's head pokes through the kitchen doorway. He smiles uncertainly at me. "I brought soup for you to heat up. Potato and kielbasa with kale. Throw the kale in at the end. Cook it for less than a minute. I shaved it really fine so it stays crunchy. That's how they do it in Portugal. Sort of Portuguese-Polish. The Portuguese add olive oil at the end but with the kielbasa ..."

"Victor, stop. I'm sorry I was so abrupt yesterday. With Manfred." He looks at me, clear grey eyes. "I really do appreciate everything you do here."

Dad's looking at me too.

"Well, you're welcome. I have to go. Manfred's got a dentist's appointment."

"Hungry?"

Dad shakes his head. "They're good men, you know."

"I know."

"It's all right," he says. "Take your time." His eyes roam the room.

"A kit?" I look around too.

"Pieces came already cut. Numbered. A picture to follow."

"I always thought you designed it yourselves. I thought it was a perfect expression of the two of you."

"Perfectly square, you mean?"

"Why didn't she tell you?"

"She liked to have the edge. Know a little more than you. Didn't matter mostly. But." He shrugs. "We were equal," he says, "until then. A team."

"You never found out where it came from, the money?"

He shakes his head.

My mind is spitting out questions but I don't say anything. After a minute he says, "I always did want to build that log house. I can still see it in my mind's eye. I'd been thinking about it ever since Dorothy and I drove all over Western Canada. Imagining the choices I'd make, if ever I had the chance."

"Perhaps I should build myself a log cabin here. You could design it." The words slip out. He looks as startled as I feel. And pleased. Which he carefully smoothes away.

"Nice and dark and low to the ground," he says. "Moss to pack in the cracks forever. Spiders. How the spiders loved those old log homes."

"Like the trapper's." I'm back there on the bed, half asleep while they talk, the glow of pipes in the shadowy room. "It was like a cave. I felt safe. It might have been the first time I felt truly safe."

"At Moira's?"

"Falling asleep. I've always remembered that. I went to sleep under the blanket of your voices. Nothing could carry me away. I was always afraid. To go to sleep. When nobody was watching I could be taken away."

The words sink in like water into sand.

Finally he says, "You were always watching, weren't you?"

"I was always afraid. But less. After that visit. I went to sleep so softly and when I woke up you were still there, talking, and you were glad I was awake. It was like waking up in a shaft of sunlight, the two of you glad I existed."

"Ah Meg, we were always glad, beyond glad, Polly and I."

I nod but I want to cry. It wasn't with Mum I felt that ease. Mum who cooked and cleaned and asked me questions after school. Because she never had that easiness. Dad is like the mountains. He's here. Mum, she was always proving something.

I drop the bundle of finely-sliced kale into the boiling liquid, stir it once then ladle it into the bowls I set out.

We're silent for the grace Mum would have said, pick up our spoons at the same time.

"Mmm," Dad says after the first mouthful.

"Mmm, mm. I never thought I liked kale."

"No," Dad says with feeling. Mum grew it for a couple of years. Limp, brownish and tasting of old cabbage, it was a completely different beast. Perhaps she didn't like it either because it slipped off the menu.

"Whole wheat or rye?" I ask. "To go with this? Not that I have either here," I hasten to add, seeing Dad's hopeful look. "I haven't felt like making any lately. I suppose with all the potato it doesn't really need bread."

"*Reason not the need*," Dad says.

"*King Lear.* Lear speaking, I think."

"Correct," he says.

It's a game we used to play the other way round. I'd bring home whatever play we were studying in English, read a phrase. He could almost always identify the character. Often he'd carry on the speech or the dialogue. *Lear* and *The Tempest* he knew word for word.

"I read *Twelfth Night* again the other week. Manfred and Victor said you recommended it to them. I was curious. Was it all the gender bending stuff or was there something I missed?"

"No, mostly it amused me. When I was alone, prospecting, I'd read it at night by the fire. I was ... Well, I was quite lonely in those days."

"After you'd become a man?"

"And before I met Polly."

"I can't really imagine what it was like, to live with that sort of secret. Because you were afraid, weren't you? When you talked about Mum coming into the clearing, you said it was the moment you'd dreaded."

"Mm. What I dreaded was that I'd fall in love with someone. And then what?"

"Were you in love with Mum? Before she followed you?"

"Oh yes. But so were half the fellows. They were good-natured though, when Polly made it clear she favoured me."

"The one who gave you birch syrup to make your life together sweet?"

"Jean. Yes, he was one."

Dad's smiling as he spoons in the last of his soup.

Washing up while Dad takes his nap, I think perhaps I'll stay tonight as well. Leave early enough tomorrow to catch the Mustard Seed at noon. I'd have a couple of hours at home before work. Which reminds me I haven't called my voicemail today.

There are two messages, the first from Val. 'Just checking up on you. Give me a call sometime.' Then Judy's voice wheezes down the line. 'Call me, Meg. There's someone you should meet.' Pause. 'Just a lead. Not ... Don't get ...' She coughs hard. 'Excited. But call me. He's only here today and tomorrow.' She left the message at eight o'clock last night.

Chapter Fifty Seven

THE FORESTRY ROAD goes on and on, lodge pole pine and spruce to either side, now and then a clearing surrounded by chain-link fence. A pump jack, some pipes and valves, or a compressor station. No views of the mountains here. It might have been quicker to go up to Drayton Valley but my hands turned the car south toward Rocky Mountain House. One way or the other you have to backtrack once you've crossed the river. The reserve is only forty clicks as the crow flies. Three times that far to drive. And it's not easy driving, the last half, dirt road rutted from logging trucks. My car doesn't exactly have a lot of clearance. But then nor does Judy's boat of a Buick.

He. A 'he' who is only here until four today. I wasn't thinking of a 'he'.

The car jolts into a pothole and out again. They're getting deeper and more frequent. Hard to spot, too. No shadows under a gunmetal grey sky. Finally, the road branches. Five corrugated minutes later I'm outside Judy's trailer. *First house you'll come to on the right. The tidy one.* Looking across the road it's not hard to see what she means. There's an old van on blocks in her yard too but it's tucked behind a little shed. Otherwise the space around the house is clear. Smoke snakes up from the chimney in the middle of the trailer. The drive's already full of dented trucks and one sleek black rental car. The whole journey's been like this, my mind busy with details. Should I have brought Judy tobacco too? Today could be the day. I look down at my jeans. Clean enough. Angle the rear-view mirror so I can see my face. "This could be the day."

I knock on the flimsy aluminum storm door. The inner door opens and a blast of noise greets me. Judy waves me in. "Turn the volume down." She tries to yell but doesn't have the wind. I step right into the living room, every seat occupied by an array of dark-haired men, except for the Lay-Z Boy with the oxygen tank parked next to it. A couple of the men glance my way. Mostly they're staring at the screen. The room smells of cigarettes and aftershave and detergent and, under that, a slant of sage and sweet-grass.

The noise stops. Judy, standing by the TV with her sparse brown hair and round face, waits for the complaints to fade. "Leroy, Shawn, Paul,"—she gestures to the three young men squashed together on the chesterfield—"this is Meg. Meg, these are Danielle's brothers" —they all duck their heads—"and this is Roger, Danielle's uncle." Hair cropped so close it's almost shaved. Military? Fifty-ish. The rental car driver. He actually meets my eyes. "Meg ... well, why don't you explain?" She's looking at me.

What? Shit. Before I can start Paul says, "Turn the sound up, auntie. Come on." He's got the longest hair and the pudgiest face. I can see Danielle in him easily enough. When I look more closely, the other two have the same shaped faces. They all look bleary but I can't smell any booze.

"Nope," Judy says.

"Where's the frigging remote?"

"Go watch the game somewhere else."

"Yeah, where we can drink our frigging beer. Let's go."

They all heave up out of the chesterfield at the same time.

"Take your coat off," Judy says to me as they migrate to the door. "Have a seat. Want some tea? Coffee? Soda? You hungry?"

"No thanks. I'm good."

"See ya." The door closes behind the three younger men.

Judy collapses into her chair, her face grey. She reaches for the oxygen tube, fits it to her nose. There's something intimate and desperate in the way she inhales. I look away.

The uncle is a jowly man with a hooked nose, meaty arms. His eyes are on the screen. Men armoured like insects run around for two seconds then everything stops. It's not even hockey. It's American football.

"Roger," Judy says. Reluctantly he looks at her. "Meg might be your niece."

Brown eyes examine me for a moment then swing back to her. "Could be," he says.

"Your niece Theresa."

He doesn't react.

Theresa?

Judy looks at me. "Roger's brother Dan was Danielle's father. You're what, nineteen years older than Danielle?"

I nod.

"Dan was married to a woman called Lisa back then. They had a daughter who'd be your age now. Who nobody has seen since Dan and Lisa split up."

Roger's eyes have drifted back to the TV.

Theresa. For years I tried out names on myself. I'm not sure I ever thought of Theresa. Nothing in me answers. Not to the name, not to this man who seems as tightly stuffed as a sausage and about as warm as the day outside.

Judy's watching me.

"How long ago did they split up?" I ask.

"Roger?" Judy says.

The screens fills with the image of a bottle of Molson, sweating lightly.

He looks at Judy. "Got to be thirty years."

Thirty years ago I'd have been twelve. Give or take.

Roger's scratching his chin, a rasping noise that crowds my ears.

He snaps his fingers. "He got a job at the Luscar mine the year I joined the service. 1969."

"The mine in Cadomin?" I lean forward.

He nods. "They'd split up by then, him and Lisa. They had been living in Whitecourt. She and the kid moved to Winnipeg. That's what he said. He didn't keep that job long." He shakes his head, glances at me. "He never could settle to anything, Dan."

"He's dead?"

"Died five, six years ago."

"And you never saw the daughter again? What about her mother?"

"Never saw either of them again. Nobody did. No word, nothing."

"Do you have photographs of any of them?"

Roger shakes his head. "Dan looked a lot like me except not so handsome."

I try for a smile.

"Everyone called him Rabbit. On account of his eyes were kind of far apart."

Judy says, "He drove a truck for a while. Up and down to the States."

"That's what he was doing when he and Danielle's mother met?"

"They'd known each other their whole lives," Judy says. "But it's what he was doing when they got together. Jenny always said she preferred men who wouldn't clutter up her house and steal her booze." Judy sighs.

"Would she have a photograph of him?"

"If she did, Danielle has it now. She was all over everyone, Danielle was, when she first got here. Photos, stories, anything."

"Well," Roger says, glancing at his wrist.

Shit. "Before you go, can I write down some information?"

I get the pen and scrap paper I put in my jacket back at the farm. "So it was Daniel ... Laboucan?"

"Yes."

"When was he born?"

"October 24th. He was ten years older than me. 1936."

"Where?"

"Just up the road."

"And Lisa, were they actually married?"

He nods. "She got pregnant and they tied the knot. The way you did, those days. I was twelve, thirteen."

"So that would have been 1958, 1959? Do you remember her maiden name?"

He shakes his head. "Some Ukrainian name. They weren't best pleased with her, her family. Getting knocked up by an Indian."

"What did she look like?"

He eyes me. "Lot like you. Brown hair, wide face. You know." He looks at his watch again.

"What about their daughter? Theresa."

He shrugs. "She was just a kid."

"Did they have any other children?"

He shakes his head, stands up and holds out his hand. "Glad to meet you, Meg."

After a momentary manly grip he turns to Judy. "Don't get up. I'll let myself out."

Judy looks at me when we've both listened to his car drive away. "It could be," I say.

Judy waits. When I don't say anything else she says, "It could." "You met her? Theresa?"

"Dan was here a few times with Lisa and their girl. For the holidays. They liked to party. Everyone did. Dan and Roger's parents, they'd be leading the pack, eh? There was always a parcel of kids running wild. Theresa was one of them."

Things are colliding in my chest. I stand up. "I need to get something from the car."

When I come back in Judy's leaning back in her chair, inhaling oxygen. When she's done I hand her the photograph in its wooden frame. She looks at it and me and it again. Dad's squatting by the water's edge, head turned to face the camera. I'm standing in the rippling stream, eyes wide, about to freak.

"When was this taken?"

"Nineteen sixty nine. About nine months after I got there." I'm on the cusp of puberty in the photograph. My limbs have stretched, my face has lost some of its childish roundness, but I don't think I look that different.

Judy shakes her head. "I'm sorry. It's possible. But I can't swear to it. She was one in a parcel of kids. And I was heavy in my own addiction then." She hands me back the photograph.

I swallow. "The last anyone heard, they were in Winnipeg?"

"That's where they were headed. According to Dan." Judy takes another couple of drags of oxygen. "I didn't see Dan for years. He went off on quite a tear. Spent a bit of time in jail."

"What was he like?"

Judy purses her lips. "Nowadays," she says, after a pause, "you'd say he had FAS. You know what that is?"

I nod, seeing Joey with his buzz cut hair and prey animal eyes. "*Rabbit*," I say.

"Any little thing frustrated him, he got mad. He had a kind heart but ..." She shrugs.

Chapter Fifty Eight

TRAFFIC'S HEAVY INTO the city for a Friday night. I'll be twenty minutes late for the Alano Club meeting. Could just go home.

Val looks over as I walk in the door, nods. A few others smile hello but the room's crowded, faces I don't recognize. Getting a cup of coffee I see a cake in the kitchen, forest of candles waiting to be lit. A birthday meeting. Speaker's a black guy. Thick African accent. I don't remember what country. He was a Member of Parliament, the youngest ever elected. Came to Canada to get a PhD. Didn't know anybody. Nobody knew him. "I was a big man in my country. In Canada,"—he shakes his head—"you didn't understand how important I was." People laugh. "Inside,"—he pats his chest with a big hand—"I didn't feel like anybody. I wasn't good enough unless I was the best."

By the sound of it, if Dan and Lisa Laboucan were my progenitors, I scored a hundred on the genetic crapshoot for this disease. Dan and Lisa and their daughter Theresa.

Val comes over at the end. "Coffee?"

I hesitate but she's the closest thing I have to a sponsor these days.

"Talk to me, sistah. How goes the search?"

"I might have found them. My name might be Theresa Laboucan. Or not. It could just be a coincidence."

When I've told Val the story she stares down into the dregs of her coffee, turning the mug, coral fingernails against the white china.

"So you'll try to trace Theresa Laboucan? And the mother?"

I nod.

"Steve who goes to the Mustard Seed? He works in the reference section of the Public Library. Helps people with their genealogy research."

"This is sort of the opposite. If I find Theresa then I'm not her."

Val studies me. "There was a story I was going to tell you, but I'm not sure it applies anymore."

"Tell me anyway."

"You know I had a daughter, right? After I got sober I decided I had to find her. It became an obsession. I'd see her on the street. Follow her home. Realize at the last minute it wasn't her.

"It got to be all I cared about. Quit going to meetings. Good thing I had a sponsor who didn't give up on me. You know Beth C., right? She showed up at the shop when I quit returning her calls, said she'd make a scene if I didn't have lunch with her."

I nod, picturing Beth, built like a block of wood, hair sprouting from the mole on her lip, trademark grey sweatpants, in the middle of the swank Glenora boutique.

"She got me talking. 'I have to know,' I said. 'I have to.'

"She raised her hand, looked at me long and steady. 'You want to,' she said. 'The only thing you have to do is not pick up a drink or a drug today.'

"I opened my mouth to argue but she just kept looking at me." Val shrugs. "The fight went out of me. I knew it was true. I want to know. I still want to know. I pray one day I will know. But I don't have to."

I look at her smooth oval face, the *eau de nil* turtleneck, wool like a warm cloud, long gold earrings showing off her elegant neck. I make myself meet her eyes again. She doesn't look away, and I can't.

I tremble at the bareness of it. She's sitting there, so beautifully put together, sitting with that terrible naked wanting, letting it be. Letting me see.

"I don't ..."

Her eyes shift. I must have said the words out loud.

"I don't know if I want to know. I'm ..." I stall out.

She waits.

"It could be just another place I don't belong."

She nods. "I've thought about it a lot from my daughter's point of view. If the family she grew up in was a happy one, perhaps she wouldn't want to find me."

"Oh Val, I'm sorry."

"It's okay. For today. Every day I turn it over. Every day I live my blessed life. And every night I thank my Creator for life exactly as it is."

Chapter Fifty Nine

ON THE FAR side of the dome the little white ball dribbles away from the net. Joey and Janice are playing. He must have blown his pass privileges. She would have, if she'd had any to lose.

Back at the desk, Jay is entering a room check in the log. "Quiet, eh?" she says, looking up at me. "Tanya's coming in at five."

"How's her mother?"

"She stopped eating. Her kidneys are failing."

"So why's Tanya coming into work?"

"Brenda refused to give her any more time off."

"To look after her dying mother?"

"According to Cathy."

"I don't suppose Cathy's standing up for us?"

"What do you think? She says Tanya has to apply for compassionate leave. Like anything's ever been that formal here. She also told Tanya they want to make the evening shifts into full-time positions."

"Make this a regular job?"

"Sick days. The whole nine yards. So they can recruit a 'better calibre of staff.'"

"They haven't mentioned this to any of us."

Jay shrugs. "Tanya figures Brenda's looking for an excuse to fire her. I told her, 'You go, I go.'"

The phone rings. Jay swivels the chair, reaches for the receiver.

"Doug, how you doing? ... Okay, okay .... Anyone call Cathy?"

She laughs, "Isn't that the way?" She hangs up, looks at me. "Tanya's mother's gone into a coma. Doug's got the girls so he can't come in. Heather's away for the weekend."

"Did anyone call Cathy?"

"Nope. You want to?"

"Not much."

"She'd come in for the evening."

"Sighing mightily." At this exact moment the idea of being in the office with Cathy makes me want to scream. "There's Laura."

"There is Laura." Jay's using her perfectly neutral voice.

The door dings again.

It's Shannon and Warren and a couple of others festooned with plastic bags. There's not much in the bags. A box of tissues, a pack of smokes, an undershirt.

"Have a good time?" Jay asks.

Warren actually looks at her and nods.

Shannon says, "We met Ash downtown. She's clean. Harry's going to help her reapply."

"That's great."

"Theresa's been taking her to meetings. She's got a job at the Friendship Centre."

"Theresa does?"

Shannon nods. "She got a place. We can stay there when we get out." She glances sideways at Warren. He almost smiles.

"And James?" Jay asks.

Shannon looks away.

Warren says, "His girlfriend kicked him out."

"Because he used?"

As they head off down the corridor I say, "Shit. I guess it's not really a surprise but shit anyway."

"He was doing it for his girlfriend, eh? But Ash, that's good. And Theresa, working at the Friendship Centre."

Theresa, Theresa, Theresa. The name ought to ring some kind of bell, oughtn't it?

The door alarm chirps again. Jay glances over then she's on her feet, a single fluid motion. I wonder suddenly if she studies some kind of martial art. "Ready for this?" she murmurs.

Don and Danielle come in together, Don swinging his truck keys. It's not him, it's Danielle.

"Come on back, guys, one at a time," Jay says.

I stay on the desk, call to Danielle as she starts to slip off toward the bedrooms, "Hold on Danielle, we've got to check you out."

"I need to use the washroom."

"Use the one out here, please."

She doesn't look at me as she crosses the open area in front of the desk. I don't catch a whiff of anything but there's something different about her.

In the office Jay checks the bags of snacks and new clothes Don brought back, logs in his cell phone and keys, puts them in the safe, all the while chatting about his day.

When she joins me at the front desk I tip my chin toward the washroom door. "She's been in there a while."

"She take her bags in?"

"She wasn't carrying anything."

The washroom door opens.

"Come on back," Jay calls, her tone light.

Danielle keeps her head turned away from me as she comes through the gate.

Jay's standing just inside the office. "How was your day?"

"I don't want to talk about it." Her lips clamp shut.

I come back to join them, Danielle still avoiding my eyes. Then I catch it, under the toothpaste, the rank, familiar tang.

"So Danielle," Jay says slowly, "did you pick up today?"

"No."

"Sit down."

Jay does, I do. After a minute Danielle does too.

"Thing is, I can smell it, the booze. And you don't look yourself."

Danielle huddles, a bird cornered by two cats. Any moment she'll break into fluttering, panicked protestations.

She doesn't, so we sit there.

Eventually Jay says, "Come on, Danielle. You know the rules. You can reapply in thirty days."

"I didn't."

We sit some more. I remember being fifteen, principal badgering me about being high. Demanding I tell him. 'You're lying. You're lying. Admit it.' The hate that twisted in me. Cornered. Humiliated. Because of course I was lying and he knew it and I knew it and the only thing I had going was to keep lying which I did until he gave up. It didn't feel like winning.

It isn't in Jay, that desire to humiliate. Which is probably why, after a while, Danielle starts to cry. "I had a really shitty day," she says so low we both have to lean in. The door alarm beeps. I go up front, shutting the door behind me. I check out the next two clients' bags on the bench by the desk. They look at the office door. It's almost never shut.

When it opens again, Jay comes out first. "Danielle is calling her aunt," she says.

I nod, flip open the medication binder, begin the paperwork. My heart is thudding.

Danielle, her back to us, talks into the phone. Then she turns, holds out the phone to me. "She doesn't want to talk to me. She wants to talk to you."

I shake my head. "I can't speak with her right now."

Danielle keeps on holding the phone out to me. I keep not taking it. I can hear Judy's voice. "Hello. Hello." Finally Danielle says, "She won't talk to you," into the receiver. She turns away again.

I can't hear Judy's reply. Nor can Jay but I feel her eyes on me. I keep on looking at Danielle's back.

After another minute the receiver slams down. "'Call her when I'm sober.'" Danielle's looking at me. "I thought she cared."

"Hard-line," Jay says. "We'll call a cab."

"Where am I going to go?" Danielle starts crying.

"Should have thought of that before you picked up," Jay says. "You know the rules. Use and you're out for thirty days. Then you can come back, try again." Her voice softens. "Lots of people don't make it the first time."

Danielle just shakes her head, fat tears rolling down her cheeks. "I'm such a fucking loser. Why did I ever think I could be any better?"

"I'm calling a cab now," Jay says. "Meg, will you help Danielle pack her things?" She gives me a long look.

When half the plastic garbage bags are stuffed with clothes, Danielle slumps down on the bed and begins to sob. "Nobody cares," she says, between sobs. "Why should they? Even if you are my sister why would you want to have anything to do with me? I'm such a fucking loser. Oh, what am I going to do now?"

I can hear the booze in her voice, feel the bit of her that's watching to see what effect she's having. I know better but I say, "What happened out there, Danielle? After all you've been through?" I sit down on the other bed.

"I'm just a fucking fuck up. A no good fucking loser like the rest of my fucking family except they're just poor drunk Indians on some no hope reserve in the ass end of anywhere. I'm a fucking whore. That's what I am. A piece of ass."

"*Poor me, poor me, pour me a drink.*" Danielle stares at me. "You're no better and no worse than a thousand other drunks."

She's stopped crying. "You wanna know what happened?"

"Yes."

"I'm pregnant."

"What?"

"I did two tests."

"How? How did you get pregnant?" I stop. Stupid question.

She's staring at the piles of clothes on the bed, the shoe-stuffed sack on the floor by her feet. Then she looks straight at me. "Okay, I'll tell you." Suddenly she doesn't sound drunk. "One last trick, before I came in. So I'd have some money. He paid extra, doing it without a rubber. I quit taking the pill in jail. I was changing my life. Now look what's happened. I got what I deserved."

I don't know what to say, and then I do. "You think God's punishing you."

She nods, just a small nod but definite.

"You think God would create a life as a way to punish someone?"

At last she shakes her head.

I take a deep breath. "And last weekend, when you said you saw your aunt?"

Danielle looks away. "I called him up," she mutters.

I wait but she doesn't say anything else. I stand up. "Keep packing. I'll be back in a few minutes."

Jay's just finishing up with Mona and Geoffrey. They look uneasy even though they can't have heard yet. As they stalk off toward the bedrooms Jay turns to look at me.

"She's pregnant."

Jay's eyebrows go up.

"Pocket money for rehab," I say. "What are the rules?"

Jay studies me. After a moment she says, "Any pregnant woman who applies gets the first bed that opens up."

"And the thirty day waiting period?"

"Doesn't apply. She found out today?"

I nod.

"Who's her counsellor?"

"Angela."

"Hard-ass. We could let her have her beauty sleep."

"Make the decision ourselves?"

"Or call our supervisor."

I reach for the phone.

"Call the cab company first," Jay says.

"I thought they'd be here by now."

"I told them an hour. Remembered how much shit she brought with her."

Julie and Deborah come in as I'm hanging up. Jay looks at me, one eyebrow raised. "No reply. I asked her to call. Urgent but not an emergency."

"Guess we'll decide. Do you want to tell her?" Jay asks.

"I think you should."

Jay studies me a moment then nods. Almost smiles.

"Hi Julie," I say. "How was your day?"

As Julie's headed down the corridor Jay and Danielle appear, walking toward us. Danielle doesn't look at Julie as they pass each other. When they get to the desk Jay clicks open the gate. "Go on in," she says. She looks at me. "One of us needs to stay with her until she sobers up."

Chapter Sixty

"COFFEE?"

"You don't like me, do you? Thing is, I love you, Meg. Like a sister. You're my sister under the skin, you know?"

Soulful eyes search mine. She seems to be getting more drunk, not less.

"Did you take anything beside booze, Danielle?"

She shakes her head. Her face has that smudged look.

"I'm pregnant. I told you that. You're going to be an aunt."

I look at the cross around her neck, the pale puffy skin. Kudzu accent looping around me.

"You don't want me to be your sister. You don't want some fucked up whore to be your sister." She giggles. "Not proper Meg. You got a stick up your ass, you know that? You and Judy both."

"Drink your coffee."

"Don't want it."

She shoves the mug away, slopping some. We both watch the puddle of black liquid spread across the vinyl surface.

"Are you going to clean up your own mess or are you waiting for someone to do it for you?"

"Sorry," she mutters, reaching for the box of tissues.

"Here." I reach back for the roll of paper towels by the coffee maker.

Meticulously she blots the coffee then drops the sodden paper towel in the waste basket only she misses it. "Shi-it." She starts to laugh. "I'm fucked up. I blew it." She's crying. "I stayed sober in frigging jail. On the frigging reserve. Came to treatment an' I got drunk."

The door opens. Jay's head appears. "How's it going?"

"It's going," I say.

Danielle opens her mouth but Jay's head is gone.

"Coffee," I say.

"I want to go to my room."

"Well, you can't, not until you've sobered up."

"Why not?"

"It's not fair to your roommate."

"Julie wouldn't …" She stops and her eyes fill with tears. "Julie likes me. You don't want to be my sister. You don't want a whore for a sister. And now I've got a baby growing in me, a baby with a john for a father. A skinny guy with a comb over and a wife and three kids and a little dick. What am I going to tell her? What am I going to tell my baby?" She's looking at me, red-eyed, beseeching. "I'm going to have a baby." Then she's sobbing.

"Whoa, whoa. One day at a time. Come on, breathe. Keep breathing."

The sobbing stops. She reaches for a tissue.

"You have some options but right now all you have to do is sober up."

"I'm not killing my baby. That's what you mean by options but I'm not killing my baby. I can't kill my baby." Her voice has risen to a wail.

"Danielle, listen to me. Nobody's going to make you have an abortion. Nobody's going to make you do anything you don't agree to."

The office door opens again. Jay collects the basket of sarongs then we hear her voice announcing ceremony.

"Where'm I going to live?"

Tell me she's not looking at me hopefully.

There's a clatter outside then voices.

"Fuck you." The words are loud even inside the office.

"Stay here." I open the office door. Jay's disappearing round the side of the dome.

"Come on Mona darlin', the beast is showing." Geoffrey's voice.

A grunt then a chair falls over.

As I round the dome Jay is saying, "You want me to call the RCMP? You'll both be in remand." She snaps her fingers.

They're in the cafeteria, Mona and Janice, facing each other, three feet apart, Mona's face bright red, Janice's eyes small and squinty as a pissed off bear. They're both breathing hard. Jay's blocking the doorway, arms spread out, a cluster of clients on this side of her but there are more clients already in the cafeteria.

"Chief," Jay says. "Council."

Eleanor and Don come forward.

"Stand here, please. Don't let anybody else go in."

She turns, sees me. "Where's Danielle?"

"In the office."

"Shit. Come with me."

Back behind the desk she pulls down the metal gate that covers the meds cupboard.

"Danielle, go back to your room and stay there. Meg, lock the office, call the RCMP then find me."

"Come on, Danielle."

Jay's already on her way back to the cafeteria.

"Wha's happening."

"Your room, now."

"Okay, okay. Don't get your panties in a wad." She snickers. "Tha's Canadian for knickers in a twist."

"Go, now, please."

I've dialled the number by the time she's lumbering down the corridor.

"A disturbance?"

"At Dreamcatcher Lodge. Two clients on probation."

"Civic address?"

My mind goes blank. "Outside Stony Plain." Fuck. I'm staring around. There's another crash from the cafeteria then I remember, flip to the front of the log book, read it out to her.

"How long?" I ask.

"Officers will be there as soon as possible. Please stand by in case they have questions."

"Sorry," I say. "Got to go."

In the cafeteria chairs and tables have been shoved aside. Peering between clients' shoulders I see Janice and Mona circling each other, knees bent, arms wide. They've each got something in their right hands. Something that glints. Jesus.

"Excuse me. Excuse me." I get in closer to the doorway which Jay is occupying again, both arms spread out. "Hey Jay," I say, loud and clear, "the RCMP are on their way."

Janice shows no sign of hearing me but Mona's eyes flicker.

"You hear that? You'll both be spending the night in jail if you don't step back and drop the knives," Jay says.

"We're fucked already," Mona says. She darts forward but Janice is faster than she looks. She steps sideways and then she's behind Mona, an arm wrapping around her throat. Mona's kicking and flailing but Janice's forearm is against her throat. She's lifting her off her feet. Mona's gasping.

"Oh Jesus," voice behind me. "Do something. Fuck man."

Somebody pushes past me, ducks under Jay's arm. Warren. He's behind Janice. He swivels away from her, snaps out some kind of karate kick. It hits her back low down, off to the side.

Janice screams, drops Mona, falls to her knees, gagging.

"Mona, get over here." Jay barks. "Warren, that's enough."

"Everybody back," I say. "Come on, move it."

"Chief, council, help us. Everyone to your rooms, now. Warren ..."

"Fucking cops," somebody says, then I hear it too, the siren.

"Mona," I say, "come to the office." I take the knife from her. It was just one of the regular cafeteria knives

Jay scoops up the other. Janice is still kneeling, shaking her head from side to side.

Warren follows Mona and me toward the office.

"Good job, man," Joey says.

The door alarm sounds. As we round the dome I see two Mounties walking toward the desk, heads swivelling.

"The fight's broken up," I say. "Hold on. I'll get ..." My voice trails off. "What do you need from us?"

"I don't want a baby. I don't want a baby."

Breathe. Fuck. "Time to pray," I say. "Ask for help. You don't have to do this alone."

Fresh tears spill down the freckled puffy cheeks but then she sits up straighter on the bed, bows her head and presses her hands together. Her lips move. Jesus, she looks like a pudgy little six-year-old. I look away. "God. Creator. Whatever, help Danielle. Help her baby. Help Janice and Mona."

"Amen."

I open my eyes.

Danielle's gazing at me. "Thank you. I forgot. That's what I have to do. I have to pray. I have to keep praying. When I'm praying I feel okay, you know? Like ... like I'm not ..." Tears well up.

"Keep praying," I say. I could say, 'Jesus died for your sins.' I could say, 'You're forgiven. Washed in the blood of the Lamb'. God knows, I know the rap. If there is a God, He or She has a hell of a sense of humour.

There's a knock on the door. "It's Julie. Can I come in?"

I get up and open the door.

"Jay told me," Julie says, looking at Danielle. Her voice has the smoker's rasp but it's gentle.

Danielle's eyes fill with tears. "I'm sorry. I let everybody down." I wait for her to slide down into the morass again but she doesn't. She just looks at Julie.

"It's a bastard," Julie says, "this disease."

Jay's voice crackles over the speakers in the hall. "Ceremony. It's time for ceremony."

"Is it okay," Julie asks, "if Danielle and I stay here?"

"Yes. Come to the desk if you need anything."

The phone is ringing. Jay picks it up, mouths "Cathy" to me and goes into the office. I haul out sarongs, collect glasses and jewellery.

Jay emerges as the blanket closes behind the last client. "Danielle in there?"

"No. I gave Julie permission to stay with her in their room. Danielle's calmed down but I figured she shouldn't be alone. The Mounties took Mona and Janice?"

"They didn't want to but what the fuck were we going to do with them? More to the point, what was Harold going to do with them overnight? Counsellors will talk to their probation officers tomorrow. I laid it all out for Cathy. We're cool on the Danielle decision but the rest ..." she shrugs. "Cathy was hot and bothered about Tanya. I think she knows Brenda is going to use this."

Chapter Sixty One

THE PHONE JOLTS me awake. A dream slips away. I grope across the bedside table.

"Meg?"

Shit. I struggle upright. "Hello Judy."

"Where is she?"

"Danielle? I really can't ..."

"What happened? I haven't slept a wink ..."

She breaks off. The coughing jag gives me a chance to swing my feet out of bed, scrape the sleep from my eyes.

"I've got to have boundaries. I know I've got to have boundaries but ..." I can hear her gulping, trying not to cry. "I know the Creator will look after her but I have to know where she is."

"Judy, the reason I can't answer questions about Danielle is because of client confidentiality."

"You're her sister."

"I might be her sister. But think about what I just said."

There's a silence then Judy says, "Oh. You mean she's still ... if I call Dreamcatcher, ask to speak to her ..."

"Or leave a message."

"She'll call me back?"

"That'll be up to her."

"Will you see her? Can you tell her I ... I'm concerned about her?"

"It would really be better if you called."

"How come she's still there? She drank, right?"

"You'll have to ask her about that."

There's a silence. Then Judy says, "There are no coincidences, eh? You coming to work at Dreamcatcher right when Danielle's there. I was mad at her for giving you my number but hey, Creator's got His plans for us."

Well. Here it is on a plate. "Judy. I have a confession. I lied to you. Danielle didn't give me your number."

"Where did you get it then?"

"From her file."

"And you had the nerve just now to come over all hoity toity about confidentiality."

After a moment I say, "I'm sorry."

There's a pause. "She knows you've been in touch with me, right?"

"No."

"What's the big secret?"

Judy and Laura should team up. Throw in Tanya too. No avoiding confrontation here.

"I don't know why I haven't told her. I should have."

"And now ..."

"I'd prefer to check out this Theresa Laboucan first. I don't want to get Danielle's hopes up."

"Is that the real reason?"

"I don't know."

"*The truth will set you free. John 8.32.*"

"Meaning I need to tell her now?"

Silence, then Judy says, "I'm not going to lie if the topic comes up but I won't bring it up. Not in the next week."

"Thank you."

I hang up, shower away the reek of stale adrenaline, make coffee. While it's brewing I check on the bread I started last night. The dough's doubled in volume, dimpled and puffy. Danielle's tear-stained face. Danielle, belly expanding, waddling down the street.

I spread my hands on the surface of the dough. Press it back down. Sprinkle flour on the counter, scrape out the bowl. I fold and knead and fold, knuckling into the bread flesh. Flash of Warren executing his kick.

The phone rings again. The phone never rings. I scrape dough off one hand.

"Hello?"

"Meg?" A guy. Manfred? "It's Doug."

"Oh." Sag of relief.

"Bad time?"

"No. No. Hold on."

Hands clean, coffee poured, I pick up the phone again. "Hi. Sorry. I was making bread."

"Want me to call back?"

"No." It comes out too strongly. Christ.

"I just thought I'd call, see how you were doing. I heard you had a pretty intense night, you and Jay."

"You could put it that way."

"You okay?"

There's real concern in his voice. "I don't know. Truth is, I'm pretty useless when push comes to shove. Jay, she snapped into action. I get sort of paralyzed."

"The way I heard it, you did really well."

"I did?"

"Coming in, saying good and loud the Mounties were coming. Keeping Danielle out of the picture."

"Oh." My voice sounds small. Pathetic, really. Doug doesn't say anything. It's a comfortable sort of silence. Leaving me room to say whatever I need to say. "It's weird," I say at last. "Since last Monday. There's so much happening all at once. Like I warped into some other dimension. I don't know if I'm having a spiritual experience or a nervous breakdown." That's supposed to be a joke but it doesn't come out that way.

"Want to have lunch?" Doug asks. "Take a walk after? I'm dropping the girls off at their other grandmother's. Plus I scoped out a Guatemalan restaurant."

Chapter Sixty Two

IT'S IN THE rough end of Chinatown which isn't the best of neighbourhoods to begin with, a hole in the wall restaurant with six small tables and one long one. A pink and green hand-woven cloth spans the back of the restaurant over the cash register. Beyond the register an open doorway gives a glimpse of a home-size gas range and a battered wooden table.

"For one?" A woman appears in the doorway, wiping her hands, dark hair pulled back in a pony tail, a roundish face, tired eyes.

"For two, please."

I choose the table closest to the kitchen, and the chair with a view of the door. She sets two menus on the table.

"You have eat Guatemala food before?"

I shake my head. The door opens and Doug walks in. I nod in his direction. "He might have."

"*Buenos dias*," he says to the woman and her face lights up. A volley of Spanish follows. Doug replies, smiling at her and then at me, pulling out the chair across from me. "Shall I order?"

"Yes please."

He and the woman enter into a discussion long enough for me to study her face. She reminds me of something. After a minute the image floats to the surface: a pottery mask or was it a jug? Pre-Columbian. Mayan. The lips and eyelids pinched so they're prominent. The poster for an exhibition at a museum in Vancouver. We were supposed to go see it as part of an anthropology class.

Doug and the woman whose name is Irena wind up their conversation. She bustles off to the kitchen.

"I think you made somebody's day."

"Imagine coming to Edmonton from Central America. Never hearing your language spoken. Hardly ever, anyway."

"Where did you learn Spanish?"

"New Mexico. The communes were mostly near the old Spanish villages."

Irena comes back with a stack of warm tortillas and a small jug. "Salsa," she says, setting down the jug. "Guatemala salsa. I make tortillas fresh." She claps her hands lightly and I can picture the discs of dough she's shaping. I nod and she smiles at me. It's like the smell of fresh corn, the kindness she exudes. Doug is smiling too. Spanish flows around me again. I don't mind that I don't understand.

The tortillas are sweet and earthy dipped in the thin tomato-y sauce, now and then a flicker of charred flour. "I'm not sure I've ever tasted anything that has so much of the feel of the hands that made it," I say.

Doug nods, his lips curving up.

Irena appears with more food, setting the dishes down between us with a flourish. *"Mas salsa*, yes?"

We hardly talk, biting through crisp fried crust to mild melted cheese, unwrapping banana leaves to inhale the steamed starchiness of corn and pork.

Behind Doug, beyond the plate glass window, wind whisks grit and garbage down the avenue. Across the way a line is forming. The soup kitchen at the Native Church. The men, it's mostly men, hunch against the cold. I glance back at Doug. He's sitting there, smiling. "You're good at enjoying things," I say. I didn't mean to say it aloud.

"You are too."

"Am I? Yes, maybe. I learned that from Dad."

"How is he?"

"He's good. How about your daughters?"

"They're okay. The grandmother they're staying with is great. Her son—the girls' father—is a piece of work. So was their grandfather, by the sound of it, but she's tough as moose hide, funny, loving. She's been through everything—residential school, the whole nine yards—but she's like an ancient tree. She grew where she had to, to get the light. Crooked, twisted, big crack in the trunk but her roots go deep enough to hold her steady."

He nudges the tortilla basket my way. I shake my head. He takes the last one, tearing off pieces to wipe up the juices on his plate.

After a while I say, "You were going to tell me about getting sober."

"I will but I want to hear about last night. I know the bare bones."

Irena appears. "It was good?" She's smiling.

Doug and I both wave our hands at the table. There's not a scrap of food left.

"Dessert? Coffee?"

"*Dos cafés, por favor.*"

Doug looks at me. I nod.

When Irena's taken our plates I say, "Jay was great but it was Warren who saved the day. Karate kick to Janice's kidney stopped her in her tracks. Which could have gotten him sent back to prison if things had gone bad. But they didn't." I shrug. "I think we were all lucky."

"Including Danielle," Doug says.

"If getting pregnant by a john counts as lucky."

He raises his eyebrows. "I didn't know that detail."

"She wants to keep the baby."

"She's got an aunt, right? On one of the reserves."

"Firestick."

Something in my voice makes Doug look at me.

After a moment I say, "I've gotten into a mess. Jay thinks they'll use last night to fire Tanya. But I'm the one who should get fired." I tell him about the phone number and Judy and the reserve and Danielle's uncle and Danielle drunk saying I don't want to be her sister and Judy on the phone last night wanting to talk to me and Judy on the phone this morning.

Somewhere in the middle of that Irena brought the coffee. When I'm done he puts his cup down.

"So you drove out to the reserve."

"On Friday."

"And met all these possible relatives. How was that?"

I shrug.

He waits.

Finally I say, "I shut down last night. Danielle, drunk, crying about me not wanting to be her sister. I don't know. I don't know if I am. If I want to be. I don't see how I'm going to know. I thought I would just know. By instinct. But, shit. How am I ever going to know?"

"Do you want to?"

"Yes." The word comes out as if I've been holding my breath.

"I know a bit about finding people. Would you like my help?"

"Yes. Please."

"So tell me if I've got this right: Danielle's father's name is Daniel Laboucan. He and his wife Lisa had a daughter your age who disappeared from sight when she was twelve."

"Eleven or twelve."

"He was a Cree man born on the Firestick reserve in …"

"October, 1936."

"Who died about five or six years ago. What did he do for a living?"

"He was a trucker. Before that he worked at the Luscar mine."

"When?"

"When it first opened."

"In 1969. You know where that is?" Doug asks. His voice is different.

"On the way to the Cardinal Divide. Where we went every summer, growing up."

"When was the last time you were there?"

"Five years ago."

"Did you ever go to the general store in Cadomin?"

"Every time we went." I feel like I'm being grilled. "What are you getting at?"

"Hubert's got photographs of just about everybody who lived or worked in the area."

"On the walls." I remember Mum and Dad and me reading bits of newspaper clippings, waiting for our sandwiches.

"He's still going strong. Well, maybe not strong but his memory is good. He can put a name to every face."

"You think ...?"

Doug shrugs. "Want to take a ride up there sometime soon?"

"Yes." I look at him. "What's your connection to the Divide?"

"More coffee?"

"Let's take our walk. I'll make coffee at my place after, if you don't mind. I've got bread rising."

Chapter Sixty Three

WE'RE DOWN BELOW the Capillano, out of the wind. Traffic rumbles overhead. The stand of willows tugs at me. "I think I dreamed about this place last night. This is where my father cut off his hair. Her hair. Where she became he."

"This exact place?"

"In the dream." He waits but words are far away.

"A birthplace," he murmurs, hands stuffed in the pockets of his canvas jacket. "And a death place, I suppose."

We walk on toward the other bridge. Strangeness washes over me. I'm moving slowly, Doug matching his pace to mine. To my right I see a familiar gnawed stump. "Beavers live in that lodge." My voice feels rusty but it sounds okay.

Doug's eyes scan the river then settle on the dome of the lodge where it bulges out from the bank. He stands there in his jeans and his soft paw boots, dun coloured hair hiding most of his face, just looking. Somehow he's familiar. I don't know much about his life but I know him. He's quiet and strong and he's not afraid. He's not afraid of losing himself.

"They're making a comeback," he says. We start walking again. "After being trapped almost to extinction. By my people, among others. You ever thought what the fur trade meant to the animals? Before, people took pretty much what they needed, a few extra to trade. Then the Europeans came. It was like some monster on the far side of the ocean opened its maw."

He shivers. I'm cold too.

When I lift the lid off the cast iron casserole, the blast of heat makes me look away. The moment the dough touches the hot metal it puffs up. I slip the lid back on.

"Smells good already." Doug leans back on the chesterfield, stretching his legs and feet out. Thick blue wool socks meticulously darned in brown on one toe.

"Wonders of technology. I set the oven to come on half an hour ago. Here's more of the same." I point the remote at the gas fireplace. Blue flame flickers around the fake logs. "So are you going to tell me your story?"

"You wouldn't rather tell me what you meant when you said you weren't sure if you were having a spiritual experience or a nervous breakdown?"

"You have a frighteningly good memory. Later. I want your basic *What it was like, what happened, what it's like now.*"

"Okay. I was born in the Royal Alex, grew up where I live now. My folks were good people but anxious, controlling. Turns out both of my grandfathers were alcoholics. My parents went the other direction. With an extra layer of shame. The drunk Indian thing. They turned their backs on their heritage. My mother didn't have an easy time having babies. There were five years and two miscarriages between me and my brother. After he was born they took out her womb. So there we were, Douglas and Bernard and a whole lot of expectations. In a way they were like the cliché of immigrant parents, willing to sacrifice so their children could make it in the new country. We were about to be a disappointment, both of us. Not at first. We were good little Catholics. But I never felt like I fit in. First time I drank a couple of beers I felt good. Comfortable in my own skin. This is what normal feels like, I thought. You've heard that a thousand times."

I nod. It's in almost every AA story I ever heard. Though I figure if you're gay it has some extra punch.

"I didn't care for school. Seemed like everybody wanted to tell me what to do and who to be, but the times, they were a-changin'. I told you that bit, me and Bobby McGee hitching out of town. I spent seven years in the U.S. I did come back to see my folks a couple of times, say hi to my brother who was going through his own rebellion. Only in his case he looked far more Native than anyone else in the family so he was getting that shit too." Doug looks at the clock on the mantle but he's not really looking at it. He hunches his shoulders then relaxes them. "I was young and selfish. Full of all sorts of ideals but the more I drank and got high the more it was all about me. Right from the start I could drink men twice my size under the table. Though I was always susceptible to drugs. Didn't care for downers, loved hallucinogens, came to lean on weed as much as booze.

"I had a few relationships but mostly I prided myself on being a free spirit which meant if you got anywhere close to anything vulnerable in me, I was gone. In a VW bus with a cracked head. Travelled all over the Southwest, commune to commune. The Tokin' Red Man. A legend in my own mind."

I smile but it's a joke I've heard before. Somehow I'm not getting much of a feel for who Doug was.

"That's how it went for most of the time I was in the U.S." His eyes stray to the clock. "I told you about the draft dodgers and the deserters. I got pretty involved, finding new identities for people. I travelled around, looking for the places with separate birth and death registries. Even cut my hair. Got all duded up. I liked being undercover. I felt important." He shrugs. "I don't mean it was all an ego trip. I believed in the peace movement. And I wanted to connect to my roots. I read Black Elk, I talked to elders on the reserves. Did a Sun Dance, sweat lodges. Even sniffed around the edge of A.I.M. but they scared me. I was raised to be a middle-class white boy, you know? The real activists, the people who made stuff happen, they didn't have a lot of time for me." He shrugs. "They were right. By the end it was all about getting high."

There's something he's not saying. About being gay? A long, charred log he's carrying, cradled to his chest. It's almost more than he can carry. I've never seen him like this. He's always seemed so steady. Except that time with Geoffrey. And after the two spirit talk.

"What time do you have to head out?" he asks.

"Soon as I take the bread out."

"I'd better be on my way."

"Is everything all right?"

"Yes."

"You are going to tell me the rest of the story?"

"On the way to Cadomin?" His eyes crinkle and he looks like himself again.

WEEK SIX

Chapter Sixty Four

THY WILL BE *done on earth, as it is in heaven.*

Hai hai drowns out *Amen.*

Laura's rounding up the flock, driving them out the door. Where they scatter, grazing on cigarettes, chatting and laughing. Her eyes flick about. She'd rather they were closer together.

The bus pulls up. Laura boards first.

Danielle sidles up to me. "Can I sit with you?"

"Sure. Why don't you grab the front seat? I'll join you in a minute."

"Thanks for bringing them," Vince says. "I pray for them, every one of them." His battered Marlon Brando face breaks into a smile. "And it's always good to see you, Meg. Don't be a stranger."

I do the roll call then drop into the seat next to Danielle. There are the usual catcalls when we pass the Beverly Motel. She stares down at her knees.

"What's up?"

She shakes her head but then she says, "I wish I could cut her out. Cut her out of me."

"Who?"

"The one who ..." She lifts her chin at the motel.

"Oh."

"Not my baby." She turns frightened brown eyes on me. "It's me. I'm …" She shrugs, tears filling her eyes.

"She's you, Danielle, but she's only part of you, a part that was scared and didn't know what to do."

"No, Meg." Her eyes are suddenly fierce. "A part of me that likes nice clothes and expensive food more than virtue, more than decency. That likes money more than God."

"Don't you think you're being a little hard on yourself?"

"If I ever forget to feel ashamed, I'll be right back out there, peddling my ass."

"Danielle, come on, we all make mistakes. That's what the 8th and 9th Steps are all about. Making amends to the people we hurt. Including ourselves."

Led Zeppelin's *Stairway to Heaven* is playing. The driver hasn't turned the volume down yet though the bus is quiet now, all but the back seat. I hear Laura's bark of a laugh. Twisting in my seat I see there's only Deborah in the seat behind us and she's snoring.

"As a matter of fact," I say, "I need to make an amends to you myself."

Danielle turns to look at me, puzzled.

"I took your aunt's phone number from the information in your folder."

She looks confused. "I told you I needed to get permission from her."

"I'd already taken the number and called her when I asked you for it. I was trying to cover my ass."

"Oh."

"But that's not all. When she asked where I got her number, I told her you gave it to me."

"Oh boy. Guess she was pleased."

"Probably not but I have set the record straight with her."

"You've been talking to her?"

"Yes."

"That's how come she wanted to talk to you the night I … the night that I slipped. Why did you want to talk to her?"

The eagerness in her voice makes my chest ache.

"To see if I might have come from Firestick originally. She agreed to ask around then the other day she invited me to meet your uncle Roger."

"That prick."

"Why do you say that?"

"Oh, he tried to grope me in the john about two weeks after I got to the reserve."

"Ah, well, I didn't exactly warm to him myself. But it was useful to meet him. He says years before you were born, your father was married to a woman called Lisa. They had a daughter named Theresa who would be my age."

"Theresa," Danielle says. "Theresa."

"Judy thought you might have a photograph of her."

She shakes her head. "I never heard tell of my father being married before. Didn't sound like he was the marrying kind. He was a bad alcoholic, that's what I heard. His car broke down one night just before Christmas a few years back. They found him a couple days later three, four miles away in the middle of a field under a pump jack, frozen stiff as a stick of firewood." She shrugs. "I hope your mother was better than mine. Lisa. Lisa what?"

"I don't know if she is my mother."

"We'd be half-sisters, right? We'd have the same last name."

"Danielle, this is a long shot. I don't have much to go on. But I'll try to find out."

She looks at me, earnest brown eyes, tear-stained freckles. "I forgive you, Meg. My sister. I hope. Thank you for telling me about the number."

Chapter Sixty Five

"THEY'RE LIKE HENS pecking up the old sun. I've always liked pump jacks. I know I shouldn't but ..."

"They're human scale," Doug says, "plus they look like something a clever engineer in ancient Egypt might have come up with. And they do have that chicken rhythm."

"Sort of stately and funny. Walking and bobbing their heads at the same time." I gaze out at the wide November fields, flat as far as you can see. I'm so used to driving this road myself, it's pleasant to be a passenger, Doug's big knuckled hands resting on the wheel.

I glance over at him. "Danielle told me that her father froze to death under a pump jack, in the middle of a field."

"Car broke down and he started walking?"

"Drunk, most likely."

"Did you tell her about Judy?"

"On the bus coming back from the Beverly meeting. She was very forgiving."

A truck is barrelling toward us, double trailer stacked high with logs. Doug pulls over tight to the shoulder. The truck blasts pasts, tires on the centre line.

"Arsehole," I say.

Doug just shakes his head. "Go on."

"Judy, Danielle's mother's sister, is on a mission to clean up the reserve. She wants Danielle to help. She's a force of nature, Judy. Her health is horrible. She can hardly breathe but her will is powerful. It's like a wind blowing you where she wants you to go."

"Her will or her mission?"

"Are they different?"

"Could be."

I wait.

"Sometimes people are tapped on the shoulder, given a job. Mostly they don't want the job. Often they try to get out of it. But somewhere inside they know they have to do it, whatever it is, so they do, but it's not their will. It's not about them."

I'm about to ask if he has a job like that when he says, "Does Judy have her sights set on you too, to save the reserve?"

"If I turn out to be from there."

"Assuming Danielle's father was status, you would be too."

"If I could prove he was my father."

"Easy enough with Danielle's DNA to compare to."

"Oh."

"How do you feel about being a Laboucan from Firestick?"

He hasn't pushed me like this before. I don't like it. "It's nothing I would choose," I say after a moment.

Doug glances at me. When I don't say anything else, he nods. "I guess that's how my parents felt. They had a choice and they chose to pass." He stares at the road ahead. His hands are tense. At last he says, "My brother couldn't pass. I could have but I didn't. Not because I was brave. It was a time when, in certain quarters, it was cool to be an Indian. I explored the identity a bit, exploited it in a way."

"How?"

"Oh, people wanted to see me as this naturally spiritual, in tune with Mother Earth guy. As long as it included free drugs and booze, I was happy to fulfill their fantasies." He shrugs.

"And now?"

"Environmental issues really get me. Especially being back in Alberta."

"Where it's definitely not cool," I say.

"Maybe it is in my blood, to feel that bond with the earth. I don't know. For a while I was obsessed. Like it was the End of Days and why didn't everybody else get it? Then I talked about it to the girls' other grandmother. The one I was telling you about the other day."

"The tree?"

"Millie is her name. She looked at me, this tiny old Cree lady—she's about four foot ten—she said, 'We've had our apocalypse. Now we're just trying to do what we can.'"

Doug glances at me.

"That gave me goose bumps," I say.

He nods. "'We've had our apocalypse.' She has the kind of eyes, they've seen everything. She doesn't waste energy judging. Things are what they are."

"My father's like that too."

"I'd like to meet him."

My spasm of unease is wiped away as we crest the slight rise. Mountains stretch across the whole horizon.

Doug pulls over.

It's clear enough today to see range upon range, a rough ocean of rock, crests gleaming in the sun. To the north, a band of violet cloud. After a while I say, "My father cried the first time he saw the Rockies. She saw them. She and her friend Dorothy in a boxy old van, taking Christianity to the settlers' children."

"When was that?"

"1921."

"Tail end of the apocalypse." After a moment Doug says, "Shall we get back on the road?" And I say, "I need to pee," at the same time.

There's a stand of scrappy fir I've visited before. In among the trunks I squat, facing the mountains. Bill pushed hard for me to take him out to the farm. I kept putting him off. *You just like to keep us all in our separate boxes.* I knew they wouldn't get along. But Dad would like Doug.

"Your father came here as a missionary?" Doug asks when we're on the road again.

"The way he tells it, it's mostly an adventure story. Two young women escaping the constraints of the old world. The woman he was with was more serious about the religious part."

"Does he talk about Native people in his stories?"

"No. Not until the sixties when a Cree man called John worked on the ranch."

"They must have been there."

"But not in his stories. It's like there are all these separate worlds slipping past each other."

"The settlers worked pretty hard to put Native people in a separate world. The few who were left." He looks across at me. "Ninety percent had died by the time the first Europeans actually settled here."

"Jesus."

"Best estimate. And it didn't stop. Eliminate or assimilate."

"Residential schools did both, didn't they?" I hesitate.

Doug looks at me. "What?"

"It's weird, not knowing which lens I'm looking through. I'm used to it on the receiving end, how people see me as Native or not, depending on how I'm dressed, what I'm doing, but it's the other direction too. Am I the Ukrainian settler? The displaced Cree or Blood or Dene?"

Doug nods but he doesn't say anything. Buildings appear on either side of the highway, then a traffic light. Lovely downtown Hinton.

"Want a coffee?" I ask. "Lunch?"

"No. You?"

"I'd just as soon wait until we get to Cardomin. If you think the store will be open."

"Long as the mine is running, Hubert's open. He's been trying to sell the store for years but it's hard to imagine him anywhere else."

We turn off the Yellowhead onto Highway 40 which, unlike the other roads we could have taken, is paved almost all the way.

"What you were saying," Doug looks across at me, "about people trying to figure out if you're Native or not. Maybe it's good for people to be unsure. It's kind of the same if someone's gay. If it's obvious—like Geoffrey, like my brother ..."

"Your brother's gay?"

"Was."

He's got the same look he had after the two spirit talk. I wait.

Eventually he says, "He killed himself." His eyes are on the road. "He was nineteen years old. Last time I saw him alive he was seventeen. Very flamboyant. He got beat up a lot. I told him maybe he should tone it down. Dress normal when he was on the street. I remember the look on his face, like I'd just punched him. He counted on me to be on his side. To understand. To love him the way he was. And I told him to hide. Like he should be ashamed."

"Jesus Doug, you were young too."

"Five years older than him." He glances at me. "I was scared, scared he was going to get killed. I could have come home, looked out for him. But I didn't want to. I was having too good a time getting high. Then someone brought a letter from my father. Mailed a month earlier to the last address he had for me. Bernard slit his wrists in the bathtub of the apartment he was sharing with two other kids. It was too late when they found him."

"Oh God, Doug."

"I was outside. It was July. Sun beating down on my head. I stood there reading that letter. Hung over. My hand was shaking. I wanted a joint. That was the first thing I thought of. My brother killed himself and I wanted a joint. I saw what I was. I remembered what I'd told him. His face. I couldn't imagine how to live with that. But I knew I couldn't get high any more. Or drink."

He shrugs, looks at me. "I came home. Moved back in with my folks. Kept my mother company. All my father did was work and watch TV. My mother went to church, cleaned house. She was dying inside. Fucking priest refused to bury him in the cemetery. A faggot who killed himself. Christ I came to hate the church. But it was all my mother had.

"I was going crazy. I was so angry. At the church, the world, my brother, myself. I started carrying a knife. Mr. Peaceful Hippie. Hung out where the gay kids were. Like I had some superhero fantasy I was going to spring to their defense. Course nobody knew what the fuck I was doing hanging around there. I looked like a psycho. Which I was. I'd been white-knuckling it for three years.

"There was a defrocked priest who worked with the street kids. Big old Irishman with a broken nose. Pat was his name. They kicked him out of the priesthood when they discovered him and his housekeeper had five kids. That was back in County Cork. Anyway, he sat me down one day, made me talk to him. He wasn't a guy you argued with. That night he took me to a meeting.

"He was my sponsor until he died twelve years ago. My father died a year before Pat. My mother went a few months after."

"Christ, Doug."

"I started going to the Tuesday meetings at Dreamcatcher. Did some sweats. Connected with some Métis people. It still wasn't doing it for me. I was pretty much flapping in the breeze. So I decided to do a vision quest. There were new age outfits in the U.S. taking groups out into the desert, leaving them to fast for three days by themselves, praying for a vision. The Sioux were complaining about cultural appropriation which was fair enough but it still sounded like something I needed to do.

"Right around then a guy in a hardware store told me about this ATV trip he'd taken along the sub-continental divide. He told me how, on one side of the divide, all the rivers drain into the Arctic ocean. On the other they end up in the Atlantic, via Hudson's Bay. That's how I came here for the first time." He points his lips at the road ahead. "It seemed as good a place as any. And it was. I didn't have any big vision but all the bits of myself that were swirling around began to come together. I couldn't see the shape but I could feel it happening. If that makes sense?" He looks at me.

I nod.

"Pretty soon after that I took a labourer's job up by Fort Mac. I saw what a few men with big machines can do to the land. Tailing ponds the size of a small town. Right on the Athabasca river. You could see an oily sheen on the river some days. Naturally occurring bitumen, according to the company geologists. Which could have been true but there was no way to tell because they weren't monitoring the river. Syncrude wasn't, the province wasn't and the feds sure as shit weren't. So it was whatever the company said. But the people on the reserve downstream, they saw changes in the fish and the animals.

"I worked there on and off a couple of years. Whenever I was home I'd come up here, hike along the Divide. Just the wind and birds. Then one day there was another pick-up truck in the parking lot, guy sitting staring out the windshield. I saw his face. He looked like somebody had died. Then he saw me. Got out of his truck, walked over to me.

"'You like this place?'

"I nodded.

"'See that valley over there?' He pointed off to the north-east. 'They're going to dynamite that.'

"'Who is?'

"'Cardinal River Coals. They've got a lease to the whole valley. Twenty three kilometers long, three and a half wide. They're going to blast off the cap rock, dump all the rubble in the stream beds and valley bottoms. Then they'll dig twenty six pits. Haul out the coal, ship it to Asia.'

"We stood there looking out at the valley. After a while I said, 'I can't let that happen.'

"He looked at me for a minute then he said, 'Okay. I know some people we should talk to.'"

Chapter Sixty Six

"LONG STORY SHORT, I got pretty involved. That was around the time Tanya and I got together. I couldn't go up to Fort Mac anymore. Came to work at Dreamcatcher for a while. Tanya too. We weren't making any money but it was good work."

We're passing the Luscar mine. The land looks oddly abstract. Smooth snow-covered cones. Too smooth. Spoil piles pretending to be hills. A sign announces reclamation. At the turn off to Cadomin there are more new signs, one to *Mountain Park Ghost Town*, the other to the *Whitehorse Wildland Provincial Park*.

"Since when has there been a park here?"

"Our big victory. Three years ago."

"That's great."

"Except we got word two weeks ago the mining company's making a deal with the province. They're going to bypass the whole Environmental Impact Assessment." Doug pulls up in front of the general store.

A bell tings as we push open the door. An old wooden counter on the right fronts racks of cigarettes, fishing flies and tackle, knives, ammunition. On the counter are bags of homemade fudge, postcards of trout and grizzlies. The floor space is filled with ranks of shelves: some lined with cans of beef stew and evaporated milk, boxes of mac and cheese and hamburger helper; others with gear and supplies for ATVs.

The walls haven't changed either except maybe the quilt of clippings and letters and photos is thicker. The guy who runs the store has shrunk. Shrunk in height but also his face has shrunk into itself, like a mushroom collapsing. Deliquescing. One of Dad's words. Doug's leaning against the counter, chatting to the owner. They look my way. I go over and Doug introduces us.

"Seen you before," Hubert says, eyes glinting out of the creased skin. "Not in a while though."

"I used to come in here with my parents. Ben and Polly Coopworth."

He nods. "How's old Ben doing? I was right sorry to hear Polly passed away."

Of course he'd be an avid reader of obituaries. "Dad's very well." I don't want to be the one to ask about Daniel Laboucan.

Doug's looking at me. He raises an eyebrow. I nod.

"Hubert," he says, "you don't happen to remember a fellow who worked in the mine when it first opened?"

"I remember all them fellows. What was his name?"

"Daniel Laboucan."

Hubert's brow furrows, creases growing creases. He's about to shake his head when he clicks his fingers. "Native fellow? Only there a month or two." He mimes lifting a bottle to his lips. "Always the trouble, eh?"

Doug and I look at each other but Hubert's already off his stool, headed down to the far end of the counter. He lifts a short stepladder off a spike in the wall and sets it up.

He's on the top step, one hand braced against the wall, squinting up when we reach him. "Damn walls are growing," he says. He looks at Doug. "You'll be able to see." He points at a yellowed clipping. A photograph of a double line of men facing forward.

Doug gets up on the ladder. He leans back to read the caption then leans in again.

"Second from the left, back row," he says.

Standing on the top step, staring up, I can't read the caption but I can see the dark-haired man, his roundish face, straight nose, eyes slightly too far apart. The men to either side look sombre and determined. He looks startled. I glance along the rows. No other obviously Native men. And no women, of course. This could be my father. My biological father. I climb down off the ladder. Doug and Hubert are back chatting by the cash register. I wander further along down the aisle. Stop at the article about the white man who staked his claim to this land after a Native woman told him about 'the rock that burns.'

"Meg?"

I jump.

"Sorry. I didn't mean to startle you. What do you want in the way of a sandwich?"

"Liverwurst with mustard, onions and pickles. On a roll."

He's grinning.

"What?"

"Guess what I just ordered for myself? My clean eating friends cringe."

"Dad and I always ordered it. Mum couldn't stand the smell of liver in the house."

"Hubert says the road's still clear up to the Divide. Want to eat up there?"

"Yes but, if I'm going to do the occasion justice, I need potato chips and an iced tea."

"What flavour chips would madam like with her liverwurst?"

We drive in silence. When we pass the graveyard Doug glances at me. "How was it, seeing that photograph?"

I shrug. "Maybe it would be different if I knew I was Theresa. But how am I ever going to know?"

"You can know you're not her."

"If I find her? That's true, but where do I start? Someone thought they might have gone to Winnipeg. Thirty years ago."

"From what you told me, it should be possible to get the mother's maiden name. If Lisa and Daniel Laboucan got married in White-court it'll be in the registry there. She may have family in the area still. Shall I see what I can find out?"

The gravel parking lot is empty, the wind scouring and cold. Doug parks the jeep so we're looking out across the saddle of alpine tundra.

Cloud shadows race each other across the slopes. Vast and supine, the foothills spread as far as you can see in either direction. Jagged peaks stand guard over the horizon, clad in their perpetual white.

Down here, snow shelters under the skirts of wind-shrunk spruce. I can see the lip of the hollow where the glacier lilies grow in July but the water is invisible, an eye staring straight up at the sky. I shiver.

Doug notices. He doesn't ask but I say, "The high mountains, they feel eternal, unchanging. I know they're not. I know they're eroding and the glaciers are retreating and all that, but they feel untouchable, above it all. This,"—I wave my hand at the expanse—"I don't know if I can explain, it's like the body of a woman, spread out." I stop, embarrassed.

"Go on." Doug's voice is muffled. He's staring out, head slightly turned away.

"It's the pelt of the Earth, the skin. The forests are like fur. Here, where the trees don't grow, it's like the places on an animal's body where the skin is bare and you can feel the heat." I stop. It's easier, talking about it as an animal's body, but I don't think I'm the only person who's uncomfortable here. Maybe he doesn't like thinking about women's bodies. A blast of wind rocks the jeep.

We reach for our sandwiches at the same moment, unwrap them. I tear open the chips and offer some to Doug before embedding a layer in my liverwurst. He watches and smiles but he's thinking about something else.

When we've licked our fingers and scrunched up the wrappers I ask, "What else did Hubert tell you?"

"He thinks he'll be able to sell the store in the spring."

"Meaning he thinks it's going to happen, the new mine?"

"He figures it wasn't really the public pushback or even the EIA—the Environmental Impact Assessment—that stopped it before, it was because the price of coal dropped. Now China's gearing up to make a lot of steel, price's going back up. I thought once we had an EIA that showed what a rare habitat this is, what damage would be done to species at risk, I thought that would be enough. We could all agree there are places too pristine to trash."

"But no?"

"The valley they want to destroy is right in a grizzly migration route. So they're offering a Carnivore Compensation Package."

"You're joking."

"I wish I was. Want to get out, walk around a bit?"

I don't, especially, but he looks so bleak I shrug on my jacket. The wind snatches the door of the Jeep from my hand, smashes it against the frame. I fumble in my pocket for my toque. We walk together to an outsized cairn of stone and concrete.

"This is new," I say but the wind tears the words from my lips. There are bronze plaques embedded in the sides. Ones at eye level have letters cast in the metal. At hand height they're in braille.

Doug leans close to my ear. "They tried painted signs first. Wind and grit sanded the letters right off."

My eyes are watering too much to read. I move around so the wind's at my back.

The Cardinal Divide is home to the woolly lousewort, Pedicularis lanata, common west of the Rocky Mountains but extremely rare to the east.

I look up. Doug is staring north, hands in his jacket pockets, hair streaming. Clouds chase each other across the washed blue sky.

Eventually he turns, looks at me. His eyes are watering. When I get closer I see he's crying. I walk up, slip my hand in his pocket. His fingers close over mine.

"Let's get out of here," he says. He keeps hold of my hand, wipes his eyes with his other sleeve.

'I could love you,' I think, walking back to the jeep, side by side, heads bent. Which is just great, given that you're gay and for all I know you have a partner at home. But in some weird way it doesn't matter.

"Ready to head back?"

I nod. He's concentrating on the rutted road so I can study his profile. He's told me a lot about himself today but there's a big fat piece missing. Even if he only realized he was gay after Tanya, when he talked about his brother, wouldn't there have been some mention there? But I guess if telling his brother to tone it down came out of how deeply closeted and ashamed he was himself ...

Doug glances at me. I look away quickly. "So you came here as a child?"

"Every summer when I was growing up. Memorable in part for the fact that we got store-bought lunch. It's my father's favourite place. In fact, he was planning to die here."

I tell Doug about Mum and Dad's plan.

Doug's laughing, shaking his head. "I shouldn't laugh but the garlic sausage ... I'd really like to meet him."

"Now?"

He glances at the clock on the dash. It's only 1:30.

"Why not? My neighbour's coming to ride her horse this afternoon. She'll feed and water both of them. Do you need to call your father?"

"Dad's used to me showing up. Though if I did call ahead the brothers might make us some supper too. The not-brothers." I glance at Doug. He's grinning, eco-sorrow at bay for the moment. I like how he doesn't get stuck.

Then he looks down at his faded jeans. "Am I ...?"

"You look fine. I can guarantee Dad's pants will be older."

Chapter Sixty Seven

"SORRY WE'RE SO late. We had a flat tire."

"In the middle of a mud puddle," Doug says.

"Come in, come in." Dad's wearing a crisp white shirt with a light check of orange and blue lines I've never seen before and a brand new pair of canvas pants.

"Dad, this is Doug Fletcher. Doug, meet my father, Ben Coopworth."

Doug wipes his hands on the sides of his jeans, smearing the mud further. He's wearing the darned blue socks and a red flannel shirt that's faded almost to pink.

"I'll give Victor and Manfred a jingle."

I've never heard Dad sound so British. Doug's still standing in the middle of the room when Dad hangs up. All he said was, "They're here."

"What will you have? I'm afraid we don't have any beer."

"I'll put the kettle on," I say but before I've even filled it there's a knock on the front door.

"Chicken soup with dumplings," Victor announces, holding the orange enamelled casserole out in front of him with both hands.

"And roasted root vegetables with preserved lemon," Manfred says, waving a covered dish.

They proceed through the living room, Doug looking faintly bemused.

When the soup's on the stove they shake hands with him in turn then we all stand there.

"Have a seat," Dad says to Doug, waving at the chesterfield. "Victor, bring in another chair from the kitchen." Now he sounds too hearty. "Meg," he waves me to sit next to Doug. "So, you were out and about?"

Doug glances at me. Shit. I should have told him Dad doesn't know about the whole Laboucan thing.

"Um, yes," I say, "we thought we'd take a ride. The road up to the Divide was open so we ate lunch up there."

"Windy, I bet," Dad says.

"Ferocious." Come on Doug, say something, but he sits there, smiling. "Did you know it's been declared a provincial park, the whole Divide?"

Dad nods.

Well fine, we can all play this game. Including Victor and Manfred who are sitting there like a couple of sparrows on a gate.

Eventually Dad says, "So Doug, do you hail from the city too?"

"No, I live about an hour this way, out by Lac Ste. Anne. On land my parents bought in the thirties."

"And you work at the same place as Meg?"

"For now."

This silence drags out even longer than the others. At last Victor says, "Well, the soup should be warm. We'll leave you to it."

"You're not going to eat with us?" Dad says, something like alarm in his face.

The earthy sweetness of the beets and carrots and parsnips is transformed by the tang of salted lemon, slightly caramelized. Doug stops after the first mouthful, fork in the air and says, "Yum."

Dad nods and then he smiles. My shoulders relax. "It changes everything, doesn't it?"

"Where did they get them from? I've eaten preserved lemons in Moroccan food."

"Local supermarket. The lemons that is. They did the preserving themselves. Said it wasn't any harder than making sauerkraut."

"Wow. Where are they from, Victor and Manfred?"

"Manitoba." Dad clams up again. Of course. He doesn't know that Doug knows that the brothers aren't. And he doesn't know that it's okay for Doug to know. Shit. He doesn't even know that Doug knows about him. If we'd planned this visit I'd have talked to Dad ahead of time.

"Meg told me they're interested in growing organic wheat here and that you know about the old varieties. That was something my father was interested in."

Dad jumps on the topic, thank God, and they're off on Red Fife and Marquis, landraces versus F1 seed, the folly of growing one variety. When they get to milling techniques they both look at me.

"I'd love to have access to freshly ground grain. And of course I'd like to try different varieties. But maybe where they're grown makes a difference too."

"The terroir of wheat?" Doug asks, smiling.

"It sounds pretentious but ..."

"I wasn't poking fun. I like the idea. I mean, wheat is the original agricultural commodity. The goal of most of the processing is to create a completely uniform product so when you buy a bag of whatever kind of flour it will behave exactly the same as every other bag you ever bought. It's food freed as much as possible from place and weather and time."

Dad's nodding. "And the farmer's supposed to be separated from all that too in his five hundred thousand dollar climate-conditioned combine except he can't be because the wheat is still a seed that goes in the ground. The farmer's where those two systems meet. He's the one who always gets creamed."

"So instead," Doug says, "go in the other direction."

"The other direction," Dad says, "is where I was always trying to go. Because it's not just wheat. Whenever you're producing a commodity the middleman makes the money. Take lamb ..."

Doug's leaning forward, listening, hair hiding half his face. They've both pushed their plates aside.

Standing at the sink the dark outside seems absolute. The curtainless window gives back the image of the kitchen, the white range and fridge, turquoise Formica table in its alcove, black and white cat clock on the wall, two pert ears above the numbered face. Mum's kitchen. Only it's not any more. Or it is and it isn't. I try to picture what she'd have made of food from Morocco, Jamaica, Guatemala. Doug is comfortable in the world somehow, as are Victor and Manfred. But so is Dad, even though he's lived in this rural backwater for sixty years. He was always reading, thinking, experimenting. For Mum, this was her fortress. Or her prison. My eyes drift to the doorjamb.

The kettle shuts itself off. I fill the pot, put it on the tray with plates and mugs and milk and the dark, dense brownies Victor and Manfred brought.

"You play the fiddle?" Dad's asking when I set the tray down.

"Not very well."

"How did you get started?"

"I went to one of John Arcand's fiddle camps."

"I've heard of him."

"He's trying to keep the Métis traditions alive. Music's a big part of that."

"You're Métis?"

"Yes."

"Can I ask you a question?"

"Of course." Doug sounds slightly wary. Please God, don't let Dad ask some stupid racist white person question.

"To be Métis, do you have to be descended from the offspring of the French voyageurs and Native women or is it looser than that? If you don't mind me asking."

I let my breath out. Doug relaxes too.

"It depends a bit who's answering. For the Métis Nation it's much looser. Anyone of mixed aboriginal/European blood qualifies for an official Métis status card. There are various ways of showing aboriginal ancestry, for example, genealogical documents which describe someone somewhere in your family tree as, quote, 'Métis, Half-breed, Indian, Non-status aboriginal, Inuit, Savage, Infidel etc.'"

"I wonder what comes under 'etcetera'?"

Doug shakes his head. "It has a Jesuit ring to it, that list. They were great ones for lists. My favourite is their ranking of all the groups in Canada in order of value: white French; black slave; savage

Indian; protestant English; Métis. They found the Métis particularly resistant to being saved."

"No bad thing," Dad says.

Doug smiles. "The Cree called the Métis *Otipenisewak*, meaning *their own boss*. As opposed to the English and the French whom the Cree considered slaves to their Company. Especially the English."

Dad tips his head sideways. "Substitute the word corporation ..."

I've never really inquired into Dad's politics. Mum's came straight from the preacher so we both learned to avoid anything that led there. I always figured Dad would be like all the other ranchers around here: averse to being told what to do by anyone.

"By some reckoning," Doug says, "fifty percent of people living in Western Canada today have some aboriginal blood in their veins. But no one's really beating down the doors to claim Métis status. The whole blood thing anyway,"—he shrugs—"Indigenous traditions almost always include ways to adopt people, children or adults, into the band."

"And your family?"

"Goes back to the Voyageurs on both sides."

My eyes trace the craggy profile. *I could love you.*

"My mother descended from François Belanger who came from Quebec and married a Cree woman. Or at least she was what was called a country wife. I doubt any priest blessed the union. Belanger worked for the North West Company then the Hudson's Bay Company. My father's ancestor was a Scot named Flett who seems to have married an Anishnaabe woman. Somewhere along the way Flett became Fletcher."

"What is it like, to be Métis? If you don't mind me asking."

"I don't mind but I don't know how well I can answer. I wasn't raised to think of myself as Métis. My parents were eager to assimilate. I could have passed, like them, but I chose not to. I had a brother who looked much more aboriginal."

"That's interesting. I hadn't thought about that. People in the same family having different ... options."

Is this weird for Dad, talking about passing? Of course, he doesn't know that Doug knows. They're focused on each other, Dad with his eagle's beak, his crumpled, papery skin. Doug's is fissured, leathery. His nose has its own raptor's curve.

"By one set of official standards," Doug is saying, "if a person of mixed blood could be taken for white, then they weren't Métis. So my brother would have been Métis and I wouldn't. That was actually the starting point for the A.F. Ewing Commission, generally known at the time as the 'Half Breed Commission.'"

"In the thirties?"

"Nineteen thirty-four to thirty-six."

Dad nods. "I heard about it."

"A Métis man who's a hero of mine was a part of the Commission, Malcolm Norris. Norris didn't buy the argument that if you could pass you weren't Métis. His version was: 'If a person has a drop of Indian blood in his veins and has not assimilated in the social fabric of our civilization, he is Métis.' I like to think that Norris, who was a Marxist, wasn't completely sold on European style civilization."

I've never really heard Doug talk like this. He sounds formal. Almost academic.

Dad's nodding. "I had a friend. A Scot from the Orkneys. She was married to a Native man long back. She had the same view of the English as the Cree you were talking about. She said her people were more like the Métis and Native people, they valued freedom and the clan over money. She told me she might even be a little bit Métis herself. Well, she said half-breed." Dad looks apologetic.

"Back in the day," Doug says, "Métis meant you had French blood, half-breed was for the offspring of the British. But go on."

"Well, apparently the Hudson's Bay Company recruited a lot of Orkneymen because they were known to be tough and resourceful. Many of them settled down with Native women and had children. Most left their families behind when they went back to the Orkneys but a few brought their wives and children with them. When this friend came to Canada and saw a Cree woman for the first time, she almost fell over, the woman looked so much like her grandmother. Then when she heard the fiddle music the Métis played, it sounded awfully familiar. What do you think? Is that possible?" Dad's leaning forward, his eyes turquoise and intent.

"I don't see why not. I've never heard about Métis people living in the Orkneys but until very recently people kept quiet about those drops of aboriginal blood. And the music, well, Métis fiddle tunes are mostly derived from Quebec and Scottish tunes so they would have sounded familiar anyway though they were also influenced by Native drumming."

"What does the drumming do?"

"Some pretty unusual things with the rhythms. Makes the tunes hard to learn. It's easier to demonstrate than describe ..." He tails off.

Dad's staring down at his hands.

"Sorry, am I boring you?" Doug includes me in the apologetic look.

Dad looks up. "Not in the least. I was thinking. I have a fiddle. I haven't been able to play in years." He holds out his hands.

Twisted fingertips, swollen knuckles. "Doug," I say, "when do you need to get back?"

They both look at me, surprised. Doug shrugs. "Doesn't matter."

"It's getting late. If you're dropping me off in the city, you still have to drive all the way back out to your place."

I feel Dad's attention sharpen.

Doug stands up. "Excuse me a moment."

He heads for the washroom. Dad's studying me. "I'll just clear these away," I say, gathering mugs and plates. In the kitchen I stare at my reflection in the darkened window over the sink. 'What are you up to?' Whoever's looking back isn't talking.

The toilet flushes. Doug's footsteps cross the living room. "It's been very nice meeting you," he says. I can hear the smile in his voice.

"Likewise," Dad says. "Come again. Perhaps you'll give the old fiddle a little exercise."

"I'd like that."

Chapter Sixty Eight

IT'S DOUG ON the phone. "Thanks for taking me to the farm. I enjoyed meeting your father. I hope I didn't tire him out."

"Dad? He goes to sleep when he needs to."

"I thought perhaps you were concerned, at the end there."

"No, no. I just thought it was getting late." I take a deep breath. "It wasn't really that. I just ... I wasn't ready for you to play his fiddle."

"Oh."

"I don't know why."

"No big deal. I'm on my way out to pick up the girls. Give everybody a break. Thought I'd catch you before you went to work."

"How's Tanya's mother?"

"Hanging on. She's one tough old lady. But the main reason I called is that I went to see the town clerk in Whitecourt this morning."

"You drove all the way out there?"

"Some things go better in person."

"What did you find out?" My heart is beating faster.

"The clerk, Sarah, looked up the marriage. Lisa Laboucan's maiden name was Holinski. She came from Swan Hills originally." He pauses.

"Go on."

"As it happens, Sarah went to high school with Lisa's younger sister, Louise. They're still in touch. Lisa died of breast cancer several years ago but Sarah's pretty sure she did have a daughter."

"Does she know where she is, the daughter?" My voice sounds even but now my heart is thudding.

"No, only that nobody has seen her for years. Sarah thinks she must have moved away."

"Jesus." I'm trying to think. "What about her mother's funeral? Wouldn't she have come back for that, if she was ..." Christ, this is weird.

"If she was somebody other than you?"

I nod. "Perhaps we can find someone who went to the funeral."

"I think I have an easier way. Sarah offered to call Louise and ask her if she would be willing to talk to me. I gave her my number to pass on."

"Wow. So ..."

"We wait. Give it a week. See if she calls."

"God, Doug, what did you say to the clerk? It's amazing, how helpful she was."

"I told her the truth, some of it anyway. That the family had fallen apart but recently and rather miraculously one of Daniel Laboucan's daughters had come back into the family's life. Now we were wondering about the others. Hoping we could reach out to them."

"It sounds like a soap opera."

"A very Christian one. She was wearing quite a large cross. I laid it on a bit thick about the prodigal daughter, a chance to heal the family."

"And who did you say you were?"

"I didn't. But I expect she thought I was a relative."

Chapter Sixty Nine

I COULD HAVE a name. Date of birth. Place of birth. Parents. Blood parents. Who are dead.

Sisters and brothers. Cousins.

Aunts. Not just on the reserve. Lisa's sister. Louise.

Is going to call Doug.

Maybe.

Kids racing everywhere. Dogs barking.

One in a parcel of kids.

Not mute. Not withdrawn.

Scarred.

Yes, okay, two drunk parents who didn't actually live on the reserve. Still.

The man in the paper, those wide apart eyes. A Cree father. Ukrainian mother. What did she look like? Lisa. Louise would have pictures. Does Louise have children?

More cousins.

Have to concentrate on the trail down to the river. Pocked, grimy, but the wind is billowing snow across the river ice. Like a fresh sheet floating down onto the bed you're making, that moment before it settles. I could walk out onto the footbridge but my feet turn right.

I could just belong. Like a normal person. 'Yes, my mother grew up in Swan Hills. I was born ...' wherever I was born. It won't be hard to find my birth certificate.

Lisa and Dan would be my real parents.

Who somehow misplaced me.

But would have been glad to get me back.

If they weren't dead.

Fuck.

But Judy's not dead. Danielle's not dead. They'd be happy to have me. And the others? The sisters I didn't meet. The brothers. Would shrug and go back to watching TV.

But I'd have a right. A right to be there. In the family. On the reserve. Status. A status Indian. Because of my father, Daniel Laboucan. May he rest in peace.

And Dad?

My unreal father?

Dad and Mum who took me in and loved me.

Tomorrow I could know.

I could go to the place where I was born.

Someone could say, 'Isn't she the spitting image of so-and-so?'

I could look at them and see myself.

Chapter Seventy

"ARE YOU UP for taking them swimming?" Heather's standing by the whiteboard, pen in hand.

"Sure. How many new clients came in?"

"Three," Jay says.

"Anyone we know?" Heather asks.

"Old white guy; young white guy, and," Jay pauses, "Jeanette."

"Prossie Jeanette?"

"The one and only." Jay looks at me. "I don't think you've met Jeanette."

I shake my head.

"How's she looking?" Heather asks.

"Skinny as a shoelace. Yellow. Hep C, eh? It's fucking sad. Only thing worse than being a young ho's got to be being an old ho."

"Blow jobs in a back alley for ten bucks."

"You ever really talked to her? She's so smart. Frig, she should be running the country, not the morons we've got, but no, she can't forgive herself for what she's been. Look in her eyes, that's what you see. She's thinking, *I'm a ho. I'm a ho.*" Jay looks at the clock and reaches for the phone. "It's suppertime. It's suppertime. New people, follow the crowd."

When I come back into the office Heather's saying, "It's the shame, eh?"

"Here. Have a seat." Jay shunts the third chair around.

I put my tray down, pick up the fork. I stare down at the pale blob, the scatter of green spheres. *You don't want a whore for a sister. Not proper Meg. If I ever forget to feel ashamed.* Danielle. And Mum. The cane she kept. To remind herself.

I look up. They're both eyeing me.

"It's not that bad," Heather says.

"What?"

"The macaroni."

I look at Jay. "Your mother, she got saved, right? Why, do you think?"

"What need did it answer in her?" Jay shunts the last couple of peas around her plate. "That's probably why I'm studying psychology. She went from being this vibrant, sexy, funny woman to, to being a joyless stick. It was like she aged ten years. She cut off her body, Desire. Sexuality. I mean okay, her personal life was kind of a mess. She was always dating men who turned out to be married. But she laughed. She was pretty and alive and warm. She wore bright colours." Jay shrugs. "In case you haven't figured it out, it was the worst trauma of my life. Her conversion. I was eleven, just starting puberty. That was part of it, I think. She felt she had to set me a better example. It was like she didn't know how to manage her own sexuality so she found somebody else to do it for her. A bunch of fucking men who hated women. She was their shadow, you know? Everything they rejected in themselves. But they didn't make her join their cult. She chose them. At first I kept hoping it was a phase she was going through."

Jay tries for a smile. "Poor Mum. When I came out to her ... She really believes I'll burn in hell for all eternity. They pray with her for me. Makes me puke, thinking about it. Sanctimonious arseholes."

Heather's nodding. "Catholic church's no different. They're all afraid of pussy, eh?"

Startled I look at her, the well-cut silver hair and pale blue turtle-neck. But then there's the lipstick and the full breasts, the glint of laughter in her eyes. "I think I shocked Meg. But seriously, how many of those arseholes are fucking their kids? Or, in the case of the priests, someone else's kids? Some pure, pre-pubescent body they can possess."

Standing in the doorway to the kitchen I spot Jeanette. It must be her, stringy, jaundiced, standing off to one side, listening to the clatter and splash of silverware being rinsed, the joking and joshing.

Something grey and wet flicks past my feet. "Sorry." I step aside. Joey grins and swabs where I was standing.

"Is this good?" Edward, face earnest. Hair's growing back on his shaved head like the curly pelt of a newborn lamb. He's in charge of clean-up tonight.

We walk around the central bank of stove and counters, check the empty sinks with their clean strainers. "Excellent," I tell him.

He ducks his head, pleased. He travelled to Canada by himself from Somalia when he was eleven. Cathy told me his story. His family was in a refugee camp. Forces on one side or another would raid the camp, snatch kids, make them into soldiers. His mother sent him to Edmonton to live with an aunt but the aunt had her own troubles. A gang became his family. I haven't heard the details of the stuff he did. I don't really want to know. He looks younger now than when he came in but his forty nine days is almost up, and what's he going back to? Even if they don't manage to deport him, which is the government's plan for him.

"Really good job," I say. "Well done."

"Meg," he says, "you okay? You looking sad."

Heather and I sit in the glassed-in room watching the lifeguard usher out the parents and kiddies. There's a moment when the pool is empty then our mob swarms in. The whistle's blowing moments later but whoever's pushing who into the water has already done it.

"Have you talked to Tanya?" I ask.

"Jay has. Her mother's holding on longer than anyone expected. Tanya's still spending most of her time at the hospital."

"Has there been any fallout from her not coming into work on Sunday?"

"Not yet."

"Are they really going to fire her?"

"Jay thinks so. They're just holding off until her mother actually dies. We've been talking about it. If they do, we're both going to quit. I've got my pension. I don't need this job. The income's nice but if they're going to be arseholes ... It's not just Tanya. Ever since they axed the aftercare program ... You never met George but he was excellent. A junkie from Glasgow. He knew what it was like to come from nothing, have nothing, eh? And he was good at talking to people. Not just clients, bureaucrats, social workers, politicians. He made them want to help. 'My junkie charm,' he'd say in this thick Glaswegian accent. He built up a network of people at all the agencies, people he could call on to iron out problems. Landlords who were willing to rent to our clients. Then Brenda got her knees under the exec desk and he was out of a job faster than he could say 'Fock me,' which he said a lot."

"Why?"

"Word was he looked like a threat to her. They'd never have hired Lily White George—that's what he called himself sometimes—to run this place but he wasn't afraid to stand up to her. Brenda doesn't care for that. Same thing with Tanya. They were a hell of a team actually, Tanya and George. I always thought he was a little sweet on her."

"Where is he now?"

"Nanaimo. Running aftercare for a big rehab there." She shrugs. "I saw it in the civil service. You get a boss who gets rid of the people who stand up to him, pretty soon all you've got is mush like Cathy."

"Would Doug quit too?" My voice isn't casual enough but Heather doesn't seem to notice.

"He's not going to stand by and watch them fire Tanya. What about you?"

"I don't know. It wouldn't be the same without all of you. I'd miss the clients too."

"It gets into your blood, doesn't it? Plus, after all the years working in offices, I like that you never know what's going to happen. And evening shift, we're really our own bosses. Brenda never sticks around past five. None of them do."

"Except Cathy."

"Who doesn't count."

"I don't think she's so bad."

"The counsellors told her to back off on the touchy-feely groups. I guess the clients were showing up all triggered on a Monday morning. Too much work, eh?"

"If most of the evening staff are ready to quit, couldn't we try to use that?"

"To do what?"

"Stop them firing Tanya? Reinstate the aftercare program."

Heather considers me. I never noticed she had violet rings around her irises. "Why not?" she says finally. "It won't work. Brenda would never lose face like that. But if we're going to quit anyway, what do we have to lose?"

Chapter Seventy One

TWO YOUNG WOMEN on horseback smile at the camera, one riding side-saddle, the other astride. *The Mazey girls set out to round the cattle home*. A Roedean girl stooks grain in a white shirt and tie, a calf length duster half hiding the britches underneath. The last photograph in the book is of six aboriginal people in front of a brick wall, the bottom corner of a high window just visible. They gaze unsmiling at the camera, two girls and a boy in the back row; in the front a round-faced young woman sits next to an ancient looking couple. The young woman wears a European style dress with a belt, the toes of her boots just visible. The children wear western clothes too. Dresses for the girls, a jacket and cap for the boy. Meanwhile the old woman huddles in a blanket, her hands wrapped inside it, holding it close. On her feet are moccasins. The old man wears them too. His hair is long and grey. He's wearing a fringed jacket, holding a slender stick. The young look well-fed, the old have hollow cheeks and sunken eyes. The caption reads, *The present phase of development in Father Hugenard's work for the mother country*.

Ah yes, *The children of the darker race* receiving *the consolation of religion*.

That must be Hiawatha's starving granny.

What if I am Theresa Laboucan, status Indian, daughter of Daniel Laboucan and Lisa Holinski, half-sister to Danielle and some, perhaps all, of her lovely siblings? 'Hello, my name is Theresa and I am an alcoholic.' That, still, always. Sober Theresa pitching in to help Judy and Danielle. Taking part in the sweat lodge. Learning the ways of my people. I'll know where I began. And maybe I'll find out what happened. How my blood mother lost me. And never tried to find me. I picture myself back before I remember. One of a gang of dark-haired kids and skinny dogs.

No memory stirs.

Make yourself some hot milk.

Which Mum used to do when I woke up from a nightmare. Somehow she'd know I was up even though they slept upstairs.

She'd stand over the range in her flannel nightgown, dipping the tip of her little finger in the pan of milk. She'd pour the milk into her cup with the yellow roses on it. We'd sit side by side and she'd hum a hymn tune while I drank it.

Chapter Seventy Two

HEATHER'S SITTING UP front with Deborah and Don. I've got the door. My eyes find Danielle by the curve of her skull, the tilt of her cheek. Doug's at the end of a row next to Jeanette. He's leaning forward, listening to the speaker, brown hair half hiding his face. Then, as if he felt my look, he turns and smiles. My groin clenches.

Great. That's going to make it easy to love him like a brother. I force my mind back to the meeting. Two rows ahead of me two girls are chatting in an undertone. Geoffrey flicks irritated glances their way. Gordon, sitting between Geoffrey and the girls, is still as a rock, his braid hanging straight down. My eyes roam the rows of seats, the backs of so many heads. The few who've stayed sober. The many who are trying. More who've given up. *We've had our apocalypse.*

It's the planet's turn now.

I could say this to Doug.

In the office, once the clients are all in ceremony, Jay says, "Tanya called while you were at the meeting. Her mother passed away a couple of hours ago. Tanya and her sisters were there. Do you need to go, Doug?"

"No. We already worked it out. The girls will stay at their other grandmother's until after the funeral. I'm going to walk the perimeter."

I try to see his face but his hair covers it as he walks past me.

"How's Tanya doing?" Heather asks Jay when the gate has clicked behind him.

"Pretty good, considering. I mean it's kind of a relief but that's when it really hits you, eh? I don't know what I'll do when my mother dies."

My eyes prickle. Shit.

"It hasn't been long for you." Heather's looking at me, her voice gentle.

I shake my head.

"Takes a couple of years," she says. Double shit.

"Excuse me." Mona's voice.

"Yes," Jay's on her feet.

"I need to use the phone. My counsellor gave me a letter from my daughter. She's got a new boyfriend and he doesn't want me ..."

Instead of making Mona stay on the bench until the end of ceremony, Jay puts a hand on her shoulder. "Why don't we go over there and talk?" They head for the alcove on the far side of the dome.

Heather shakes her head. "Where's she going to go? They released her right from jail to here. George would have been on the phone ..." The gate clicks.

"George?" Doug says from the doorway. "I was thinking about him on the bus. Geoffrey's all set. He owns his condo. Warren and Shannon are going to his sister's. But Janice ..."

"Mona too."

"I told her I'd make some calls but I wish George ..."

"Was here." Jay swings into the office. "I'm so frigging sick of this place. They fire Tanya ..."

Heather nods. "I'm ready," she says.

"Me too," Doug says.

They all look at me. "And me," I say.

"Tell Doug and Jay your idea," Heather says.

"I like it," Jay says. "It won't work but I like it."

"What about Laura?" Doug asks. My gut twists.

"Laura is John Wilson's plant here," Jay says.

"We don't know that," Doug says.

"Tell you what." Heather looks back and forth between them. "Why don't we wait to tell Laura until they've actually fired Tanya."

"That's when we tell them we're quitting?" Jay asks.

"Then it won't matter if she tells Brenda or Don what we're planning to do."

"But if we're going to try to make a difference," I say, "shouldn't we do something sooner? Once Tanya's actually been fired, isn't it going to be harder to get them to reverse course?"

"Too much loss of face," Heather says, nodding.

"Bearing in mind that none of this is going to work," Jay says, "you have a point. So what should we do?"

"In an ordinary organization," Heather says, "we would bring our concerns to our supervisor."

"I can see it now," Jay says. "Cathy sprouts a spine, goes and confronts Brenda."

"Even if it won't do any good," I say, "maybe we should follow the proper procedures."

I glance at Doug. He nods.

"It might help us get Employment Insurance anyway," Jay says.

"Not if we quit," Heather says.

"They've approved EI for people who quit Dreamcatcher before. They've seen so many workers come and go from here ..."

"What are the proper procedures?" I ask. "I don't think I've ever seen an employees handbook."

"There's one in the safe, vintage nineteen eighty something."

"Somebody was going to revise it a couple of years ago," Jay says.

Heather looks around. "So which lucky person is going to talk to Cathy?"

Post-it notes rest like bright butterflies on wall-charts and calendars and piles of paper. At the edge of the desk, a tray of art supplies tilts off a heap of folders. Plastic glitter beads pool along the bottom lip.

"Cathy, could I speak with you?"

"Of course Meg, come on in." She clears an inbox tray from the spare chair. "Have a seat. How are you doing?" She gazes at me with brown, concerned eyes. "I wanted to tell you how well you handled the ... situation the other night. The fight. And Danielle. Although,"—her chin comes up—"you and Jay should have called me when you knew Tanya wasn't going to make it in."

"You're right," I say. "We should have. You just brought up one of the reasons I wanted to speak with you."

"Oh." I don't think people tell Cathy she's right very often.

"We, meaning Jay, Doug, Heather and I are concerned about rumours that Tanya is going to be fired. Is there any truth to them?"

"Oh. Well." Consternation crumples her broad face. "I'm afraid ... well, I can't speak to rumours. Tanya did commit a serious breach of procedure."

"Have you given her a warning?"

"I can't comment on personnel issues." She clamps her lips shut. She wants to chew one of them. Instead her left hand strays up to the ends of her hair. She looks about seven years old. I can see exactly how the other kids must have tormented her.

"The other issue ..." I pause, letting the silence stretch. She twists a lock of hair around her forefinger. "The other issue we wanted to bring up is the need for an aftercare worker. What's the use of getting people sober if we send them back into the same bad situations?"

Cathy's nodding, relieved. "I couldn't agree with you more. I made some suggestions myself. The matter is under discussion. At the highest level."

I look at her to see if she's joking but her face is utterly sincere.

"Between us, I've been pushing hard to create the position."

"Re-create it," I say.

"Actually, this will be a different job description. But"—she puts a finger to the side of her nose and taps it—"I think I can promise it will be more helpful than what we had before." She leans back, smiling.

"Well. We'll look forward to hearing the details," I say. "Thanks, Cathy."

"*At the highest level*," Heather says. "My Jesus, it's a good thing it was you in there not me. Brenda and Johnny boy discussing *at the highest level*. Christ but that woman's thick."

Usually I defend Cathy but it's too easy to picture how Brenda controls her: here a little pat on the ego, there a sharp flick of her blood red fingernails. They aren't literally blood red. She paints them a pinkish beige that blends in with the rest of her beige look. She's not the sort of snake that advertises its venom.

"Penny for your thoughts," Heather says.

"Sorry. I was thinking about Brenda."

"Scary, eh?"

"Mm. I think we should write her a letter, all sign it. Have it ready."

"I bet they'll fire Tanya on Monday."

"So on Sunday night whoever's on puts the letter in Brenda's box. That way she'll find it first thing."

Jay walks over to the schedule. "That would be the three of us and Laura."

"And for Monday night, Brenda, Cathy and Laura," Heather says. "Maybe Brenda will think twice."

"Maybe."

"Who's going to write this letter?" Jay asks.

"Excuse me?" A hoarse smoker's voice. Jeanette. "Could I get my meds."

When I go back into the office Heather's the only one there. She says, "What do you say to the two of us getting together to write the letter this weekend?"

"If the others agree," I say, surprised and yes, flattered. Cathy's not the only weak ego around. "How's Sunday morning?"

"What time?"

"Eleven. Want to come to my place? I'll make you lunch."

"That would be nice." Heather looks pleased.

"Nothing fancy, just a sandwich."

"All the years I cooked for my kids, husband too when I had one," she says, "I can't be bothered to cook for just me."

"I never had kids so I don't know what my excuse is. My last relationship, he liked to barbeque. Didn't matter how cold it was. So that's what we ate."

"But you bake bread. I remember that loaf you brought in. I was quite impressed."

"You were? I thought you thought I was daft."

"Well, you'll never see me doing it but I was impressed."

"By what?" Doug steps into the office.

"Meg's baking."

"Me too." His eyes smile.

My mouth goes dry.

Chapter Seventy Three

"I'M GLAD I caught you."

"Coffee?"

"Yes, please." Doug holds out a paper bag.

I peer inside, raise my eyebrows.

"New vendor."

"Have a seat."

He settles into the corner of the chesterfield. "Do you mind if I just stare blankly for a moment?"

"Tired?"

"I took the girls to the Farmer's Market this morning. The funeral's this afternoon."

When we've dunked our croissants and sipped enough coffee Doug says, "Theresa Laboucan's aunt, Louise, called me."

"Oh."

He looks at me. "Are you okay?"

No but I say, "Yes. So?"

"The short version is, you're not Theresa."

"Oh."

"Disappointed?"

"You're sure?"

"Theresa is alive and well, married to a U.S. Navy SEAL. Two kids. They live in Pensacola, Florida."

"Oh."

"It was a short conversation. Sarah told Louise about the attempt to reunite the family. Louise called Theresa. Theresa's answer was 'No, thanks.'"

"That was it?"

"I didn't get the feeling that the name of Daniel Laboucan evoked warm feelings."

"Poor Danielle. It might have been nice for her to have some other relatives."

He studies me. "What about you?"

I shrug. "It was like opening a door into somebody else's house, the whole Danielle thing. I thought if it was true, I'd feel different, knowing these were my people. But they aren't, so that's that. End of story."

Doug's sitting there, looking at me.

"What?" I sound irritated. I am irritated. "Look, the childhood I remember was in this quiet, orderly, kind home. As it turns out, it wasn't quite the way it seemed but that was still my experience. I look at Danielle's family, I listen to the stories, the violence and tragedy and loss and poverty ... I know this sounds terrible. It's not their fault that their lives are such a mess. All the awful shit that was done to Native people is why things are the way they are. But it's still a mess, a huge, horrible, intractable mess like everything else now, the planet, what we're doing ... I don't know how to finish this sentence."

"Back to you, maybe." Doug's voice is mild.

I close my eyes. He's right. This is bullshit.

"Meg."

I open my eyes. He looks worried.

"I need to go. The girls want me to be with them."

And their mother, and their grandmother. "Of course," I say.

"Are you okay?"

"Yes." I stand up. "Thanks, Doug."

Chapter Seventy Four

PUSHING OPEN THE front door I call out, "Dad, it's Meg." Still no answer. His boots are missing. And the battered old barn coat he's taken to calling his smoking jacket. Outside again I sniff the air.

He's on the east side of the house, on a bench I've never seen before, head tilted back. The morning sun gilds his hair and skin. The pipe smoulders in his right hand.

"Hello, Dad."

He turns and his face creases into a smile.

"Hello, Meg." He slides over, pats the spot next to him. "What a nice surprise. Come and try out Manfred's latest." I don't move. "Has something happened?"

I shake my head, say exactly what I rehearsed in the car. "Dad, it's time for you to tell me where your name comes from. Because it's my name too. It's the only name I've got."

He studies my face, eyes melt-water blue in the sunlight. Then he looks away. There's not much of a view to the east. Mostly sky and scrubby pines. After a moment he nods. "Very well. But let me tell this in my own way."

I sit down next to him.

He puts his pipe to his lips, draws on it until the tobacco glows, then exhales. When there can't be anything left in his lungs, he says, "It was the second of November, 1918. I was driving the wounded from a field dressing station to the field hospital, further back behind the lines. We were shelled. The nurse and two of the wounded were killed. One soldier survived, barely. A young infantryman. He had burns to his face and one arm already. They'd only just brought him in to the field hospital when I arrived. We loaded him onto the ambulance. He was in terrible pain."

Dad's tone is level but there's a twitch under one eye.

"Now he had a jagged gash to his thigh, blood pumping out. The ambulance caught fire. I dragged him clear. He was screaming. It was raining, a cold hard rain. Near dark. I tied a rough tourniquet above the wound. Fifty feet away I saw a rotting shed.

I got him to his feet, took most of his weight on the side that wasn't burned. He helped, hopping on his good leg. He was shorter than me and slight. Mousy hair, fine features. Just a boy. When the petrol tank blew it knocked us both over. We crawled the last few yards. It was an old pig shed, by the smell of it, but at least it was dry. Things scuttled around in the dark. I could hear his teeth chattering.

"I sat down next to him. It was all I had to give him, my own body's warmth. I knew I should keep him awake.

"'What's your name?'

"He didn't speak but his fingers started scrabbling at his neck.

"'Can I help you?' I thought perhaps he was reaching for a crucifix.

"He got a hold of something, pulled it over his head. 'I'm dying, aren't I?' A high, rasping voice.

"I reached down and touched the tourniquet. It was warm and wet.

"'Please.'

"He held whatever it was out to me. The cord with his identity discs on it, by the feel. Now he was fumbling at the front of his tunic.

"'Let me help you.' He must have been in agony. Someone had cut away the left sleeve of his jacket. I could smell them, the burns."

Dad's holding the bowl of his pipe in his right hand. He looks down at it then back out at the sky.

"I reached over, tried with one hand but I couldn't get the buttons so I turned and knelt and undid them with both hands. I was holding my breath against the smell.

"He reached into the inside breast pocket, took something out. He pressed it into my hands. "'Please.' He sounded desperate.

"It was a pouch of some sort. Oilcloth.

"'I'm dying, aren't I? Aren't I?'

"'I think so.'

"'Will you do me a favour?'"

Dad's eyes flick sideways to me. "The words were so incongruous I almost laughed. 'Of course.'

"'The things I gave you, get rid of them. And when ... and when I'm dead, take off my uniform. Get rid of it.'

"'But your family ...'

"'My parents are dead. It's just my brother and me. Please.'

"'But what about him? Not to know ...'

"'Please.'

"I sat in the dark in that stinking pig shed beside a dying man. I could say yes, decide later. But I couldn't. I couldn't lie to him.

"He started to cry, half whimpering, half sobbing. 'They'll find out. They'll find out and they'll shoot him.'

"'Who? Who will they shoot?'

"'My brother.' I thought he was rambling but his voice got stronger. 'Everyone kept asking him, "When are you going to join up?" He ignored them. But when we turned eighteen, he got his papers. He was so scared. It was so stupid. I wanted to go. To serve my King and country.'

"'I don't understand.'

"He didn't say anything for a while. I could hear the rain drumming on the roof tiles. Rats scuttling. The shed shook when the mortars pounded. For all I knew the Germans were advancing. We weren't far from the front. But there wasn't anything to do about that. We could have been in one of the observation balloons they sent up above the front. Or in a life raft, the two of us alone in a sea of war.

"Eventually he said, 'We used to pretend to be each other. Dress up in each other's clothes. He even got a wig. I put my hair up under a cap. We walked down the main street of the town near where we lived. It was fun. He ... he told me once if he could, he'd be me always.'

"That's when I understood.

"She must have felt my astonishment. She said with a quaver, 'Well, now he can.' "

"Wait a minute. The soldier was a girl?"

Dad nods.

"And nobody knew?" He doesn't answer. 'Her brother's name was Ben Coopworth?"

"Yes."

"What was her first name?"

"I don't know. She wouldn't say. Sometime in the night I must have fallen asleep. When I woke she was dead. At dawn I took the uniform off her body. Took everything. I left her naked, nameless body in that rat-infested shed. If there had been a shovel. Anything. I scraped together what straw there was. Walking away that morning. I was carrying the uniform. Stiff with blood. I kept seeing her body, gleaming, pale, like the belly of a fish. I was walking away from the shelling but I came across old trenches. I don't even know if they were our trenches. I dropped the uniform into one. Kept walking. Eventually somebody saw me. I was given a lift to the field hospital I'd been trying to reach. Reported that the ambulance had gone up in flames. I was the only survivor."

He reaches in his pocket, pulls out his knife, opens the small blade. He scrapes the bowl of the pipe into the palm of his hand. He's frowning down at the charred tobacco. His hand is pale, knobbled with blue veins.

"What was in the pouch?"

"His papers."

"You kept them?"

"The identification discs too. I wasn't easy in my mind about what I'd done."

I let out a breath I didn't know I was holding. "So you didn't plan to use them yourself?"

"Back then?" He stares at me, eyes hard. "No, I did not."

I don't say anything.

After a moment he says, "Shall we go in?"

I nod, aware suddenly I'm shivering.

I stare out the window. Blackened stalks of sunflowers lean, heads bowed. The kettle shuts itself off.

As soon as I sit down, Dad says, "Ask what you need to ask."

I don't know where to start. After a moment I say, "How could she possibly have got away with it? I mean they must have had medical exams. The recruits. I don't imagine the barracks had private showers."

He's shaking his head. "I asked her. In the night. Trying to keep us both awake. She was rambling mostly but now and then she'd be clear as a bell. As far as I could make out, at the end of their training, the recruits got a couple of days' home leave before they shipped out. After the leave, she reported at the train station in his place. Nobody gave her a second glance. She said a number of times how much alike they looked."

"But Dad, she went to war with no training at all, with men she was supposed to know."

"And she died a week later. They didn't know, either of them, what she was getting into. Nobody knew, unless they'd been there. You could get on a train at Victoria station, be in hell in hours."

"But if she got caught. When she got caught ..."

"He would have been court-martialled and shot. If they'd been able to find him. I don't know what would have happened to her. I don't imagine they thought it through. It was an idea that took on a life of its own. I suspect she'd always been his protector. She told me several times how frightened he was. And that she was older than him. By three minutes. They were only eighteen and alone in the world. You can do some stupid things. I wasn't quite eighteen myself and I'd just done something equally impulsive. Something that changed my whole life."

"Going off and driving an ambulance isn't the same."

"No but I understood how you could have an idea and just act on it."

I look at him, at the shock of white hair, the craggy nose, deep grooves around his mouth. It did always amaze me, how fast his reactions were.

"Okay, so the other bit that seems incredible is the coincidence. You becoming a man too."

"But it wasn't a coincidence. I've thought about this quite a lot lately. It must have made it easier for me to act. On the idea of passing myself off as a man. I don't mean the practicality of having papers.

That didn't feature much in my thinking back then. Because it was just a temporary measure. To solve a problem."

"What, then?"

"Well, I'd seen it with my own eyes. That it was possible." He looks at me. "Most days, for the last seventy years, I've thought about her. Just for a moment. I'd do it again, you know."

"What about the brother? The real Ben Coopworth."

Dad shrugs. "I imagine he was living somewhere as his sister."

"You didn't try to find him?"

"She wouldn't have wanted me to."

He picks up his mug of tea, takes a sip.

Finally I say, "So that's it. That's the story of my name. My last name. And Meg?"

"Was the aunt who gave Polly the fare to leave home."

"Mum never told me that. She just said she liked the name. Why didn't she tell me that?"

Dad shrugs again.

Something boils up in me. "Why are there so many damn secrets?"

No answer.

"Okay, while we're on the subject of mysteries, where do you think Mum got all that money from?"

He looks at me for a long moment then he says, "I told you, I don't know. It's time you went back to the city."

"You're telling me to leave?"

"Yes." He closes his eyes. It's as if the flesh has melted from his face.

"Dad."

"Please go."

Chapter Seventy Five

I PULL OVER in Stony Plain. Lean my forehead on the wheel. I want a drink. It's the loudest thing in my head. I just fucking want a drink. And why, look, here I am in front of a liquor store. Isn't that just dandy? Everything is shit and I want a drink.

A drink?

Fuck off.

Just the one?

I can taste it. Warm brown burn. No, of course it's not going to be one fucking drink. I'll drink the bottle. Then another. Blow up my life. What life? What the fuck is there anyway? I'm forty-two, can't keep a boyfriend, can't keep a job.

Whoa. Get out the violins.

Fuck off.

Poor me, poor me ...

Pour me a fucking drink, okay? I turn off the engine, pull the key from the ignition.

Shit. I'm going to do this. God. Whatever ... I'm shaking.

Meggie, you okay? Dora reaching down her big, bony hand.

Dora. Fuck. Help me. I'm going to drink.

Tomorrow, Meggie. You can drink tomorrow. Use tomorrow. Do whatever you want tomorrow. Not today.

Not today. I take a deep breath, then another. Jesus. Put the key back in the ignition. Start up the engine. Fuck. I'm still shaking. Breathe. Signal. Look.

"I parked in front of the liquor store in Stony Plain. Val, I was going to fucking go in there. I've been sober nineteen fucking years."

Val's taking the cash drawer and slips, putting them in the safe. "You had anything to eat today?"

I don't remember.

"There's a Lebanese around the corner. They make good sandwiches."

We sit down at a tiny round table in the back. "Talk to me, sistah," Val says. "Start with today."

"Today I found out I'm not Theresa Laboucan. I'm about to lose my job. I've fallen in love with a gay man who I took home to meet my father who's really a woman who stole the name he gave me from a dead soldier who was really a woman too."

"So this morning you woke up ..."

Fuck. Breathe. "I woke up late, because I worked last night. Woke up in the never pit. You know?"

"Tell me."

"After Mum died. I'll never walk into a room and see her look up. I'll never hear her voice. Like a bird against a window, beating at that never. And the other. What I'll never have. My blood. That belonging. By birth. Birthright. It doesn't matter how much I want it. I can't have it. Ever. Unless. Unless I am Theresa Laboucan.

"Then Doug, the gay man, told me Theresa is alive and well in Pensacola, Florida."

"Meaning you're not her."

"Correct. So I went stomping off to the farm. Demanded my father tell me where he got his name. Which is my name. Or at least it's the only damn name I have. Even if it's a stolen name."

Val shakes her head. "Run this part by me again."

So I give her the very short version of Dad's story which sounds as ridiculous as a Shakespeare plot when you leave out all the pretty speeches.

Val considers me when I'm done. "And what does this have to do with you?"

"It's my name. Coopworth. Meg C." Of course. She doesn't even know my last name.

But she's shaking her head. "Why is it your business?"

"How my father got the name he gave me?" I glare at her.

She gazes back at me, perfect nose, brown eyes, cream cashmere turtleneck, dark hair drawn back in a chignon.

"Fuck," I say at last. "You wouldn't understand."

"Try me."

I open my mouth but I don't even know where to start. "All I want," I say at last, "is to know where I came from. Everybody else knows. Why can't I just ..."

Shit. Even I can hear the self-pity.

"You want to know," Val says. "Of course you do. Have you done everything in your power to find out?"

"Everything I can think of, except remembering. I mean if I could just remember my own life. Like a normal fucking person."

Val waits.

Breathe. "Yes, I've done everything I know how to do."

"Then how about turning the rest over to the Creator. God. The doorknob, for all I care. If you don't let go of this, Meg, you'll drink. You just proved that. How many meetings have you been getting to?"

"Hardly any. I go for work but ..."

"Picking up the drink, that's the end of the slip."

She's seen it; I've seen it. Starts with skipping meetings. More important things to do. Then you get edgy. People don't do what you want them to and it pisses you off. Before long you're back pretending you're in control of your own life. So you can drink. So you do.

I take a deep breath, let it out. Feel my shoulders drop. I'm power-less over alcohol. Drugs. My father. My mother. My job. My past. Remembering my past. My life feels completely fucking unmanageable. I think it's a disaster that I'm not in control. But it isn't. It's okay. Even if I don't believe there's a God who is in control, it's okay. For today.

Val smiles at me. Sadness creases the skin around her eyes.

"Ah, Val," I say.

She shakes her head. There are tears in her eyes. *"Life on life's terms,"* she says. "You coming to the Mustard Seed tomorrow?"

"The correct answer to that would be yes," I say.

"Two chicken shawarmas," the guy at the counter calls out.

Chapter Seventy Six

HEATHER PULLS OFF her fleecy boots and looks around. She's wearing the jeans with sequins sewn on the back pocket and a grey angora turtleneck.

"Thanks for coming earlier. Sorry about lunch."

"No problem. Nice place." Heather smiles at me. Her eyes are almost violet in the morning light, catching the hint of mauve in her sweater. The wire rims of her glasses have a faint lavender iridescence. I've never seen her earlier than four in the afternoon.

"Want some tea? Coffee? I've got some good coffee."

"You've been hanging out with Doug."

"He's a nice guy, isn't he?"

"I don't trust charming men but yes, I think he is. And he's good with the girls. Not like one of those absentee fathers buying their love. My ex-husband played that game."

The phone rings. "Hello?"

"That you, Meg? This is Doug. I just spoke to Tanya. Brenda called her half an hour ago. Offered her condolences then told her that her services were no longer required. An official termination letter awaits her at Dreamcatcher. She can pick up her personal effects before 4 pm today. After that she will not be welcome on the premises."

"Jesus."

Heather's watching me. Now she draws a finger across her throat. I nod.

"Well, I wanted to let you know. You're meeting with Heather?"

"She's here now. I guess this simplifies the letter. Did you talk to Jay?"

"Not yet. Talk to you later."

"They really did it, the day after her mother's funeral?" Heather says.

"Yup."

"Well, I'm done."

"What about tonight?"

"Shite."

"Maybe we just stick to our plan. Work this evening. Leave the letter for Brenda so she gets it tomorrow morning. I'd like a chance to say goodbye to the place. Some of the clients. Even if they don't know."

"It's going to be hard on them. Not too much stability in most of their lives, eh?"

"You think we should tell them ourselves?"

"No, I don't. Do you?"

"No. But ..."

"You having second thoughts?"

"Not really, just sad."

Heather nods. "Crazy as it is, I'll miss the place."

"I don't deal with change all that well, myself."

"I'll miss our little gang. Maybe we can get together."

"Maybe."

"I know," Heather says. "I thought I'd go on seeing a couple of the women I worked with after I retired but we really don't have anything in common."

I wave goodbye from the stoop. Sunlight find its way down between the bare branches of the elms. I tip my face up. It's warm for the end of November.

Dad took apart an old apple barrel once, worked the bottom band all the way down, worked the top one up then pulled it off. The staves all fell outward. Lay in a ring on the ground. I stared at them. Couldn't see where the barrel had gone. How the pieces had ever made a barrel at all. Something stout you could fill and roll.

Ego strength. Lip-tooth speaking. Something I lack, according to her. I was trying to explain it, that feeling that you can just fall apart. There's no middle. You disappear.

You're afraid you will disappear.

Yes, but also you want it. It would be a relief. To disappear. Stop trying to hold yourself together.

Are you having suicidal thoughts?

Sober fifteen years, it wasn't gone. That call of the dark. Of dissolution. Annihilation.

'The beast,' Val calls it. 'Don't feed the beast.'

Chapter Seventy Seven

GUY FROM P.E.I. is telling his story. He only moved here a year ago. Sober ten years. No work back home.

I sit back in my chair. I'm in the right place at the right time doing the right thing. Whatever else happens in the day.

"Never got into the meetings here," he's saying. "I was used to knowing everybody. Three months after I got here, I walked into a bar, ordered a beer. Like it was the most natural thing in the world. Which it is for an alcoholic. Got away with it for a couple of weeks. Two, three beers a day. This is great, I thought, then fucked if I wasn't on my arse drunk. 'Scuse my language. Stayed drunk. Lost the job I moved here for. Got a D.U.I. so now I'm not going to be getting another job." He looks around. Pale stubbly face, receding brown hair. "I'm a truck driver, right? I was mad, picked a fight in a bar, got the crap beat out of me. So if any of you are thinking it's gotten better out there, look at me." He holds up his left arm. "I got enough frigging hardware in my wrist now, I set off the metal detectors. But hey, that's what it took to smarten me up. I'm back. I'm sober. I pray I'll never take that for granted again. One day at a time. So thank you. Thank you for being here today. Without you, I'm dead meat."

"Good speaker, eh?" Val's at my elbow.

I nod.

"How you doing?"

"Better. Thanks for yesterday."

"Keeps me sober," Val says.

"Hey Meg, is that you?"

I turn. Theresa's standing there, long black hair shining. Her skin is glowing. She's glowing. "Wow, Theresa, you look great."

"Meg, is it true they fired Tanya?"

"That was fast," I say.

"Teepee telegraph," Val says.

"Well, that's fucked."

"Theresa, do you know Val?"

They smile at each other. "Val's been helping me. Book-keeping, all that stuff. I'm doing it, Meg. The concrete business. Did Warren tell you him and Shannon are going to live with me until they can get on their feet? I could use some muscle in the business. He's really strong, you know."

I nod. "It's great to see you doing so well."

"Good to see you. Say hi to the gang. See you, Val."

Val's eyes follow her. She's smiling. Proud.

"So she's been coming to the Mustard Seed?"

"Says it keeps it green, what it was like."

"It's gotten worse, the neighbourhood, hasn't it?"

"First crack, now crystal meth. So they fired Tanya?"

"We're all quitting in protest, the evening shift."

"That's what you meant about losing your job." Val shakes her head. "I never could stand bad management. That's why I work for myself."

"You own the boutique?"

"I bought Madeleine out over six years. Half of every pay cheque. So what are you going to do?"

"I'm not working in an office again, but that's all I know."

"Why don't you go into business for yourself?"

"Doing what? When I quit my job I read a couple of those books. Stalled out on the first question. 'What is your passion?' I felt like such a loser."

Val waves a long-fingered hand as if clearing away smoke. "Your mother had just died. You weren't ready. Pray on it. You'll get an answer."

Val knows I'm not big on praying. Except when I'm about to pick up a drink.

"Keep an open mind, hon. I gotta go."

Chapter Seventy Eight

"MEG, YOU'RE THERE. I tried calling earlier. Can I stop by?"

"Where are you?"

"Just around the corner."

I see his shadow through the cloudy glass of the front door a moment before I hear his soft rap. "Come on in. The kettle's on."

"You're okay?"

"Yes. I just got back from a meeting."

"I was worried I dropped the 'you're not Theresa' bombshell on you and then I had to go. I debated delaying telling you but that seemed ..."

"Condescending? Good call. How was the funeral?"

"Beautiful. Real."

"And the girls?"

"They're fine. They're in good hands, between Tanya and Millie."

"And Tanya?"

"Pissed off but not surprised, about Dreamcatcher. Sad and relieved about her mother. It was a peaceful death, her children around her."

"What would you like? Coffee?"

"Just water, please."

When I come back into the living room, he's leaning back, legs stretched out in front of him. A different pair of darned socks. His face looks more creased than usual.

"So we're all going to be out of work tomorrow," I say, handing him the glass.

"Will you stay here or are you thinking about moving to the ranch?"

"I'm not sure Dad would have me right now." His eyes are on my face but he doesn't say anything. "I pushed him to tell me stuff he really didn't want to talk about. He told me to leave." I take a deep breath. "I came as close to drinking as I've come in almost twenty years."

Doug sits up. "Because of that or because you found out you're not Theresa?"

"Because I haven't been getting to enough meetings. Because too many things came together. But yes, finding out I'm back to square one as far as knowing where I came from was part of it. My sponsor thinks I'm going to drink if I can't accept not knowing."

"What do you think?"

"She's probably right. But it's crazy. It's in there. In here"—I point to my head—"the information I need. I just can't make it come out."

"And you really do want to?"

"Yes."

"So tell me a story." Doug leans back again.

"What kind of story?"

"Whatever comes to your mind. Make something up."

"Anything?"

"Anything."

"Okay. There was a girl who had a friend. Which was good because she needed a friend. Her mother was high. Her father was worse. She had a dog. Who died."

I stop. "Sorry. I can't help it."

"Hey, it's your story. Take it wherever you want."

"But I don't want." I stop. "Maybe I do. Okay. The dog died. The mother died. Or something. The father. The father was a nice father. Except when he wasn't. When he was drunk he was happy. Except when he wasn't. He had friends. They came and played cards and they drank beer and sometimes they argued and got into fights. After the men were gone her father would come upstairs. He would stand in the door of her bedroom. She would screw her eyes tight shut. She wouldn't move a muscle."

I stop, stomach curled so tight on itself I could throw up. I say, "This isn't my story. This is my mother's story." My voice sounds far away. Everything is far away.

"Her mother had a stroke. Her sisters left home. They told her it was her turn now. They laughed."

"Your mother told you that?"

"She told me what the sisters said. But I didn't understand what it meant. So it's her story."

I stop. Doug has that sorry-for-you look that made me want to rip the heads off assorted therapists. I open my mouth but then I shut it because he's nodding and there's something else in his eyes.

"Everywhere you look." He says it softly. "My girls. Lorraine. A man Tanya was dating. Girls and I talked on the phone Sundays I was up north. Lorraine didn't sound herself. She told me." He shakes his head. "I paid my whole month's wage to get on a chopper that night. Called up Tanya when I landed. Told her he'd better be gone. I'd have killed him." Doug's voice is quiet, matter of fact.

"Is she ... your daughter okay?"

He nods. "Bastard suggested something. Told her it would be their secret. She'd be his 'little princess.'"

"Tanya didn't know?"

He shakes his head.

I feel tired and sad and wound up. I open my mouth, say, "I have scars on the backs of my legs."

He looks at me, face serious, waiting.

"Sorry. I don't know where that came from."

He looks puzzled.

"I mean it's true. It's just ... I don't know why I told you that."

Only I do. I want him to fly in on a helicopter, chase away the bad guys. Take me somewhere safe. I want it so much my chest is caving in with the wanting. And I'm completely embarrassed. I'm forty-two years old, talking to a co-worker.

But it's real and clear and true, that wanting.

"I wanted to be rescued," I say.

I wrap it into myself. I wanted to be rescued. I know this. This is something I know.

Chapter Seventy Nine

MY FINGERS SINK into rough fur. I breathe in sage and sweet-grass and aftershave. My eyes travel up the courses of stone to the opening at the top.

"Creator, Spirit, Whatever, please help me accept my life as it is, right now. Even if I never know anything more than that I wanted to be rescued. Please help Danielle and Edward and Geoffrey and Gordon and Don and Deborah; Warren and Shannon and Joey; Mona and Janice. Help Ash and James and Wendy and all the others come back and try again. Help Dreamcatcher and Cathy and ... yes, Brenda too. And Theresa and Val and Judy; Tanya and Millie and the girls. Help Doug and Jay and Heather. Laura too and Harold. And Bill. Help Manfred and Victor and Dad and Mum, wherever you are if there is a life after this."

I'm sitting in the dome, eyes closed, fingers buried in the coat of a long dead bear. It spreads out like ripples in a pond, the prayer.

"Amen," say the people in the circle. "*Hai hai.*"

The blanket is drawn back and we stand, blinking, Jay and Heather and I spread out among the female clients.

Laura's pushing a pad and pencil across the counter. "Write down the number," she says, "and your name."

"That's not ..." Don says.

"It's how I do it," Laura says with a swing of honey blonde hair.

She dials the number from the pad, hands him the receiver and writes down the time beside his name.

He turns his back on the desk, stretching the cord.

She taps him on the shoulder. His head snaps around but whatever he was going to say goes unsaid. He rolls his eyes then turns so he's facing the counter.

"Who's next?" Laura asks, holding out the pad.

"The list is born again," Jay murmurs to Heather who is folding sarongs. "I'm going out on the floor." She catches my eye.

"And I'll do a room check." I reach for the logbook but Laura beats me to it.

22:27 Meg doing room check, Jay on floor, Laura on desk, Heather in office.

I trail my fingers along the belly curve of rock. Jay's waiting for me on the far side. She glances around. Most of the clients are in their rooms already, tired from their Sunday pass.

"Doug called earlier. We're all invited to his place on Thursday. A farewell to Dreamcatcher barbecue. Partners invited. Not that Annie will come. She's had her fill of Dreamcatcher stories. She's not going to miss me working here."

"And you?"

"Fuuuck," Jay says. "I should be glad but ..."

I nod. "I have the letter for you to sign. What do we do about Laura? I assume Doug didn't tell her. It feels weird, skulking around behind her back."

"Then let's tell her."

"Should we ask Heather?"

"She doesn't care. Brenda's not going to back down from firing Tanya."

"So, Laura," Jay says. We're all in the office. I'm counting cash, Heather's at the computer.

"Yes?"

"You heard that Tanya was fired yesterday?"

"Yes."

"Well, the three of us and Doug are quitting as of tonight. In protest at that and at the lack of aftercare."

Laura nods. "I warned Brenda," she says.

"Oh?" Heather turns in her chair.

"What did you say?" Jay asks.

"That the evening staff were tight. They were unlikely to accept the dismissal."

"And what did she say?" Heather asks.

Laura looks around at us. "She said, 'Evening staff are a dime a dozen.'"

"And what did you say?" Jay asks, her voice perfectly neutral.

"I said, 'You get what you pay for.'"

Heather's eyebrows go up. "And what did Brenda say to that?"

Laura shrugs. "She knows the board is discussing making the positions full time. With benefits."

"Well," Heather says, glancing at the clock, "I expect we should do the overview. Let's see. Mona?"

"Good but anxious," Jay says.

"Jeanette?"

"Struggling."

"Danielle?"

Jay looks at me but it's Laura who answers. "Working on her issues."

Chapter Eighty

SO HE'S GAY. So he's not going to be my boyfriend. I have a friend who calls up and offers to bring lunch.

Thinking of Heather and Val's soft sweaters sends me on a search through the plastic tub under the bed. I pull out the angora boat neck I bought in Val's boutique a couple of years ago. When I had a real pay-cheque. My good bra. Silk undershirt. Or just the soft wool against my skin. Black jeans. Perfume?

Meg.

It's not really perfume. A lemon verbena cologne. I brush my hair until the doorbell rings.

Doug's looking kind of spruced up himself, or at least he's wearing a new plaid shirt and his hair's a couple inches off his shoulders. Freshly cut. Brushed too.

"Nice sweater," he says, smiling down at me. Sunlight catches threads of silver in his hair.

"Nice shirt," I say and we're just standing there, smiling at each other in the little glassed-in entry.

Then he shifts the carrier bag in his hand and I step back. "Here, let me take that."

He takes off his boots and follows me into the kitchen.

The tripe is mild and rubbery in the aromatic broth. The beef's sliced thin, pink and tender.

"This is the best pho I've had since I left Vancouver."

"How was the last shift?"

"Interesting."

We help ourselves to seconds.

"Did you hear what Brenda said to Laura?"

Doug nods.

I smile. "It's not that interesting, is it?"

He shakes his head, smiling back. "I'd rather hear how you felt."

"Different. We all went into ceremony. I really prayed. There were a lot of people to pray for. People I cared about. I felt grateful." I shake my head. "It's hard to talk about. Not *hard* hard, just difficult to find words for. I felt ... I am grateful to you for helping me get to that feeling. About being rescued. Even though I find it embarrassing." I look at him. He's watching me with his quiet brown eyes. "I was praying to accept my life as it is, including all the not-knowing, but it does feel good to have this one thing I know from before."

Doug opens his mouth, closes it again.

"What?"

"Well, I don't know if I should go there."

"I didn't say I was happy about not knowing."

He studies me. I meet his eyes. Hold them. I don't mind, I think. I don't mind him seeing me. And I have the odd feeling he's thinking the same thing.

"Well," he says, "perhaps you were rescued."

"What do you mean?"

"When we were driving to your father's place the other week, on the back roads from the Divide, I thought how far it was from anywhere. If you'd been on foot you'd have had to cross the river. If you were coming from the west. And from the east ..." He shrugs. "I wondered if someone brought you there. Dropped you off."

"Dumped me, you mean. Like a litter of unwanted kittens."

"Meg, I'm sorry. I shouldn't ..."

"No. Say what you were going to say."

"It was something you said about Manfred and Victor. When you were figuring out that they were a couple. I said they were lucky they ended up on your father's farm and you said, 'Too lucky.' "

"What are you getting at?"

"You showing up at the farm. Whether you got there by yourself or somebody ... somebody left you there, wasn't it an incredible piece of luck that it was that particular farm?"

"What are you talking about?"

"What were the odds that the people would take you in? Treat you as an answer to their prayers?"

I stare at him. "You mean it was someone who knew Mum and Dad? But why would they do that?"

"To get you out of a bad situation?"

Something's balling up in my stomach. "Fuck. Why don't I remember anything?" I push my soup bowl aside. Stand up. "Sorry. I need to move around."

He nods, worried eyes following me.

"Want some coffee?" I ask.

"Please." He gets up, brings the bowls into the kitchen, goes back for the glasses.

"I'm okay, Doug." But I'm not. My heart is thudding. I grind the coffee, tip it into the French press. Then it's as if a scroll's unfurling in my mind.

I go into the living room. "I could tell you a story," I say. "Maybe that's all it is, but what if they were hiding the girl? They took her out of a bad situation, wanted to make sure her people couldn't find her. They couldn't take the girl themselves because the people would come looking for her. If they told Ben and Polly the situation then they would have to lie to the authorities. Whereas if they didn't know, if the girl just showed up, they could do what they did. Tell the truth. It was such a crazy story ..."

When I don't go on, Doug asks, "Who are they? Are they 'the friend'? From the other day?"

I can't breathe.

After a moment he says, "It would all depend on you not talking."

"Well, I didn't. I couldn't."

"I know, and that was very convenient."

"You think I was doing that on purpose?"

"No. Or not exactly. It's just ..." He stares off into space, brows furrowed. "It's too convenient. Not just that you couldn't talk. You couldn't remember. Even your own name."

"I didn't make that up." It bursts out of me.

"No, no. That's not what I mean."

"People do forget. Traumatic amnesia. It happens." Inside, great black wings are spread, are beating. Beating at the walls. There's no room ...

Stop. Breathe.

Not working. Hold my breath.

I'm dizzy. Gasp for air.

"What's happening?"

My heart's pounding. Something's coming, huge and black, filling all the sky. I gasp for air. I'm panting. I shrink to the ground. Doug's squatting on the floor beside me.

"What is it?"

"I can't. I can't." I'm sobbing and gasping. Dread twists every fibre. "Something. Something terrible. Jesus. No. No." My voice is frantic. Pleading.

Breathe. Let it. Let it come.

"I can't. I can't. I can't." A great black wave is curling above me. Is going to break ... I'm on my feet.

Yes you can. Let it. Let it come.

And I do.

I stand there and the wave breaks and I breathe and the water fans out around me, wide and shallow. It ripples across the sand and I'm standing, breathing in the sunlight. Nothing happened. I open my eyes, look at Doug. He's still squatting, one hand on the floor. His eyes are golden brown, clear.

Nothing happened.

He shifts and his knees crack.

Nothing.

"What just happened?"

"Nothing. The thing I've been afraid of my whole life. It was nothing."

He stands up, stiff.

"Um. I'm sorry."

He shakes his head. "Don't. Please."

I nod.

"Shall I finish making that coffee?"

"Yes."

In the bathroom I throw water on my face. Dry it. Peer at myself. I look different. I feel different.

Doug's back on the chesterfield, mug in hand. A second mug steams by my chair. "Will you tell me what just happened?"

I nod, sip my coffee. It tastes purple and rich, eggplant purple, almost black. Glossy. Black wings. No words.

Try again. Like breaking through a paper wall. Okay. "This is going to sound weird. When you said it was convenient. That I couldn't talk. Or remember. I got frantic. Something terrible was going to happen. The worst thing you could imagine. I think someone told me that's what would happen. Convinced me."

"To keep you silent. Stop you telling." Doug is nodding. "Abusers do that."

"Yes. But this might be different."

"What do you mean?"

"It sounds crazy."

"Tell me anyway."

"The story. If a person ..."

"You mean the person who ..."

"Took me out of the bad situation ..."

"Scared you into keeping silent?"

"Like a spell." My voice has slowed down. "If I talk. If I tell anyone who I am, where I come from, then this terrible thing will happen."

Doug waits then asks, "What terrible thing?"

"The worst possible thing I can ever imagine happening. Something huge coming at me, cornering me, smothering me so I can't breathe.

"Jesus."

"I might have supplied that."

"From what had already happened to you?"

I nod.

"The wall I always hit in therapy. I've tried for years to get close to that fear. But I'd always panic. Today I stood there. Let it come." I'm still feeling it, the wave rippling out over the sand, the sunlight.

I look at Doug. "I think I've been trying to do that my whole adult life. Let myself feel. What I was so afraid of. Somehow you being there to ... to witness. Somehow it was possible today. Thank you."

"Do you ..." He hesitates.

"Remember anything useful, like my name and address? No, but I know what just happened was real. Because it's such a relief."

He nods.

"It's weird but I feel better. Solid."

His eyes stray to the mantelpiece. To the clock. Ten past three.

"Which is a good thing," I say, "because you need to go, don't you?"

"Yes, but I could make a call, see ..."

I shake my head. "I'm okay. I really am. I need a little time to digest. Then I need to call Dad."

"Shall I give you directions now, to my place? For Thursday. You can come, can't you?"

WEEK SEVEN

Chapter Eighty One

"DAD, I'M SORRY about last time. That I pushed so hard about the name."

He looks straight at me. "You came very close to suggesting I kept Ben Coopworth's secret for my own purposes rather than out of respect for his sister's wishes. That was not the case."

Even though I'm standing and he's sitting down, I feel about three feet tall. But I'm not. I'm forty-two, sober, willing to admit when I'm wrong. "You're right. That was insulting. I'm sorry."

He nods. "Now sit down and tell me what's brought you here first thing in the morning."

Out of the wind, the sun is warm on my face. I close my eyes. Somehow that makes it easier to ask. "Dad, do you think it's possible someone you or Mum knew brought me here?"

"Brought you here and left you? Why?"

"Someone who was desperate to get a child out of a bad situation." I sense him turning to look at me. "Someone who knew how much Mum wanted a child." I open my eyes. He's shaking his head. "Please Dad, think."

"Meg, this doesn't make sense. Where did you get a story like this?"

I made it up. I don't say that out loud. But it isn't crazy. I don't know how to explain it but it isn't. "Would Mum have told someone in her church?"

"She'd never have told them that."

"Did you tell anyone?"

He's silent. Eventually he says, "I told Moira. But Meg ..."

"Dad, please, humour me."

"Very well, but let's go inside."

Once he's settled in his chair I ask, "Did you tell Moira about Mum wanting a child before or after I came to the farm?"

"Before."

"Was there anyone else you told?"

"No."

"Will you tell me about Moira? How you met her. What you said to her. Every little detail. Please."

"Very well. The first I heard of Moira McFie, it was in the autumn of 1966. Or it could have been '67. The tannery in Drayton Valley had gone out of business. Old fellow couldn't get any of the young men to work for him, including his own son. Pembina oil field was in full swing. Somebody told me about a trapper over by Rocky Mountain House, a woman no less. She'd tan hides so they came out soft and supple as rabbit skin. She lived out in the bush but she'd pick up and deliver hides on a Saturday morning in one of the bars in town.

"So, one Saturday I slung a couple of bales of hides in the truck and drove down there." He stops, stares out at the mountains though they're hidden by cloud then looks at me. "I wasn't in a good way. Polly's drinking was bad by then. She hadn't started banging her head but she raged, shrieking accusations, taunting me, and I, well I wasn't in my right mind by then either.

"I parked the truck behind the bar, tried to pull myself together. My plan was to get a look at the hides she'd already tanned before committing myself. Moira was where they said she'd be, in Happy Joe's Bar and Tavern. The only woman. Her hair was wild and mostly grey but you could see it had been flame red once. The triangle of her cheekbones and chin somehow made your eyes settle on her mouth.

"I tipped my hat to her, asked if she were the lady trapper who tanned hides."

"'Trapper,' she said, considering me, a little smile.

"I met her eyes but only for a moment. I felt stark naked, standing there in that bar, her looking at me with those green eyes.

"'Moira McFie.' She held out her hand.

"It was smooth and cool. 'Show me what ye've got,' she said with a strong Highland lilt. She stood up and I followed her out.

"She reached into the back of the truck, fingered hide and fleece. Nodded. 'Drive me down the road a piece,' she said.

"She smelled of smoke, wood smoke and tobacco, both. Neither of us said a word. It looked as if we were heading back across the river but just before the bridge she pointed left. We took a rutted track as far as the truck would go.

"'Would ye help me carry them?'

"I hesitated, surprised. From what I'd heard, nobody even knew where she lived. Besides, we hadn't come to terms. But I nodded, swung her the first bale, hefted the second. When I settled it on my shoulder I looked around. She was gone.

"'Here.'

"I jumped. She was behind me. I looked down. She was wearing moccasins now, the boots nowhere to be seen. We wove through spruce and fir for several minutes. She must have been in and out of there at least once a week but I couldn't make out a track. At last we settled to a straighter course and I could see the wear in the ground. We can't have been far from the river, the trees tufted with old man's beard, moss underfoot. Then moss rose up in front of me, moss on wood shingles. I made out a low doorway. She set the hides to the left and I did the same.

"'Come ye in.'

"I took off my boots. Light filtered in through a single window. Well, you've seen the place. I'd been in enough cabins in my travels with Dorothy I knew more or less what would be where. There wasn't anything I wouldn't have seen forty years earlier.

"'Have a seat,' she told me, pumping fresh water into a bucket. The gush and squeak of that pump brought Dorothy to mind so clearly it was as if she were standing in front of me.

"Moira spooned tea into a pan on the stove. We didn't say a word while the water came to the boil. Without asking she put sugar in my mug before passing it to me. We sat some more, each clasping our mugs with both hands, spurts of flame visible through the open drafts.

"'I don't care for it,' she said at last, 'going to town. But I don't fight it.'

"She sounded less Scots than in the bar. One hand let go of her mug. There wasn't much light but I could see the fist she made. 'I fight it, it has me, yes?' Head tilted to one side she studied me, eyes like moths fluttering over my face.

"Slowly I nodded.

"'I let it be ...'

"Her hand unfurled, palm up. She spread her fingers. They were long, tapering. 'Everything passes. If I let it.' Now her eyes were steady on mine. 'Live by yourself in the bush,' she said so softly I leaned forward, 'you can go mad. Live with anyone else in the bush, you can go mad that way too.'

"She waited, her silence then a pool of still water. Like a deer, I lowered my head, drank it in. I drew that water deep and deeper. Every cell sang in the relief of it.

"I thought it was just her. Drinking. But now it's me." My voice startled me.

"After a while she said, 'I was married to one the booze owned. There was no end to his thirst. He could vow by everything sacred. An hour later be drunk again.'

"What happened

"'I went mad myself. Angry, all the time. Fast as I could pour his drink out, he'd find a place to hide more. One day, I was behind the door, spying on him. Nothing but a little shack, me hiding behind the door. Suddenly I saw myself.'

"'What did you do?'

"'Started laughing. He dropped the bottle. It rolled across the floor, spilling all the way.'

"'What's so funny?' He was scrambling to pick it up.

"'I stepped out from behind the door. Couldn't stop laughing. Then he was laughing too.'

"Did he stop?

"'Drinking? No. But I stopped hanging my happiness around his neck.'

"'What happened in the end?

"'I found my own peace.'

"'To him?'

"'He hung himself.'

"I opened my mouth.

"She shook her head. 'There was a lot he had to deal with. In himself.'

"'That must have been ... What was that like for you?'

"'Sad.'

"She said the word so simply, and somehow I understood. 'It didn't have to do with you?'

"'No.'

"That was when I told her I couldn't give Polly what she most wanted in the world which was a child. I didn't care if Moira guessed why. It was such a relief to tell someone. And then, when the words were in the air between us, I could see how we were both doing it, Polly and I. Hanging our happiness around each other's neck. She blaming me for the drinking. Me with ... with my own unhappiness. Moira didn't say a word but the quiet came back into me then."

His face is thoughtful under the wild eyebrows.

"You think she knew you weren't born a man?"

"To be a good trapper you have to see what's in front of you. Most people are lazy. It's easier to sort the world into categories than it is to look. If you give them what they expect to see they'll toss you into the usual box, no questions asked. Moira was not somebody you could fool that way."

"She's dead, isn't she?"

"Yes. About twenty-five years ago some company bought the mineral rights to the land around her place. Cleared a road right next to the cabin. Their equipment suffered a lot of breakdowns." He shrugs, the skin around his eyes creasing in a smile.

"It didn't stop them. In the end she moved to the Territories. Seven, eight years ago, I got a letter from the man who was her nearest neighbour. He'd mushed into Yellowknife. When he came back out a couple of days later he didn't see any smoke from the chimney. Went to check on her. She was frozen solid. Heart attack, they thought. The only name and address he found was mine."

"She didn't have any family?"

Dad's brow furrows. "Well yes, she did, at one point. A brother-in-law, anyway."

"How old was Moira when you met her?"

"Younger than me. I was sixty-six. She could have been sixty. Thereabouts."

"And the man she was married to ..."

"He was Cree, I know that much. Which would have been ..." He shrugs. "She said something once about service, being in service. Some Englishwoman who thought she was getting a lady's maid got a scandal instead. If she went off with a Native man it would have been a scandal all right. White men shacked up with Native women, everybody knew that, but the other way round?" He shakes his head.

"Went off with the man she married, the alcoholic?"

"It's possible."

"How old was she when she was with him?"

"Young, I think, but all I remember her saying was 'long back'."

"Could she have gotten pregnant?"

"Nothing she ever said made me think she had borne a child." He stares out of the window then looks at me. "Somehow I think she would have told me."

Chapter Eighty Two

OUTSIDE, THE WIND has picked up. The sun's behind a veil of cloud. Moira knew Mum wanted a child. But that's all I know. I'm standing in the driveway. Can't even decide which way to walk.

The door to the machine shed slides open. Manfred emerges wiping his hand on an oily rag.

"Coffee break," he says. "Will you join us?"

"That would be nice." No snarl, nothing.

He's probably got whiplash from my moods. But they're both welcoming. The trailer is too. The butterscotch yellow's cheery, and the apple green curtains have been washed and ironed. It's far more of a home than my house.

"Cream in your coffee?"

"Yes, please."

"Have a seat."

I sit on the bench on one side of the table, they sit side by side on the other.

"So," Victor says, "tell us about Doug."

Manfred says. "Don't mind him, Meg. Have a brownie."

Coffee and orange weave through dark chocolate. Suddenly I feel as cheerful as I was tormented ten minutes ago. "Magic," I say, waving the brownie at them. "What do you want to know? Not that I can tell you a lot. I work with him. He's a nice guy. I haven't had a guy

friend in a long time. It helps that he's gay. I mean he's emotionally
literate in a way a lot of straight men aren't."

"Gay?" Victor looks at me with wide eyes.

Manfred's shaking his head.

"What makes you think he's gay?"

"Victor."

"Well, he's not."

"What do you mean he's not?"

"Honeycakes, the only person on this farm that man had eyes
for was you. He adores you."

"He does not."

Victor raises his eyebrows and purses his lips.

"He does not." I look at Manfred.

He tips his head sideways, raises one eyebrow.

"When did you two become so camp?"

"In the heart of ever rugged rural gay man," Victor thumps his
chest, "beats ..."

"A fluttering fairy," Manfred says.

"Stop it. You're trying to distract me. Are you serious?"

"Yes." A pair of grey eyes and a pair of brown eyes are suddenly
and thoroughly earnest.

"Why would he tell me he was gay?"

"He told you that?"

"Are you sure?"

"He's the go-to guy at work for any gay issue. Besides his ex ...
His brother ..." I trail off. "Shit. There have been things that didn't
seem right. But ..."

"Why don't you ask him?"

"What and look like a complete idiot? Besides it would sound
like some weird come-on. 'Hey, are you gay because if not ...'"

They're both looking at me, identical smiles on their lips. "You
like him, don't you? Ben said ... Ow." Victor yelps. Manfred smirks.

"Ben said what?"

"He worries about you."

"Being a lonely spinster?"

"Being alone in a big city when most of what you care about isn't
there."

"Oh."

He adores you. I want to ask, 'Are you sure?' Which of course I don't because I know it's not true.

Doug is not interested in me. If he's not gay he'd have made some kind of move by now. Besides, all he's seen is that I'm a complete fucking basket case. He's a friend. A good friend.

"More coffee?"

Victor's holding out the pot.

"No thanks. I should go back to Dad's."

"Well here, take these with you for lunch. Kale spanakopita and a Greek salad."

I shake my head. "You guys are amazing."

They shrug the same shrug then laugh, looking at each other. "Together too long," they say.

For a moment I want it so fiercely I can't breathe, that ease with another person. The being known.

Chapter Eighty Three

"WHAT'S FOR LUNCH? I saw you bringing something over."

"Spanakopita. Shall I put them in the oven? They're supposed to bake for twenty minutes."

When I come back into the living room I ask, "Dad, why do you think Moira was so secretive about where she lived?"

"I wondered that myself. At first I assumed it was because she was a woman living alone but, once I got to know her, that didn't seem likely. I don't think she was afraid of much. Besides, she was well armed."

"What then?"

"She liked knowing no-one would come knocking. She didn't have much time for people."

"Except you."

Dad nods. "I think she enjoyed my company. But she didn't need company, you know?"

"Did you? Do you?" The question surprises me as much as it does him.

After a moment he says, "Yes. I learned that, prospecting alone." He stares off at the mountains then turns to look at me. "Funny you asked me that, about company. When you were out for your walk I was thinking about the settler and his dog. The terrible loneliness. Men who'd served in the war, they were entitled to a free quarter section of land. He wasn't the only ex-serviceman we encountered who was in a bad way. Shell shock, isolation, grinding work. You got to know the look in their eyes. Haunted. And ashamed. You were supposed to come back and get on with life. As if nothing had happened."

"Were you affected like that?"

I'm not sure he's going to answer but then he nods. "The first season in the Monashees. A local shopkeeper was fronting me my gear, feed for the horse and me. In return for half of any stake I claimed. Half of nothing was nothing. We both knew that. But there was no work to be had. Nobody had money to buy his goods. We agreed on a general area I'd explore. Copper. Silver. Gold. I spent the summer in the mountains. Alone except for my horse. I wanted to enjoy it more than I did. I found I wasn't easy in myself. But certain places helped.

"There was a little glade, just below the tree-line, nothing spectacular but I always felt comforted when I sat there. The trees wrapped around you but you could still look out across the ranges. Then lightning struck and that part of the mountain went up in smoke. When I walked into it, my little glade, all charred and acrid, the war came back. The pig shed. The dying soldier. All the dying soldiers. The moaning. Screaming. Cursing, praying mangled men. The horses. I tried to make it go away. But it wouldn't. Or only for a few minutes. I couldn't sleep. I couldn't eat. I certainly wasn't collecting rock samples. I could hardly look at my horse. Because suddenly I'd see him torn apart." He shakes his head. "I'd had flashes, before. Bad dreams. But I could always set them aside, go on about my business. One night the settler came into my mind. I remembered Dorothy walking right up to him, sitting down next to him. I could see her eyes, so clear and steady.

"She was showing me what to do. That's how it felt. I had been trying to push away the images. My experiences. I was afraid they would destroy me. Instead I saw I must allow them in.

"The strain went out of me and I slept for the first time in a week. My dreams were terrible and I woke weeping. It was several days before I could go about my work but I had come through to the other side. The memories would return but I wasn't afraid of them. Not the way I had been." He looks directly at me. "Does that make any sense to you?"

"Yes. Yes it does."

He lifts his nose and sniffs. I smell it too. Something beginning to burn.

They're not too bad, the spanokopita, just a little darker than golden. As soon as we sit down to eat Dad asks, "How's work?"

"Over," I say. "We all quit."

"Oh."

He's disconcerted. His neutral topic evaporated.

"You don't think they'll ask you all to stay on?"

"Not a chance."

"What are you going to do now?"

"I'm not sure. I may be able to get E.I.—Employment Insurance—while I figure it out."

"And Doug, he resigned too?"

I nod. Dad wants more. I relent enough to say, "He has a business making harnesses. We're all going to get together at his place tomorrow for a farewell barbeque."

"Will you miss it, the job?"

"My co-workers, definitely. And the clients."

"Has it affected you, working somewhere like that? You must have seen a lot, heard a lot." Dad's put down his knife and fork. He's considering me, head tipped to one side. More blue jay than hawk.

"People have been through so much. It's painful to listen sometimes. But, well, at least I'm feeling. Feeling for people, you know? It'll just swell up in my heart, sadness but also a sort of wonder. That people survive what they do. And can still love.

"I pray for people because I don't know what to do with all the feelings. I don't have any idea what I'm praying to, but I pray anyway, for something to help them along the way."

"And do you believe there is help?"

"Something helped me get sober. I'm not sure of much else. What about you?"

"A lot of religion seems childish to me. A demand for certainty in an uncertain world. On the other hand, I have had my angels. It seems rude not to acknowledge them."

It's my turn to nod but I'm shy suddenly of his eyes. And hungry. I haven't touched my spanakopita. Forget the knife and fork. I pick it up and bite into buttery filo then dense kale and salty feta.

Dad forks in the last mouthful he'd left politely sitting on his plate.

"Yum," I say, trying not to scatter filo everywhere.

Dad licks his forefinger, dabs up flakes from his own plate and transfers them to his mouth.

"Mum wasn't a good cook, was she?"

Dad shakes his head. "Even when she wasn't so inclined to frown on the pleasures of the flesh she tended to boil things to death. Might have been the lumber camps. They weren't famous for haute cuisine."

"Was it unusual for a woman to have that job?"

"She always knew how to keep the boys in line." His voice is light but a shadow crosses his face. After a moment he says, "It does help."

"What does?"

"Talking about things. We didn't, you know. Talk about the war. Afterwards. There I was in London. No family. No one to welcome me back. But it was more than that. There wasn't any place for me. For what I'd experienced. I wasn't the only one in that boat. Maybe there were some who swam right back into the lives they'd lived before but for most, well, it was an adjustment. Nowadays you'd be encouraged to talk about it. Then, even if someone did want to hear—which mainly they didn't, *least said soonest mended*, you know—but even if they did, it was another world.

"You were back among lighted windows, rain shining on the streets, women drinking tea in Lyon's Corner Houses. An ordinary world and all the time you knew there was another world which was equally real which was mud and rats and wire and mines and screaming and the booming of the guns and men gassed and burned and maimed and dying and all you could do was know them both, both worlds, as if you were walking along a crack in the world, a foot on either side. There wasn't anything to say, you see?"

"I think so."

"The worst was the war people wanted. The women especially. They wanted champions. Glorious exploits. Men would give it to them, that war. Those who spoke of the war at all. Because who could explain that in the end they fought not for home or country or King or Empire? They fought for each other. For the ones who lived and died in that other country." He falls silent.

"And what about you? What about the ambulance drivers?"

"And the nurses, the women in the canteens." He shrugs. "We were supposed to go back to our husbands. Or our fathers."

"But you didn't. Did you want to?"

He shakes his head. "I don't seem to have a reverse gear. I couldn't imagine going back any more than I could imagine returning to England at the end of the Sunday School mission."

"You and Dorothy, didn't you talk about the war?"

"We didn't see each other for a while. She wasn't best pleased when she learned that, far from having my father's blessing, I had deliberately flouted his orders. She felt, correctly, that I had misled her. It put her in an awkward position, living, as she and her father did, quite close to my family, and moving in the same circles."

"She forgave you enough to tell you about needing a driver for the mission van."

"She wasn't one to hold a grudge." He yawns. "Sorry."

"Nap time?"

"Twenty winks."

"I think I could do with a few myself. I didn't get much sleep last night."

Upstairs, I lie on my back and stare at the ceiling. It's really just painted boards nailed to the undersides of the rafters. Must get cold up here in the winter. I turn my head. Where the four slopes of the roof meet, there's a wooden block with something carved into it. I've never seen it before, but then I've never lain on this bed in daylight. It's a circle with two strong lines dividing it into four, plus two fainter ones dividing it again. Like the Medicine Wheel Emmett drew. Like a compass, more likely. And yes, at the end of the line pointing north, two short lines spread out from the tip. If I moved back here this would be my room. If Dad would have me. I couldn't stay up baking all hours of the night. And what would I do for a living?

And Doug?

What about Doug?

He adores you.

He does not.

But he likes me.

And I like him. Oh yes I do. A silver bubble rises in my chest.

He likes me enough to call me up and bring lunch.

And walk with me through the valley of the shadow of death. What?

Whatever it was that happened the other day, he was there. Clear and steady.

And something did happen. I'm different.

Drifting into sleep I smell tobacco smoke, feel soft fur under my hands. Safe. Safe in the warp and weft of their voices.

Chapter Eighty Four

I WAKE FROM a dream I don't remember, thick-mouthed. Sodden with sleep. I hate sleeping during the day. Hate waking up in my clothes. Did enough of that in the old days. Staring around trying to figure out where I was. Who was lying next to me, half the time.

The toilet flushes. Dad's back in his chair by the time I get downstairs.

I sit down. "Dad, why did you take me with you that time, to deliver the hides?"

"To Moira's? She asked me to."

"To what?"

"To bring you." He's looking at me, surprise in his face.

"Why?"

"I don't know."

"How did she know about me?"

"I told her."

"When? How did that conversation come about?"

"A few days after you arrived she phoned. I remember the timing because I had just made an appointment to talk to a social worker."

"Did you tell her about me then, on the phone?"

He nods.

"How did the topic come up?"

"You mean, did she ask some leading question? She didn't get a chance." He smiles. "I was half-way to agreeing with Polly that it was a miracle, first Polly stopping drinking then you appearing like that."

"When you told her about me, what did she say?"

Dad frowns. "I'm trying to remember. Nothing much. I told her about the appointment. That it looked hopeful that you could stay with us while we applied for approval as foster parents.

"She told me she was going away again. That was why she was calling. She'd let me know when I could bring more hides. I didn't hear from her for almost a year. When I did, that was when she asked me to bring you. She said she'd like to meet you. I didn't think anything of it."

"Where did she call from?"

"The bar in Rocky Mountain House let her use their phone. I'd given her my number."

"Had she called you before?"

"No."

"Would you have expected her to let you know if she was going to be out of town?"

Dad's brow furrows. "No. No, I wouldn't."

"You told me about the first time you met her, taking hides to the cabin. What happened next?"

"About a month later she dropped me a line saying the hides were ready. I was to meet her at the bar. I thought we'd go back to the cabin again. Or at least I hoped we would. I'd tasted what it was like to talk to another human being without reservation. It left me hungry for more.

"But this time she was all business. We went out behind the bar. She had an ancient car tucked into the trees at the edge of the lot. My hides were on the backseat along with a bedroll. They were beautiful, the hides. The best I'd ever seen but I couldn't swallow my dismay as she pocketed the money and turned away. She turned back, looked me in the eye. 'I got some family trouble of my own,' she said. 'I'll be back.'

"I just nodded. Watched the car pull out of the lot. She turned left not right, headed for the mountains. I felt empty then." He tries for a smile, doesn't quite make it.

"Oh Dad."

"There have been easier times in my life. But it had helped, the earlier talk. There'd be hours in a day when I wasn't consumed by my ... my thoughts."

I want to ask but there's a rawness to his face that makes me reach for the teapot instead.

"I don't know exactly what Moira meant by 'family trouble,' if that's what you're wondering. I didn't see her again until the next spring. I got a note saying she was back. I was about to start lambing and besides, I didn't have any hides to take her. Nothing to justify the petrol. I went anyway. Time was Polly would have noticed but by then she was just eager to have me out of the house so she could get on with drinking herself silly."

"What year was this? Yesterday you said you met her in '66 or '67."

"It must have been '67 because Polly didn't get really bad until that last year before you came."

"So this would have been April or May 1968?"

"That's right. This time Moira asked me to give her a ride to the cabin. I don't know what had become of the car. If it was even hers. It wasn't suited to the terrain. Most of the snow was gone but the ground was still frozen or I don't think we'd have made it in my truck.

"I paid close attention to the route this time. She noticed. 'Next time you come,' she said, 'come here or they'll all be flapping at the bar.'"

Dad holds up his hand making the mouths moving sign.

"'Me driving off with a strange man.' She laughed then and there was something in the laugh made me almost certain she knew.

"When she'd made us tea and we'd lit our pipes, I asked how her trip had gone.

"She looked blank.

"'The family trouble.'

"'Ah. My husband's brother. Lives up by Creston.'

"'The husband you told me about?'

"'One was enough.'

"I waited.

"'He wrote to me, said his niece was in trouble. I could come, spend the winter, my own cabin, run a trap line or two, maybe she'd talk to a woman.

"'He's a good man. Funny. Lost his wife to cancer. They never had children. The niece is the closest thing he has to a daughter.'"

"Niece as in Moira's husband's daughter?"

"I'm not sure. Moira didn't say anything to indicate she'd had any part in raising the girl. But her husband could have had a child with another woman. Or there could have been another brother or sister who had a child. I'm afraid I don't know."

"So what did Moira find out?"

"The niece wouldn't see her. She'd been in the States. Came back with some man. The uncle thought he was a bad lot. That the niece was scared of this man but the niece swore blind she loved him and everything was good. According to the uncle it wasn't. He'd seen bruises on her wrists. And she was yellow, as if her liver was packing in. She wouldn't go to the doctor. Or her man wouldn't let her. The uncle thought he might have been dodging the law."

"Did she have any children, the niece?"

"Yes, she did. She had a daughter."

"How old was the daughter?"

"I don't know."

"Think, Dad. Please. Anything. An impression."

"Not a baby," he says slowly, "but still a child."

I wait.

He shakes his head. "That's all I can think of. She never talked about them again."

"And you never asked?"

His brows furrow. "I might have, once, but I don't believe she answered. I'm sorry. I wish I could tell you more."

"Do you?"

He gazes at me. That look.

"Sorry. I'm sorry, Dad. But I think this is it."

"Will you tell me why? I'd like to understand."

"Just don't laugh at me."

"Of course not." He's surprised. Hurt.

"Sorry. That was uncalled for."

I tell him about the wings. Feeling something terrible will happen if I speak. "I think someone told me that. I think I was so scared I shut everything away."

He nods slowly. "When you came here you were tucked far down inside yourself. I had the feeling you'd made a place for yourself and nobody was going to get to you ever again. I knew—we knew—something awful must have happened to you. Beyond just the scars on your legs. I don't mean just but ..."

"I know. I've spent years in therapy, trying to release those memories. But I always hit that wall of silence. Until the other day when somehow I was able to stand still, let it come. The fear behind the wall.

"It was Doug who pointed out that, if someone took me out of a bad situation and brought me to a place no-one would think to look for me, the whole plan would have depended on my silence."

"So the way you couldn't talk, or wouldn't, it was because you were afraid to?"

I nod.

"And you think it was Moira who did that? Moira who scared you into silence?"

"I can't think of anyone else."

At least he doesn't immediately reject the idea. Instead he says, "Let me smoke a pipe and think about this."

When he's sitting down again he says, "A few weeks ago, when we were talking about the time I took you to Moira's cabin, you said you felt safe there. You weren't afraid of being stolen away when you fell asleep. It stuck in my mind."

I nod. "It echoed in my head after I said it."

"But if Moira did what you think she did, wouldn't you have been afraid of her? How could you have felt safe in her cabin?"

"I don't know." He's right. Of course he's right. It doesn't make sense. I felt safe when I shouldn't have. A wave of tiredness washes over me and I taste whisky. Just for a moment. That moment before you swallow the first mouthful. I stand up. "Can I see the newspaper, Dad?"

Chapter Eighty Five

"ARE YOU ALL right?"

"Mostly. I could use an AA meeting but there aren't any around here tonight. Will you tell me more of your story? About what happened after you became Ben."

"Mary and I camped in the river valley until it was too cold. Chased any rumour of work. Ended up in Red Deer for the winter. In the spring she met a fellow. Went off to B.C. with him. I got a job as a ranch hand. Near Drumheller. Big spread owned by a remittance man. Too fond of the booze. Aristocratic family was happy to pay him to stay on this side of the ocean. He wasn't awash in money but he kept a good stable. Said the horses liked me. I was glad of the work."

"You'd been living as a man for how long?"

"A year."

"And with Mary gone you were alone with your secret. Was that hard?"

"There was someone else back then I'm pretty sure knew."

"Who?"

"I don't want to shock you."

"Come on Dad."

"Drumheller was like Moose Jaw, a wide open town. Playground for the whole Red River Valley. Used to be coal mines all over. There were still a few hanging on. Enough to support a couple of establishments." He glances at me. "The miners mostly went to May Roper's place but the fellows from the ranch favoured Fanny Ramsley's. I went along."

"God, weren't you ...?"

"Nervous? Yes but the older fellows had told so many stories I felt as if I'd already been there. Besides, on pay day all the hands went. I didn't want to stand out.

"Fanny's place was in a coulee less than a mile east of town. It was a substantial building. The living room must have been thirty feet square. They had a piano. Used to be a coloured cook called Mamie Carter, the best cook in the valley, they said. She played the piano whenever she wasn't cooking and Fanny worked the bar. Fellows danced and drank and played poker and sat about. I'm not saying there was no sex going on.

"Along two sides of that big room ran a corridor with half a dozen rooms opening off it. But even in my day there were plenty of men there for the music and the cooking and the company. In the old days, when the mine operators were having a get-together, or the miner's union, the Legion, the Elks for that matter, that's where they'd go. Dinner at Fanny's. It was the most comfortable place around. A lot more civilized than the bunkhouse at a ranch or a miner's shack or any homestead.

"The girls didn't lack for offers of marriage. It was always a worry to Fanny, keeping staff. 'They don't know what they're getting themselves into,' she'd say about the ones who went off to marry a miner or a homesteader. Working for her, the girls had some comfort and time to themselves. They'd sit around and do fancy work or read or tend to the flower garden. One girl kept chickens, the Polish ones with a silly top-knot. They could buy the finest clothes any store in Drumheller carried, but the smart girls saved their money. In time they'd go on to set up a house of their own. Not too many other ways a woman could come to own her own property in those days."

It sounds like such a sensible business proposition. Like Theresa with her escort service.

"So you see it was different then. There wasn't a lot of prejudice. In the early days it was how most of the women came to the prairies."

The white women, but I don't say that out loud. "What about the police? Wasn't it against the law?"

He shrugs. "Fanny said as long as you were outside the city limits, the police wouldn't bother you. If the girls started parading their finery down Main Street that might cause trouble. Especially if they were better dressed than the first ladies of the town. Then worthy citizens would start some sort of Moral Reform Society to put pressure on the authorities, but generally the police just made a show of doing something. They knew the trade wasn't going away and they'd just as soon deal with a known quantity." Dad yawns. "I think it's time for bed."

"There's something you haven't told me."

"What?" He gazes blandly at me.

"You said someone back then guessed your secret."

"Fanny, I think. Not that she said anything but the girls didn't tease me the way they did the other shy fellows. As a matter of fact ..." He hesitates.

"What?"

"Well, I've wondered since whether she was interested in me herself."

"Was she gay?"

"I don't know. It didn't go anywhere. I was ridiculously naive. We enjoyed each other's company. She liked to read. She liked books by the Americans who lived in Paris. Fitzgerald. Hemingway, Anais Nin. 'The French know how to live,' she used to say. She was teaching herself the language. So she could read Collette in the original. She'd dreamed of taking a trip to France but trade wasn't what it used to be." He's looking at me, a half smile on his lips.

"Where did she get the books?"

"The fellow who ran the local newspaper had literary ambitions."

"What was she like, Fanny?"

"Fiercely intelligent. She wasn't beautiful—her features were too big for her face—but she had great vitality. According to her, she was what the French call *jolie laide*."

"And she was attracted to you?"

"She seemed"—he hesitates—"alert when I was around."

"But you didn't think of yourself as gay?"

"No."

"What did you tell yourself? About who you were?"

"Or what I was? To a degree that must surprise you, I didn't. As long as I didn't have a name I could just be myself. Perhaps I stayed in a state of innocence so I wouldn't have to find a name for myself, for what I felt. That was what was so astonishing about Polly. That moment in the clearing. Walking into her arms. *I know what you are. And what you are not.* I walked out of my un-knowing. It was gone. From now on we would know together."

"Expelled from Eden?"

"It was time."

Chapter Eighty Six

WE EAT OUR oatmeal in silence. Dad seems far away, the way the mountains do some days. I woke with the smell of spruce and smoke in my nostrils. The feeling of safety that makes no sense. Makes nonsense of everything.

When he puts his spoon down I say, "You're going to tell me about Mum, aren't you?"

He's gazing at the window, no sign he heard me.

"About the money Mum somehow acquired."

Silence.

"You must have asked her about it."

"She asked me not to." His voice is flat.

"And you didn't?"

"No, I didn't."

"But what did you think?"

"About what I think now."

I wait. Finally I can't help it. "That whole happy brothel story yesterday. I'm not stupid. I live ..."

His eyes stop me. After a moment he says, "This is not mine to tell."

"Mum's dead, Dad."

"I'm aware of that." He glares at me. I glare back. "You don't know what you're asking."

"I think I do."

He stares at me. "Very well. But first I'm going to smoke my morning pipe. Alone."

Beyond the window, beyond the blackened stems and shrunken heads of the sunflowers, the mountains march across the horizon, rank upon rank. The Mum I knew stood here. And the one who banged her head until it bled, who drank and raged. The other mother. I close my eyes, grip the edge of the sink, dizzy the way I'd get dizzy lying on my back watching the wind chase clouds across the sky. I'd close my eyes then, sun red behind the lids, the buzzing of bees in the flowers, a fly tickling my arm. Under me the springiness of twigs, thin turf over rock. Mum spreading out a picnic, Dad striding toward her, me lying further up the slope, invisible in a slight hollow. 'Lunch,' Mum would call, her voice echoing from the rock faces.

Dad takes his time settling back into his Morris chair. He's lost the angry raptor look. At last he says, "It really was different, you know, back then. And what was she supposed to do? Fourteen years old, out on her own, no money, no education, no family."

"It's why she chose that church, isn't it? She couldn't forgive herself."

"Forgiveness." Dad snorts. "They talked about forgiveness all the time but they never let anyone forget their sins. Too busy feasting on them. Give me a brothel over a church any day."

"Please tell me what you know."

"All right. The money she left you. Polly always had a head for business. She'd read the financial pages, study the stock prices. I used to tease her. 'Dreaming of making us rich?' Now, I think she had money invested. Whatever was left over from buying the house and the land. I really don't know how much that was or where it came from."

"But you suspect."

"You're sure you want to know about this?"

"Yes."

"There were two things she let slip. The first was in the early days. We'd both had a bit to drink. We were sitting on a rock and she hoisted up her skirt, stretched out her leg, twisted her foot this way and that. For some reason she didn't have shoes on. 'I used to be a dancer,' she said, 'on the stage.'

"'You're still a dancer,' I said. I was thinking about the step-dancing she did.

"'Not like that,' she said, then she clammed up."

"That was it?"

He nods.

After a bit I ask, "Is that where the cane comes in? It was part of some sort of stage show? A burlesque?" Mum a burlesque dancer. Fishnet stockings and a top hat. That's *Cabaret*. "Did they have burlesque shows in the Prairies? Or was it before she came West."

The look on Dad's face tells me it's not going to be this easy. "What was the second thing?"

"When the drinking got bad, there was one particular night. I must have remonstrated with her about something, I don't remember what. She was beside herself, her face all twisted up.

"'You're nothing.' She spat the words at me. 'You can't do it. You can't give me what I want.'

"No arguing with that. The harsher the words she hurled, the further inside I went. It maddened her. Perhaps that was what I wanted. *You can't get me.*

"But she could. That night she said, 'Men who had their pick, real men, they picked me. They'd ask for me.' She caught herself then but it was too late."

His eyes are scorched. The skin surrounding them is ashen.

"Dad, I'm sorry. I shouldn't have pushed."

"Let me finish. We never spoke of it again. But it took hold of me, that image. I'd be out with the sheep, checking the water troughs, wind ruffling the grass, all I could see would be the girls parading around for the men to choose. As if I was outside, looking in at a lighted room. I couldn't look at Polly without seeing the men taking their pick.

"It got worse and worse. I didn't want to be around anyone, didn't want anyone to see me. To see what was in my eyes. Winter was coming and the prospect of the two of us in this house, nowhere to go but the barn. An idea can sink its claws into you and you can't shake it off. Whatever sense you try to talk to yourself, it's bigger than you. It's got you.

"I'd have done almost anything to get the peace back in my mind. Tried drinking too but it didn't do anything for me." He looks at me. "It was like the time in the Monashees, the way the images kept coming. Polly, parading. The men, choosing. That was the state I was in, the first time I met Moira. Driving down to Rocky, I started picturing my gun. I could put an end to it. Not just me. I could make sure none of them would ever possess her. I knew it was madness. I was afraid. I was afraid I could really do such thing."

"Oh Dad."

He's gazing out of the window the way I've seen him do a thousand times. Shadows drift across his face. Eventually his lips move. I lean forward. He turns to look at me. *"This thing of darkness I acknowledge mine."*

Prospero, *The Tempest.*

"It humbled me, to lose control of my own mind. Perhaps the flaw was always there, the fear that I couldn't deliver what a real man could."

"Isn't that what most men are afraid of?" The question just pops out.

Dad looks at me, startled, then he laughs. He laughs until there are tears in his eyes and he looks like himself again.

"You know," he says, wiping his eyes with one of his big soft handkerchiefs, "I've thought about it, over the years. Why it hooked me like that. Things had gone sour with Polly. We'd always"—he hesitates—"enjoyed each other. But at the end there she didn't want anything to do with me. A fact she made abundantly clear. In her cups she had a deadly instinct for the sore spot. I think the more I felt like a man, the more I felt it that I wasn't a real man. But I wasn't a woman either. It wasn't that I was both, I was neither."

"You were always you."

"I had to be or I was nothing."

"There wasn't any scaffolding to hold you up."

He studies me. "You don't have any scaffolding either."

There it is. The thing I've been mad about my whole life. I could laugh or I could cry. "Sometimes I feel so flimsy. As if I could just disappear. You, you've always been so solid."

"I filled my pockets with stones."

"The mountains?"

He nods.

"The way you became the oak pew thing in church?"

"Yes." He looks surprised. "Exactly."

"Being a part of everything ..."

He nods. "But I forgot. I forgot, that last year with Polly before you came. I felt the most alone I'd ever felt. It wasn't just Polly who needed saving."

"Oh Dad."

"If Moira was somehow responsible for you coming here, well, I've even more to thank her for." He yawns.

Chapter Eighty Seven

I PUT THE bowls in the sink. Wind slices across the field. Turning from the window I see the kitchen as it was the day I arrived, the old wood cook stove where the stairs are now. The table nearby and the bench I sat on, observing them, these strangers. The woman with bulgy eyes, the man with golden hair. They left me by the stove, went into a room and closed the door. I heard the murmur of voices then hers, an eagle screech, *No.* His: *Polly, we have to.* In all the years after that I never heard him raise his voice to her again. Nor she to him. They never fought. Pursed lips now and then. Dad's livestock schemes. *I told you* so thrumming in the air. Discussions about where the stairs would go when they built the bedroom. They went round and round on that one.

I've done my time on the wheel of sexual jealousy. It's not hard to picture how that image consumed Dad. If I forget it's Mum and Dad we're talking about. My experiment in non-monogamy ended in a dose of obsessive picturing. Which I dealt with by running away. Dad though, Dad cut a hole in the roof and built a new room. Not a fortress, a fastness. A mountain fastness. Or a nest. A nest on the roof of the house. Where somehow they found their way back to each other.

Sunday mornings he'd make tea, take it up on a tray with flowers in a little vase. Or rose hips. Or sprays of dried grasses. I had a job, first thing. Mum's main flock of chickens lived in the coop and laid their eggs in nest boxes but then there were a few who lived in the barn and roosted high up in the rafters. They fed on stray grain, scratched up the bedding, laid wherever they felt like laying. During the week I gathered eggs from the obvious spots but those hens were crafty. On Sundays, my job was to hunt for the ones I'd missed. Then I'd take them down to the river and throw them as far across as I could. It wasn't until years later I thought to ask Mum why we didn't float those eggs in a bowl of water the way we usually did to check for freshness.

She blushed.

Outside, I leave the shelter of the house, cross the field where my life began. My remembered life. I walk right up to the edge of the bluff, slide my toes to the lip. The river, twenty feet down, is directly under me, carving into the bank. It's gone, the place where I used to stand, throwing the bad eggs across the river. The possibly bad eggs. So Mum and Dad could have their marital bliss in peace. What Connie from my old job used to call it. *Our marital bliss.* I only once met her husband Steve and he didn't seem much to write home about but she was happy. Content. Never joined in the hatefulness of the other women, talking about their boyfriends, their husbands. That weary contempt. I'd think, why bother then? *Can't live with them, can't live without them,* someone would say eventually and they'd laugh. I can't seem to live with either gender so I'm not one to talk.

It's too cold to stand around. My feet take me into the shelter of the cottonwood grove. The trees are different, old ones fallen down, new ones growing up. It was like a summer river, the flow of days here. No shouting or screaming. Until I hit adolescence. At fifteen I flung words like stones. Splashed them like acid. Some part of me appalled at the wantonness of it, like swinging a sledgehammer in a roomful of glass. Only of course I didn't believe I had the power to hurt. Didn't believe it could matter, what I said, any more than that it would matter if I disappeared. Leaving them to guess if I was alive or dead.

"Do you have time for lunch? It's cream of parsnip soup."

"Victor stopped by while I was out?"

"He did. Have you decided?"

"About what?"

"The lease."

"No. Sorry. I've had other things on my mind."

"I know."

But. He doesn't have to say it.

"Can I ask you another question?"

He nods and puts down his spoon.

"How did you deal with it, that jealousy?"

"Meeting Moira helped. Not that I talked about it but I had the feeling of being understood. Sitting there in her cabin, it was as if I remembered things I already knew. From the time in the Monashees." He looks at me and I nod.

"Eventually, instead of trying to push it away, I invited it in. Listened to what it had to say. Which was that I was afraid there was no place for me. Not now, nor would there ever be. Nobody would ever choose me. Not if they knew. Poor little cuckoo. It went back long before I became a man. Didn't matter that Polly and I had loved each other for more than thirty years.

"I wanted Polly to solve my problem and for many years she did. She chose me. But now it was up to me. Dorothy was in my mind quite a bit those days. Perhaps everybody has an image of the eyes of God, whether or not there is a God. I tried to imagine meeting Dorothy as Ben, revealing myself to her. Or being recognized. But I couldn't picture it. Trying made me see the gulf that divided my life. Far deeper than merely crossing the ocean. More than just changing my name. I had become somebody nobody would recognize.

"Moira, though, Moira looked out at you from a deeper cave. Dorothy had the solid loyalty, the clarity of spirit I found in my dogs. Moira wasn't one you'd trust the way you'd trust Dorothy. But by then I understood life wasn't simple." He stops, rubs his chin. "I'm rambling, aren't I?"

"No, I like listening to you talk like this but I really should get back to the city." I gather up our bowls. "We're all—the Dreamcatcher crew—meeting at Doug's this afternoon. I could use some clean clothes."

"You could always leave some here."

"Maybe I will."

"And invite him over again. I'd like to hear him play the fiddle."

"Dad, I should have told you this last time. He knows about you. And Manfred and Victor. I thought it was okay to tell him because he was gay himself. I thought he was. Now I'm not so sure."

"But you trust him?"

"Yes, I do."

"That's all right then. Oh, hold on. Here's something I remembered when you were out walking. Something Moira said. Something the brother-in-law told her. He said the niece thought her man was 'all that and a bag of chips because he made movies.' No, 'because he was a filmmaker.' It was that phrase that came back. 'All that and a bag of chips.' It was so incongruous, coming from Moira's lips."

"A filmmaker," I say. The hairs are standing up on my arms.

"That's all I know. It's not very helpful."

"It might be."

Chapter Eighty Eight

IT'S NOT AT all what I expected, a sprawling log cabin style house varnished a glossy orange brown. One small barn; a paddock; fenced pastures. I recognize Jay's black Honda Civic and Heather's silver one. No Tanya yet.

"Come on in." Doug's smiling in the doorway, red and tan plaid flannel shirt, jeans that perfect faded softness.

"Hey Doug." He steps back to let me through at the same time I hold out the sack I brought. "Bison steaks," I say as he says, "Come in" again and we stall in the doorway. I inhale leather and hay, looking up at him. He's oddly serious, looking back at me.

There's a scatter of gravel in the driveway. Doors open and slam. "Dad." It's Lorraine or Mina, the younger girl anyway, barrelling toward us.

Doug steps forward to catch her as she throws herself into his arms. The other girl is close behind. Tanya's getting something out of the car.

'They're the real family,' I think.

"Meg, is that you?" Heather's voice, from inside the house. "Come on through."

A hallway lined with knotty pine and framed photographs leads to a deck that faces west. Two horses graze in the distance. A cold wind ruffles faded grass.

"How are you with fires?" Heather asks, brushing bits of bark from her fingers into the fire pit. "Doug had it going nicely but ..."

"Hey Meg." The collar of Jay's jacket is turned up, framing her pale face.

"Might have been a bit big," I say gazing down at the unsplit log smothering the fledgling fire. I grab some smaller pieces and a length of metal bar that's obviously been used for this before. Levering up the log I slip twigs and branches underneath then let it back down. We all watch. Nothing happens. At last one flame licks up the side of the log, then another.

"Good thing he's got a barbeque too," Heather says. I glance around, betting on real charcoal.

"What are we eating?"

I jump at the voice behind me.

"Mina, my girl," Jay says, "how are you?"

"Hungry. Starving."

"Well," Heather says, smiling at her, "I brought potato salad and Jay brought smokies and Meg brought something." She hooks an eyebrow at me.

"Bison steaks."

"And Mom brought hamburgers and Dad will have steaks. Regular steaks." She casts me a look. "And buns and relish and ketchup."

"Maybe," Jay says, "I should get those smokies on the grill right away."

Mina nods vigorously.

"Have you met Meg?" Heather asks.

She shakes her head.

"Meg, this is Mina. Mina, Meg."

She considers me for a moment. "You work at Dreamcatcher too."

"I did."

"You all did. This is a goodbye party."

"Smokies coming up," Jay says.

Mina races after her.

"They're good kids," Heather says.

Jay and Mina are side by side now, Jay looking down at Mina who's explaining something.

"How old are they?"

"Ten and twelve. It's so different," Heather says, "how kids grow up now. My mother would have had my hide if I'd busted in on a grown-up conversation like that. But you're only young once. You've never had kids, have you?"

"No. I don't think I'd know how to raise them." I stop, embarrassed, but Heather shrugs.

"Doesn't stop most people."

When everyone is milling around the fire pit I go off in search of the washroom.

The house puzzles me. It's definitely nineteen seventies, down to the pale blue shag carpet on the stairs. I open a couple of doors onto bedrooms which haven't been used for twenty years, judging by the mix of dust and ancient furniture polish. Finally, there's the washroom then a room with boards laid across two file cabinets. A computer and a printer. Posters on the wall. Most to do with the Cardinal Divide. And bookshelves. Anthropology. History. Music. And then 'The Manly Hearted Woman.' 'The Spirit and the Flesh.' Footsteps sound in the passageway. Shit.

They turn into the bathroom.

I scoot past. Back in the kitchen I see that another, larger room opens off from it. There's a Navajo rug on the floor, an older one on the wall plus a saddle blanket on the stone chimney above a large fireplace. A Morris chair with wide, flat arms is drawn up to the fireplace, a book splayed open on the leather covered seat. Same era as Dad's chair but the legs are square, the slats under the arms rectangular. The oak's stained a darker brown too.

The sound of flushing sends me back into the kitchen where I fill a glass with water.

"How are you doing?" It's Jay. "Nice place, eh? The girls love it here. You haven't seen the basement, probably, but they have it set up as their den. Grown-ups by invitation only."

"Did they all live here, when they were together, Doug and Tanya?"

Jay gives me a sideways look. "No, they were in the city. I don't think Doug spent a lot of time here until after they split up."

"Wow, that bison steak was good." Doug's chasing the juice around with a scrap of bun.

"Delicious," Heather says. "I didn't think I'd like it. Country food, you know. Back home the Newfoundlanders were always trying to get me to eat moose." She wrinkles her nose.

"You marinated it," Doug says.

"The place that sells it did. On 118th and 60th, I think. Not that far from Yvonne's."

"Next to the cake place, the shrine to icing?"

"The butcher's brother raises ..."

"Eh hem."

We turn. Tanya's looking round the group of us, plates on our knees, in the room with the rugs. The girls are outside, swinging on a rope hung from the branch of a pine tree. The cobalt blue has faded from Tanya's hair. Raven's wing black, it frames her long cheeks. She's another one with perfect lips.

"Since we've got a moment of grown-up time," she says, "I just wanted to thank you for standing up for me. At the cost of your own jobs." Her voice is ragged. "This is a hard time, eh? Even though Mum was ready to go. It means a lot to me." She sits down abruptly.

"You're welcome," Heather says. "You're very welcome. And, speaking for myself, it was a pleasure. I've had to swallow and smile enough in my life to get by, you know? It felt fine to say 'No. No, this is no way to treat a person.'"

Jay's nodding. "Hear, hear. My only regret is, I'd like to have been a fly on the wall in Brenda's office on Monday morning."

"Well," Tanya says, "I did get a call from Pam, Brenda's secretary. Brenda wasn't too fazed by us quitting but guess what? There's a new aftercare coordinator."

"Who?" Heather asks.

Jay narrows her eyes. "Laura?"

They're grinning, Tanya and Jay and Heather. "Watch out Brenda," Heather says.

Tanya nods. "According to Pam, Brenda looked like she swallowed a toad."

"She might be good," Heather says. "Landlords won't know what hit them. But what about us? Anyone got plans?"

Jay's nodding. "I'm going to finish my degree. But I was looking at the job boards and I saw something I might like. Pay's decent too. I'm going to apply."

"What's the job?"

"Store detective."

There's a moment when we're all looking at Jay and then everyone is nodding.

"You'd be good," Heather says.

"You like observing people," Doug says.

"Still get your drama fix," Tanya says.

"What do you think, Meg?"

"Do you get to wear a fedora?" They all laugh. "No, I agree. I can picture it."

"And you?" Heather's looking at Tanya.

"I'm going to apply to the RCMP. Been thinking about it for a while. Girls are old enough now. They may not take me." She shrugs. "It's not just you they do the record checks on, it's your whole extended family, eh?"

"Jesus, they ought to snap you up," Heather says. "You'd be great."

It's not hard to picture Tanya, stern-faced, standing by my car while I wind the window down. Tanya the Mountie.

Doug's smiling at her but it's okay. Suddenly I get it, how different they are. The way Bill and I were different. Too different. You fool yourself for a while but then something makes it obvious and after that you can't help seeing it. It takes a hold of you, the knowing.

"What about you, Meg?" Heather's voice filters in. They're all looking at me.

"I want to bake bread and sell it."

"Open up a bakery?" Jay asks.

"No. I'd sell it at the Farmer's Market in the city."

Doug's studying me. "Where would you set up?"

"My Dad's farm. I could rent out my house in the city, use that to live on. Borrow against the house to buy equipment. If it all worked out, I'd sell the house, pay off the loan."

"You've really thought this through," Heather says.

"No, I really haven't. It just came out of my mouth."

"But it sounds good," Jay says.

"I've seen the money people are charging for food at the Farmer's Market," Tanya says. "City's changing, eh?"

I look at Doug. "What about you?"

"I like working with leather. Plenty of people buying acreages. I'll be good until the next bust. Might even learn to make boots. Cowboy boots for the well-heeled. Underwrite my unpaid activities." He smiles at me. "I watched my Dad try to make a go of farming. People pay more for the things they don't need."

"Proves you're a member of the leisure class," Jay says. "And you, Heather?"

"Well, I don't know. I've got my pension but ..." She shrugs. "I was at a meeting last night. Somebody asked if I'd heard about the new treatment centre for women with eating disorders. Thought I might contact them. Of course I could go on a Caribbean cruise. But I think I'd rather talk to someone about throwing up, you know?"

Chapter Eighty Nine

I RINSE THE soap off a plate. "So when was this house built?"

"Nineteen seventy eight. The old place burned down three years after my brother died. I thought it would kill my mother but in an odd way it seemed to help. They sold most of the land. Dad's heart wasn't in it. He was already working another job to make ends meet. They built this with some of the money. Plus the insurance."

I hand him a plate and he wipes it dry, looking around at the varnished logs.

"The house I grew up in, it was a plain little hip-roofed prairie house, not that different from your Dad's place. Before the addition. Which is, by the way, very cool. This place, it's somebody's idea of a log cabin." He shrugs. "It's an imitation of a real thing, you know? But I love the land. I love the smell when the sun touches the grass in the morning. The colour of the earth. It's hard to explain."

"You don't have to."

I hand him another plate and take a deep breath. He looks as if he's about to say something but I need to do this. "Doug, you're not gay, are you?"

"Me? No. Where did you get that idea?" His eyes narrow. "Wait. Tanya told you."

"Not directly."

"But you believed it?"

"I didn't have any reason not to."

He gives me a long look.

"Well, why wouldn't I? Everyone looked to you to talk to Geoffrey. When James was being a jerk. And the others. You stood up in front of everybody. You said ..." I squint, trying to bring the words back, Doug standing there, head swivelling, hooded eyes ... "You said, 'It's nobody's business what he is, what I am, who we love. We all deserve the same respect.'"

"You never heard of solidarity?"

"And then you gave me that whole spiel about keeping people guessing. What was I supposed to make of that?"

"It seems I succeeded." He tips his head to one side, a funny look on his face. "What else?"

I probably shouldn't say this. "You're too sensitive and emotionally smart to be a straight man."

He stares at me then he starts to laugh.

"And anyway, I'd never have invited you to my place for coffee."

He stops laughing.

"What?"

He shakes his head.

"Come on. I just made an idiot of myself."

"I was starting to wonder if maybe you were a lesbian."

"Me? What made you think that?"

"The way you talked about the land. When we were up on the Divide."

"I have had women lovers but ..."

"And when you invited me back to your place the first time we went out, then you pretty much pushed me out of the door ..." He shrugs. "I figured one way or the other you weren't interested. Easier on the ego if you're gay, I guess. Same reason Tanya decided I was. And you do treat me like a brother."

"But you never flirted with me." My face gets hot.

"I wanted to but then you were ..." He stops.

"Too fucked up?"

"Too vulnerable."

"Oh." He wanted to.

"On Sunday, when I brought the pho, I told myself it was now or never because, once we left Dreamcatcher, I was afraid we wouldn't see each other."

"Oh."

"I was going to ask you out on a date date. Then there you were, all dressed up. You were even wearing perfume. But ..." He shrugs. "It went in another direction. I had been thinking about how you got to the farm. I just wasn't necessarily going to bring it up then."

"But once again I was a basket case."

He's standing there, dishcloth dangling from his hand. He's waiting for me to meet his eyes. They're golden brown with darker rays.

"Meg, you're a brave woman."

"Brave? I hardly ..."

"Brave. To let it come, the old pain. I spent years running from it. It ran my life, fear of what I felt. Until one day I did what you did the other day."

I'm watching his lips move. Soft, rosy lips above the jut of his chin.

"It changed everything. My moment of liberation. It was so simple. But it took everything it took to get there. To be willing. To accept." He smiles a crooked smile and my heart squeezes. "Not that everything was right, proper, God's will, all that. Just that it was what it was and there I was, big enough to feel it."

"The other day," I say slowly, "was a kind of liberation. That's a good word. But I have another question for you."

"Okay." He looks wary.

"Do you still want to flirt with me?"

Like a gust of wind reaching across the surface of a lake, a grin wrinkles his face. "Maybe."

"I'm not very good at it."

"I'm kind of rusty myself."

"So there's no one else?"

"No. You?"

I shake my head. "We could practice."

"I know," Doug says, putting down the cloth. "Why don't you come and sit on the chesterfield with me?"

"I could do that."

So I do. I like the smell of him but I'm twitchy as a mouse.

"You don't have to," Doug says.

"It's not that."

"It was easier when I was gay?"

"Mm. Are you laughing at me?"

"With you. I'm laughing with you. I'm nervous too."

"And I have kind of a disastrous track record."

"I consider myself warned. Besides I'm not so good myself at the relationship thing."

"How come? Sorry, that's not exactly a sensitive question. But I'm surprised."

"Maybe I like being by myself too much. I like to play my fiddle, ride my horse, eat, walk, think, make stuff. I love Mina and Lorraine but I'm not a family man, you know? I never felt a burning need to have kids of my own. I don't like noise and TV and parties and sports."

"Not even hockey?"

"Definitely not hockey. Ping pong maybe."

"You don't have much to prove."

"The older I get the clearer it is that very little in life is about me."

"That's what Dad says too."

"I'm not that old."

"How old are you?"

"Forty nine. You?"

"Forty two. Ish."

He studies me a moment. "I've tried to imagine what it's like to be in your shoes, but I didn't even think of that. Not to know your own birthday."

"Mum and Dad always celebrated the day I came to the farm."

"And you?"

"I did too. We decided I turned ten that day. It's even my official birthday. On my driver's license."

"What day was it?"

"The sixteenth of September, 1968."

"Do you still celebrate it?"

"Yes, and I always have a hard time on that day. But ..." I shrug.

He reaches an arm around my shoulders. I lean into him. There's a new smell like the yeast on wild berries, and then there's something strange and sweet, like the incense that spreads through the air first thing in the spring when the buds on the balsam poplar grow sticky with resin. It makes you lift up your head, flare your nostrils. His eyes are two suns shining on me, so much light I almost have to look away. I stare back into them and I'm going in and in. Room opens onto room.

"Doug."

"Mm."

I'm lifting my face and he's coming to meet me.

Chapter Ninety

THE SILVER APPLE *of the moon, the golden apple of the sun.*

. Waking, those words drift through my mind. And an image. A low doorway. Moss covered shingles.

I'm glad I didn't stay last night. Though I wanted to. Silver bubble in my chest the whole drive home. It's still there.

He adores you.

Maybe.

You're not the beggar at the feast. Old Lip-tooth. Me and my *scarcity mentality.*

Okay, so I've known Doug for … He started working at *Dreamcatcher* when Danielle arrived. A week after Geoffrey came. And Geoffrey should be leaving this coming Wednesday. So forty-nine days minus twelve days. Equals five and a half weeks. That can't be right.

We didn't make a plan. For when we'll see each other. Because we're taking it slow. Like mature adults.

The phone rings. I grab it. Drop it. Shit. "Hello?"

"Meg. How are you?"

"Good. Happy to hear your voice. Um, how about you?"

"Really good. I was, well, I wondered if you wanted to go for a drive?"

I look out of the window. It's grey and windy. "That would be lovely."

"I know it's not exactly …"

"We could go and visit Dad again. He asked me to bring you."

"I'd like that. Plus ..."

"A chaperone," I say.

"Exactly." I can hear the smile in his voice.

"So the guy was a filmmaker." We're in the jeep, headed south on 22. "That means something to you, doesn't it?"

"Mum and Dad only ever took one photograph of me. When I heard the shutter click I lost it. Started shaking and hyperventilating. I was standing by a river. The North Saskatchewan, up where it rises. All the rocks looked glassy. In the water. I don't know how to explain it. Like they were separate and I could crawl in between them. Disappear. That was what I wanted. More than anything in the world. I wanted to disappear. Dad tried to put his hand on my shoulder. I shook so hard I felt as if my teeth were rattling. I had that metallic taste in my mouth."

"Adrenaline."

"And then I was just panting. Nobody moved. Dad was by the water with me. Mum was further up the bank. I don't think they knew what to do.

"After a while my breathing slowed down and Mum said, 'Come here, you're freezing.' I couldn't stop shivering. She wrapped Dad's sweater around me." I shrug. "Maybe there's no connection. I don't know. It's not as if it was a movie camera. But my mind went right there when Dad told me the man made movies."

"And you didn't tell me this last night, or any of the other stuff you and your father talked about."

"I really, really didn't want to be a basket case again." We're passing Mum's church. "Hey, slow down. Actually, would you mind backing up?"

He pulls over and backs up.

Read the Bible. It'll scare the hell out of you.

He looks at me, eyebrows raised.

"They changed the sign. This is the church my mother belonged to."

"Nice. What did the sign read before?"

"To get to heaven, turn right and go straight."

"Somehow I missed that last time."

"It was dark when we drove past it. Oh, by the way, I did tell Dad that you know about him and about the brothers."

"Was he okay with that?"

"Mm. I told him I told you when I thought you were gay but now I wasn't sure."

"Ah."

"But Manfred and Victor know you're not. Turn right at the blue thing."

"What is that, anyway?"

"The hood off our old Chevy."

"No, I mean, what's it supposed to be?"

"An ostrich."

"Ah."

"One of Dad's less successful schemes. He wanted to get rid of it, the sign, but Mum claimed to like it. It's possible she was rubbing his nose in it. He was always coming up with schemes. She was the one with some business sense." I shrug.

Doug glances across at me. "Are you really all right, with the stuff you found out about her?"

"Oh, I'm still digesting. But it does make sense. Finding out Mum was an alcoholic was more of a shock. Now, the idea of Dad having the ... well, there's no other way to put it, the balls to go and hang out in a brothel ..."

Doug grins. The trailer comes into sight, smoke drifting from the chimney. "How did they know?" he asks. "That I'm not gay."

"Victor and Manfred? Something in the way you look at me. Which apparently I hadn't noticed."

His smile broadens.

Chapter Ninety One

NOBODY ANSWERS WHEN I knock on the door. And I don't smell pipe tobacco anywhere. We walk around the house anyway then knock again. "He's probably asleep. Let's go in."

He's not there.

"Might he have gone for a walk?"

"I'll check the brothers' place first."

Victor opens the door before I've even knocked. "Meg, how nice to see you. You too Doug."

"Um, have you seen Dad?"

"He's not in the house?"

I shake my head. My temples feel tight.

"Where does he like to walk," Doug asks, "when it's not too cold?"

Victor's face clears. "To the bench by the river. That's where he'll be."

We hurry out past the machine shed and across the field then through the scrim of poplars and shrubs. Doug slows his pace. A moment later I catch a whiff of tobacco. When we reach the edge of the little hollow Dad's head swivels our way. His eyebrows look particularly springy today.

"Meg, Doug, what a nice surprise. Have a seat."

Doug selects a sandy hummock. I take the other half of the bench. Dad tips his chin at the mountains. "See that?"

The mountains have disappeared behind a wall of cloud. Overhead the sky is thickly quilted. The wind is weirdly warm.

"We don't get many here," Dad says to Doug, "not compared to Calgary. Always makes me restless."

"The horses too."

"You have horses?"

"Just the one, but I stable a neighbour's horse with him."

Dad nods. "I kept a couple of donkeys with my horse. Good guardians for the sheep too, donkeys. I miss riding out early in the morning. Or at dusk. I loved to be out at dusk. That moment when the colour drains from the world and the birds fall silent."

"In Celtic lore the veil between the worlds is thin just then."

Dad smiles and draws on his pipe. I look at Doug sitting there, so easy among the yellowed fronds of wild asparagus, his knees sharp in their soft jeans, eyes brown and friendly. Dad's not even wearing a jacket. His sweater swells out. I try not to stare. He's gained a little weight. So of course he'd put it on there. 'Watching his figure' must have been easier with Mum's cooking than Victor's. Or is he doing it on purpose?

"Old Hal," Dad's saying, "he lived to be thirty-two. I rode him until the end. We'd both slowed down by then. I knew I wouldn't get another horse"—he shrugs—"but I miss the company. Dogs and horses. My wife felt that way about her hens. She could watch them by the hour."

Must have been after I left. *The devil makes work for idle hands* was Mum's motto when I lived here.

There's a little silence then I say, "Dad, I had an idea. I'd like to make and sell bread using locally grown organic wheat. And maybe other things that grow here. Sunflower seeds. Saskatoons even."

"Where would you do it?"

"Well that's the thing. I could try to set up in the city but I'd rather do the baking here. If you were okay with that."

"Where would you sell it?"

"At the farmer's market in Edmonton. If people are buying croissants and baguettes I bet there's a market for local organic. Nobody else is doing it. Not yet anyway."

"So if Manfred and Victor ..."

"Exactly. You couldn't get any more local. The thing is, I think I'd need to live here. I don't know if you could stand that, for me to move in."

He looks more thoughtful than overjoyed. Doug is studying the mountains. Shit.

"I wouldn't have to be here full time. If I get E.I. I wouldn't need to rent out my house right away. I could ..." I stop. I'm just digging myself in deeper.

"Well," Dad say after a moment, "Manfred's using one end of the machine shed, but you might be able to take the other end. It's got a good concrete floor. And power. Or there's the big chicken house." He wrinkles his nose.

"Hold on. What about me moving in here with you?"

"That would be fine."

"Dad, seriously, are you sure? I might drive you crazy."

"This is your home."

A shadow crosses his face. "What is it?"

His eyes flick toward Doug who's gone to stand on the lip of the bluff, looking down toward the invisible river. The wind whips his hair back off his face. In profile he looks like a brave among the buttes in some old Western.

"Um, it turns out he isn't gay but we're really just checking each other out. And whatever happens, he has step-daughters and a horse and a place of his own he's very attached to."

"Near Lac Ste-Anne," Dad says, nodding.

"You were paying attention."

He shoots me a don't push it look. "I like him," he says. "It's not that."

"But it is a very small house."

He nods, frowning down at his pipe bowl. The wind blows out two matches and his lighter. I stand up to block it and make a cup of my hands. He nods, drawing the flame into the bowl.

Doug's come back to join us. "Look," he says.

The wall of clouds to the west is fraying. The peaks reappear, reflecting the light of an invisible sun, while overhead the cloud quilt is a dense, unbroken mauve. The band of sky between cloud above and cloud below is a luminous, limitless pale blue.

Dad's head's thrown back, the beak of his nose sharp as a mountain ridge. After a while he says, "I haven't seen one like this in years."

"Maybe it's a sign," I say.

"Do you believe in those things? Signs and portents?" He looks at me, eyebrows raised, face a map of wrinkles.

"Not really." I shrug. "But ..."

He nods. "I was thinking earlier how right it felt, you showing up here. A gift. It wasn't just Polly who felt that." He glances at Doug. "I never asked myself the question you asked, whether it was too much of a coincidence. It's a very good question. If it wasn't a coincidence, and ruling out divine intervention, there is only one person who could have brought Meg here."

"Except," I say, "as you pointed out, I felt safe in Moira's cabin. That's one of the few things I actually know. And I can't see how I would have if she was the one who kidnapped me and scared me into silence."

Doug nods. "Even if she was rescuing you from a terrible home, a child wouldn't experience that sort of abrupt dislocation as safety."

"So," I say.

"But ..." Doug says. He stares of into the middle distance, the wind tugging at his hair.

"But what?"

"Okay, bear with me. During the Vietnam war—" he looks at Dad—"I was in the US and I became involved, in a very minor way, in helping draft dodgers and deserters escape to Canada. Under cover of a hog transporting business. We went to great lengths to keep a low profile but, near the end, we had the feeling the feds were closing in on us. We suspected there was an informer. So a couple of us laid a false trail. I talked about growing up on the Alberta/Montana border. The other guy cut his hair and started wearing straighter clothes. Just before the hog transporter arrived we went and bought a big old van. Paid cash."

"A red herring," Dad says.

"Exactly," Doug says, "to cut a long story short." Amusement glints in his eyes.

Dad actually looks embarrassed.

"Go on," I say.

"Okay, so we think there were two adults who were concerned about that child's welfare."

"Moira and her brother-in-law, the child's great-uncle." Dad's leaning forward.

"Let's assume the abusive guy was the girl's father and let's assume Moira and the great uncle found out something about him. Something bad. The kind of movies he made, for example." Doug glances at me.

My mouth is dry. "Go on."

"Say the mother's liver fails and she dies. The great uncle could try for custody but if the father is an American citizen, all he has to do is take his daughter across the border. They'll never get her back. Perhaps they suspect he's getting ready to do that anyway. So they take her. To get her to safety, they trick the father into following one of them while the other hides the girl."

"You're saying the great uncle could have been the one who took the girl, not Moira. Took the girl and, perhaps, scared her into silence." Dad pokes at his pipe then draws on it until the tobacco glows.

"So I might never have seen Moira," I say slowly, "until the day you took me to her cabin."

"That's right," Dad says. He looks at Doug. "Moira phoned within a few days of Meg arriving here. Ostensibly to tell me she was going away but perhaps she reckoned—correctly—that I'd tell her that Meg had shown up as planned."

"And if I hadn't?"

"I don't know. My guess is that the great uncle would have been watching from the other side of the river."

"So, what, he carried me across the river, up the bank, popped me over the top and set me on my way like some wind-up toy?" I shake my head. "Sorry. It's just so weird that I can't remember any of this. It can make all the sense in the world but I'm never going to know if it's true."

"Would you be sure if you did remember?" Doug's voice is gentle, his eyes on my face.

He's right. The story is so outlandish I'd still be wondering if I'd made it all up. Just so I could have some kind of explanation. Doug turns to Dad. "Meg made an interesting point. About how exactly she was brought to the farm."

"The way she just described it sounds right," Dad says, "if you wanted to make sure no one saw a strange vehicle approaching the farm. One with BC plates, for example. He'd have parked on one of the forestry roads on the west side of the river then carried her across."

"Would that have been hard to do?"

"No. It had been a dry year and this is a wide, shallow stretch. She could probably have made it across on her own. With help it would have been easy."

"Will you describe it to me, where she was when you first saw her? What happened?"

"I was ploughing the field you walked across to get here. Mostly I was looking back over my shoulder. I noticed Moss staring at something. My dog. I followed his eyes. At the edge of a chokecherry thicket, a little figure was standing, completely still. In that strip of shrubs and trees between here and the field.

"I shut off the tractor, climbed down. Made my way across the field. It was a child. A girl, I thought. I stopped well short. Way she was standing, she was ready to bolt. I greeted her. She didn't say a thing. Flimsy clothes, shoes but no socks, filthy dirty, hair a tangle. I moved slowly, spoke slowly. 'Are you lost?' I couldn't tell if she understood or not. 'What's your name?' She didn't seem to register my words but every creature knows a gentle voice.

"I started moving slowly toward the house and after a moment she drifted along with me. She had a strange look. Not dreamy exactly—she had that wariness—more as if she were watching herself walk across the field."

Doug looks at me. "Where does your memory begin, exactly?"

"On this side of the river. I remember pushing through bushes to where there was more light. I could hear the sound of an engine. When I got to the edge of the field I stopped. I watched an orange tractor turning over the earth. A man with gold hair was driving it. Mostly he was looking back over his shoulder. I didn't think he could see me. Then I saw a dog off to the side of the field. He was staring at me. He wasn't growling or barking, he was just staring."

"Were you afraid?" Dad asks.

"I don't know. I felt cold all the way through. The tractor stopped and the man got down. He walked toward me. The dog followed him. The man reached one hand back behind him, his fingers spread out, and the dog stopped. The man was wearing a faded blue shirt, a faded red bandana, tan pants. The way he stepped across the field, he was like an animal. A deer. Wild and curious. He wasn't like anyone I'd ever seen before." I look at Dad then at Doug. "He asked me questions. I didn't have any words. My legs were ready to run but I didn't. I followed him when he started walking. He went around the edge of the field. After a while I could see a roof. A red roof." I stop.

Mum told this story a hundred times. How she watched us walk toward her. How her heart filled with joy and she knew this was God's work. She told it so many times it was smooth as a stone in the river. And I've certainly told enough therapists my version, but Dad and I, we've never told each other.

They're both watching me. Dad's eyes are a lighter turquoise now. Back then a chalky almost green. Doug's eyes are amber with dark flecks. He asks, "Was it significant, the roof being red?"

"I felt something when I saw it. Relieved?"

"As if you were expecting to see it?"

"Maybe. The house had a red door too. It opened and a woman stood there. A woman with dark hair. She held her hands out a few inches in front of her, palms up. She was wearing a pale blue apron over a skirt, a blouse buttoned to her neck. We were sliding toward her, the man and the dog and me. She stood completely still. When I got close enough I saw her eyes stood out like a frog's.

"'She's thirsty,' the man said.

"'Come in.' The woman turned and went back into the house. I followed her. Behind me I heard the man stamp his boots. I looked down at my shoes. The left shoe, the leather had cracked by the toe joint. The right shoe the lace must have broken. It only reached through two of the holes. I didn't have any socks on.

"'Come in,' the woman said again.

"I pushed off the right shoe with my left toes. Had to bend down and untie the left one." I look at Dad. "It was simple. I don't remember thinking anything. Mum gave me water and a blanket. You asked me more questions. We ate stew and Mum gave me a bath. It didn't feel strange, the house. I don't mean I felt safe. At one point you moved your hand and I flinched."

Dad nods. "I remember that."

"But there was something. Maybe someone did describe it to me."

"Moira, you mean? She'd never been to the house."

"That you know of," Doug says.

"You mean she would have come and 'cased the joint out?'"

"So she could give the great uncle directions. One of them could have described the house to Meg. The outside at least."

"Perhaps," Dad says, "but I've recognized places I've never been. In the mountains sometimes. I used to wonder if I'd dreamt them." He turns to look at me. "The other week, when you talked about putting down the drink, you said"—he squints into the distance—"you said it was as if a door opened in front of you and you walked through it. Your exact words were, 'You could say it was a decision but it felt like an acknowledgement. Of something that was somehow already true.' That's how it was. A girl with no name, no voice, walked out of the bush, walked across the field, walked into our home and we welcomed her. It seemed right. Fitting. I can't explain it but it did."

Doug's nodding. "That feeling of familiarity. You recognize something—a place, a person, a moment—even though you've no reason to. You know it's yours somehow. But don't you always have a choice? It's always about courage. Whether you have the courage to do whatever it is that is yours to do. You know. And you're known." Doug's eyes find mine. "But that doesn't mean it's destined to go a certain way." He's looking at Dad now. "You could have decided it was too risky to keep Meg with you. Because it was a risk, wasn't it?"

Dad nods.

"There's something I used to tell the clients at Dreamcatcher, about the difference between what's probable and what's possible. It's probable that an addict will pick up again, destroy themselves and damage everyone around them. But it's possible they'll stay clean. However improbable it is, you can choose the possible."

Dad says, "I know quite a lot about the improbable, actually. When your life crosses that line. It can happen in a minute. The probable is reason's territory."

"And the possible?"

"Belongs to imagination. To instinct."

Doug's nodding. At ease. Like Dad. Two cats on a sunny window-sill. Then they're both looking at me.

"I'm all right," I say, "and look." Like cotton worn so thin it parts and parts again, the clouds that hid the mountains are in tatters. The sky behind is the pale blue-green of a bird's egg.

Dad looks at Doug, "How would you feel about playing a tune or two?"

"I'd be happy to."

"I'll get it," I say, standing up.

"I could come with you," Doug says.

"No. Stay here. I'll be back. Anybody want anything else from the house?"

They shake their heads.

Chapter Ninety Two

KNEELING TO REACH under the bed upstairs, Mum's at my side. Hands folded, eyes firmly closed. *Forgive us our trespasses as we forgive those ...* Her nose tilts up, almost a snub nose, wide mouth, little lines fanning out from the corners, dimple in her chin. The gravy smell of her. The first night she showed me how to pray by the chesterfield where I was to sleep. The words to the Lord's Prayer unfurled inside my head as she spoke them. I stole glances at this stranger with her froggy eyes. She thanked Jesus for answering her prayers. She asked Him to bless me. Her fervour confused me.

Mum before she cut her hair and started getting it permed into a steely helmet. Back then glossy black curls framed her face. Another face swims over hers. With a flick it's gone. Grief grabs me. Squeezes my heart until I'm gasping. I push my forehead down into the bed but I can't make it come back. That other face.

Tears are pouring from my eyes.

They stop as suddenly as they started. I wipe my eyes on the blanket. After a moment I reach under the bed. My fingers find the stiff, rounded end of the case. I pull it out, wipe dust off the domed black cover with my sleeve.

In the bathroom I wash my face then meet my eyes in the mirror. The face looking back at me is serious.

Trust the shadows.

I nod and turn and go out into the Chinook, fiddle case in hand.

Chapter Ninety Three

"SO HOW DID you do it?"

Doug's voice carries on the wind.

When I come out onto the bluff he's standing next to the bench. They're both staring down at the ground. Dad reaches for the cane. He draws something in the grit at his feet. I set the fiddle down.

"The house is 20' by 24'. I cut both dimensions in half which made it 10' by 12'. I couldn't see any reason why I couldn't half the rafter lengths too. That way the pitch of the roof stayed the same, and all the angles."

"But when you cut through the existing rafters, which you had to do ..."

They're completely immersed in their manly talk. I must have laughed out loud because both heads swivel my way.

"Meg," Dad says, "do you remember the day Jimmy and Russ came over and we cut the hole in the roof?"

"Yes. I thought Mum was going to be sick."

"She didn't," Dad says to Doug, "have complete faith in my carpentry skills. And in truth, without the original plans and the example of the house in front of me, I'm not sure I'd have tried it."

"So who built the house?"

"I did, but from a kit."

"From Eatons?"

"Aladdin Mills. *From the forest to your home.* Eatons had stopped shipping by then. Same idea though."

"So that's why it looks familiar. If I picture it without the addition."

"*The Whitehall.* Introduced in 1930. Floor plan G.

"There are a good few around, aren't there?"

"None quite like this," I say.

"Here." Dad leans forward, holding out the knife he always carries in his pocket. There it is again, the gentle swell.

Doug opens the smaller blade and trims off the broken hairs. He passes the knife back to Dad, his straight square tipped fingers almost but not quite touching Dad's twisted ones.

Doug sets the bow down and lifts the fiddle out of the case. He puts it to his chin, tries a note or two.

Dad winces and shakes his head. "It's a crime, to leave an instrument un-played. I should have passed it on."

His voice is matter of fact but there's a creak of sadness. He'd come and play here, by the river, when he was learning a new tune. Or sometimes just when the weather was good, late on a summer evening. Chores done, Mum and I would walk out to listen in the twilight, owls hooting in the pines. Later, when I came back, I used to get out of my car and listen. I'd listen to the silence after the roar of the city. Sometimes, when my ears had adjusted, I'd catch the lilt of a tune across the fields.

Eight or nine years ago I realized I hadn't heard him play in a while. When I asked he held up his hands. His fingers looked like the roots of a tree growing on rock. I didn't know what to say. It's a one way ticket, old age. The thought of it scares me, how loss follows loss. *Life pries your fingers loose*, my first sponsor used to say, trying to explain the concept of letting go. She seemed ancient then. She was probably in her late sixties. The age Dad was when I came here. He's watching Doug, eyebrows curling out over hooded eyes, alert as a hawk on a fence post. Doug's standing there, hair half hiding his face, tightening knobs and plucking strings. He starts into a tune then stops again for no reason my ear can detect.

Eventually he nods and looks at Dad who nods too. He swings into what even I can recognize as a waltz. Dad leans back and closes his eyes. Doug segues from one tune into another. His eyes are open but they're fixed on something far away, or perhaps inside. I remember this look on Dad's face, sombre, inward, however lively the tune was. I pictured him reading the music as it spooled off some reel inside his head but he said no, it was his hands that knew the tunes.

Doug's hands are bigger than Dad's, same length but broader in the palm. Steady, competent hands. Dad likes him. He fits easily here. The way I did. I fit right in. It brings the lump back into my throat. Hearing Dad say what Mum said a thousand times in her way. I wish I could have trusted that belonging. But it wasn't mine by right and I couldn't forget that. I suppose it's what teenagers do, but I tested it to the max. Waiting for one of them to say, 'We didn't have to take you in.' They never did, either of them, ever. I don't know what more they could have done. *They could have told me the truth.* Would that have helped? To know their secret. Or would I have thrown it in their faces? Used it whatever way I could to drive them away. Because it hurt too much to want what I was sure I couldn't have.

Doug's drawing out a note in the way that means the end of the tune is near. The bow lifts away from the fiddle.

Dad says, "It'll take a while to open her up but she sounds better already. You learned to play from John Arcand?"

"Then from some Métis old timers. In the Red River settlement in the eighties. I was supposed to be doing research for a thesis but I was more interested in hanging out with the old guys. What about you? Where did you learn?"

"I studied piano," He considers Doug for a moment. I know what he's about to do. "When I was a girl."

"Uh huh," Doug says. I could kiss him.

"So I could read music. And I was lonely. Fiddle's the closest thing to a human voice. Besides, I never really knew what to do with myself in a group of men until I had an instrument in my hands. Then it was easy. I didn't have to talk."

Doug's nodding, his eyes soft, the curve of the fiddle resting on his thigh, denim worn almost to white, the lacquered wood rich and golden brown.

"Do you know *St Anne's Reel*?" Dad asks.

"I think so."

Doug lifts the fiddle to his chin.

"Can we listen too?"

I jump half out of my skin.

"Sorry. Didn't mean to startle you."

They're each holding a wooden folding chair, Manfred in a blue and black plaid flannel shirt, Victor in rust and ochre, their matching belt buckles holding up more perfect jeans. Time for a trip to Value Village if I'm going to live here. Or I could try Dad's baggy canvas version.

Doug lowers the fiddle.

"Don't stop. It was lovely, the wind carrying the music."

He picks his way through the reel the first time. When he falters Dad hums the notes. Then he plays it through twice, beautifully, the low notes rich and throaty, the high ones clear. Dad's foot is tapping in time. Then Doug slides into a tune I've never heard before. After a while Dad's foot falters. His eyes are open, watching Doug's hand on the fiddle neck. Doug's looking at Dad, nodding.

"That's one of the Métis tunes you were talking about," Dad says when Doug finishes.

Doug looks at me. "There are some beats missing."

The brothers nod.

"What's that tune called?" Dad asks.

"*The Devil's Reel.*"

"Here's what I'd like for my big birthday." He's looking at me. "For Doug to come and play my fiddle. At the Cardinal Divide. All of us, we could go up there, buy sandwiches at the store. Have a picnic, the way we used to. Remember?"

"What do you mean, your big birthday?"

"In July."

I stare at him. "You're not ... No wonder you didn't want to celebrate." I look at Doug. "When he supposedly turned a hundred. In March. He said it was because of Mum. He was in mourning."

"No, I said it was too soon. Which it was. I was born on the 9th of July, 1901." He looks around.

"Jesus Christ." Doug and Victor and Manfred are looking from one to the other of us. Three little marionettes. It's almost funny. I look at Dad. "This one's yours to explain. Excuse me."

I walk upriver, close to the edge. Water murmurs over shallow stones. I can't see the stones but I can. They're shining, each one rimmed in silver. The river joins them all. It flows on and on from the mountains through the prairies all the way to Hudson's Bay. In the city the river's frozen bank to bank. The beavers rest in their lodge. And the coil of golden hair, it isn't there anymore.

Acknowledgements

Quotations from Georgina Binnie-Clark, *Wheat and Woman*, Toronto 1914
Lyrics from *I Will Survive*, Freddie Perren and Dino Fekaris, 1978
Snowbird, Gene MacLellan, 1969
Walk on the Wild Side, Lou Reed, 1972

As a gender queer child, as a lesbian who's been called 'sir' for forty years, as someone who enjoys messing with people's categories, I have been researching this book my whole life. At the same time I want to express my gratitude to particular individuals and institutions.

Thank you, Richard Jenkins, Cree/Métis educator and activist from Moose Mountain, Alberta, for sharing traditional Cree understandings of gender and sexuality with me, and for the work you have done to gather and preserve this precious knowledge.

Thanks to the Alberta Native Friendship Centre who hired me to research and write about the situation of two spirit youth.

Thanks, too, to the Provincial Archives of Alberta, a remarkable resource where I first encountered the Sunday School Bus.

The Clarke Historical Library of Central Michigan University is a digital treasure trove of Aladdin Mills' kit house catalogues from the early twentieth century.

I acknowledge the support of the Province of Alberta through the Alberta Foundation for the Arts.

I recognize the support of the Province of Nova Scotia through the Department of Communities, Culture and Heritage.

Thanks to my editor, Lindsay Brown, who spared me an embarrassment of verbal tics and lazy phrases.

Special thanks to Anne Bishop for our years of winter meetings, for talk and critique, encouragement and companionable complaint.

I live in Mi'kma'ki, the traditional and unceded territory of the Mi'kmaw people. I am grateful to this land which sustains me in every way; to our sheep and dogs and chickens who amuse and instruct, and to Alexa Jaffurs, my beloved companion in trouble and fun. A woman of few words, she wields a sharp pencil.

About the Author

Nina Newington's first novel, *Where Bones Dance,* won the Writers' Guild of Alberta *Georges Bugnet Award for Novel* in 2008. She is currently finishing a memoir about living illegally in the US for twenty years. A former Kennedy scholar with an MA in English Literature from Cambridge, she makes her living designing gardens and building things. English by birth, she and her American wife immigrated to Canada in 2006. They raise sheep on unceded Mi'kmaw territory near the Bay of Fundy in Nova Scotia.